FAMILIARS

Other Anthologies Edited by:

Patricia Bray & Joshua Palmatier

After Hours: Tales from the Ur-bar
The Modern Fae's Guide to Surviving Humanity
Temporally Out of Order * Alien Artifacts * Were-
All Hail Our Robot Conquerors!
Second Round: A Return to the Ur-bar
The Modern Deity's Guide to Surviving Humanity
Solar Flare * Familiars

S.C. Butler & Joshua Palmatier

Submerged * Guilds & Glaives * Apocalyptic
When Worlds Collide * Brave New Worlds * Dragonesque

Laura Anne Gilman & Kat Richardson

The Death of All Things

Troy Carrol Bucher & Joshua Palmatier

The Razor's Edge

Patricia Bray & S.C. Butler

Portals

David B. Coe & Joshua Palmatier

Temporally Deactivated * Galactic Stew
Derelict

Steven H Silver & Joshua Palmatier

Alternate Peace

Crystal Sarakas & Joshua Palmatier

My Battery Is Low and It Is Getting Dark

David B. Coe & John Zakour

Noir

Crystal Sarakas & Rhondi Salsitz

Shattering the Glass Slipper

David B. Coe & Edmund R. Schubert

Artifice & Craft

Stephen Kotowych & Tony Pi

Game On!

Troy Bucher & Gerald Brandt

Last-Ditch

FAMILIARS

Edited by

Patricia Bray
&
Joshua Palmatier

Zombies Need Brains LLC
www.zombiesneedbrains.com

COPYRIGHTS

Table of Contents

SIGNATURE PAGE

Patricia Bray, editor:

_____

Joshua Palmatier, editor:

_____

Brian Hugenbruch:

_____

Lawrence Harding:

_____

Jean Marie Ward:

_____

Jordan Bricco:

_____

Alexander G.R. Gideon:

_____

Gini Koch & Bebe Bayliss:

_____

Russell Hugh McConnell:

_____

Kari Sperring:

_____

Alicia Cay:

_____

Jim C. Hines:

_____

Sharon Lee & Steve Miller:

_____

Shanna Germain:

_____

Jacey Bedford:

_____

A. Katherine Black:

_____

Jason Palmatier:

_____

Justin Adams, artist:

_____

Through the Smoke

Brian Hugenbruch

Life is change, Je'an tells me: a cacophony of ever-shifting smells, and sounds, and colors that all but assault all twelve of your eyes. I've never believed this. I've not known change, save one, to be a source of joy. And all those who cling to the idea of progress, or revolution, or advancement? Liars all. Change is a trebuchet hurling dung against the walls of time.

But whenever I explain all this to Je'an, she simply smiles, scoops me up from my glass enclosure, and offers a drop of perfume for my antennae.

"Gill," she says as she toddles along the tall, long counter of her shop, "you're a caterpillar. Your life is held up by humans and elves alike as the epitome of change. How can you fear it so?"

My parents were eaten well before I'd hatched: a silver snake had coiled in wait near the milkweed and taken them both for supper. The whole grove was harvested by butterfly-catcher-humans—

"Lepidopterists," Je'an murmurs.

—yes, those. Nature exists to be cruel, and the humans most of all. How a venerable elvish creature like Je'an could live in one of their habitats of broken stone and piled wood—

"A city," she says.

A *city*. A place of charnel smoke and monsters rending flesh and hide from bone in ways that would make dragons blush. A place that thrives on change. Why misunderstand me as fearful? I don't fear it. I hate it.

"Gill," she sighs, setting down a vial of cloudy green liquid, "your time is coming, you know. I think you would understand better if you allowed that metamorphosis to happen. Understand humans, in fact, and yourself as well. Is that not something which would appeal?"

It's not. I've no wish to understand. I'm content as I am: safe and protected in this perfumery. I enjoy the vibrations of the chiming bells as someone enters. I delight in watching Je'an find the perfect scent—or some non-magical concoction—for those who wander through the doorway. And milkweed always grows here, so I may dine while sitting next to a candle of particularly lovely scent and taste.

Speaking of which, surely supper must precede any exhausting talk of transformation?

Je'an laughs as she sets me back into my small glass cage, where milkweed, branches, and leaves have been placed in imitation of what might have been my natural life. It reminds me of the past as sharply as her perfumes act upon the humans. I watch their enormous eyes—so big they need but one or two— glaze over in the presence of that one scent, and suddenly time catapults backward to some other when. It's nearly always a more pleasant time, and they pay Je'an handsomely for this magic.

"Hardly magic," she chides, wrinkled fingers setting me near the milkweed. "And just as well. Magic's illegal here. No, the humans are like the elvish: we love to remember. There are a few so enamored of the past they can't escape it, but that's no fault of mine. They don't understand how to change with grace." She pulls her hands away, leaving me alone in the warm habitat. But I can hear her voice in my mind, stronger than the whispers she breathes: "Now you, Gill—change would come most naturally."

But must it?

"It must. Shall we make a trade of it?"

I could feel my fur crawl at the offer. This isn't a figure of speech. Despite the efforts of years, my chrysalis is days away. And while humans loved the idea of cocoons being spun from silk, my chrysalis would emerge from underneath dead flakes of my flesh. It's not something of which poets would sing.

Slough off one self and, if you're lucky, the same one is underneath. But my luck had run out, and she knew it. She had me in a corner. But what could I trade?

"I'll undergo chrysalis for you," Je'an murmurs. "I have just the potion for it, though most of the work will be done by our bond. You'll live life as an elven boy for five days while I molt in the stockroom. And when I'm done, you can return to your caterpillar state if you so choose."

What a strange notion. Could even magic do that? I know the answer before Je'an has the urge to speak, because I can feel her confidence through our bond. Of course it can, and she's been preparing such a potion for *months*.

Her feelings are open to me: I can sense she feels I'll learn a lesson, or regret the decision. But I still can't figure out what she'd gain through all of this.

"Your peace of mind," she answers, "one way or another. Also, I love the idea of having wings, and I'd like to see if they'll support my body. I won't know for certain until I try, right?"

I'm born with enough knowledge to understand her wings would need to be vast to lift her enormous, fleshy elvish body; and at her advanced age, the strain might stop her heart. The idea of the old woman leaving me behind forever causes me to balk—I'd take the pin to any of my ten hearts before I risked risking her.

"That's very sweet," she says, "but it's not true, and besides—that will be afterwards. I won't go anywhere, so long as you keep the stockroom safe. Deal?"

I can feel her self-assuredness, like a mountain in her mind, and her thoughts are like a balm the humans buy to soothe their chapped and flaky skin. It doesn't feel right. But it's what I want, and what she wants, and I don't fight it. When someone gives you a path around inevitable horror…you examine it, yes, you sniff it, you taste it with your antennae. But if it looks right, you take it.

"Good," she says. "I'll go get the potion."

* * *

The first day went smoothly. Je'an staved away her metamorphosis for a few hours while she let me practice speaking (such weird thrashing of the tongue and throat!) and other bodily necessities. I quickly found I could draw on Je'an's centuries of knowledge in the field of leaf-usage and proper sanitation. Harder was the use of ears and a mere two eyes, instead of antennae and feet, to feel my way around the world…but the witch-woman helped me comprehend this oddly bright, oddly textured world.

At the end of training, she left the key to the store on the counter, telling me to lock the door each evening, and to douse every candle save the one by my old habitat. Then she reminded me that I'd find milkweed poisonous; I would have to spend the next five days eating like one of the monsters whose shape I'd taken.

"You didn't mention that before," I say.

"You didn't ask," she answers as she closes the stockroom door behind her.

The bond persists despite our role reversal, and I can feel her settle onto a silk hammock and then wriggle her way out of layer after layer of dead skin, the chitin of her chrysalis peeking through the spaces that used to be cheek or shoulder.

In my new form, the feeling makes my stomach churn, so I push it aside and busy myself about the store. With two eyes and a lot more height, the place looks dazzling in its clarity: veritable rainbows of liquids contained in faceted bottles, with a long counter of dark oak hewn from a fallen tree. Trapped as I was inside my glass enclosure, I'd never appreciated just how much the shop itself carried the feel of the forests.

In the back of my mind, I can feel Je'an feeling smug about this.

A few clients wander in throughout the day, and they look at me as though I'm an elven boy—that is to say, coldly, but not as though I'm a caterpillar masquerading as a two-legged omnivore. None of them attempt to haggle—a good thing, since the numbers mean little to me. Instead, they provide coins, which I place in a secure container, and I wrap their vials with the same muscle memory of care Je'an uses each day.

I watch each one leave with a vague sense of satisfaction at helping. I'm not certain if this is my thought, or Je'an's, but it's a nice feeling all the same. And when my stomach rumbles and gurgles like swamp gas, I lock the door, put out all the candles, and find food in Je'an's personal quarters. She's brought me in here from time to time, if just to stretch all my legs, but I've never seen it as a biped, so I've never understood it as cramped.

She puts so much of herself into these perfumes, I realize, and doesn't keep anything for herself. I've always known this, but I've never *understood* it—as a caterpillar, I watched her mixing and sniffing mostly as a means of entertainment between meals and naps. I'm not certain how often she herself slept, save that she seemed to think it was enough.

I'm not convinced about this, and part of me worries for her now in her transformation…but I can't bring myself to look upon the pile of fetid meat on the stockroom floor. All I can do is be glad the perfumes mask the stench of it.

* * *

Matthieu arrives at the shop's door the next morning. He's rapping at the glass with an ivory-tipped walking stick loud enough to wake me. The sun's not out; I know for a fact that we're not due to be open yet. But the Magistrate's son, with a mustache so drenched in wax that it could burn as a candle for days without running out, does not let the affairs of others impede his own immediate gratification.

He's a near-constant patron, though; even I recognize him from the number of times he's drifted passed my habitat. So I unlock the door; he's swept past me before I can even eke out a good morning.

"Where's Je'an?" he demands. "I have a new request; Trakand City's Autumnal Tryst is in three weeks, and I *must* have a new scent for it."

"Je'an has gone to visit family," I tell the human. "She should be back in a few days. She's asked me to mind the shop for her. If there is anything on the shelf which would—"

I have a well-rehearsed script for known problem customers, and Matthieu has no interest in letting me fall back to it. "Boy, absolutely not. Her commodity parfums—" he never says the word the way the other locals do "—are sterling for peasants, yes, but I…no, I must have something dazzling. How acquainted are you with the art?"

"I know next to nothing about it," I tell him truthfully.

Matthieu's glare shifts from imperious to contemptuous. "That is unfortunate. Now—what did you say your name was, boy?"

I haven't, and he knows it. "Gill," I say.

"Gill. How pedestrian. Very well. I hope you know your letters, because I… oh. Oh wait. What…what is that?"

I turn and follow his gaze in the direction of my little caterpillar habitat.

He's walked past me on any number of occasions. While I paid him the sort of mind one does of passing giants, he'd scarce glanced in my direction, or seemed to notice the glass case at all. Further still sits the candle, unlit, that Je'an had set next to it for light.

Not for light. The thought comes unbidden to mind, and I'm once again uncertain whose it is. She'd bade me not extinguish it, and I'd been so hungry that I'd hurried through my chores. And here, in the early morning, a petulant man with wealth and want seems entranced.

"Boy," he calls. "Gint."

"Gill," I tell him again.

"Yes, yes. Since when does Je'an possess a Thrice-Banded Red-footed Swirler?"

I feel sick to my stomach in ways that have nothing to do with the bird-like food the elf woman keeps in her larder. "A what?"

The soft, oiled man whirls on me. "Don't play the fool. A Swirler of any sort carries a distinctive musk, and the Thrice-Banded Reds are all but extinct. Where did Je'an find such a creature, and how long has she been hiding it from me?"

"She hides nothing," I say. "And her business is her business. Your lordship, do you wish to place an order?"

"I do." He slaps an uncalloused hand down on the oak counter; a couple of bottles clink together in polite protest. "I want a cologne made from the musk of the Swirler, and the creature's body when I return. Before its change, if it can be helped, but I'm happy to add the butterfly to my collection instead."

"A collection?" I'd known there were lepidopterists in the city; somehow, it doesn't surprise me that I've met one on my second day as a two-legged being. Though I should be glad I wasn't still in my enclosure.

"A point of personal pride," he says, buffing his painted fingernails against a garishly violet silk coat. "Will you accept the order?"

"I'll make a note," I tell him. "Je'an will need to confirm whether the perfume is something she can make, or if your Swirler is available."

"It must be," Matthieu says with finality. "I'll pay any price. I'll buy this shop from her if I must. I'll buy the city block, if I must. When will she be back?"

"In four days," I say promptly.

"Unacceptable. I'll return tomorrow."

"Sir, that's not necessary, I—"

He leans over me. He's a skinny man, one who's never had to run from danger or exert himself if he had no wish to. But there is still enough height to his frame that his gold-stitched clothing fills my field of vision. And while I'm a lot bigger than I was two days ago, he's still several spans taller, and he knows it.

"Do not presume to tell me what to do, boy, or I'll have you beaten for your insolence. If—"

"Excuse me," a voice calls, "is there a problem here?"

I can't see over Matthieu's shoulder at first, but when he tenses after he turns I can assume the woman is someone he did not wish to see. After a moment, I'm able to skirt around and see for myself: a human taller than either of us, carrying enough metal on her person (in her shirt-rings, in gauntlets, in well-worn weapons) that no volume of perfume will cover the stench of it. But whether she smells of sweet nectar or vilest swamp vine is of less import than her attention on Matthieu.

For his part, the rich human's face twists and contorts in a manner wholly unfamiliar to me. Je'an never grows angry, never loses her calm, so both seem out of place on a symmetrical face such as his. And his words sound ever stranger to my ears: "This is no concern of yours, guard. Be elsewhere."

The woman places her hand on the pommel of her blade, or at least that's what I assume it to be; Je'an knows of such things, and I can feel a wary contempt for the item come across our bond. If the woman is a law keeper, though, I feel like she must be a friend. At the very least, she's the enemy of someone who's rapidly becoming my enemy.

"Master Loisel," she says, "we have enough complaints of you badgering and coercing the local tradesfolk to keep us busy for months. Do you really want to add assaulting an elvish boy to the docket?" She smirks a bit and adds, "It won't paint a darling picture for your cohort at the Autumn Tryst, now will it?"

Matthieu visibly pales and takes a step back. "You wouldn't!"

"My day is worse off whenever I meet you, milord. Don't try me."

The human man still gives me a glare and says, "Four days. And it had better be ready!" With that, he sweeps up his varicolored velvet cape and brushes his way past the guardswoman. The effect seems muted by the way he bounces off of her like a pebble off a tree's trunk. He tries again, gathering his belongings all the more dramatically before pushing the door open with his cane and shambling out into the morning light.

The guardswoman gives me a bow. "I don't know you, kid, but I know Je'an, and I definitely know Matthieu. If she's due back in a couple of days, I can ask my fellows to keep an eye on this place, if that would make your life a bit easier?"

I think on this for a moment. It's not in my nature to trust—I'm not part of a caterpillar cohort, and while instinct tells me my kind would huddle together for warmth, that's mostly led to a lot of dead kin in the forest. Je'an's memories tell me that some other sorts of caterpillars collaborate on foraging or fighting off predators, but this clearly wasn't my people.

But as I think through the matter, I realize I don't have much chance against Matthieu alone. I can't lock the door forever—that's not part of my agreement—and I have to keep Je'an safe above all things. She's the only one who can turn me back into a caterpillar, when all of this is done! Moreover, I wouldn't want anything to happen to her; she's been kind, and I feel strongly about returning that kindness.

The woman cuts through my thoughts, though. "Shy, huh? Well, I owe Je'an from way back, so while I won't get too close, I'll be by from time to time, see if you—"

"Yes," I blurt. "Please. He scares me."

She smiles sympathetically. "Poor kid. Well, you have Ngaire of Third Watch with you, at least until Je'an returns; and I'll make sure there's someone nearby in case you need a hand."

"Thank you," I say, and I mean it.

She leaves the shop without buying anything. At first I'm confused about why this bothers me...then I realize that Je'an, while dozing in her chrysalis, watches me as though she's dreaming. The connection between us has always been in two directions, ever since that day she found me, and part of me is a bit unnerved that this persists even inside her wall of chitin.

But it's to my benefit, connections. Because now I can understand what these rainbow liquids all do, besides making pretty scents; and if Je'an's bottled anything which can help keep Matthieu at bay, she'll know how to use it...and by extension, so will I.

* * *

I spend the rest of the evening rigging traps around the shop. The elvish woman had used mirrors to maximize the amount of sunlight flitting about the shop, but windows were few and far between. Points of entry were limited. So were points of exit, but I wasn't leaving this place.

After I finish my work, I relight the candle by my old enclosure. I find it stinks horribly; my eyes water a bit as I stand near it. I'd never minded it as a caterpillar, but my antennae served for both smell and taste, and I suspect humans (and elves) have wildly different ways of using noses than I did.

So I step away from the enclosure. The pain in my nostrils eases instantly. Then I reach out through the bond, just to see if Je'an is awake: <Why did you rescue me, really? Was it for the musk this man wants?>

The thought that comes back through feels so groggy that I catch myself yawning with it. <The musk is a benefit, but I brought you because you seemed scared. And we bonded because I wanted to see the world from your point of view.>

What a strange answer. <Me? What does my point of view matter for?>

<Your antennae smell and taste the air around customers—you'd make a wonderful salesperson. Have you never looked through my eyes?>

I have not. I'd always known it was an option, but I didn't consider it worthwhile. Why would I, if I were going to live a long, healthy life as a caterpillar and nothing else? Of course, given the circumstances, I feel foolish for not accepting what was so freely shared.

I glance back at the enclosure. <Is the musk really useful or rare?>

<It is—the secretion can be made into a cleansing potion. It's not magic, and it does not give beauty or eternal life, but a fool like Matthieu might think it such. Also…it doesn't smell of anything. He's just never smelled milkweed before. That's what has him so intoxicated—the scent of what life outside Trakand is like.>

The thought that the rich man had no concept of proper food almost made me feel sorry for him. Then I thought about his other words. <He wants me, too.>

<He wants a prize. Please don't give it to him.>

The sound of glass breaking in the far corner of the shop pulls me away from whatever Je'an might have said next. I hear high-pitched shouts and, grabbing a walking stick from behind the counter, I rush outside.

Matthieu stands in the middle of a cobblestone street, clutching at his face. A bottle of perfume, broken, sits near his feet. I'd set it up to swing at anyone silly enough to open the back window. Not only would he smell of peaches for three days, but it would soil his pretty clothes.

Ngaire and a handful of similarly armored beings come running up the street. "Everything all right?" she asks me.

I nod at Matthieu. "Seems like he's had an accident."

"If my clothes are stained," he growls, "I'm sending you the invoice!" He steps forward unsteadily, cane at the ready, but Ngaire is already between us. She doesn't move, but with eyes full of perfume, he bounces off of her and falls backward onto the cobblestones.

She looks over her shoulder and says, "We'll handle this, sir."

I step back into the shop and lock the door behind me. I have no doubt the mess outside will be cleaned up…but I can't help but think this isn't over yet.

I had no idea being a biped meant I'd have to be as on my guard as I'd been when a creature in the wild.

* * *

The next two days pass without incident.

I kept a knot in my stomach well into the first afternoon; every time I smelled something remotely close to a peach, I looked around fast enough that clients would ask me if I were all right. The script Je'an had given me had somehow accounted for this, though; I suppose she must have realized I'd be new to being nervous.

But Ngaire and the Third Watch wandered by from time to time—never to buy, but always with a watchful eye—and whatever had coiled in my chest slowly subsided. I ate supper and fell asleep without incident. And with the stink-candle lit, not a soul gave the enclosure any sort of notice. I suppose I could have moved it into the back room…but it seemed impolite to make Je'an move it back someday.

Okay, that's not true. If I moved it, then I would feel as if it's not coming back.

I don't know what time it is when I wake to a red and orange glow. Je'an has a word for this coming through the bond, but even creatures of the forest know the signs of oncoming fire. I don't smell or taste smoke, however. Fire, and nearby, but not here.

I rush out from Je'an's small chamber and into the main shop floor. No fire here, either, but the glow is far brighter, and wisps of smoke wind their way around the shelves. From the sounds of shouting outside, it's another building not far away, and wagon wheels, laden heavily, trundle over the cobblestones. I can hear a few familiar voices from the Third Watch at a few different distances, all down the street.

But the smell of peaches is overwhelming. The front door has been taken off its hinges and leaned back into place; it's not a door I could hope to move on my own, and the windows are rigged with other perfumes and strange potions.

Matthieu looms over the enclosure, ripping out small branches and piles of milkweed. "Where is it??"

"Get out!" I shout.

He whirls on me and I take a step backward. His face, a cream color when he'd first come, had also been stained and looked as though he were wearing blueberry pie. But while that's a shock, it's the eyes that scare me. They remind me of a hawk, or owl, or snake: anything that would eat me without hesitation.

And I'm trapped inside with him.

"Where is the caterpillar, boy?" he demands. "I must have it! I'll tear this place apart if I must!"

"I thought you liked Je'an!"

"Oh, I do, and I'll compensate her just fine for all damages. I'll have a new shop built for her, in fact! One far nicer than this cramped, putrid little place."

Instinct tells me it's unwise to provoke something that wants to eat you. But all I can think about is Je'an, in the unlocked stockroom, bound in the final stages of chrysalis. I have to stall this man as long as I can.

"I'm sure she'd hate that," I tell him.

"I didn't say she wouldn't," Matthieu says with a wave of his hand. "But what choice would she have? No witnesses around, are there boy?"

"There's me," I say.

"You? You'll hide behind the guards, and my solicitors will have a field day with you. No court would convict me."

Time for another tactic. "It's me," I say. "I'm the caterpillar."

"You—" Matthieu's eyes widen, then they narrow. "That makes no sense."

"It's true. Je'an's transformed me."

The rich man stares at me for a moment. "If I didn't know any better...but no, you have three red bands in your hair, don't you? Unless that's the fire, and your eyes...but no. You're not acceptable as a boy. I need you as a caterpillar!"

"What, for a collection?"

"You?" He spits on the floor. "Boy, I'd keep you alive! No pins for you. Your kind secretes a special substance on your back—if the witch-woman's ever swabbed you, you'd know what I mean..." He watches me for a moment, and he nods knowingly. "Keeping it for herself! She's more clever than I thought. But never mind her. Change back."

I could feel unfamiliar biped emotions rising in me—thoughts of betrayal and trust. Je'an had certainly cared for me from time to time, and we'd never discussed what was done with the musk. I suspect she would have told me if I'd asked. I never asked. And there were times where I, so desperate to be a simple caterpillar, had shut down discussion in favor of food or sleep.

If it had gone into the restoratives, and she'd used that money to buy milkweed for me, I could hardly complain. Moreover...I'd deliberately left her in charge of my own destiny, and she'd catered to my simple wishes. If I were going to be my own person—my own caterpillar, or butterfly, or something—I would need to rise to that challenge.

"I can't change back," I say.

"Can't?" he scoffs. "Or won't?"

I put my hands awkwardly on my hips. "Either."

"Be that as it may," Matthieu says calmly. "I know Je'an; she won't have taken the reversal spell with her. It must be in the stockroom—"

"No!"

"Aha! Your final mistake," he says, eyes glinting in reflected firelight.

He runs toward the stockroom. It's not locked from either sde, so he throws the door open and staggers back when it swings easily. He gawks at the glow coming from inside. And as I skid to a halt behind him, I do much the same.

Je'an, an old but sprightly elvish woman, has started to struggle through her chrysalis. Through the smoke we each can see tanned wizened skin now sparkles and gleams in ways that have nothing to do with firelight; the glow streaking out of the cracks shifts in color and tone with every breath. I can't see if she's grown wings or not; she's still two-legged, at least, but I could swear I see antennae near her hairline.

"Monstrous!" the rich man blurts. Then he lifts his ivory-handled cane. "No matter. I suspect we can dissect her and find what we need to turn you back!" He readies the stick as though he intends to use it as a pin.

I lift my arms toward Je'an out of instinct, but only because it helps me reach through our bond. I don't want just to see through her eyes—I want to take the magic back. The metamorphosis back. The chrysalis back. Everything I should have been. I choose to be more than I am—not just to save her, although it helps, but because I'd only seize my destiny by being me. Really, truly me.

Streaks of light burst out of the chrysalis, through Matthieu and toward me. The rich man grabs at his eyes instinctively, trying to ward away harmless light, and trips into a shelf. A stream of fragile bottles land on the ground beside him, shattering at once and sending him into a tizzy. I don't know which potions or perfumes they might have been, and don't care; I only know he's running toward the door and moving it, badly, of his own volition.

Soon the lights all go out, save for the faint and fading flicker of firelight from the street, and I'm fluttering in the air above Je'an. Her hair's turned the color of rainbows, but she has neither wings, nor antennae, nor has she changed in age or shape.

I beat my wings and settle onto her shoulders. We look at one another, and our bond tells us two very certain things about one another. First, each of us is in the shape we're in because we *choose* to be. It's who we are. And secondly… we're both really hungry.

* * *

Ngaire comes to visit a few days later. I flutter down from a shelf and transform into an elvish boy. She takes a step back and says, "Now that's new. I don't know that I would do that often, kid—the city still has a dim view of magic, however accidental."

Je'an chuckles from behind the counter. "Lieutenant, no magic is practiced here, and never has been. But I'm certain Gill will be more careful from now on."

"I will," I say, and I mean it. "But how can we help you?"

"I'm here to help you," she says. "Matthieu was taken into custody—we apprehended him leaving your shop the night of the fire. Charges of trespassing and destruction of property. We think he set the fire as a distraction, but we can't prove much. The Magistrate has recused himself from judging his own son, but someone will make a decision soon. You won't need to come downtown, though, either of you."

"That's good to hear," Je'an says. "What does he remember?"

"Not much. He was covered in a lot of different fluids, so we thought he'd been drinking heavily. Possibly eating imported mushrooms. Would explain some of the dreams he said he had, to be certain."

Je'an gives Ngaire a bow. "Thank you for keeping us informed, and let us know if there's anything we can do."

The tall woman bows in return. "I shall. Be well, the both of you."

It's only when the shop is empty that Je'an says, "She's right, you know. You do need to be careful. This is not a kind city toward anything that seems magical. Even if it's not."

"I understand," I say. "But...I also understand that I won't have a life unless I fly out into the world from time to time. I'll simply exist."

"Was it so very bad?" she asks.

"Not at all. But...I like the feel of this more. Even with the risk."

She inclines her head. "Then, my dear friend, I'm glad to have suffered through some days of cramped living for you. Go, have a flight about the block. Just be back for supper."

I give Je'an a smile and shift back into a butterfly, beating my wings as soon as I no longer feel the ground beneath my feet. The elvish woman, now huge beside the counter, waves her hand ever so slightly, and I take off in the direction of an opened window in the back, flittering between varicolored bottles before bursting out the side of the house and into the open sky. A serene blue, streaked with white, hangs over the orange tiles and white wooden planks in this portion of the city, and there are neither birds nor snakes anywhere in sight.

I catch a breeze and drift upward, looking down and taking in all my ever-expanding world.

A Case of Missing Trilobites

Lawrence Harding

Loretta Winstanleigh was somewhat disgruntled as she entered the reinforced witches' carriage of the three forty-five to Paddington. The guard had been rather short with her, or rather with her familiar, which naturally meant her by proxy. His attitude when he shut the door firmly behind them seemed entirely unnecessary. After all, Quintinum *had* given him his hat back, with only the smallest possible ink-stain. He was being positively well-behaved; at least, more so than he had been at Lord Corrigan's soiree, which Loretta had elected to leave early. Lord Corrigan, at least, was not present to be offended. Though he was known for being fashionably late, it seemed gauche to be so when hosting. Loretta had responded in kind by leaving fashionably early, as soon as Quintinum provided the excuse.

Quintinum trotted alongside Loretta with his idiosyncratic five-tentacled gait. One galaxy-speckled eye was fixed lovingly on her, while the other roamed the carriage in curiosity. The latter eye fixing on something, Quintinum clacked his beak in quiet excitement and scrambled away. Loretta followed at her own pace. It wasn't as if he could go far.

From Quintinum's chirrups, Loretta guessed that the object of interest was another familiar. This was intriguing; everyone who was anyone in the witching world had been at Lord Corrigan's soiree. Anyone who wasn't was either of no interest at all, or very interesting indeed.

When they met the familiar, it was like no creature Loretta had ever seen. It was mostly two feet of segmented shell, like an overgrown woodlouse. Its armored headplate culminated in three spines that swept back like a tricorn hat. There were no eyes to speak of, barring two stalks covered in glittering lenses. Quintinum planted himself in front of the creature and, when two antenna dropped down to investigate him, he batted them like a kitten with a string of yarn.

As she took in the scene, Loretta realized that she had, in fact, seen such a creature before, albeit long dead. All manner of specimens of this type had been recovered from the Dorset cliffs in recent years, of considerably smaller creatures that roamed the world countless ages before man. She therefore had an inkling who the trilobite's witch was.

"Am I correct in assuming that I am addressing Mr. Michael Kennelowe?"

The witch finally looked up from his book. Though no longer a young man, he was certainly a good deal younger than Loretta's forty-four. His coat, several years out of fashion, was more an elaborate network of patches than a garment in itself. Likewise, his mousy beard seemed largely the product of apathy. He smiled at Loretta in a way that suggested he did so because it was what one did when addressed, but did not stand.

"You are indeed. Do I likewise have the pleasure of the company of Miss Loretta Winstanleigh?"

Loretta raised an eyebrow. Insofar as the magical community was aware of him, Kennelowe was notorious for his reclusiveness. He preferred to dwell with his collection of fossils than socialize with fellow practitioners. She had certainly never met him.

Kennelowe chuckled. "Come now, Miss Winstanleigh. How could I not recognize the infamous Quintinum?" Quintinum looked up, clacked his beak and waggled a tentacle in greeting, then returned to toying with the trilobite's antenna. Kennelowe chuckled. "I may not attend the galas, but I do keep abreast of the papers." Loretta allowed her chest to grow a little with pride as he glanced down at the familiars. Likewise, his own smile grew fonder. "I see that he and Humphrey are already getting along famously."

This was certainly the case. Humphrey had accepted Quintinum's interest and was allowing him to dangle from his antenna, one tentacle to each, while both familiars conversed in clicks from Quintinum and a low musical hum from Humphrey.

It seemed unkind to separate them. Loretta took this as an invitation to take the seat opposite Kennelowe. He moved his feet so as not to intrude upon her space, but almost immediately returned to his book. He made every appearance of being engrossed in it, though the thumb and forefinger of his right hand worried the corner of the page without ever turning it. Something was on his mind, and Loretta decided it would be an amusing distraction to discover what.

"What business brings you from Dorset, Mr. Kennelowe?"

She did not expect a direct answer; nor did she get one. "My own business," came the reply, without even a glance from his feigned reading. "Though I could ask the same of you, Miss Winstanleigh. I understand that the great and good of the witching world are currently at Lord Corrigan's soiree. It appears they are missing your presence."

Loretta chuckled. "I don't deny that there was an incident that made a quiet exit advisable." She glanced at Quintinum, who was currently sitting between Humphrey's eyestalks and trying to make eye contact with both of them at once. "No doubt it will be in your papers tomorrow."

"Then I look forward to reading about it."

Loretta leaned back. "Needless to say, Lady Pyesmythe is currently in need of a new fascinator and Quintinum is once again squid *non grata* with her familiar, but that is very much my business."

"Indeed. I hadn't asked for a preview."

Loretta frowned at this dismissal of her invitation to gossip. Her retort was interrupted by a commotion at the door between the witches' carriage and the rest of the train. A small man in faded tweeds, with a similarly thinning thatch of straw-like hair, was trying to force their way in against the guard's protestations. The guard was trying to prevent them from entering and failing to do so, partly due to the eagerness of the interloper, and partly due to the ginger cat weaving between his legs.

Kennelowe finally looked away from his reading. His eyes narrowed and he rose to his feet. "It just so happens that *he* is my business."

The fellow had made it into the carriage and was making right for them. His gaze had fixed on Kennelowe, his eyes now alight with admiration. Kennelowe strode into the aisle, his expression anything but. Humphrey shrugged Quintinum off and scuttled in his master's wake.

"Mr. Kennelowe? My name is Silas Bartelby—"

"I know who you are," replied Kennelowe. Bartelby didn't seem to notice his curtness, for he beamed wider and looked past Kennelowe to his familiar.

"And this must be—"

Kennelowe snapped his fingers. Humphrey launched himself at Bartelby's chest, pinning him to the floor. Bartelby's greeting was smothered as the air was driven from him.

"Now." Kennelowe stood over him. "I could hex you, but that would be too quick. I could let Humphrey gnaw on you for a while, but I haven't the patience. So tell me, Mr. Bartelby—where are my fossils?"

"Mr. Kennelowe!" Loretta pulled herself up to her full height. "What is the meaning of this?" She crocked her arms, hands on hips, and tried to look authoritative. Quintinum leapt up to dangle from her right elbow, ready for action but detracting from the overall impression.

"This man stole from me, Miss Winstanleigh. I have it on good authority from my man in Exeter that he has contrived to pilfer my property—property that is precious to me, and infinitely more so to Humphrey." He looked at her sidelong. "Would you suffer someone to steal the bones of your kin, however distant?"

Loretta met his stare. He seemed deadly serious, with an emphasis on deadly. She had no desire to get in his way, especially in so confined a space. What's more, she felt something of a hypocrite. It was not as if she was averse to causing a little chaos herself, or even a lot of it. Nonetheless, there were certain standards even she held herself to, and that included using one's familiar as an attack dog.

"If I may interject?" Bartelby's voice was muffled beneath Humphrey. "Surely if I *had* stolen anything of yours, I would hardly rush to greet you?"

"Ah, well." Kennelowe shrugged. "What better way to conceal your guilt than by hiding in plain sight? A classic double-bluff!"

Loretta scoffed. "Does he seem like the kind of man capable of a double-bluff?"

"A harsh assessment, madam, but one I will accept," grunted Bartelby, as he endeavoured to worm his way free. He collapsed with a gasp as Humphrey pinned him down still harder, his low hum increasing to an angry whine. Quintinum squawked and spat out a stream of silvery light across Humphrey's back—only a warning shot, but enough to get the trilobite's attention. Bartelby managed to extricate himself up to the waist as Humphrey shook himself and grumbled.

Kennelowe was incandescent. "Restrain your familiar, madam—this is none of your business!"

"Well, now, it is very much my business, for no one tells me or my familiar what to do. Let the poor fellow go, Kennelowe, and talk to him like a civilized gentleman!"

"I shall do no such thing." Kennelowe scowled and folded his arms. "He is a thief and a scoundrel."

Loretta's choice words of reply were lost beneath the train's sudden whistle. They entered a tunnel, and were plunged into darkness.

* * *

It was pitch black, but that didn't mean Quintinum couldn't see anything. He could see a cloud, or something like one. It bounded down the aisle, liquid and gas all at once, corporeal and incorporeal, all quicksilver and snapdragons and sea salt and danger.

Quintinum had never seen anything like it, and if Quintinum was a slave to anything it was curiosity. As the cloud suddenly veered towards Humphrey, Quintinum swung himself into its path and took it in his tentacles.

* * *

When the train emerged from the tunnel, Loretta was reeling on the floor like a drunk in a common brawl.

"Quintinum? Where's Quintinum?"

Kennelowe blinked. "He's probably just scuttled off somewhere."

"No. Not like that. I can't feel him. He's *gone*."

And so he was. Ever since he'd first appeared when she came into her powers as a girl, Quintinum had been her constant companion, whether present or not. He could be rooms away in the house, satiating his endless appetite for curiosity and chaos, but she could always feel him at her side, as it were. Now there was nothing, not even an absence, which would at least have been something.

Loretta paced the carriage, checking beneath seats and on overhead racks. There was no sign, as she'd known there would not be. She stormed back down the aisle, pointing a trembling finger at Kennelowe and Bartelby in turn.

"One of you took him! How? Why? How could you? Give him back!"

"How could I from here?" protested Bartelby, whose legs were still beneath Humphrey.

"And I was next to you the whole time, as in the dark as you were. Furthermore, I had no idea you'd be here today. How could I rig up a trick like that, on the assumption you'd throw yourself from a party at this exact time to get this exact train? Even if I knew how?"

Loretta stared from one to the other, then sagged. "Whoever's to blame, he's gone. I can't feel him."

Kennelowe frowned. "Well, he must be *somewhere*. Familiars can't just disappear. It's unheard of."

* * *

It was dark—a very different kind of dark from the tunnel. Quintinum had no idea where he was. He was definitely inside something, but the darkness was beyond even that.

He was alone. Completely alone. For as long as he'd waddled along this plane, he had never been alone. There had always been Loretta. Quintinum clacked his beak in mourning and frustration. He didn't like being alone.

"Now, let's see what we have here, then."

The voice was muffled, vague, and somehow familiar. It continued to mumble to itself as a latch clicked. The darkness was then cut in two by a sliver of light, at which a slate-gray eye appeared.

There was only a crack, but that was enough for Quintinum. He thrust out two tentacles to grip either side of the opening, and a third directly into the offending eye. His jailer fell back, shouting words Quintinum had only ever heard Loretta use in private. They were not good words. Quintinum prised the gap wider and leapt to freedom.

He landed on his jailer's chest. As he took stock of his surroundings, Quintinum recognized the ink-stain he'd left not half an hour earlier. He'd *known* there was a reason this human was wrong. He chittered to himself and bounded away. The man, however, managed to grab his rearmost tentacle and had Quintinum in his grasp once more.

Quintinum writhed against the grip. The man continued to spit out bad words. Quintinum managed to twist himself round to face him head-on. He took the opportunity to add to the ink-stain, this time with a direct shot to the mouth. His jailer fell back, spluttering, pawing at his mouth, and, most importantly, letting Quintinum drop from his grip.

Quintinum didn't reach the ground. He hung in the air, able to move his limbs only sluggishly, as if through fizzing treacle. Somewhere behind him, a cat was purring.

* * *

"What if he's dead?" Loretta paced on the spot, trying not to panic.

"You'd know." Kennelowe smiled grimly in a way he apparently thought was reassuring, but he was clearly used to conversing with dead things rather than humans. "You know that. You'd be a husk right now, mindless and soulless, or dead, if you were lucky. You know what happened during the wars in France, and the Crimea. We pay our subscriptions, same as for other veterans in need. I had an uncle—*have* an uncle. He was at Balaclava. His gryphon…" Kennelowe paused but kept his eyes trained on Loretta. "You would know."

"So where is he then? How can you be so heartlessly calm? Have you never lost something precious?"

"Yes, actually. That's rather why Humphrey and I are here, though I appreciate it's not quite the same thing."

"No, it's *not!*" Loretta whirled to face Kennelowe. Faint sparks licked about her fingertips as she raised her hands.

"Aha!" Kennelowe clapped his hands, which did nothing to ease Loretta's mood. "You have magic!"

The sparks faded as Loretta blinked and looked at her hand. "Which means—"

"—that Quintinum is still very much alive, somewhere, even if you can't feel him."

Loretta clenched her fist. In some ways, this felt worse. Was being separated from Quintinum worse than having to mourn him? "But where?"

* * *

"Now, why are *you* here?" the newcomer purred as he walked in a slow circle around Quintinum as he hovered in the air.

He was a broad man of middling height, dressed in an impeccably tailored frock coat that was just begging for Quintinum to ruin it. Not that Quintinum would dare. He hadn't liked the first man, but this one was worse. Even Loretta was wary about Lord Corrigan, which was why Quintinum had contrived to remove Loretta from the soiree as soon as was least socially unacceptable. He wouldn't have if he'd known he'd be here. The ginger cat, Lord Corrigan's rather aloof familiar, padded over and sat beneath him. It looked up and fixed him with its emerald green eyes in rapt disinterest.

"I expected you to disgrace yourself and your mistress at some point," Lord Corrigan continued, "though I didn't expect it to happen before the canapes. Winstanleigh must have truly outdone herself."

The wheels of the train squealed as they slowed before the next station. Corrigan scowled. With a flick of his wrist, he sent Quintinum floating back towards the packing case he had burst from. The guard leaped to redeem himself, hefting the case back into place and holding the lid ready. Corrigan dropped Quintinum inside and the guard slammed the lid shut as the train pulled into the station.

Quintinum was left in darkness once more. He was but dimly aware of the outside world but, if he concentrated, he could smell the magic that began pouring off Corrigan the moment the case was closed. Not enough, however, to taste the spell itself. He concentrated hard, trying to glean clues from his captors' muffled conversation.

"Regrettably, this rather complicates matters."

"Still, milord, it proves it works! One familiar or another, does it matter?"

Quintinum could sense the guard's eagerness to prove to Corrigan that he had not, in fact, let him down. It was all too clear that Corrigan could tell, too. He was taking far too much enjoyment in making the man squirm to cover the mistake in his own handiwork, even if it risked distracting him from whatever conjuration he was performing.

"It matters because Kennelowe is a reclusive non-entity. I had to find someone in Exeter willing to lure him out, and that cost a pretty penny. People would take longer to notice a mishap with his familiar, if they noticed at all. Whereas if there's one thing the Winstanleigh woman relishes, it's being noticed."

"Ah. A problem?"

"Nothing we can't solve. A witch *sans* familiar can only be so strong, after all—and any attempts by her to resist will be most instructive."

"So, are they permanently separated, sir?"

"Ha! If only. The spell, I believe, has severed their link, but should they touch again the connection will be restored. Even I cannot overcome the power of proximity—yet. So keep him locked up tight, you hear?"

"Loud and clear, sir. Little bugger is a lively one, I've no wish to wrangle him again."

"He is rather, isn't he? Still, this might be to my advantage. I wish to see the effects on a familiar when deprived of its living witch. It might be more instructive to use a familiar with a little more life to it." He paused, then his voice became softer, as if talking to no one but himself. "Yes…a lively familiar is a better base line. If I am to prove to the Ministry that we can sever a familiar from a witch and still make use of it, one with a bit of spunk will be ideal. Once they see the potential…applications, they're sure to abandon their pious qualms. There'll be no more Balaclavas, thanks to me. Except for our enemies, naturally."

At this point, Quintinum had lost interest. He'd learned what he needed. A touch. That was all it would take. He threw himself against his prison again and again. But of course, he was in no ordinary packing case. Not only could he not break it, he couldn't even touch its edges. He simply ricocheted off a numb, empty void. There was nothing he could do but gnash his beak and hope for a miracle or, even better, Loretta.

* * *

The train blew its whistle and pulled into Barchester station. As it came to a halt, Humphrey's antennae suddenly straightened upright. He scuttled off Bartelby and began clambering onto the seats on the platform side. Bartelby immediately leapt to his feet and brushed himself down.

"I'm terribly sorry," he babbled, clearly feeling an explanation was warranted, if not actually wanted. "I fear there has been some sort of misunderstanding. I simply overheard the guard telling his cat about the remarkable creature in the next carriage, and from the description I knew it must be you and Humphrey! As an enthusiast and keen follower of your work, Mr Kennelowe, how could I pass up the opportunity? I can only apologize for the intrusion—"

Humphey jerked an antenna towards Bartelby and let out a sharp squeak. Loretta, beginning to at least try and regain her composure, raised a hand abruptly, silencing both Bartelby and Kennelowe, who seemed about to interrupt with some choice words. "Talking to the cat?"

"Yes, you know, the way people do." Bartelby paused. "It was curious, though. It looked like it was listening to him, actually listening, not just staring at him politely like most cats would. Very odd."

Humphrey whined, now jabbing his antennae towards the window. Loretta and Kennelowe hurried to the window to see what the matter was. Loretta immediately saw what had caught the trilobite's attention—a large ginger cat accompanying two guards carrying a heavy packing case. As she looked, the cat turned and fixed her with emerald green eyes so vivid that they could not be natural.

"The cat's a familiar," she hissed.

"Whose?"

"No idea. Ginger cats are ten a penny. Anyway, come on."

"Why?"

Loretta frowned. She wasn't used to having to convince people. "If there's another witch around, then they must have something to do with Quintinum. Who else could it be?" She didn't add that, being without a familiar, she had never felt less safe. Something decidedly magical was afoot, and she didn't want to lose sight of the only practitioner about who might not be hostile. She sought for some other reason to tempt Kennelowe. "And I'll bet a thousand guineas that that case holds your trilobites. It's big enough." In her heart of hearts, however, she hoped it held a certain squid instead, and damn the guineas.

Kennelowe's eyes narrowed. Humphrey waved his antenna urgently, which seemed to assuage him. He nodded at Loretta curtly.

The whistle blew. The train was about to depart. The witches made for the exit, Kennelowe pausing to grab Bartelby by the collar and stare him in the eye.

"Rest assured, I'll be back. If you're lucky I'll only bring the law with me." And with that, he and Winstanleigh were leaping onto the platform as the train began to pull away.

Their pursuit was immediately hampered by the crowd. Barchester was an unexpectedly popular stop, and the platform was packed with holidaymakers, businessmen, and other sundry travellers. Despite Humphrey's presence causing a stir, Kennelowe and Loretta were forced to shoulder their way through the press. The guards were just visible at the center of the platform, making their way steadily to the stationhouse at the end.

"You there! Stop! That's my property!" cried Kennelowe.

They did not stop, nor acknowledge being hailed. Loretta snapped something unladylike at them and, taking advantage of a gap in the crowd forged by Humphrey, she let fly at them with a hex. It was far from her best, far even from what her weakest would be if Quintinum were there, and barely fizzled out against the rearmost guard's back.

Kennelowe glanced back at her, aghast, but said nothing, for the crowd was now at least scattering from their path—and screaming. Beside him, Humphrey made full use of the clearing platform for a run-up. The trilobite took a flying leap at the rearmost guard and bounced straight off. The guard didn't so much as falter, or make any sign he'd noticed the impact at all.

Kennelowe now reached the guards himself and tried to take one by the shoulder. The moment his hand touched the guard, he withdrew it with a gasp. He faltered for a moment, shaking his hand as if trying to get the life back into it. None of the guards reacted to his touch or his cry. Even the cat paused only to arch its back and lick a paw before ambling on.

By now a crowd—small, wary, and keeping their distance, but a crowd nonetheless—had gathered. Among them was the stationmaster, a tall and imposing man with an equally impressive hat. He was doing his best to appear stern and authoritative, while fully aware he was dealing with people who could turn him to ash if the mood struck them.

"Now then sir, madam, can you please explain yourselves?"

Kennelowe rallied, still shaking his hand back to life and pointing at the guards, who were still walking on in the direction of the stationhouse as if nothing had happened. "I believe that case contains my property—stolen property, in fact."

"I see, sir." The stationmaster nodded, tight-lipped. He then raised his head to address the guards. "All right, lads. Come back here and let's get this sorted out."

The guards made no reply. They simply carried on walking, and as they reached the stationhouse door they disappeared entirely—case, cat, and all.

"What the devil?" cried the stationmaster as the crowd dispersed in panic.

"It was an illusion." Kennelowe's voice was quiet and flat below the uproar. "A damned good one, but still. We were tricked."

Loretta's heart shed another scrap of hope and sank. "So that means Quintinum must still be on the train." Both turned east, the direction the train had departed in.

* * *

Bartelby had not been fool enough to follow the witches. He made his way back toward his compartment, in the vain hope it was still available. Fear of the dire consequences threatened by Kennelowe were yet to sink in; rather, his heart was heavy from having come into the presence of a titan in his field only to find his presence was an insult. And worse, to be accused of such things! To be regarded as an enemy! He wished he had not taken up the last-minute invitation from his friend in Exeter, and so ended up on this train.

As he entered his original carriage, however, something caught his eye that stopped him in his foot-dragging steps. Ahead of him, a familiar flash of ginger disappeared between the legs of newly-boarded passengers. It was the train's cat—the very same cat he had just seen disappear along the platform pursued by Winstanleigh and Kennelowe. Bartelby frowned and forgot his melancholy, instead concentrating on pursuing the cat.

The increasingly full train meant that his path was often impeded, but there was only so far the cat could go and only so many compartments it could hide in. Bartelby checked each as he went, but his search only bore fruit when the guard's carriage came into view. Outside its door sat the cat, licking a paw, before turning and languidly pushing the door open and disappearing inside.

That confirmed it. Something uncanny was certainly happening. Bartelby hurried to the door, then paused. Now that he had reached his goal, he wasn't entirely sure what he intended to do. To burst in and demand an explanation? That would only earn him mockery at best, and at worst? If his suspicions were correct it didn't bear thinking about. Still, newfound bravery had brought him this far. He felt he would never forgive himself if he should turn back now. He opened the door a crack. As he did so, a voice became audible. It had clipped, urbane tones, and certainly did not belong to a guard.

"Winstanleigh will be no threat to us for now, not without her squid. Now, leave me be. I must make this illusion last as long as possible. We need Kennelowe off the train in case he comes looking for his damn fossils. Go and make sure he took the bait. If we're lucky, he took her with him."

Various suspicions seething within Silas came to the boil. He had been looked down upon, mocked, sneered at, occasionally even pitied. He was perfectly aware he was not the most adequate of men, but even he had his pride. Never had he been so shamefully used. He would not stand for it. He pulled the door open and hurled himself into the guard carriage.

Directly before him was the guard. Silas was only slightly built, but he had surprise on his side. He bulled into him, sending him off balance and tumbling back. His fall resulted in two crashes, and two cracks.

The first crash was the guard hitting the boxes stacked against the wall, enough that the topmost rocked dangerously, its lid opening just enough to spill part of its cargo—two of the most perfect specimens of trilobite Silas had ever witnessed. The first crack was the guard's skull as he was rendered unconscious.

The second crash was the crate the guard had been attending to being knocked to the ground in the fray. The second crack was its latch giving way. The lid flew open, and Quintinum was free once again.

The familiar came bounding out, tentacles flailing, beak snapping angrily. One star-whorled eye fixed on Bartelby, who feared he was about to be hexed on sheer instinct. Fortunately, Quintinum's attention was otherwise occupied by the witch rising from the corner, roaring in frustration.

Somewhere, presumably, an illusion had faded. Kennelowe would realize then he had been wrong; hope flared in Bartelby's heart that he might forgive him. He quickly abandoned this mistimed concern and began to seek cover, for the witch was now glaring at him and bore a fizzing ball of emerald light.

Time slowed, in the manner that it does when one's consciousness makes the most of its last moments. Bartelby was not particularly observant, but even he was able in these brief seconds to take in details he would not normally have noticed—the gloved cat rampant upon the witch's ivory buttons, the stray threads on his frock coat, and—gallingly—Bartelby's address on a luggage label. The label was attached to the topmost packing case—a case that was certainly not his.

Bartelby felt movement by his feet. The damned cat (which, he now realized, must be this witch's familiar) was leaping to its master's side. Bartelby lashed out desperately with his left foot, striking the cat in the flank. The cat yowled; the hex left the witch's hand early and incinerated a hatbox behind Bartelby's right shoulder.

The witch cursed, and cursed all the louder as Quintinum rose to the occasion and doused him liberally with steaming ink. Then—because this was a day for discovering hidden depths—Bartelby took three swift steps forward and struck the witch firmly on the nose, reddening the ink-stained face.

Time recollected itself as Bartelby's soul decided it had more life in it after all. Everything became a rush. Quintinum leapt onto Bartelby's shoulder, chittering triumphantly. The squid secured himself to Bartelby's forearm and raised one of his tentacles. The chittering became a screech, and the side-door of the carriage burst free.

The wind whipped Bartelby's face. It was clear what Quintinum intended, even as the squid prodded him meaningfully in the side. And why not? At this point, he might as well trust Quintinum's judgement. Some instincts, however, overrode all others. As Bartelby stepped forward, he scooped up the two fallen trilobites. Then, and only then, he leapt from the train.

* * *

Magic exploded on every side as Quintinum was borne down the embankment. Corrigan immediately made chase. He was not a man to let an insult lie, which was the only reason Quintinum had never inked him. There were some risks even he wouldn't take—until pushed. Normally, Quintinum would be having fun right now. But duelling wasn't fun without Loretta. It was terrifying.

Even scarier to Quintinum was having to rely on Bartelby. Bartelby had no magic. If Corrigan caught them, he could be no help. Besides, Humphrey hadn't liked Bartelby because he'd thought Bartelby had done bad things. Maybe he had, but he'd also helped save Quintinum. That counted for a lot, especially now that shrubs all around them were erupting in lilac flame. It was a more complicated situation than Quintinum liked to deal with, but he felt bound to return the favor. He would help save Bartelby. He might even bloody Corrigan's nose as well.

Bartelby was running very fast, even managing to stay upright on the slope. Quintinum was impressed and grateful, because it made his job easier. Bartelby was not an easy target for the enraged witch. Quintinum coiled a tentacle around Bartelby's forehead and planted another on each shoulder. The man barely flinched, earning him a few more points of respect in Quintinum's tally. Now properly braced, Quintinum began hurling silvery balls of energy back at their assailants. He chittered happily as one singed the cat—but only singed, and the cat continued to advance, back arched in irritation. Quintinum wasn't as strong without Loretta. As he hurled another ball, he hoped he could be strong enough.

* * *

A flash of lilac illuminated the skyline, followed by a shimmering penumbra of silver. Loretta's heart soared. She'd know that color of magic anywhere. "It's Quintinum!" she cried, her joy cracking her voice as much as her composure.

Kennelowe turned and seized the stationmaster's shoulder. "When's the next train?"

The stationmaster stared at him. "Not for half an hour, sir, I'm afraid you'll have to wait."

"No need. That's perfect." Kennelowe clapped his hands. "Come on, Humph."

Humphrey scuttled to his master's feet and Kennelowe stepped onto his back. Placing his legs securely in the notches in Humphrey's tricorn crest, he turned and offered a hand to Loretta. "Get on. He's perfectly safe."

"There's not much room."

"And not much time to get to Quintinum, I'm sure."

Loretta thrust out her chin, took Kennelowe's hand as if she had never doubted, and mounted his familiar behind him. As she secured her arms around his chest, two antennae swept back and curled around their ankles, holding them firmly.

"Hold on," warned Kennelowe. "He has quite a turn of speed when he wants to."

The crowd scattered as Humphrey trundled to the platform edge. His carapace began to glow with streams of flickering aquamarine. When he leapt onto the tracks, there was a crack like thunder, and then he was racing towards the magical explosions, the two witches hanging on for dear life.

* * *

Quintium was flagging. He was used to being stronger. While mere moments ago he had been able to score some satisfying hits upon Corrigan or his cat, Quintinum was now very much on the back limb. He had managed to parry everything so far, but he feared his luck was beginning to run out.

As for Corrigan, he was relentless, and he was gaining on them. Just a few more paces, and he would no longer need to cast spells. He would have his hands on Quintinum and Bartelby, and there would be no parrying after that. Quintinum willed Bartelby on in vain, but he, too, was beginning to tire and stagger.

Quintinum's shot went wide. The next hit home, but simply rolled off Corrigan's coat and damaged nothing but his pride. The lord grimaced in rage, and a ball of scarlet light began to form in his hand, bigger than any previous missile. Quintinum would not be able to parry that. The witch snarled and raised it high.

There was a sharp crack like thunder, a flash of aquamarine, and Corrigan was tumbling over. The spell flew at them. Bartelby was hit in the midriff, but Corrigan's aim was off enough that Quintinum cushioned the blow. Bartelby was left only stunned. They fell to the ground, while Corrigan himself disappeared into a bank of smoldering shrubbery. The object that had sent him flying flew past Quintinum and Bartelby and came to an abrupt halt. Two figures stepped from it, staggering as they encountered firm ground once more.

Quintinum's hearts soared as he leapt into Loretta's arms. He wrapped his limbs around her head, nipping and nuzzling her ears as a warm and golden feeling of rightness flowed between them once more. He was dimly aware that Humphrey was there, and he chittered his thanks, but Humphrey was tired. The trilobite only wanted to sit and accept the praise of his witch, who knelt beside him and scratched his gills.

"Quintinum!" cried Loretta as she peeled him off her face. "It's so good to see you!" She held him before her, and her rapturous joy became something softer and fonder. "It's good to feel myself again."

Quintinum clacked his beak. He, too, had felt their connection reforging in each other's embrace. He, too, was more glad than he could say.

* * *

When Loretta turned to face the man rising from the bushes, brushing cerulean embers from his coat, she crooked her arms and frowned. "Lord Corrigan." She was very good at pretending to be less surprised than she was. "You stole my familiar."

"And my trilobites," called Kennelowe. Both ignored him.

"And now, I suppose," continued Loretta, "you intend to silence me." Corrigan glowered.

"That's the very least I'll do to you and your damned squid," he growled. Loretta was gratified to note as he walked closer, carefully concealing a stagger, that his face was blackened not by magefire but by ink. *Well done, Quintinum.* Corrigan raised his hands and took up a duelling stance. His cat arched its back and hissed.

Loretta raised an incredulous eyebrow. "Are you challenging me to a duel, Corrigan?"

"Woman or no, I will have satisfaction."

"'Woman or no' doesn't come into it," snapped Loretta. "How dare you? What right have you to expect that decorum from me—*me*—after all you have done?" Her hands began to hiss with power as she drank deep from the well she and Quintinum could only draw from together. "I know you think little of my temper, Corrigan, but you have to admit, it has its uses."

There was nothing Corrigan could do to fend off the barrage Loretta and Quintinum unleashed. He was powerful, but he was drained. Certain of victory, he had overcommitted. He was angry, but Loretta was furious.

"That's enough!" cried Kennelowe, as the tenth round of hexes left Corrigan and his familiar sprawled on the soil. "Loretta, that's enough."

Humphrey whined in agreement with his master. Even Quintinum let his arms fall and clucked into Loretta's ear. After a long moment in which a final, overlarge silver fireball formed in her hand, Loretta scoffed and let her power drop.

"You're right. He's more trouble to us dead." She walked to the unconscious bodies and nudged them with an over-firm foot. "Besides, I want to see his face when he encounters consequences for the first time." With a flick of her fingers, she conjured ropes gleaming with adamant and bound them securely. "Now, we just have to decide what is to be done with him."

* * *

What was to be done was largely decided at Barchester station. The stationmaster had not been best pleased at their return, even more so because he was now in charge of the custody of a powerful man, both magically and politically. He was currently telephoning the authorities with all due haste. He had no wish for enemies and was endeavoring to get the entire matter off his hands as quickly as possible before any of the affair stuck to him. Others could decide who had the right of it. In the meantime, Loretta, Kennelowe, and Bartelby had taken choice seats in the waiting room. It was otherwise empty, the presence of two witches and their familiars being enough to disquiet most people.

Humphrey and Quintinum were curled up at their masters' feet. Both were fast asleep, and their witches were content to let them rest, with not a little envy.

"I suppose I shall have to return to the party and explain why their host won't be attending," mused Loretta.

"To get ahead of his story?" Bartelby leaned forward, trying to look calm and assured, but ended up wincing over the poultice bound about his midriff. He kept forgetting about the pain; inside he was still trembling from the afternoon's excitement.

"That would be a good idea," conceded Loretta. "Though I was rather thinking what a treat it would be to break the news and see everyone's faces. Whether they believe me or not."

Kennelowe barked a laugh around his pipe. "You certainly live up to your reputation, Miss Winstanleigh."

"Gosh, I should hope so. Would you care to join me?"

Kennelowe shook his head. "Humphrey would never forgive me if we delayed recovering his cousins." He glanced down fondly at the slumbering arthropod, whose antennae were crooked protectively around the two specimens returned by Bartelby. "I'll go on with you, Bartelby, if you don't mind."

Bartelby could not suppress his grin. "Of course! If we're lucky the fossils may have already been delivered to my address." He frowned. "Though it galls me that his lordship tried to implicate me, it does rather seem to have worked out in the end."

"Indeed." At a whistle outside, Kennelowe looked up. "That will be your train, Miss Winstanleigh." He fished into his pocket and produced a faded calling card. "Do call on me soon. Humphrey's taken a shine to you, and I'm sure he'd like to give you both a tour of our collection." Loretta took the card with a smile and pocketed it.

"I'll take you up on that offer, Mr. Kennelowe. We're sure to have much to discuss."

Kennelowe nodded, then offered an identical card to Bartelby, whose mouth fell agape; he only just stopped short of grabbing it. Loretta chuckled and nudged the dozing squid gently with her foot. "Come on Quintinum. Time to go."

Quintinum stirred, chunnered sleepily to himself, then clambered onto Loretta's shoulder. When she raised a hand to scratch him, he grasped it tightly in a tentacle. He did not let go until their journey was done.

The Alien Method

Jean Marie Ward

A research station parked over a world taking its first steps toward interplanetary flight is a sweet ride. You settle into high orbit and play peekaboo with space junk. A clutch of scientists follows events on the surface and debates whether the jumped-up primates currently in charge will achieve interstellar travel—and whether they should be invited to join the Cooperative if they do. The military component is larger, since we run the joint, but our main duties consist of keeping those debates from escalating to antenna pulling and preventing space pirates from following the trails of said planet's first Voyagers to their source and trashing the place.

But sweet gets sucked out the airlock when a Primus of the High Council decides to take a taxpayer-funded vacation—*ahem,* "fact-finding tour" of said solar system. Suddenly it's all high-stepping, synchronized wing-and-weapon maneuvers in the main hangar bay. My squadron and I looked like the dancers in the video of *42nd Street* we watched as part of our Earth Culture Sensitivity Training.

It wouldn't have been so bad if this particular Primus hadn't brought along his first-hatched, hereafter known as "Junior" to protect the guilty. Junior had just completed a brief, undistinguished stint in military service, and daddy was checking all the boxes to qualify him for a career in politics. (Star-faring gods preserve us.)

Meanwhile, our station commander, Colonel G'rrll'n, was trying to elevate her ranking on the current general's list through strategic butt kissing. "Junior," she churred, "I understand you passed your pilot's exam."

On the fourth try, and only after the former academy commander was encouraged to retire.

"How would you like to take a spin over the continent that looks like an Aviann in flight?"

That's how three of the station's burliest marines, cultural anthropologist Dr. V'nnnn'lll, the requisite tub of the sapient fungus known as Gunk, and I, Lieutenant K'nn'bz Rch, found ourselves on a shuttle disguised as a dirty ice ball buzzing the Capitol of Earth's United States in the middle of a summer heatwave. Clueless doesn't begin to cover it.

"Take that you ugly hairy-headed arthropod oppressors!" Junior crowed, shaking his forelimbs at the viewscreen.

The shuttle pitched forward. *Shithead was flying manual!* I slammed the override on the copilot's cradle and hauled the yoke back with my forelimbs while my mid-limbs danced over the controls. The shuttle's nose crept upward. I banked, manipulating the shuttle's magnetic response to the Capitol's iron dome. Our hull screeched against one of the dome's ribs. Then the repulsion factor kicked in. We shot down a street of stone buildings and old row houses toward the Potomac.

Exoskeletons don't sweat, but I swear my joints were leaking. Unlike Junior, I passed all my flight tests on the first go and had collected hundreds of hours on the station's shuttles, which is how I wound up babysitting him in the first place. But this exam had no retakes. It wasn't until we were over the river (I can land anything on a river) that I could spare a thought for anything other than staying airborne.

The readings on all our key systems looked good. But our close encounter with the Capitol had damaged some insulation scales on the outer hull. Without repairs, this shuttle was troposphere-only.

I turned to explain the problem to Junior and discovered his cradle was empty. In addition to disabling the autopilot, he had uncoupled his safety harness. He slumped against the port hatch. The sight recalled the nasty crunch I heard in the middle of our "course correction." I swallowed and returned my attention to the flight screens. But having compound eyes means you have three-sixty vision. His ichor-covered thorax was always in view. Based on snatches of conversation between Gunk and Dr. V'nnnn'lll, he was missing most of his left eye and parts of both antennae. Forget the shuttle, Junior was too banged up to survive escape velocity. We could be stuck on this dirtball indefinitely.

Fortunately, our home world has an atmosphere and gravity nearly identical to Earth, and everybody had their shots. Since we're roughly the length of a human finger, with ships sized to match, we're also easy to overlook—one of the reasons we excel as observers. I scanned the clustered towers across the highway from the Pentagon. The canyons between them offered plenty of cover. A wealth of deserted balconies promised shelter and access to resources.

I set the shuttle down on a neglected upper floor balcony masked by closed fabric blinds. While Gunk directed triage, I transmitted our coordinates to the station and asked to speak to Colonel G'rrll'n.

The colonel sensed something was wrong. She decamped to her quarters before taking the call. Propped against her lectern, she crossed both sets of forelimbs over her thorax. "How bad is it?"

"The ship? Gunk estimates three Earth days, tops. Junior…"

I cocked my head toward the medical action happening beside the hatch. Under Gunk's direction, Dr. V'nnnn'lll had pumped Junior full of the good drugs before starting work on his injuries. Junior responded by stridulating a sexual invitation that would have gotten him arrested back home. The colonel's antenna went rigid.

"Yeah," I deadpanned. "He's gonna need a full molt."

"How did this happen?" she demanded. "The sensor log shows everybody harnessed at take-off."

"Junior said the straps crimped his wings. I haven't checked the log, but my guess is he mid-limbed the buckles when he disabled the autopilot and strafed the Capitol."

Her jaw clenched. None of this was helping her promotion prospects. "I'll have a pair of relief shuttles at your location one Earth hour after dusk."

"With all due respect, sir, he wouldn't make it to the station. Besides, you don't want the Primus to see him like this. He'll never believe he did it to himself. He'll turn the station upside down trying to prove it was negligence. Let Gunk handle it. Seven Earth days and Junior will be good as new. In the meantime, tell the Primus he and Dr. V'nnnn'lll are communing with the local arthropods."

"Setting aside the fact the local arthropods barely qualify as sentient…"

True. We may look like cousins, but that's parallel evolution for you. Taxonomically speaking, we're not even part of the same domain. We're barely part of the same galaxy. But the Primus, like his son, had flunked biology.

Colonel G'rrll'n continued, "What happens when Junior makes it back to the station? Has Gunk figured out a way to rearrange his memories?"

She made it sound like a good thing.

"Not that I know of," I said. "When the time comes, we tell the Primus the truth. We didn't want to worry him. As for how it happened, blame snipers. It's America. It's always snipers."

After ending the call, I assigned Corporals Ph'rrr'd and B'rrrrphl to guard the shuttle and prepare the party for transit. Corporal H'kkk'nn and I headed out on recon with one of the shuttle's electromagnetic spreaders and a pair of marble-sized, camouflage-skinned drones. Our sensors said the apartment was empty, but you always double-check.

We disabled the doors' lock and slid the spreader into place along their bottom track. The room beyond was a giant beige box with a cube cut out of one corner for the kitchen. Directly ahead of the doors, a mammoth gray sofa faced a runway-sized coffee table, cabinet, and wall-mounted screen. To our left, four chairs surrounded an enormous table. Posters of colorfully costumed humans and strange animals dotted the walls. (Dr. V'nnnn'lll later identified the animals as "familiars," though the blue stag, cat-wolf, and four-eyed sloth were as alien to Earth as they were to me.) Happily, my scent receptors detected no insecticide or, worse, scented candles.

A breakfast bar separated the dining area from the kitchen. The business side of the counter featured a stainless-steel sink and dishwasher. The waste bins were tucked under the counter between the sink and the passage into the dining room. Safe air, water, shelter, and food—it wasn't exactly the high life, but it was doable, with enough dust mites and aerosolized cooking grease to keep Gunk fed and willing to make all necessary repairs.

I hustled everybody out of the shuttle as soon as Junior could be moved. We should have had plenty of time to relocate before local workplaces emptied for the day. But we were still in the open, midway between the sofa and the table, when the deadbolt on the front door *thunk*-ed. Everybody except Junior, who was snoring, and Gunk, who didn't breathe except to speak, held their breath. The camouflage skins on our hover sleds can mimic the color of their surroundings. My people can't. The brown of our carapaces didn't match the rug, and humans can be…volatile.

The sweaty, rumpled, hairy-headed human who opened the door was a middling specimen. He was only as tall as the doors to the research station's hangar bay. He wasn't a happy hulk, either. His perspiration stank of anger as much as overheated flesh.

"Shit," he snarled, "it's hotter in here than outside."

Our forearm communicators supplied the translation. The thud of his backpack hitting the ground added emphasis. He cursed again, closed the door with exaggerated care, then stomped past the sofa into the darkened hallway leading to the apartment's two bed- and bathrooms.

We'd already deployed our drones, but visual projections where the humans could see them were strictly verboten. I ordered the team to shelter in place and spread my wings.

I landed on the edge of the passageway. The human tapped a small box on the corridor wall. A dim, greenish glow illuminated the bridge of his nose. He compared the reading to the screen on his phone.

"Eighty-four! Eighty-fucking-four! How does she do it?" he asked the ceiling. "One more lousy degree, and I could report her ass. Augh!"

Shaking his head, he retreated to the larger of the two bedrooms. I followed. He dropped his clothes on the carpet and headed for the ensuite bath. He turned on the shower. I gave the order to move and rejoined my crew. But nobody relaxed until everyone and everything were secreted behind the waste receptacles.

"They're so big," Corporal H'kkk'nn hissed. Her fellow marines nodded, their antennae stiff with tension, alarm pheromones pumping overtime.

Dr. V'nnnn'lll and I exchanged sympathetic glances. You can study Earth's civilization for years, amass storehouses full of artifacts, and crawl all over their buildings. But you can't comprehend the size of these creatures until you see them for yourself. It's like watching a skyscraper pull up its foundations and tramp across a city, pulverizing everything in its path. Then it sinks in how dangerous they are. It's not a pleasant realization, but no marine ever crapped out on me yet.

Corporal Ph'rrr'd raised a forelimb. "Permission to speak, sir."

My pheromones signaled assent.

"Why was he complaining about the heat?" he asked. "It's nice in here."

I turned to our cultural anthropologist, but Gunk got there first. "Inferior thermoregulation. It's the downside of having a skeleton instead of a carapace," burped the gelatinous, bubblegum pink fungus who had neither.

Dr. V'nnnn'lll bit down a grin. I was beginning to like her.

To everyone's relief, the human didn't linger. He left the apartment a short time later in a fresh shirt and shorts, smelling of cologne. He didn't return for three local hours, after the apartment's temperature had cooled to the number posted on its thermostat, seventy-three degrees Fahrenheit. He grabbed a can of soda and bag of corn puffs from the kitchen, then settled on the sofa for two hours of gaming before heading to bed.

Gaming and sleeping proved to be his primary at-home activities. He avoided the multi-computer office occupying the smaller bedroom, preferring to handle his after-hours business by phone beneath the large, ceiling-mounted fan in the living room. Over the two remaining days of the planet's five-day work week, he left the apartment early and returned later than the statistical norm. Meal preparation was spotty but included enough organic matter to keep us fed and Gunk working overtime.

The marines and I split the time between ship repairs, helping Gunk with Junior, and look-out duties. Dr. V'nnnn'lll Gunked the building's electrical systems, as well as our host's hard drives, servers, and cloud storage. Threading Gunk fibers thinner than spider silk into the apartment's information systems, and recording and interpreting the data, was every bit as demanding as repairing the shuttle. But from the way she acted, you'd think it was Clutch Day, Planetary Union, and Swarm all rolled into one.

"You know, Milt's right," she told us at dinner the third day—Friday, per the locals. Her pheromones fizzed and eye facets sparkled under Gunk's thread lights. "That's his name: Milton Cleveland Garber. Milt to his friends. By now I feel I know him well enough, even if we never meet socially. Anyway, his landlady, Ida Cristillo, is tampering with the air conditioning. She's placed regulators on the systems feeding her units. It's illegal, but Milt can't prove it without hacking her data systems, which is even more illegal than what she's doing to his HVAC."

The marines stilled. They would have jumped at the chance to test drive Milt's gaming set-up, but arthropomorphizing the native primates was dangerous. To marines, dangers exist to be eliminated. By marines.

I'm no diplomat, but I know a situation when I smell it. Keeping my pheromones neutral, I asked, "What do you plan to do about it?"

Her pheromones signaled confusion with a whiff of hurt. "Nothing. I just thought it was interesting. I mean, don't you want to know why he's upset all the time?"

Now I felt like a jerk. Healthy paranoia is a requirement of command. But the professor wasn't some wet-behind-the-antennae rookie on her first insertion. She'd served on a dozen Earth expeditions and once defended her team from a broom. (A broom might not sound like much to you, but remember, to us that broom is as big as the Washington Monument.)

She was just doing her job. It wasn't the job she expected. But she was still stuck here. So, she created a research opportunity, teasing out data from our host's information systems like one of the local ants milking honeydew from an aphid. But unlike her other research junkets, there wasn't anyone around to share the thrill. The marines and I saw everything in terms of threat, and Gunk…who knows what goes on in the distributed intelligence of a hot pink fungus capable of incorporating random matter into its extrusions and chemically transforming them into everything from shuttle insulation to sickbay shrouds?

Thinking about all that professional excitement in need of an outlet got me wondering what else she might get excited about. She might not be the showiest female on the station, but her sleek brown wings were perfect, and despite our primitive accommodations, her pheromones smelled like sun-warmed grass.

Hey, I'm an officer, not a monk.

Since she was a civilian, the regs against fraternization didn't apply. I smoothed my way by asking about the cultural implications of Milt's data and was rewarded with an invitation to view the highlights in Milt's office Sunday afternoon.

Perfect. It was hard to keep from smelling too excited. We were on track to finish rebuilding the shuttle Saturday. Running pre-flight scans would take the marines all of Sunday. I wouldn't run mine until they were satisfied—Monday at the earliest.

Gunk didn't need me either. They'd finished rebuilding Junior's broken bits, triggered a full molt, and swaddled him in an organic polymer sickbay shroud to complete the undeserving nincompoop's recovery. Gunk themselves were recharging, absorbing quantities of dust mites, grease, and random spiders. Even our host seemed to play along. Saturday, he left the apartment almost as early as usual, and he didn't return until after midnight.

Sunday afternoon found me lounging next to Shrreee—we had graduated to first names—on the carpet under the largest of Milt's two desks. Screen shots on the wall behind the knee hole detailed Milt's work on military retirement systems and reports of elected officials' efforts to reduce benefits while touting their support for the military. Some things are universal, regardless of species.

I said, "All this is happening at the Capitol, right? Makes me sorry I stopped Junior from blasting the joint."

She gave my shoulder a playful nudge. (*Voluntary contact. Score!* My chances were looking better by the minute.) "Have you forgotten the whole 'nearly died' part?"

Her tone was pert; her scent, the opposite of angry. I shuddered dramatically, the edges of my wings brushing hers, testing my welcome while keeping within the green zone. "I lost a decade of my life in the cockpit that day. I'm a faint shadow of the—"

"You'll be a dead shadow if you don't get to the kitchen right now!" Gunk's gravelly glub erupted from our comms. "Junior escaped."

Damn him. I was *this close.*

"How?" Shrreee's question trailed after me as I sailed into the hall.

Hell if I know. He was tranqed to the antenna. He shouldn't have been able to move, much less escape a Gunk cocoon. All I could figure was stupidity was a superpower, and Junior's was triple strength. *What next?*

I shouldn't have asked.

The bolt on the apartment door clicked. The door opened. "Shit," Milt snarled. "It's gotta be ninety in here."

Wings tight against my back, I dove, skimming the floorboards to avoid detection. Milt tossed his backpack in front of the doors to the living room closet and clomped into the hall. I shot toward the kitchen ceiling for an overview. No Junior.

"Gunk, which way did he go?"

"Dammit, K'nn, We're a fungus, not a sniffer bot."

"ID chip? Drones?" I growled with more patience than they deserved.

"De-chipped as soon as he separated. Junior's destined for greatness, you know." It's hard for a fungus to sound sarcastic, but Gunk managed. "Nothing on the feeds. He's probably still in the kitchen."

Corporal H'kkk'nn announced the Marines had arrived in the dining room and awaited orders.

"Search the kitchen cabinets, floor up," I replied. "I got the ceiling."

It wasn't just that I was the better flier. Taking to the heights meant I'd be the one distracting Milt if he got too close. I was the most expendable person on our team. The colonel could have another pilot here in two hours. Junior needed the rest of them.

The wood-toned wall cabinets offered cover and good sight lines. I boosted my communicator's sensor settings to max, supplementing the readings with eyeball and antenna scans. My comm chirped notice of movement near the sink. It could be the marines, but…

I raced to the edge of the last cabinet.

Milt, a wet towel draped over his head, entered the kitchen and collected a soda from the refrigerator. My communicator chirped again. Junior, still translucent from his molt, clambered onto the counter.

"Found Junior," I shouted into my comm. "Counter, left of sink. Code Red! Human in the kitchen! Human in the kitchen!"

Of course, Junior wasn't wearing a communicator, and despite being newly molted and pumped full of enough drugs to kill a bird, he was still oversexed from his injuries. Or maybe he was always oversexed. It's not like we scuttle in the same circles. The point is, he was banging his head against the raised edge of the sink like the smeary image he saw there was sex on six sticks.

Milt straightened. I seized control of a kitchen drone and set it to dazzle. But as he turned from the frig, the towel dropped over his eyes. Three familiar pairs of antennae crested the side of the counter. All they had to do was grab…

Milt yanked the towel away. The soda bottle hit the floor. He shrieked, "Roach! White Roach!"

The marines charged across the counter. Junior kept banging the sink. I buzzed down to help. The marines surrounded Junior and herded him toward the wall. Turning to our host, I triggered the drone's distraction program and bunched my legs to leap.

The towel stretched between Milt's fists started to shake. "They took it away. They took it away! The roaches are working together!"

He screamed again and ran out of the kitchen.

The marines and I retreated to the trash cabinet. Shrreee joined us a minute later. While Gunk grimly swaddled Junior in triple-layered sani-shrouds, I patched into Gunk's drone feed and projected Milt's progress on the cabinet's inside wall. Aside from the translator, we didn't need audio. By the time he called his landlady, they could hear him in Canada.

"The damn thing was three inches long! And white! A white roach, Ida! The brown ones carried it away, like it was their king or something. The roaches are organizing, and it's all your fault."

Ida babbled something about "green buildings" and scheduling conflicts.

"I don't care!" Milt shouted. "I want this apartment fumigated tomorrow. And I want the receipt and the dead bugs to prove it, or I'm calling my lawyer, the HOA, and *Seven On Your Side*!"

He ended the call and asked his phone how to kill roaches.

"Dish soap and water in a spray bottle? How will that help? Peppermint and tea tree oil? Ida tried that. Useless. Spray insecticide. Doh. Glue traps? If they're smart enough for collective action, they won't fall for those. Boric acid powder. Now that has possibilities…"

By the time he left, the stress hormones inside the cabinet were thicker than Junior's head. I climbed the hover sled we'd been using as a lectern and addressed the troops. "Thanks to Junior, our host knows we're here. He has not discovered the nature of our presence. Mission security has not been breached. Non-interference protocols remain in place. However, our host seeks to kill us. Solutions? We got thirty Earth minutes to implement."

Corporal B'rrrrphl raised a forelimb. "Eliminate him." His brother marine's head bobbed in agreement.

"Always an option." The energy weapons in our comms can be wielded with pinpoint accuracy, but they leave traces—traces we don't want humans to find. There were also ethical and strategic issues. We look like humans' least favorite vermin. We rely on their abhorrence to move among them undetected. It would be wrong to kill Milt for playing along. Strategically… "We'll keep it as a last resort. Our ultimate goal here is expanding the Cooperative. We want humans working with us, not against us. Eliminating random specimens because we were in the wrong place at the wrong time defeats the purpose."

Shrreee nodded, her pheromones signaling something more complicated than approval, like I'd passed a test I hadn't known I was taking.

I didn't get a chance to do more than register the thought. Gunk was grousing: "You sound like Colonel G'rrll'n, We have a toxin—"

"You can rewrite his memories?"

Unlike the colonel, the prospect gave me chills. If Gunk could rewrite human brains, they could rewrite ours. But if they could do it, I'd give the order. It might be our only viable option.

Gunk burbled, "If he were a cicada. We do great work with cicadas. Have you ever seen them copulating without their heads?"

Seriously? Seeing Junior bang the sink was bad enough. "Is this relevant?"

Gunk burped, their version of a pout. "No. The coding of memory among higher sentients is too complex. You can destroy their ability to think or temporarily dull their emotions, but isolating and altering specific memories is virtually impossible. On the other hand, blunt force trauma often leads to memory loss. But you can't predict what they'll forget, if anything."

I didn't know whether to be disappointed or relieved.

"Relocate the camp," Corporal H'kkk'nn suggested. "Transport Junior, Gunk, and the drones to the shuttle. Milt never looks outside. We can shelter in place while you complete your pre-flights and Junior finishes hardening."

"It's a solid plan." And the only one that occurred to me.

Corporal H'kkk'nn's pheromones brightened.

Unfortunately, it came with a giant *but*. "The problem is we need to sweep the apartment for Gunk residue. Milt is out buying bug spray and boric acid powder. I guarantee he'll deploy them the minute he returns. That means we'll need hazmat suits to clear the place. You saw how he reacted to Junior. Imagine how he'll react to the suits."

The corporal's scent roiled. She wanted to say the marines could be careful, sneaky even. Of course they could. The issue was Junior. There was no space to contain him in the shuttle. He could fall off the balcony and get himself killed. On my watch—and I had a performance review coming up.

"Make him a familiar," Shrreee said.

"What?" the rest of us sputtered.

"A familiar. It's a kind of magical pet-slash-helper. We make him our familiar, order him to leave us alone, and go about our business. He'll buy it. All his game characters are magic users. He's a big fantasy fan on other platforms too. You should see his library!"

"How does that help us?" I asked. "Magic doesn't exist."

"Doesn't matter. It's a head game. We just need to convince him it's real."

I tried to keep my pheromones neutral and respectful. I wanted to get laid, after all. But the skepticism poured off me in waves.

Shrreee rolled her antenna. "Really, guys. Humans still use petrochemicals. We have FTL. If we can't pull a few tricks from under our wings, we need to rethink our definition of 'advanced.'"

"What will it take and how long?" I asked.

"Ten minutes. I control his electronics. All I need you guys to do is march up the living room closet in formation when I give the signal."

Shrreee's scent held no uncertainty. I thought about her research and her confrontation with the broom. The idea sounded nuts, but Milt did spend a lot of time slinging made-up spells and lobbing magic fireballs.

It was risky. If we failed, I'd have to get very creative with diversion and non-lethal force to ensure everyone evacuated before Milt started spraying. But if it worked...

I resisted for all of a nanosecond, but I'd watched too many vids. "Make it so."

Milt returned toting two clanking plastic bags, smelling angrier than ever. He kicked the door closed. Vibrations from the impact reverberated through the lintel, shaking me from pincers to haunches. Despite Shrreee's assurances, I had exempted myself from the closet parade. She believed in her plan. I belong to the Church of Cover Your Ass.

"Milton Cleveland Garber!" a window-bending human voice borrowed from Chris Hemsworth's Thor boomed from the living room speakers. The big television blinked, turning from glossy black to pale gray. Millions of black dots bloomed on the screen, undulating in response to Shrreee's electronically generated bellow.

Milt's bags hit the carpet. "What the hell?"

"Hear me, Milton Cleveland Garber. I am the Lord of the Flighted, and I have chosen you to be my familiar on this plane."

"Lord of the *what*? Really, Sid?" he demanded, naming one of his gamer buds. "I say you don't understand magic, and you hack my system to get back at me? What kind of loser are you?"

He fished his phone from his back pocket. He was probably calling Sid, but he could be calling for help. I pulsed the phone out of his hand. I'm almost as good a shot as I am a pilot.

"My phone!" Milt wailed. He snatched it off the carpet. He dropped it just as fast. The case was still hot from the pulse.

None of this was part of the script, but Shrreee didn't miss a beat. The lamp on the table cattycorner to the closet and the standing lamp on the balcony side of the television, started to strobe. The overhead fan sped to a blur. "Human, this conversation is for your ears alone!"

Milt gulped and turned to the TV. "You're not Sid, are you? Sid couldn't…" He pointed at the phone. "That…what did you do?"

"Magic." The undulating dots became a fountain of black sparkles.

"No, magic isn't real. It's a fairy tale."

"I'm neither fairy, nor tail. I am the Lord of the Flighted, and I have chosen you as my familiar."

"You keep saying that, but you can't make me a familiar. Familiars are animals. Pets. I'm a human being." Milt's voice shook. But scared as he was, he didn't back down. It's one of the reasons we want humans in the Cooperative. They don't know when to quit.

"If magic isn't real, how do you know what a familiar is or is not?" Shrreee's Thor voice dropped to a congenial grinding of rocks. The strobing lights stopped flashing. The fan's rotation slowed. "According to your dictionaries, it can be anyone you know well or who serves another. I have need of such in this plane."

"Why?" He stood squarely in front of the TV, feet wide and fists clenched. But his pheromones jittered on the edge of panic. "You're messing with my stuff like a real live Sephiroth and you're not even here. That's crazy powerful. Why do you need me?"

"My corporeal form cannot manifest in your dimension. Therefore, I need servants and a familiar to protect them as they go about their work."

Shrreee pinged our comms. The marines leapt from the carpet to the closet. They landed on the closet door roughly the length of a human hand apart in a line roughly the same distance from the floor. They marched up the door in perfect alignment, wings flaring every sixth beat, the display as precise as their intervals. The dots on the TV screen coalesced into a large arrow. It flowed left in a continuous, hypnotic loop, drawing Milt's gaze to their maneuvers.

"You want me to protect *roaches*?!"

Despite everything I said before, I was still insulted.

"I can't fix the microbiome with a rhinoceros," Shrreee snapped.

"Wait? What?" Milt's head whipped back to the screen. "What's the microbiome got to do with anything?"

"Your world is decades away from an extinction event driven by pesticides, plastics, and climate change. The trauma of such cataclysms tears holes in the space-time continuum. Many of those affected by your world's disasters are thrown into ours. The higher life forms die quickly. They can't survive here. But your viruses kill us and keep killing us for generations. Right now, we're barely holding on against the plagues we have."

Drones were recording Milt's every twitch, but I needed to gauge his reactions in real time. I flitted to the edge of the hallway. His rubbery human features slackened, and his fear scent was starting to fade.

"I don't understand," he said. "How do you know we're facing extinction if you're stuck wherever you are."

"What part of 'magic' don't you understand?"

"Sounds like a lot," he replied, showing more self-awareness than expected. "How does my protecting a bunch of cockroaches help?"

"Actually, the roaches will do fine. They've survived multiple extinctions already."

"Figures," Milt grumbled.

Shrreee let the comment pass. "You only need to protect my servants, whose job it will be to restore the biome from the ground up. Human religious texts make much of the fall of a sparrow, but they neglect to mention the grubs and insects upon which the sparrow feeds. Without them there are no crops, no birds, no animals. No you."

"But how am I supposed to tell your guys from the rest? Those guys are walking Superfund sites. Can I still kill those—the regular ones, I mean?"

Shrreee-Thor sighed. "My servants understand your language. Ask them a question. They will flare their wings once for yes, twice for no." Not being dummies, the marines promptly flexed.

"Wow. Just…wow."

"You can use glue traps and bait stations to manage the apartment's unelevated insects," Shrreee continued. We wouldn't be caught alive in them, much less dead. "Now that the stakes have been made clear, it's time to ratify our contract and take the necessary steps to cancel your exterminator appointment."

Milt shook the dazed look from his face. "Exterminator appointment? Back up there, Lord…do you have a name? All I got is your title, but you've got my whole name. Since what I thought I knew about magic doesn't seem to apply, I don't know if knowing my full name gives you power over me. Either way, it's kinda one-sided. And I'm not signing anything until I check out this insect die-off thing. Besides, if this is about that exterminator appointment, you don't need a familiar. It's never gonna happen. Ida won't call an exterminator unless the HOA starts screaming."

I pressed the thumbs of my forward pincers to the spot between my antenna where headaches grew. Milt was as bad as Gunk or Shrreee when they nerded out.

Maybe worse. There was a long pause on Shrreee's end.

"You can verify everything I've said online," she said at last. "If that isn't enough, consider this: my servants' comfort zone is the same as yours. Therefore, I have a vested interest in your living conditions. I can make your landlady fulfill the terms of your contract."

"What? No billion dollars or trucks full of gold bars?"

"Listen, kid, I'm trying to prevent an extinction event. There's not a lot of money in it. Causing disasters? Sure. Fixing them? You bet. Averting them? Not so much. But I can stop your landlady from screwing you over. Are you in or not?"

Milt nodded. "But if you're lying, the deal's off."

"Done."

The lights flashed again. Shrreee pinged the robot vacuum parked beside the closet. It zipped from its charging station to a distance roughly eighteen human inches from Milt's sneakers. Shrreee intoned her terms and solicited his agreement in triplicate. The Roomba solemnly circled him three times and docked itself. The television went black.

"That's it?" Milt asked plaintively.

Corporal H'kkk'nn flared her wings once. Ph'rrr'd and B'rrrphl flared theirs an instant later.

"You do understand. Excellent!" Milt pumped his fist. "Hey, do you want to help me research this die-off thing?"

B'rrrrphl was stuck on Junior duty, but H'kkk'nn and Ph'rrr'd were game. I trailed them to Milt's office. Shrreee had abandoned her command post under the desk for the narrow gap behind the two-drawer filing cabinet, hidden from the room's assigned drones. She met me on the floor at the corner of the cabinet and waved her pincers over her comm. Intrigued, I turned off my comm as (silently) requested.

Her scent practically sizzled. She cocked her antenna at the unlikely threesome. "How much trouble am I in?"

"For what? Convincing a human we're magical, world-saving roaches?"

"And committing us to helping him," she elaborated. "Yeah, that."

"There's nothing in the regs against deceiving humans to preserve our cover. As for helping him, I can disable the regulator and make it look like equipment failure."

"I'd like to have Milt confront Ida with it."

"As long as it fits in a hover sled," I said.

"It should. You sure you're not mad?"

I assured her I wasn't. Privately, I thought "The Lord of the Flighted" was acting more like a familiar doing favors for a human than the other way around. But it was better than getting squished or gassed.

She took a full-body breath. "We need to go bigger for Ida. I'll need a lot of Gunk and all the pincers you can spare."

In addition to the FX she'd pulled together for Milt, Shrreee envisioned a giant casting circle of the heat-activated thread lights and smoke threads. The threads presented no danger to humans or flammable furnishings. We use them for first molt parties and, Junior's antics notwithstanding, our newly molted carapaces are more sensitive than anything on the outside of a human. A water-soluble Gunk formula was used to paint "Repent!" in large, soon-to-be pink, letters on the walls between the posters.

At six the following morning, Milt received a text from his new magical boss with all the dope on the illegal regulator sitting on his backpack and his marching orders for the rest of the day. As instructed, Milt called Ida and canceled the exterminator appointment. Instead, he demanded she meet him at the apartment at six p.m. Meeting accomplished, he was free to leave for work. His only other role in our charade was to show up at five, in case Ida arrived early, and produce the regulator on "The Lord of the Flighted's" demand.

"Can I wear my wizard cosplay?" he asked plaintively. No one answered. He tried texting, but the number Shrreee used didn't exist. Shoulders slumped, he finished preparing for work and plodded dejectedly from the apartment.

We expected Ida to try to get the jump on Milt. We weren't expecting her to key the door at three. Shit! Another plan shot to hell.

I sicc'ed two drones on her and darted to the top of the door. "Shrreee, we need Milt. No time to text. Yell like a security alarm until I say stop."

The landlady was a stocky woman a head shorter than Milt, wearing a sleeveless print dress and high heels the same shiny black as her hair. She minced into the living room, a limp paper pinched between two fingers and a can of insecticide tucked under one arm. The paper reeked of alcohol. *Somebody* had been doctoring documents, not very subtly, either.

"Mr. Garber? Oh, Mr. Garber?" she yodeled disingenuously. She knew damn well he didn't leave work until four-thirty.

Shrreee blared, "Intruder! Intruder! Intruder!"

As hoped, Ida ducked outside. The drones followed, zipping into the hallway just above her head. The camouflage coding in their skins shifted to mimic the paint in the hall. Ida dialed a number on her phone. My comm relayed the translated audio.

"MIS-ter Garber, what is the meaning of this?" The door cracked open. Ida shoved her phone into the gap just long enough to catch a few "Intruders!" before retreating to the hall. "The exterminator's here. We need to get in."

Milt squawked loud enough to activate the drones' translators. "No! You can't. I don't want him. Get him out of there right now!"

"Mr. Garber, this is completely unacceptable. First you want the exterminators. Then you don't. Too bad. He's here. Now, turn off your alarm, so I can get on with it."

"Noooooo! I…" He stopped, not sure how to continue. He didn't have an alarm system. "It's complicated. Just don't do anything until I get there!"

He ended the call. I told Shrreee she could quit. Ida sniffed. "That'll teach him. These IT types think they're so smart."

She opened the door to the alarmless apartment, satisfaction oozing from every pore. She couldn't hear Gunk's despairing glug: "Junior."

Part of me wasn't even surprised. "Marines, you know what to do. Gunk, keep two drones on Ida. The marines get the rest."

Ida's scent changed. She dropped can and paper by the door and rubbed her bare arms. "It's cold in here. How can it be cold? It's not even four."

The threads of Shrreee's casting circle caught on her heels as she trotted toward the hall. I flew to my usual post at the corridor entrance and pinged Shrreee. "I got an idea. Patch me into Thor."

Ida's fingernail clicked against the thermostat screen. She pulled her phone from her pocket and checked an app. "Damn. The regulator's offline. Piece of junk! That's the last time I buy Ali Baba."

She returned to the living room. I eased myself into firing position. I waited until she was right where I wanted her. I fired.

Her right heel collapsed. She dropped to her hands and knees in the middle of the casting circle.

"Ow! Ow! Ow!" Bending and twisting to inspect the damage, she collected still more Gunk on her skin and clothes. "What is this shit? It looks like… cobwebs! Ew! Get it off! Get it off!"

She rubbed herself all over. It didn't do any good. Those threads are stickier than spider silk. Trying to brush it off just spread it around. She scrambled to her feet. "Oh my God! It's a funnel web. I'm gonna die!"

Funnel web? I pinged the shuttle computer. "*Venomous Earth spider. Native to Australia.*"

She pounded her mismatched shoes into the carpet. "Where is it? Where is it?"

Answer: nowhere. We were fresh out of arachnids. Gunk considers them a delicacy. But she didn't know that, and I was nasty enough to take advantage. I set my laser to its lowest setting, barely hot enough to melt cow butter, and played the beam over the remains of the circle. All the thread lights, including those on Ida, lit up like Higbee's in *A Christmas Story*. Ida shrieked.

"Silence, woman!" my Thor voice bellowed as I sent the drones' video to our television link. "You have been judged and found wanting. Behold!"

The screen and every light in the room flashed. The drones were still recording, but the video started with Ida's arrival. All I knew about Earth law came from Cultural Training, but that bit at the thermostat sounded pretty damning to me.

From the way she stopped trying to squash nonexistent spiders and pry "cobwebs" from her skin, I was onto something. She turned toward the screen. Her eyes widened. Her face paled. She croaked, "That's illegal! It's entrapment!"

I laughed. It didn't sound nearly as evil as I would have liked, but she cringed satisfactorily. "Know this, Ida Giustina Cristillo, if you do not stop abusing your tenants by denying them service and depriving them of comforts they paid for, I will send forth my arachnid army. They will find you wherever you hide. They will envelop you in their webs and suck your juices until all that's left is a desiccated corpse, which I will suspend from the ceiling of the lobby as a warning for landlords everywhere!"

I pulsed the rest of the threads. Smoke fountained upward. A high thin squeal escaped her lips. Seizing the moment, Shrreee strobed the lights. I pulsed the Gunk on the walls. "Repent! Repent! Repent!" Shrreee exploded the fancy square bulbs in the dining room chandelier one by one. Any second now, Ida would be pleading for her life like that miser in the Dickens vid.

In this crucial moment, when I was completely focused on Ida, on the slightest shift in movement, complexion, and pheromones, a large, brown, and all-too-familiar, over-privileged idiot flapped in front of her face.

"Oooh," Junior cooed. "You smell pretty."

Ida's fear of spiders did not extend to us. Yes, she screamed and jumped and fell on her ass beside the sofa. But she came up swinging.

I switched the drones to dazzle mode and aimed them at Ida's face. They swooped in, prisms flashing like mini-disco balls. She batted them away. They bounced back.

I sped across the room, taking aim as I flew. I had to keep her away from the insecticide. If that meant burning her fingers, I would. Blisters heal.

Before I could fire, four more disco drones flew into position. Another six circled overhead. The marines had arrived. Powering down, I ordered, "Herd her toward the closet and keep her there."

I had some vague idea of holding her prisoner until Milt arrived and told her the place was under The Lord of the Flighted's protection, with or without the regulator show-and-tell. That plan got as far as the door.

Junior landed on the peephole. "Whatcha doin'?" he asked brightly, still under the influence, but sadly still conscious.

Ida's hand whipped out. I whipped in, using the momentum of my landing to shove Junior out of reach. Junior spun to face me, head lowered, wings flared, plates rattling, hissing in threat. Ida shrieked.

"Marines," I called, "commence maneuver Square Four, Junior center."

"Huh," Junior said as I positioned myself a wingspan above and to the right of his head. The marines landed in perfect formation, completing the square. I quickly ordered eight of the drones to move in formation with us. The remaining four stayed focused on Ida.

Our wings flexed. Our plates rattled. We hissed in unison. We'd been practicing these moves ever since we learned about the Primus's visit. By now we were *good*. With the drones flashing rainbows, we were better than good. We were kaleidoscopic, like the musical climax of *42nd Street*. Junior joined in. Badly. He kept jumping off the door, trying to bite the drones.

Taking advantage of the distraction, I announced, "These are my servants, Ida Cristillo. Harm them at your peril."

Milt burst through the door. We cut the dazzle on the drones and shot into the baseboard, dragging Junior with us. All Milt saw was Ida backed against the poster on the adjacent wall, sobbing "Hail Mary" on repeat. Being a decent guy, he ferried Ida to the nearest ER and waited with her until her family arrived.

While he was out, we copied the video feeds from the relevant drones onto his main computer and some memory disks we found in his desk. Shrreee texted him where to find the recordings and advised him to purchase and install compatible security cameras to explain the videos. She assured me they would stand up in U.S. courts. Milt could film Ida in his home.

He returned after eight with a pizza and booted up his favorite game. He didn't share the pizza, but he didn't flinch when the marines landed on the arm of the sofa to watch. Shrreee and I left him expounding on the magic of his online world.

The air on the balcony was pleasantly sultry. The alien moon gleamed. Foreign stars twinkled against the purple black sky. My forelimb stroked the sensitive joint between Shrreee's head and shoulders. She snuggled closer.

"Tell the truth, K'nn, how screwed are we?"

"Screwed? We're not screwed."

"Ida saw our drones. She'll tell her doctors, and if Milt starts talking about being a familiar—"

"Nobody'll believe it."

She groaned. "My supervisor will. First contact isn't supposed to happen like this. We're not supposed to impersonate wizards!"

"First contact? Who are you kidding? That was a hundred years ago."

She pulled away and fixed me with a disbelieving stare.

My pheromones brightened to a grin. "And you call yourself a cultural affairs officer. How many times have you watched *42nd Street*? The proof's right in the credits: BuzzBee Berkley. Where do you think he learned those moves?"

The Seamstress of The Wilds

Jordan Bricco

"This is the end, isn't it?" The soft voice of Katja drifted up from the threadbare apron.

"It is." A lump formed in Cecily's throat as she ran her fingers along her familiar's side hem. The apron had been with her for a handful of years, and produced some of the most spectacular magic she had ever seen. She dropped her hands from the apron and returned to folding a few yards of sturdy slate blue canvas.

"Well, hurry up and use the last of my power then. Let me go." Katja's light pink flowers briefly re-appeared, after having faded from the cloth long ago. Calico was not the sturdiest of fabrics, but something about the choice had been *right*, and so Cecily had chosen the lightweight cotton for her fifth familiar despite her reservations.

Cecily wrinkled her nose as she packed the fabric and a few basic supplies, sewing and otherwise, in a worn shoulder bag. "If I called on the remnants of your power now, let you end the way you wish, I would have nothing left to create my next familiar. Your last moments will ensure my continued access to magic." Katja had been her best familiar. She didn't just channel magic, she was a friend where there were no others. A companion in her loneliness. "Much like the man who wished for more wishes before he found that he could not, I wish I could take the dregs of your power to keep you near me forever."

Katja whispered, "Don't measure your success by the ease of the way. You don't need my power to awaken your next familiar, it is just another wish."

Cecily closed her eyes and inhaled the dust of her oft neglected little cottage. "Then you will be gone from me sooner. It is already too soon."

Katja settled into the quiet of one who neared death. The stitches of power that held the two of them together were weak, weaker than Cecily ought to have let them grow. Cecily blew out the candle as the autumn's late morning sun finally lit her small room.

Dust danced in the light like quiet fairies. The early morning held a stillness that Cecily was loath to interrupt. But her stomach grumbled and a headache pinched at her temples. She could delay no longer, she had to start the process for a new familiar. She stuffed a handful of dried berries into her mouth and the rest into her generous apron pocket, wrapped the heel of yesterday's bread and stashed it in the bag before she slung it across her shoulder.

Outside, orange and yellow leaves pranced about in a light wind. Pine and damp decay flavored the chill air. The early sun made everything shine with the promise that all would soon be white. Katja loved winter. She channeled the ice crystals of that season with unparalleled expertise. The new familiar would be different. And if it was stubborn, as they often were, it might be a dark, lonely winter as they struggled to balance their powers.

Cecily took her chances with the spirit of The Wilds and turned to the right at the end of the path from her cottage. The forest was a fickle beast with its trails never ending up in the same place twice. She wasn't headed anywhere in particular, but trusted that The Wilds would send her where she needed to be.

Do you remember the year that we dragged the snow into the edges of summer? Katja's voice went straight to her mind, conserving the energy it would take to speak aloud.

Cecily gathered her frizzy brown waves into a bun at the nape of her neck. *We spent the rest of the summer fending off flooding and ensuring that flowers still bloomed and were pollinated. We made so much work for ourselves for a few more months of snow.*

It was worth it. Katja's response was more a feeling than a sentence, an aching that she too might miss their friendship.

Leaves crunched under each footstep. The quaintness of the sound brought a smile to her face despite the sharp pain of loss in her chest. *Yes, Katja, it was worth it. All of it. Every second with you.*

Though threadbare and faded, Katja spared some energy to radiate peace. The weight on Cecily's mind eased. Katja would be gone soon, yes, but that didn't ruin their beautiful past. She would always be there in the way Cecily moved and spoke and thought.

The third left turn after her second right turn deposited Cecily in the middle of a meadow. She knelt down and ran her hands across the now prickly grasses. Fifteen years in The Wilds and she had only seen a meadow a handful of times—it was her luck to reach it now, as the seasons shifted from one to another, seeming to die but never truly doing so. She had hoped Katja could see one more winter before her end.

She knew that losing Katja would be a change in season, not the end of all seasons, of all happiness. But that was not how it felt.

A gurgled cry rang out from across the meadow, somewhere in the forest.

Finally, Katja whispered weakly in her mind.

"Finally?" Cecily repeated aloud. "It is only late morning." She stood and readjusted the strap on her aching shoulder. Excitement and dread mixed in her gut.

Dry plants crunched beneath her thick leather boots as she strode across the meadow. The sun's warm rays were a minor respite from the chill of the morning. She wasn't old, but at thirty-three, she wasn't young either. The cold penetrated deeper than it had in years past.

Though, the fraying fabric of her familiar might be more at fault than her aging body.

Cecily ducked underneath the thick branches of an elm. She lost her balance and fell against the trunk, her hand collecting a heaping of the sticky sap. Worse, her fingers brushed against a spongy fungus. Vibrant purple lines streaked up her fingers, deadly snakes racing to stop her heart.

Her arm stung as she watched the poison spread up her veins. Of course, she had left her remedies at home, not expecting to need to heal anyone—least of all herself. The apron flashed a brilliant gold and sent warmth down Cecily's limbs. The tingling in her hands blinked away. She flexed her fingers, grateful for Katja's instinct to save her before she realized the true deadliness of the situation.

Then everything went ice cold.

"Farewell, my friend," Katja's voice trailed away with the autumn breeze—as dead as the leaves that swirled around the ground and drifted from the trees.

"No!" Cecily threw off her pack and worked to untie the apron bows from behind her neck and back, her fingers trembling and inefficient.

One final tug pulled the apron free. She cradled the faded calico in her arms and wet it with her falling tears. "That wasn't how you were supposed to go."

As she spoke, the fabric crumbled into dust and danced away along the forest floor.

Cecily stared down at her empty hands, still shaped in the protective hold. The remains of her dried berries scattered across her skirt, rolling and tumbling until they reached the ground, as lost to her as Katja was. Another wave of chill ran from her fingertips to her back. Fifteen years and she had not once been without a familiar.

She had grown too attached and now paid the price. The background thrum of power dissipated and with it Cecily felt half a person. Where was the other voice to guide her? Where was the peace only someone else could provide?

A second gurgling cry interrupted her mourning. Cecily rose and clenched her cold hands into fists. If that noise was but an animal caught in a trap, she would curse The Wilds with whatever magic she gathered from the next familiar.

Around a corner in a beam of purposeful light, a man struggled against a willow. The taller trees around the willow had backed far enough away to give it sufficient sunlight to grow even deep in a forest.

Vine-like branches dotted with elliptic yellow leaves wrapped loosely around a sturdy man's body. He clawed at his throat, where branches twisted around, squeezing. His wide blue eyes found Cecily and he opened his mouth soundlessly. Cecily twisted a branch between her fingers, silently thanking The Wilds and repenting of her wish to curse it for generations. The Wilds had provided.

Though Cecily was disappointed that she would have to make a familiar the long way since she no longer had Katja's power to shortcut the process. The only other time she had needed to make a familiar the long way was also the first time.

Give voice to one who has none. The words were cross-stitched and framed on her wall. Every Seamstress knew the key to making a familiar.

It just usually wasn't so straightforward. Cecily remembered herself and rushed forward. It wouldn't do to have The Wilds kill her new familiar before she had even made him.

In a soothing voice, she said, "These trees have a nasty streak. I'm sorry you got caught up with them." She pulled the vines from the man's neck. The tree submitted to her will and weakened its grip enough for her to peel away the branches. Not enough to be easy, but enough.

When Cecily unwrapped the last branch, the man crumpled. She caught him before his head hit the ground. "You're safe now." The man blinked his bloodshot blue eyes. She ran her hand across his sweat-slicked hairline in a soothing motion. "I'm going to set you down now." She glanced over at her pack and back again. "I have some water and a blanket that will help."

The man opened his mouth, but only managed to appear as a fish on a fisher's line, moving his mouth to no avail.

Cecily lowered his head to the ground and left to get her supplies, a huge grin on her face. It was so perfect. The man couldn't talk, he had no voice. All she had to do was help him speak again by giving him a little water and her new familiar would be made.

"You—you saved my life."

Cecily swore under her breath as she grabbed her bag. She took a moment to process her disappointment and paste a soft smile across her face. Of course it would not be so simple.

"Hush now, don't strain yourself." Cecily knelt by him and handed over a full canteen. Then she pulled out the sturdy slate blue canvas and draped it across the man. "Rest for a while and then we can go somewhere safer to talk."

The man looked up at the willow tree warily before propping himself up on one arm to guzzle down the contents of the canteen. Already she felt the invisible stitches of power start to run across the canvas. It was early to tell, but this familiar would be at least as strong as her second one, Gerard. It would just take so much more time to get there.

Cecily tugged at the man and pulled him to standing. He wobbled, then raced from under the willow, dropping the cloth along the way. Cecily ran her hands along the long branches as she slowly followed. Even without a familiar's magic, The Wilds wouldn't dare harm her, a Seamstress living in its embrace. At least not on purpose.

The man coughed and rubbed at his raw neck. "Do you live in this cursed forest?"

Cecily picked up the cloth from where the man had discarded it. She dusted off the leaf fragments and folded it neatly. The initial contact was enough. The man didn't need to feel the fabric again for the bond to take hold. She ignored his question and offered her own. "Who are you? How did you manage to get so tangled in the willow?"

"I am Julien, a craftsman from Plau." His face reddened, matching his raw neck. "There was this woman. She told me of a tree of never before seen quality that neared the end of its life in these woods. I carve wood, you see. Furniture, animals, and anything between." Julien pulled a small object from his pocket and passed it to Cecily.

The carving was of impeccable quality. A young falcon, some downy feathers just peeking through, with her wings spread in her first, awkward flight. Cecily ran her fingers over the lines and looked at Julien with new eyes. "This is incredible." She held it back out, reluctantly.

Julien shook his head. "Keep it. It isn't enough payment for my life, but would you consider it a start?"

Oh how much he would soon pay for his life. Cecily tucked the figure into her pocket and smiled again, keeping her tone easy and friendly. "Saving a life is its own reward. Now, should we find a way out of The Wilds and back to Plau?"

"The Wilds?" Julien's eyes darted around the autumnal forest, poised to run off at the wrong sound. His voice picked up tempo. "Is that where we are, The Wilds? No one survives The Wilds."

Cecily bit the inside of her cheek. A wave of her hand, while she had magic, could have taken those words away. Taken Julien back to the time when he was naive as to where he was. And the dangers it presented. Namely, herself. Not able to take the words back, half-truth would have to be enough. She strengthened the lilt to her voice that she gained in her childhood. "The wilds, as in the forest, somewhere wild? Does the term mean something else to your people?"

Julien scratched at the lines on his neck with both hands and looked around. "This is just a forest. It can't be The Wilds. This is just an ordinary forest. You're alive. I'm alive. Just a forest." Despite his words, his taut stance warned Cecily that his worries were not gone.

"Well, Julien, do you know which way you came from? I am not familiar with your town." She pulled Julien's arm into hers, linking them together. The corded muscles beneath his thin shirt pressed into her arm with the confidence only a man could have. Whatever direction Julien answered, there would be more than enough time to get what she needed from him before they arrived.

In The Wilds, directions were meaningless and would not help them find Julien's way home. The Wilds would take them wherever it wanted them to go.

"I came from the east." He glanced up at the high noon sun. "Though that doesn't help us much now." When he glanced back down, his eyes locked on Cecily's. Julien's eyes had cleared of the panic and pain of earlier and were crisp and clear. There was something there, some pain hidden far down, but he looked away before Cecily could grab onto the lead.

Cecily pulled him toward the sound of a running river off to the right. "We might as well start somewhere. Moving is good." Katja would have chided her for such clumsy conversation. But that was a Seamstress's life, devoid of contact for most of the time, except when providing magic to villagers. She didn't *converse* with people.

When they reached the gentle river, she paused to refill the canteen. Julien knelt on the bank and stuck his entire face and neck in the frigid water. A second after Cecily began to wonder if he would ever come out again, Julien whipped his head from the water and coughed.

Then burst into thick laughter. The kind of laughter that fills rooms and hearts, the kind that cannot be forgotten in an entire lifetime. Julien shook out his hair, giving it slight curls. The chill tinged his face red but his smile was bright.

It moved Cecily in a way that she did not want to be moved. She needed a familiar. Nothing else. The only companionship she needed was from the fabric in her pack and the voice she was about to give it.

Cecily dug the heel of bread from her bag and split it, offering half to Julien. "Tell me about the woman."

He bit off a large chunk as they followed the river in some direction, since east still couldn't be accurately deciphered. His mouth was full when he asked, "What woman?"

Giving voice to love would be enough to fulfill the demands of making a familiar. And the way he spoke of her, well, Cecily was sure she hit the right vein of questioning. "The one who told you the story of the tree in the forest? She must be someone special if you followed her words into the unknown." Cecily tugged her bun free to cover her neck with her thick hair, trying to find any way to minimize the unending chill.

"Oh, her. She was just some woman in the town telling stories. Everyone heard them. I just happened to be starting a project that needed different wood than I had around. She was no one." He brushed the crumbs from the stubble on his chin. The dunk in the river had invigorated his face, but when he mentioned his project, that was when his countenance brightened.

Cecily led them away from the river which had narrowed to a stream. The sun slid down behind the canopy of tall trees. What had started as a beautiful autumn day full of promise ended as a chilly evening bereft of means to warm herself and return home. Her attempts to seal the familiar bond were going nowhere. Still, she would not give up. "A particular project?"

They followed a path of brown leaves, Cecily attempting to follow the sun's directions to head east. Useless though it was, Julien had almost asked the dreaded question earlier when he thought they might be in The Wilds. She had to keep up pretenses that she was just an average human until the process was complete or she would have to start over again. And with new fabric at that. And without a familiar, finding her way back to her cottage for that fabric would be near impossible.

No, if Julien left her before the familiar was established, Cecily would surely die in these woods just as anyone else would.

"My betrothed is expecting our first child. An infant's first bed requires something special, for wood is protective of the young." Julien raked his fingers through his drying curls. "And now all I have to show for that is the worry that I've caused my Lea. I should never have come into the forest."

"Why would Lea worry? Surely this must not be the first time you've left home to travel for your craft."

A light drizzle started, the drops hitting Cecily like hail. Katja could have fixed the weather, but she was dust. Cecily clutched at her chest where the still raw ache pounded away. She had to move forward, had to finish mourning her last familiar. That magic was gone, used up, as happens with all familiars with their finite sources of power.

In a second the drizzle turned to a drenching. Cecily ducked under a thick pine and Julien followed. At least they were forced close together under the tree and some of Julien's warmth pierced through her chill. The tree, however, didn't keep out all of the rain, just most of it.

Julien looked around the branches overhead. "Can I see that blanket from earlier?"

Cecily dropped her pack to the ground and massaged her shoulder with one hand while she grabbed the familiar fabric with the other. Julien draped the cloth over three branches, snagging only once, which made a loose shelter decent enough to keep them sufficiently dry. Cecily leaned back against the trunk and inhaled the fresh damp pine. It both calmed and invigorated her enough to pull the last pins of pain from Katja's end out of her chest.

Julien joined her on the forest floor and took a deep breath. He hunched forward instead of leaning back and Cecily felt the threads overhead respond. Whatever he was about to say was enough to affect the familiar bond.

"This is a long story." He inhaled deeply, expanding his back and tightening his wet shirt.

Cecily had forgotten what it looked like to have someone so near her, breathing and living. There was a kind of power in it. A power in taking one's next breath and then the next one and on and on. That was the power that swirled up from Julien's warm flesh and into the fabric above.

Thick raindrops pounded around them, briefly deafening her. She shivered again, feeling ice in her bones. Without turning, Julien shifted closer, warming her like the dying embers of a fire.

"Lea and I were betrothed at birth. Our families had consulted with a Seamstress of The Wilds two generations back. There had been issues with childbearing in each family and the Seamstresses were renowned for their blessings. That woman draped a rich azure satin over my grandmother and an amber linen over Lea's grandmother."

Cecily frowned and interrupted. "Satin is a new type of cloth, only been used for the last twenty years. It can't have been satin. And azure at that!" She bit down on her cheek, silencing her infuriating lack of practice in pretending to be just a human.

"It is the way my mother tells it. It was long before my birth, when my mother was still a curious child watching adults from behind bushes when she shouldn't. She said the cloth covering the women spoke and said that a member of each family in two generations should be betrothed to each other. It was a portent of good luck and prosperity for Plau." Julien picked at a fingernail and whispered, "I don't know why I'm telling you this. Even Lea doesn't know that a Seamstress was involved. Those women whose blessings were curses."

Unnoticed by Julien, a coiling swirl of energy moved between the man and the cloth. Julien gave voice to something he didn't tell his betrothed. By coaxing him along, Cecily had guided Julien to just what she desired. Above, the familiar started to waken. A thread of power dropped down to Cecily; she grabbed hold with her mind.

Julien hopped up and backed into the dissipating rain. The twin moons, large and bright in the twilight sky, lit his curls white, but his face held only darkness. "You said something about the satin. What do you know of fabric?"

The swirling shift in the air followed Julien, thickening and growing, wrapping around his body as the vines had done just hours before. Julien's voice echoed in her mind from above, from the canvas, *What do you know of fabric?*

Cecily met Julien's wide-eyed fear with a shrug. She rose and stretched her fingers up to brush the damp cloth familiar. She dropped her arms and pulled on the invisible threads that bound it to her. Swirling her fingers in the air, she pulled from the familiar's burgeoning power, then sent it out to Julien.

The man's eyes clouded over and his stretched-tight face slackened. The suspicion fled from him, so that when he blinked away the temporary effects of the magic, even his body did not hold onto the fear. Julien wiped rain from his face and rushed back under the canvas. "I don't know what came over me."

"You spoke of the Seamstress and your grandmother? Was that the end of the story?" Carefully Cecily pulled more power from the familiar to warm her limbs.

The rain petered out to a trickle, so that only darkness remained around them. Julien sat and shifted his weight back into the tree trunk, though he did not move closer to Cecily again. "They died. Not that day of course, but over the next week both of the women died. When I was born, my mother decided that I was part of the prophecy and pressed my betrothal on Lea's parents. The wedding is next summer, when she is strong, after giving birth to the child."

"My congratulations to the two of you." Cecily pondered on who the Seamstress from his story might be. To make two familiars at once? She was powerful indeed.

"I don't know what luck the Seamstress thought that she blessed Plau with, but I have not seen it. My mother only had one child survive birth, and Lea only has one sister, but she is weak and unable to support a pregnancy. I think there is no luck or blessing. It is all just a curse." Julien looked out into the gray forest and pursed his lips. "It is too dark to reach home now, we should wait here until dawn." He leaned his head back and closed his eyes. His breathing slowed in the silence that Cecily allowed between them.

Cecily pulled a crochet hook and a ball of gray wool from her bag while Julien drifted into sleep. A trickle of excitement ran through her limbs, making it impossible to sleep. The growing power of the familiar energized her and she needed no sleep to recover. But it wasn't time to leave Julien yet; the transformation was not complete. Through the night she counted stitches to occupy her mind, timing them with the thudding of his heart.

By the time the morning rays woke Julien, Cecily had a pair of small socks, and had just tied off a blanket. She patted them before handing them over to Julien, with a smile. "For your child."

"It isn't my child." A final, thick swirl of golden energy ran from Julien to the fabric, where the power crisscrossed in long stitches, completing the bond. He stood without accepting the gift and pulled the canvas from the tree branches. Oblivious to the change, Julien folded the slate blue cloth and handed over the bundle without knowing what it was he had done.

"And Lea doesn't know that you know." Cecily wedged the fabric under her arm and again held out the baby gift to Julien. That was what she gave voice to, a painful secret deep in this man's chest that he otherwise might have taken to his grave.

He accepted the gift with a sigh, but the way his fingers trailed on the stitches told Cecily enough. Julien started walking to the east, home. He stuffed one hand in his pocket and rolled his shoulders. "No. It wouldn't change anything. My grandmother died for this betrothal."

She died to bring luck to the future of my village. The cloth shared the rest of Julien's thoughts directly into Cecily's mind. She inhaled the crisp morning air, when everything was right again. Her new familiar was about to be born.

Unaware of the world-changing creation of magic so near him, Julien walked through the forest without another comment.

Cecily's boots squelched on the damp leaves that littered the forest path. She held the cloth familiar close to her chest and ran her fingers over the tightly woven fibers. What form would this familiar choose? Cecily was a seamstress as well as a Seamstress and could make anything the familiar wished to be; it was part of the training. She just hoped it wouldn't be an impractical gown as Ina had chosen.

Watching Julien's sure footing and sense of direction brought back that feeling from when Cecily had first helped him away from the willow. It stirred in her heart and whispered, "He's only human." But she couldn't think like that; she couldn't have the compassion that humans had, couldn't feel the way they did.

She picked up her pace and met Julien at his side. "Was it worth it? Having a Seamstress involved in your life?" It wasn't a question for the process, but a question for herself, some deep yearning to know that all of her unseen work was appreciated.

Julien stopped mid-stride and ran his gaze over Cecily's face. He pushed the baby gift into his chest. His mouth moved in reply, but his voice came clear and strong from the canvas tucked under Cecily's arm. "I don't think losing a life is ever worth it."

Before Julien's next blink he bolted away, the sharp scent of fear spiking in his wake. His sure footing turned to a panicked run, grazing his arms against any plant in his way. He glanced back, his face drained of color. In a handful of heartbeats Julien disappeared from sight.

Cecily unfurled the fabric and stared at the pulsing stitches of power across the surface. It was nearly complete; then she could craft it into its ultimate form. As if in a vision, she saw what the cloth should become. A long hooded cloak with only one fastener, a small clip at the neck in the shape of a willow leaf. Practical and perfect. She draped the fabric over her arm and hummed a tune from her childhood as she followed the clear path that Julien left behind.

To the familiar, Cecily continued the conversation. "If the cost of a few lives kept the world running? Would those deaths be worth it then? If those deaths brought about the magic that kept The Wilds contained? If it kept the seasons changing and the plants growing? If it saved the mothers travailing in childbirth? Would it be worth it then?"

"No." The fabric familiar replied.

"I was much the same when I went to train to be a seamstress. And then I learned that the world is like cloth, woven together with fragile little threads. And those threads break or tear. With no one there to fix them, the world descends into chaos. And that was when I became a Seamstress. I stitch the world back together, mending holes with the cost of only a few lives." Cecily turned to avoid the broken branches of a short tree. A bird chirped overhead before flying away.

"No," repeated the canvas in Julien's deep, clear voice. "That isn't justification."

Cecily chuckled. "Well, I have years yet to change your mind." They reached a bend in the worn path, but she continued forward, following the disturbed foliage. More branches were broken, some lower. She was getting close.

"Years." The familiar said without a question, flat and numb.

They reached the edge of a clearing, perhaps the one from the day before, perhaps not. Julien lay on his side a few feet into the brittle grass, unmoving, a stalled trickle of blood streaked down his scratched arms. The pungent scent of fear clung to his body, a remnant of the final moments of his life.

"You're mine now, Julien." Cecily bent next to the body and grabbed the baby blanket and socks from cold hands. Then she flicked her wrist, sending out her fresh power, and the body dispersed into dust in the shape of a man.

Cecily draped her sixth familiar over her shoulders to mimic the form he would ultimately become. "Let's get this gift to Lea and her baby."

To Bite a Giant

Alexander G.R. Gideon

The shit stains on the hems of their white capes are always the most satisfying part of seeing a royal in the Rags. Most of the bastards would rather lose a finger than step foot among the poor. The hordes of starving children that infest the streets here would be happy to oblige that wish, after all. But this one stood tall and proud, the gaze she cast about the street bore the cunning of a predator. She had the eyes of an owl; dark, cold, and prepared for anything.

She stank of magic.

I'd tailed her for over an hour through the district. Others did the same, but her aura kept them at bay. She was searching for someone, and from the questions she'd asked those she passed, that someone was me. I've worked for many a royal, but I'd barely ever had a mage deign speak to me, much less hire me. I wanted to know why this one brazenly combed through the Rags.

Do you think she knows? Sauro said, her voice buzzing through my mind.

I doubt she would be so open in her search, or alone, if she did, I said, slipping my words back across our connection.

But is she alone?

I hated when she had a point. *Have you seen anything?*

No, I've been on your shoulder to keep from losing you while you stalk her.

I'm not stalk—

I'll scout around, Sauro said, our link growing fainter as she lifted off. I watched her tiny insect form disappear into the gloom of the alleyway.

"Damn all mosquitos," I mumbled. My words must have reached her because Sauro chuckled. I looked back to the mage in time for her cape to disappear from the alley's mouth. Over-eagerness can kill a thief, so I counted to ten before I left the shadowed doorway I'd tucked into. I strode from the alley with a casual gait, glancing around to see where my mage had gotten off to.

A hand settled on my shoulder.

"You're following me," the mage said. A statement, not a question. She'd waited to ambush me. I swallowed the panic skittering up my throat and let my mouth fall open like a slack-jawed crystal eater. I took in her dark carob skin, hazel eyes, and beautiful curls before I widened my eyes at her official robes and bowed my head.

"I pray you forgive me for giving such an impression," I said with as kind a smile as I could muster. "Your business is your own, and I never intended to mind it."

"A valiant effort, but I know who you are, Bashir." She glanced around. "Where is your friend?"

Now *that* sent a hot bolt of anxiety through my bones.

"Beg pardon?" I looked up at her, feigning confusion. "What manner of friend might I have here in the Rags?"

Something heavy dropped onto my shoulder, staggering me as what felt like a fist of blades gripped into my flesh. Hot blood trickled down my side and I looked up into the eyes of a horned owl staring down at me.

"This manner of friend," the mage said with a small smile. "I know you're Forbade, and I know it's why you've been so successful a thief. Call your familiar. I would do business with the both of you."

What should we do? Sauro said. Relief flooded through me that she'd returned.

She's confident in her assumption I'm Forbade, so let's give her confirmation.

Good, because I've already taken her blood.

She flooded me with what few memories she'd managed to take from the mage's mind. It was paltry compared to what we could take from an unmagical, but what we *could* see of her mind smelled of blood. Dropping my façade as a Rags beggar, I curled my lips into a wicked smile.

"I know you as well, Akilah," I said, using the name she'd abandoned over twenty years ago. Her own smile slipped enough to spot the tell. No living soul should have known that name. Her devil of a mother gave it to her. She had cast it aside when she came into her magic and had her owl, Mujiya, rip out the woman's throat.

"I see why they call you Bashir Who Knows. I think Bashir Who Knows Too Much a better name," she said, the calculations whirring behind her eyes. Her smile returned, but it had a wicked air to it, like a child intending mischief with something they ought not to have found. "If you value your life, never utter that name again. To me or anyone else."

"I pray I'll never need to. But this doesn't have to be a fight," I said, not wishing to push her into making a choice I'd regret. "You came here to do business with me. To ask me to steal something. Show me one-hundred gold sovereigns, then tell me what it is and who I'm stealing it from."

"You don't mince words, do you?" she said, still scowling.

"No, I don't. And one more thing." I pointed to my shoulder. "Get this fucking bird off me."

* * *

Master Thief Targrand used to tell me, "No one's voice speaks louder than their body." Her words always rang true. A tightening of shoulders betrays one's nerves. The tremor of an eyelid screams rage when the rest of the face remains calm; a twitch of a finger the only warning given before steel is drawn. Yet, while I can know so much of what a person intends from the language of their body, the guard before me taught me I cannot glean from a man's movements when he needs to piss.

I'll kill him if it gets on me, I said to Sauro, pressing my back against the tower wall and hoping the soldier couldn't see through the scraggly bush that separated me from his stream.

No, you won't. The blood would stain his tunic, and we need it.

I'll kill him on our way out then.

Better. I have his blood, Sauro said, landing on my cheek.

Not the face.

Too late.

Sauro's magic sparked across my skin. She'd injected me with his blood, and I felt the link between the guard and I snap into place. If I opened myself to it, I could feel the general flow of his thoughts, or glimpse into the things he saw or felt. I refrained from the latter while he had himself in his hand. I wrapped my consciousness around the link, holding it like the chain of a dog's collar, and pulled it tight. The man stiffened as every muscle in his body froze in the middle of tucking himself away. Panic beat at the cage I'd settled around his consciousness, but I pushed it away from my awareness.

Come behind the bush and give me your clothes, I ordered through his blood, pushing my power into it so he'd have no choice but to obey. Without a word he pushed through the foliage until he stood beside me. He looked me in the eye and I saw his fright, wild and hot. There was no fear like the loss of yourself.

I thought of all the guild mages who had denied me and left me Forbade. They scoffed at Sauro before turning me away, saying a mosquito was no familiar, that I'd never have power worth anything. True enough, I couldn't call storms, or burn a village to the ground. But a powerless familiar couldn't give me this kind of control. A powerless mage couldn't put this kind of terror into a living soul.

When the man had stripped to his underthings, I placed a hand on his shoulder, my eyes locked on his. *Sleep until the sun rises,* I ordered. His eyes fluttered closed and he collapsed. I slipped his tunic and armor on over the tight-fitting darks I wore.

I need eyes, I said to Sauro as I outfitted myself.

I've got a few, she said before she lifted from my face.

Make sure no one has raised an alarm.

Would you like me to bring you a drink as well?

I'd love a nice ale if you could.

She laughed as she raced off, making me smile. We knew the watch patterns from her earlier reconnaissance, but the Thirty-Three Towers were known for their extreme vigilance. Better safe than impaled on a pike on the gate.

As I waited for her to return, I wondered about this artifact, especially with how vague our mage had been when speaking of it. She described the small chest that housed it in great detail, but she couldn't emphasize enough that I was *not* to open it. She paid my fee in full and up front, so I had no plans to dishonor her request. But her protests piqued my curiosity.

Sauro landed back on my face and pushed on my consciousness. I opened to her, melding our minds and experiencing the world through her multi-faceted eyes. Empty courtyards. Guards patrolling the battlements. Bored faces, yawns all around. No thought that anyone might want inside. I slid out of the images and smiled.

Thank you, my love.

You'd do the same for me, she said. I chuckled, drinking in the affection I felt from her.

Matching the gait and solemnity of the other soldiers, I moved across the courtyard. Sauro kept a close watch around us, poised to alert me the moment she spotted the hint of a threat. Twin, iron-bound oak doors, twice my height and thicker than my chest, guarded the entrance to the tower. Thank the Gods they already stood open, or I'd never get through.

Are they watching me? I asked Sauro, glancing at the two soldiers standing watch on the turret above.

Not even a glance your way.

The towers of the Thirty-Three didn't strike an impressive visage. They stood maybe four stories tall, barely more than the trees of the Naguira Wood. Their grandeur lay in how far below ground they reached. Some said they reached the center of the earth. Even more remarkable were the series of tunnels that connected them. Whatever this artifact Akilah wanted was—Akari rather, if I didn't want her threatening my life—it held enough import to be kept under guard in the undertower.

Nodding here and there to soldiers, I matched their gait and solemnity as I headed for the center of the tower and the passage that led below. Not all soldiers had full access to the undertower after dark. This late its gates were closed to the unauthorized. A single soldier stood guard, pike in hand. I expected her to react as I approached, but she remained unnervingly still. I slowed my pace, gripping the pommel of my stolen sword.

Amazingly, bafflingly, she was asleep on her feet. Skill such as this deserved respect, as I'd never seen so thorough a master of one's craft. Shaking my head in amazement, I said to Sauro, *Let's ensure her dreams continue.*

It took only moments for Sauro to give me the woman's blood. Her thoughts flowed like tree sap in her deep slumber, slow and sticky. In them, she wore a white dress and dreamt of sunflowers. The wind's gentle passage through her braids and caress on her dark copper skin made her smile. Someone stood at her side, holding her hand. I couldn't make them out, their presence more concept than reality.

As I left her thoughts, I planted an order. *Walk among the sunflowers until the real sun rises.* There was no chance she would fight against the order. The divine knew I wouldn't. I pulled the keys from the sleeping guard's belt and unlocked the gate. Gentle as a whisper I slipped through.

That's two we've spelled, Sauro said as we descended. *Hurry.*

The strain of our magic weighed heavy on my consciousness with the distance. Our power only stretched so far, and our hold would break before long. The gatekeeper hadn't seen my face, but the first soldier certainly had.

Lead the way, I said, quickening my pace.

Since only the elite had their quarters and stations here after dark, no one bothered to patrol. I kept my footsteps quiet as I passed those still awake in their chambers, scratching away at some document or other by candlelight. A heavy scent of smoke hung in the air from the torches and lanterns; my eyes watered as I sped through the corridors at Sauro's direction.

The caravan captain's had quarters tucked away at the end of a branch passage which left only one escape route. *Shit.* I knelt before the door and peered through the keyhole, looking to confirm the captain's presence. Only darkness met me. I cursed.

Can you check for the captain? I said to Sauro, sending an impression of her scouting out the room. She rubbed her acquiescence against my thoughts and squeezed through the keyhole. Only moments later she reappeared and settled on my face.

Clear.

Targrand taught me to never set to picking a lock until you've tried the handle. It opened with a click when I did. Thinking of how she'd smirk at that, I slid inside. It was blacker than a whoremonger's cock inside, and I groped about, afraid of what I'd run into, and the racket I'd make. Sauro pushed me across the room to the table the chest sat on.

The table the *huge* chest sat on.

Running my hands across it, I estimated it at six hands tall and at least as wide as myself. *Someone* would notice a soldier dragging a giant fucking box behind them.

Why didn't you tell me about the size of this bastard?

Can you not lift it?

I tested the handles and couldn't budge it.

Shit, Sauro said, which I found extremely helpful. *What do we do?*

I don't fucking know, I said, running a hand over my face. *Maybe—*

The door opened behind us. The light of a torch blinded me when I turned, and the man in the doorway gave a surprised, "Huh?"

Sauro sped to him, taking his blood in an instant. The drawing of steel rang through the room, and the man charged as Sauro gave me his blood.

"Stop," I said. I'd not established full control and he took a few more steps and started to swing his sword before it took effect. He halted in place, his eyes trained on me, his sword paused mid-strike. I felt the spell on the guard in the courtyard break.

"How many did it take to bring the chest here?" I asked the captain with a quick compulsion.

"Four," he said through gritted teeth. So, even if I ordered him to help me, we wouldn't be able to handle it.

"Is there a way to get this to the surface alone?"

"No."

The Nemesis fuck me.

"At least not as a whole."

My ears perked up.

"You could bring the pieces inside up separately. It takes longer, but you could do it alone."

"What's in the chest?" I commanded.

"The ceremonial raiment and jewels of the Royal Arch Mage, along with the Manumit Talisman," the captain said, sending my thoughts racing. I knew of the Arch Mage's recent death. Since possessing the robes and treasury didn't make one Arch Mage, I imagined she only desired the Manumit. I'd heard tales of how it amplified the power of both the mage that wore it and their familiar.

If it can make us stronger, this Manumit might get us out of here, Sauro said.

"Do you have the key to the chest?" I asked the captain. He nodded. "Open it."

He sheathed his sword as he walked to the chest, pulling a key from a pouch at his thigh. Once he'd opened the latch and lifted the lid, he stepped back and returned to glaring at me.

"Thank you, now good night," I said, ordering him to sleep. His eyes rolled back in his head, and he collapsed on the spot.

I dug through the robes, golden armor, and precious stones until my finger hooked a small chain. A gold medallion slid out of the mess bearing the largest ruby I'd ever seen. The second I wrapped my fingers around it, my blood turned to lightning as the Manumit's power crawled inside my bones. The vigor it poured into me tolled in my ears like a temple bell, and the darkness around fled as my sight blossomed into new life. But the taste and smell of summer honeysuckle surprised me most.

Can you feel that? I said to Sauro, staring at the amulet in my hand. This new strength eclipsed anything I imagined possible. Sauro and I had never been powerless, no matter what anyone thought, but I knew now we could make the world believe it.

I can, she said, a dreamy quality to her thoughts.

My awareness flowed outward from me and I knew things in ways that escaped my understanding. I knew the soldier in the courtyard had informed his comrades of my presence, and that a group already rushed to capture us.

I also knew exactly how we'd leave this place unscathed.

Let us go, Sauro said, and I smiled savagely at the might in her.

She sped out of the room and down the corridor toward the battalion heading for us. I followed, my steps light. The soldiers halted halfway down the passage when I stepped into view, lowering their pikes toward me.

"Stop, whoever the fuck you are," the man in the lead snarled at me.

"After the things you did to that man in Breka, what power do you think you have to order me, Calitas," I said, holding his gaze. Fear painted him white when he registered what I'd said. He took a step back.

"Captain?" one of the soldiers behind him said, the point of her pike drooping toward the floor.

"Don't worry about him, Naliki," I said with a gentle smile. "And rest your mind. You are not your father, and never shall be. Your legacy will be that you became a woman worthy of all the good in the world, despite how hard he tried to kill that possibility."

Tears gathering at the corners of her wide eyes, she whispered so low I shouldn't have heard her. "Who are you?"

"I am Bashir Who Knows, and I *will* pass," I said, my gaze sliding across the other soldiers, who muttered nervously amongst themselves. I started forward and they scrambled to clear the way, pressing themselves against the walls in fear as I swept by them.

Thank you, Sauro, I said once we were clear.

It was a delight, she said as she settled onto my shoulder. *I cannot believe I could access that much of their memories so quickly. Or that I could show you over so long a distance.*

Neither can I. I never imagined the talisman could give so much power.

You aren't planning to give it to the royal mage, are you? There was a note of apprehension in the color of her thoughts. I waved a hand to dismiss the notion.

Of course not, I said, furrowing my brow. *But I think we should ask her what she wanted to do with it.*

* * *

Lions often symbolize courage. The dead, still carrying their shields and wearing their tabards emblazoned with them, littered battlefields all across the Sundered Lands. But I've never seen courage in a creature already considered a king of its kind. It may be biased, but I always thought a mosquito more courageous. What else could you call the act of biting a giant?

The Kingdom of Erqoiyu was undeniably a giant. Staging a coup and seizing control of it would certainly leave a bite mark. And so, with that intention swirling through me along with her blood, I thought Royal Mage Akari could match the courage of any mosquito.

Who controlled the kingdom mattered little to me; I harbored no love for the Royalty. If Akari's rebellion would make life easier for all of us, then it would have my support. But I could see the entire width and breadth of Akari's mind now, and I knew the kind of tyrant she intended to be. The Royals thought the commonwealth beneath them. Akari barely believed they deserved to live. Not even those closest to her truly knew how dark her intentions were. Which made Sauro and I the only ones who knew she needed to be stopped.

The Nemesis fuck me.

"Am I to take your empty hands as proof of failure?" she said, scowling at me from across the table, her chin resting on the backs of her hands.

"I am never unsuccessful," I said, taking a long drink from my tankard.

"Then where is it?" she said through gritted teeth. I set the tankard back on the table with a thump.

"I know what's in the chest."

The muscles in her neck tightened and her spike of panic made the tip of my tongue tingle. The barkeep and the patrons around us—all her mages—stiffened as well.

"Do you?" She said, forcing herself to relax. Though her mages stayed ready to send their familiars to flay me alive. "I believe you owe me some gold if that's so."

You might expect anxiety to smell like sweat, or piss, or some other vile thing. But it actually smelled sweet, like blackberry mead. Akari's thoughts raced like a dog after a rabbit: wondering if I knew what she planned, whether I'd found the Manumit, and whether I might have it on me even now.

"The answer to all of those questions, is yes." I tapped the side of my head with a finger. "You can't imagine all I've come to know. For instance, I know what Pwer behind me does in the streets at night, and that Hinyl likes to watch. Naughty boys, the both of you."

I dropped my head over the back of the chair and grinned at the two, now upside-down, men in question. They glared back at me, alarm chiseled into their faces. I turned my gaze to the woman that sat with them.

"What hatred and murder you harbor in your heart, Tiffella." She grit her teeth at my use of her name. "And what ambition. Allow Akari to do all the work, then swoop in, slit her throat, and take it all for yourself. After all, there's not a chance in all the realms you could do it yourself."

Leaving Tiffella to stammer in indignation, I sat up to face Akari again.

"Reqiip there wants inside you so bad he can taste it, and he'd have already tried if you didn't terrify him. Only dear Learji behind the bar is truly your loyal servant. Though she really would like to feel your boot on her face." I shook my head as I chuckled. "You really know how to surround yourself with the best don't you, Akari? But of course, you can't have anyone around you that could be a threat to you."

Putting my elbows on the table, I leaned across it toward the mage.

"I didn't take you for an insurrectionist when you found me in the Rags, *Royal* Mage. But I see in the shape of your thoughts the small army you've raised. And while your reasoning covers your mind like ivy, I want to hear you say it."

Her face contorted, and what it settled on I couldn't possibly call a smile. A twisted, vile, perverted thing; it carved away her lips to leave a horrid gash in her face. She leaned in and said, "Why shouldn't I rule what's beneath me? The Lord and Lady are weak. No power runs through their veins."

She crawled over the table like a risen corpse. Her thoughts turned black and red, and tasted of the smoke of a funeral pyre.

"But as a mage, it does in mine. Why should I allow their boot on my throat when a glance their way could send them to the Nemesis."

She rose slowly from the table to loom over me.

"I don't care what you think you know. You cannot stand against me. Give me the Manumit, and I may still let you keep your limbs."

"If I don't?" I said calmly, reaching for my ale. The other mages stood as one. I didn't give them so much as a passing glance, keeping my eyes locked on Akari.

"Then we take it from your corpse."

I let her hold her smirk for a few moments as I drained my tankard. Slamming it back down on the table, I curled my lips into a wicked grin.

"Sit down," I said, ordering the blood of all six at once. The utter shock in Akari's eyes when she obeyed warmed me to my bones.

"What an inflated sense of yourself you have," I said as I stood. Threading my fingers into her hair, I pulled her head back so she looked straight up at me. "What power do you really possess if a *Forbade* could do this to you."

Bashir! Sauro screamed in my head.

Releasing Akari, I threw myself back just in time for Mujiya's talons to close on empty air rather than my throat. The great owl soared low over the tables before streaking back toward me. I rolled once more out of reach.

Did you not take their blood? I said scrambling to my feet.

I did.

What a fucking time to find out that even with the Manumit, our power didn't affect them. I had already summoned royal soldiers to take Akari and her lot into custody once I'd subdued them. But if I couldn't control their familiars, I wouldn't survive that long.

I spread my awareness throughout the room, searching for the other familiars. The moment I cast the psychic net, a spark of life caught my attention next to my foot. Without even looking, I kicked at it, and my boot connected with the rattlesnake just before it struck my thigh. The serpent flew across the room. Behind me, a man cried out and my hold on him slipped. He shot up out of his chair before I could wrestle control back in place.

Fuck, this was tricky.

Mujiya swooped low, *much* faster this time, and I only barely managed to duck him. I read somewhere that all Mages with flying familiars could control air to some extent. I'd never been able to so much as blow out a candle, but I wondered...

Reaching into the connection I shared with Sauro, I wove power from our link into the shape of a spell. The weaving done, I cut the thread and pushed the magick into the world. Mujiya raced toward me, claws stretched out before him for a killing blow. Just before he reached me, air gusted into him with the force of a typhoon, crashing him into the wall. It continued to swirl around me, and I scanned the tavern for the others.

Something dark raced up. A skunk. It spun, lifting its tail and spraying at me. My typhoon caught the smell and surrounded me with it. My eyes watered like a mourner and I fought the urge to vomit. I stumbled from the vortex, desperate for a breath and barely able to see.

Send the gale through the door, Sauro shouted in a panic.

So I did. A yip and a screech reached my ears.

What was that?

The fox and cat trying for your throat getting blown back out of the door.

"Enough of this," I snarled, wiping the tears from my eyes. Again, I commanded the mages blood. The breath ceased in their throats. Their sudden alarm burned hot across my skin.

"If you want to live, call off your beasts."

All fell still and quiet. I knit another spell from our connection and the stinging in my eyes subsided, though the cloying stench of the skunk's musk still hung like a dead man in the room. The familiars all sat in a line outside of the doors, watching me.

"Everyone out," I ordered. Chairs scraped back behind me as the mages followed. Their terror blazed like the sun now, threatening to burn me alive.

The air outside tasted like the sweetest candied apples compared to the skunk's stink. The familiars retreated as we walked out, giving me space so I wouldn't kill their masters. In the distance, a battalion of soldiers rode for us on the road, leaving a plume of dust behind them.

Above you, Sauro said just before the world itself shook as the largest bird I'd ever seen slammed into the ground before us, its crimson plumage shining in the sun. The roc brought its head close, one golden eye trained on me. Relief flooded into Learji's thoughts at her familiar's appearance. I sent an order to her to act as my shield, but before she could obey, the roc leapt into the air. Keeping adrift a few paces from me, it gave a huge flap of its wings, sending a wall of air at me to break my bones.

Tapping into my connection with Sauro again, I wound the attack around me, increasing its momentum, before I sent it driving back into the hulking bird. It squawked as the wind hit it full in the chest and sent ruby feathers flying in all directions. A scream that couldn't reach her lips echoed through Learji's mind.

Let us breathe, Akari thought desperately at me, her words swimming up to grab my attention. They'd all dropped to their knees, faces blue and eyes bulging. I released my hold on their lungs and they gasped for air, gulping it down like a drowning victim pulled from the sea.

"Remain on your knees and speak only when spoken to," I said. I hadn't made it a compulsion, but I didn't have to. Eyes downcast, they nodded.

The beating of hoofs had reached us. I hailed the riders as they approached. They circled us, but only the captain dismounted. She looked us over, her eyes widening in her tawny face as she took in the scene. She glanced toward the downed roc before settling her gaze on me.

"You are Bashir, I gather," she said, resting a hand on the hilt of her saber.

"I am," I said, spreading my hands and giving her a small bow. "And these are the mages who would overthrow the crown."

"I know these men and women," she said, anger in her words. "What proof do you have that Akari, or any of the others here, would be anything other than loyal to our Lord and Lady?"

"Tell her," I said, ordering Akari to tell the captain the whole of the truth through her blood. The captain listened as she did, her brow furrowing further and further. When Akari finished, a heavy silence enveloped us as the captain weighed her words. The soldiers shifted nervously, obviously uncomfortable to know how much contempt Akari and the others held for them.

"Shackle them," the captain said at last. None of her battalion moved, and she snarled, "Now! They'll go before the Lord and Lady for judgment. Then, the Gods save us, we'll deal with this army they've gathered in the shadows."

The captain's eyes snapped to me.

"You," she said, leveling a finger at me. "You're coming with us. I'm sure the Lord and Lady would like to speak with you."

"But of course," I said, with a smile I meant less than any other that had ever graced my face.

* * *

As a boy, just after I'd bonded with Sauro, I dreamed of becoming the Arch Mage and living in the palace. With the Lord and Lady hanging upon my every word, I'd live in luxury until the light left my eyes. Walking through the palace all these years later, I realized how quickly that light would have winked out. Erqoiyu was many things: a hub of commerce, a major military force, and the largest producer of art and music in the Sundered Lands. But more than anything, it was hot. And while we weathered it far better than those of the cold south, the palace remained a hell pit.

We trudged down the largest corridor I'd ever seen, leading to the throne room. A hundred people could walk on either side of the blue carpet that ran its length. I knew this because there were at least a hundred fucking people currently walking on either side of the carpet. All those sweaty, stinking bodies put off a lot of sweaty, stinking heat. Even with the walls being more window than anything, and the airy palace linens I wore, I sweated like water was a poison I needed to purge from myself entirely. How the soldiers in full plate standing at intervals down the hall seemed so cool and calm, the Guardian only knew.

We reached the doors, and waited as we were announced. I cursed the Royal's need to list everyone's title, then all their relative's titles, and then the titles of everyone they'd ever fucked for good measure. That last took the longest since Royals fuck everyone in one way or another.

At last, they opened the doors to the massive chamber beyond. The gathered here numbered far less than in the rest of the palace, and the temperature dropped drastically. Couldn't have the Royals as uncomfortable as the rabble after all.

Time to work, I said to Sauro. She sent her acknowledgment and sped off as we stopped before the thrones.

"The Royal Mages before you stand accused of treason, sedition, and inciting rebellion," the captain said once the chamber had fallen silent, stepping forward and kneeling before the Lord and Lady. Lord Pirtomu stood, his long dark braids cascading around him, gorgeous against the light blue of his robes.

With his high cheekbones, obsidian skin, and umber eyes, he seemed larger than the chamber itself with his austere beauty. Even the sweat on his skin added to his presence, making him shine like the sun. If anyone had ever looked born to be a king, it was him.

"You have heard the allegations levied at you," he said, his voice like a song in the forest in the dead of night. Equal parts sweet in its melody, and chilling in its presence. The mages kept their heads low, not wishing to look up to the man that they'd pledged their service to. Only Akari dared to meet the imposing man's eye. He gazed back at her, his face impassive but his brow furrowed. "Will you refute these claims?"

Silence lingered in the room after he spoke, like everyone had held their breath as they waited for her response. Sauro returned, giving me the first blood she'd taken.

"I do not," Akari said at last, drawing a gasp from all attending. Lady Nirya sat forward then, her eyes blazing with a cold light.

A deafening din erupted. Too many voices tumbled over themselves; it felt like an avalanche tearing down a mountain. I scarcely heard any of it.

When the link snapped into place with the lowly noble, the rush of thoughts and memories that hit me left me nauseous. I'd linked with thieves and murderers, but I'd never encountered someone this depraved. I saw the torture he'd ordered and enacted with his own hands. I felt the blade in his hands and the smile on his face as he surgically removed the bones from a man's arm as he screamed. I saw him in the room with his daughter—

The noise ceased, and I snapped out of the noble's depravity. Lady Nirya had risen to her feet. She didn't stand as tall as Lord Pirtomu, but despite her delicate nature, she seemed even larger than him. Her skin was darker than his, but her eyes were greener than the oldest trees in Naguira. She wore robes of emerald to complement them, and when she moved to stand beside her husband, it was as if the divine themselves had descended to the earth.

"What right have you to depose us?" she said, her voice like Summer herself.

Sauro returned before Akari spoke, and I sank into the horror of another dozen nobles. The shape and taste of their thoughts were disgusting beyond comprehension. How these monsters could revel in rape, murder, pain, and suffering so wholly I never wanted to understand. It took all I had to stay on my feet as my stomach rebelled against such evil.

"Let all hear our judgment."

Pirtomu's voice filtered through the black haze. He lifted his fist to invoke the Gods.

"You will all hang as Forbade with first light and may the divine have mercy on you."

"I will not be sent to my death by cowards who can't even do the deed themselves," Akari said. With a blinding flash, her bonds shattered, and the

Lord and Lady both staggered back. My hold on her link had slipped as I swam through the nobles' horrors.

Shit.

Akari leapt toward them and I slammed a compulsion back into her blood. She halted, spitting a curse as I ordered her to kneel. I grit my teeth, doing my best to stay focused as Sauro continued to bring me hell. Soldiers raced up and pushed Akari flat onto the floor.

"That won't be necessary," I said, waving them away.

"Who are you?" the Lord said, paying me a glance as he comforted the Lady.

"Bashir, your grace," the captain said. "He subdued Akari and the others until we could take them into custody."

I looked up at Pirtomu and his eyes widened slightly when I met his gaze. If even the minor royals' minds were blacker than the deepest pits of the Watcher's Hells, then what darkness lay inside the head of this god of a man?

"You are Forbade," The Lady said, more an accusation than a question.

"I am, milady," I said, never losing my hold on Pirtomu's eyes.

"You have not always possessed so great a strength," Pirtomu said. Some emotion I didn't recognize crept into his face. "He has the Manumit."

"I do."

The soldiers rushed me the moment the words left my lips.

It is done, Sauro said, and I smiled savagely.

"Kneel," I growled, burning the command into the blood of everyone in the room.

To a man, they dropped to their knees. I felt Nirya's shock at finding herself on the floor, but the anger that burned on her brow could have melted stone. But Pirtomu had never broken his gaze, and the hope that had kindled in his thoughts surprised me.

If you can hear me, then I ask you to do what we cannot, Pirtomu pleaded.

I intend to.

He knew the evil of his nobles, and for years both he and Nirya had been unable to do anything about it. It ran too deep, and spread too far into those with power. I could count on one hand the number of royals that didn't deserve death in the throne room. The Lord and Lady didn't even have the soldiers on their side. They were little more than prisoners here in the palace, forced to sit with the knowledge that only the devils around them had real power.

I was not a good person. I have lied, stolen, sabotaged. Even murdered. No one would call me a hero, and I'd never wanted to be one. But faced with *this*? Even I couldn't sit and do nothing about the hell these demons had brought to the world.

Because I had power now as well.

Turning, I stalked back through the kneeling royals.

I have seen the vile things you have done, the dark ambitions you hold, and the way you revel in suffering, I said as I went, driving my words into their minds. *I name myself your enemy, and I* will *come for you. You shall know the pain you've inflicted before your end. I cannot be stopped. There is no power so great in this world as knowledge.*

And I am Bashir, Who Knows All.

Have Voodoo, Will Travel

Gini Koch & Bebe Bayliss

"C'mon, boy, move it!"

Sarge's shouting didn't make Veritas feel more encouraged to leap into the swamp in front of them. Not only was the water coming up past everyone's knees, cypress trees were everywhere, with massive streamers of Spanish moss hanging from branches to caress the black water. The moss held chiggers for sure, and the swamp likely had eels or alligators. In the moonlight, the whole area looked dark, disgusting, and dangerous—three things Veritas felt he should avoid at all costs.

"Move, boy, *now*, or I'll shoot you myself!" Sarge shouted again, and Veritas unwillingly stepped into the swamp. The bottom of his coat dragged in the water as he held his rifle high, determined not to notice anything that might brush against him.

Veritas and the forty or so men left in his company of Union soldiers were in the middle of a battle with some Johnny Rebs they'd stumbled upon deep in these Louisiana swamplands. Somehow his side had been winning—right up until those boys in gray had left the rise of land they were all on to run into the swamp water.

Veritas moved forward, following the others, listening to Sarge shouting at them all to keep moving and shooting at their targets, trying not to notice the water was now up to his waist. Then he noticed something new—the Rebs were running back towards them, screaming in terror that had nothing to do with his company's bullets. He immediately saw why.

A gigantic thing that looked a little like a bear draped in Spanish Moss—but more like a horrifying monster with matted fur and glowing red eyes—loomed behind one of the rebels. It swiped at the boy with a giant paw that held four long, razor-sharp, curved claws. It caught the boy's neck, claws cutting deep, and the boy sank into the swamp.

Veritas screamed, then hollered a warning as more monsters loomed up from behind the dead soldier. "Run, everyone, run! There're monsters coming!"

But that's not what anyone else seemed to see.

"Bear attack!" Sarge shouted. "Shoot 'em, boys, and we'll have food for days!"

"Run!" Veritas yelled again, as Sarge grabbed his arm to pull him forward. "Run for your lives!"

The Johnny Rebs were also screaming about bears and broke ranks, shooting wildly at both Union soldiers and monsters.

Veritas managed to get out of Sarge's grip, mostly because the man was bellowing orders and trying to shoot "bears" at the same time.

He shook his head and looked through his rifle sight. He saw monsters, not bears. But he also saw other shots hitting those monsters and it seemed like the shots were bouncing off.

While it was unlikely that what looked like fur was instead armor, Veritas didn't figure he had long to decide. He aimed for the monster nearest to him—still far enough away that Veritas was safe from attack—and aimed at the head. A glowing red eye, to be exact.

He'd had to become a good shot back on the farm in Indiana to ensure that rattlers and copperheads didn't kill their stock. He was so good that he was his company's assigned sniper. So he did what Pa had taught him—he let his breathing slow, went to a calm place, told himself that he was the one moving, not the target, adjusted for that movement, and fired.

The monster screamed. It sounded horrible to Veritas, like the death roar of birds and beasts combined, and louder than loud. But to the others it apparently just sounded like a bear dying.

Veritas backed up while spotting his next target. There were at least twenty of these monsters, and he'd only taken out one. The monsters, on the other hand, had wiped out half of the rebels and a quarter of his own company. Fear made him faster and more accurate, and he got another monster down, its roaring as loud as the screams from the boys and men being slaughtered by the rest of the thing's pack.

The swamp was getting quieter since most of the humans were dead or, in the case of a few, sobbing in terror. Veritas shot another monster through the eye, listened to its deafening death knell, and kept backing up, hoping to get out of the deep swamp and onto higher ground, the better to shoot monsters and avoid getting killed.

Of course, he probably should have avoided signing up to fight in the War at the age of sixteen in the first place but, at the time, in the relative safety of his small hometown of Laconia, Indiana, the War had seemed both necessary and a bit romantic. He'd leave the farm and go save the country, free the slaves, maybe meet President Lincoln, and get a commendation.

Now celebrating his seventeenth birthday in the middle of some wretched swamps outside New Orleans, with all the boys he'd joined up with dead or deserters, the only goal he had was to survive. A goal that wasn't looking too achievable right now.

He stumbled up the bank as one of the monsters swiped at Sarge, ripping his chest to shreds. In the time he'd managed to kill three of these things, they'd killed everyone else but him.

Now was the time to turn and run, but the monsters had already shown they were faster than the humans, and Veritas had no clear idea of where to run to, anyway. So he aimed again and fired.

Another monster screaming a death cry, sixteen monsters left. Veritas didn't have to do the 'rithmetic to know that, with what was coming, he probably wasn't going to see his eighteenth birthday...or even dawn.

"Lord," he whispered, "if you could see your way clear, I'd sure appreciate assistance here of some kind. But if not, I'd truly like to see the Gates of Heaven when one of these monsters kills me, not the face of the Devil, if I've been decent enough in Your eyes to gain such a blessing."

Nothing happened, and he didn't feel any more at peace. Veritas considered his next words to the heavens as the monsters all headed for him, reminding himself that the preacher always said that God liked a man who was willing to do His work. "And, if there's anything you might want me to take care of here before I die, I reckon I'd be more than obliged to do that, just to ensure that my soul goes to the good place rather than the bad."

No sooner was this offer made than something happened that was more astonishing than what already had.

* * *

The swamp glowed with an eerie greenish light. But the monsters were outlined in a bright red glow.

"You will *not!*" a woman's strong voice intoned, and the monsters froze—against their will if Veritas was any judge.

He wasn't frozen and he was still looking through his rifle sight. He could see the woman clearly.

She was a tall Negress of indeterminate age, slender but powerfully formed, with a full head of wild curls.

She was floating above the ground, surrounded by white light, wind making her dress flow and hair wave gently, and on her outstretched left arm perched a large, coal-black rooster, though it wasn't a rooster like he was used to on the farm.

This creature was much bigger than any rooster Veritas had ever seen. Its feathers were in wild disarray and the wattle against its large chest made the rooster look like a bizarre black snowman.

This bird stared straight at him and suddenly just looked like a very large, regular rooster. "Kneel in the presence of the Voodoo Queen of New Orleans," the bird said, its voice raspy but clear enough.

Roosters did not talk. Veritas managed not to drop his rifle, but it was a near thing. He considered what to do and decided that getting away was the safest choice. He turned and ran.

Directly into the path of a large, wild cat, who crouched before him with a look in its eyes that he knew well from seeing coyotes raid cattle on the farm. He was the prey and, if he was lucky, the big cat would kill him fast.

The cat snarled and the rooster cackled and Veritas backed up. He turned around slowly, then went back and knelt before the Voodoo Queen, putting his rifle on the ground before him.

"Thank you, Missy," the Voodoo Queen said to the big cat, who came and settled at her feet, still keeping a close eye on Veritas. "And well done, Veritas Aiden Laconne." She and the bird floated over the swamp to hover in front of him. "If a bit reluctant. You show great wisdom for one who has only just reached the beginning of his seventeenth year."

"How do you know my name?" he managed to ask.

"I know all about you," she said. "I listened to your prayer and saw into your soul. You alone saw the danger for what it was. You alone offered to complete tasks to ensure entry into Heaven."

She floated closer to Veritas and the glow around her went brighter. "I am Tanté Madia," her voice boomed. "I have seen magic from the dawn of time, I have molded it with my mind. I watched La Salle arrive here, saw Lafitte hide his gold and save his emperor, saw this world turn from new, to old, to new again. And in that time, I have learned what the few have forgotten and the many will never know."

Tanté Madia leaned towards him and her eyes were blazing even more than before. "And I, Tanté Madia, Voodoo Queen of New Orleans, past, present, and future, say that you are the one chosen to be my eyes and ears, a weapon and a salvation, to go where I cannot, to protect and serve those who have need of my power."

"Or I reckon you let the big cat kill me?" he asked, trying to keep his voice steady.

"I am Missy," the big cat said, "a jaguar, who is the beloved familiar of the most powerful and ageless Voodoo Queen who has ever lived or ever will live.

I do not kill those she values. If she has given you a mission, she finds you worthy."

Tanté Madia smiled and it was beautiful and terrifying at the same time. "You are worthy to become my chevalier, my warrior, an extension of myself. I have chosen you to help me shield the living from the supernatural, protect the supernatural from each other, and let the dead rest."

"Do I have to do anything evil?" Veritas blurted out. "I'm sorry, but if I'm going to be your shiv—"

"Sheh-*vaa*-lee-aye," the rooster interrupted. "It means knight in French. Not that I see anything much to knight here," he said as an aside to the Voodoo Queen.

"More evil than you have already done in such a short time?" she asked gently and he felt ashamed yet also understood. "No. Ours is the path of right, the path of help and healing. You will have to fight many times, but you will also need to learn how to find the way without fighting, without killing. Though some evils must be killed, and some evils cannot be killed, only diminished."

"I don't really know much about…well, any of this," Veritas admitted.

"Yet you have a gift for it. You saw the bears for what they truly are, and risked your life to save your fellow humans, even those at war with you. The Honey Island Swamp Monsters are typically less aggressive but were disturbed by your battle during a significant rite for their clan."

"What rite could we have disturbed that justified this slaughter?" he asked quietly.

She chuckled. "It is their mating season."

She turned and waved her hand, muttering something in a language he didn't recognize. The Swamp Monsters turned and went off the way they'd come. Then she turned back to him. "Such is the power of my magic that those monsters are returning home instead of killing you, you who massacred their kin. So, Veritas, do you accept?"

"Think hard, human, before you answer," the rooster said. "This is a magical obligation put on you to ensure your service."

"And safety," Tanté Madia added.

"How can I do this? I don't know any voodoo, or magic."

Tanté Madia smiled. "I know. I will give you a gift, a means of travel, and a guide. You will not be alone." She made an odd movement with her arm and something appeared in her hand—a honey-colored piece of wood in the shape of a heart.

If doing the will of a Voodoo Queen was the price to ensure that his soul went to the good place, it seemed he had only one choice. "I agree."

She held it out to him and Veritas stood up to receive this heart, which hung on a leather cord. "It is a planchette made from a yew tree and has great power. It will be your guide and lead you where you need to go. And, because of how it was created, it will also guard you and those who travel with you. This is the gift."

"Oh. Uh. Thank you." Veritas tried not to let his face betray his thoughts.

"It will work when it should," Tanté Madia said with humor in her tone, showing that his face had indeed betrayed him. "Wear it around your neck. Keep it safe, keep it hidden, and keep it out of the hands of evil."

"Yes, ma'am." He put the cord over his head. The planchette hung just under his clavicle. "Oh." He tucked it into his shirt and looked up at her. "Alright?"

She smiled. "Alright." She made another movement with her hand and Veritas heard hoofbeats coming up behind him.

He turned to see a horse that, in the moonlight, looked silver, though he knew it had to be a gray. The horse was bridled and had full saddlebags. It trotted up to him and nickered.

Veritas stroked the horse's nose. "Now, who did you throw, boy?"

"He threw no one," Tanté Madia said. "He is your means of travel."

"He doesn't look like he's made of magic."

She chuckled. "He is not. He is as flesh and blood as you are, but, like you, has been spared a hideous death in order to lead a more righteous life."

"Horses can sin?"

"Not as men can sin, no. And Moscow has not sinned so much as begged for a better life and a better way than he had."

"Moscow is a name for a mule, not a handsome horse," Veritas blurted out.

The horse whinnied at them and Tanté Madia laughed again. "He feels that a new name would be appropriate, and suggests you give it to him."

Veritas considered this, because it seemed like an important request and now that he'd agreed to help her, he felt obligated to do what Tanté Madia asked. "I think…Silver seems kinda…obvious." The horse snorted. "And he doesn't seem to like it."

"Well determined," Tanté Madia said encouragingly.

Veritas thought some more. His granddad had died right before the War and Veritas still missed the old man. "Mortimer might be nice. Morty for short."

The horse whinnied again and shook his head up and down. "He likes it," Tanté Madia said with satisfaction. The horse nickered at her and pawed the ground. "And he, in return, suggests that Veritas is a long name, and while Veritas Aiden Laconne sounds impressive, Val might be a better nickname for the trail."

Veritas grinned. "I like it, Morty." The horse nudged him with its head in a way that felt loving. Veritas, now Val, in turn hugged Morty's neck. "I think we'll do alright together."

"I agree. And now, the final part."

Val turned back to Tanté Madia. "Yes, ma'am, my assignment?"

"Oh, your assignments will be many. No, I must give you a guide."

"I thought this, uh, planchette was supposed to guide me."

"It will, and I am pleased you remembered my words. However, you will need more than the planchette—you will need someone of experience, cunning, and wisdom, who can also contact me wherever you are."

The rooster looked suspicious. "What are you suggesting?" it asked her. "Because it doesn't sound like something I'm going to like."

She pretended not to hear. "I give you as your traveling companion and confidante my familiar, the black cockerel, Merle."

"I don't know what a familiar is, but shouldn't your pet stay with you, ma'am?"

"I am no *pet*," Merle snapped. "I am the conduit for the greatest Voodoo Queen who has ever lived or will ever live."

"A familiar," Missy said, "is an animal companion that helps magic flow more freely to those we serve. Some of us are better at it than others."

Merle squawked in protest and Tanté Madia stroked his feathers. "Merle, you know how much I value you, and that you are essential to Val's success. Which is why you must go with him and Morty. I trust you to provide the connection to me that Val will need on his journeys."

"Journeys?" Val asked weakly.

Tanté Madia nodded. "You will be traveling far and wide, with my voodoo magic helping and protecting you, and you, too, will learn the ways of magic and power."

"So I can better," Val squinted as he concentrated to remember her exact wording, "shield the living from the supernatural, protect the supernatural from each other, and let the dead rest?"

Tanté Madia smiled at him. "Just so. You are what I have been waiting for." With that she kissed Merle's head then moved her arm in a way that was clearly telling the cockerel to fly off.

Which he did, looking unhappy and cawing quietly to himself, as he landed on Morty's pommel.

The jaguar stood up. "I'm here to help guide you, too, for now, since we're all aware you have no idea of what's going on."

"Thank you, much appreciated." Val gave himself a shake, slid his rifle into the case hooked to the horse's saddle, and mounted up.

Morty snorted and shook his head. "He's impressed by your ability to get onto him," Merle shared. "You're small for your age and he's twenty hands if he's one."

"I know how to jump," Val said. "And the stirrup's right there."

"He's used to his owner using a mounting box."

"I'm used to my Pa telling me to get on up." Val took the reins. "Now, where do you want me to go?" he asked Tanté Madia.

"Merle and Missy, and the planchette, will guide you. I will be watching. Be well, my Chevalier." Tanté Madia smiled and vanished.

* * *

Missy turned and headed into the swamp, though not in the same direction as the Honey Island Swamp Monsters had gone.

"I guess Tanté Madia doesn't think too much of my skills," Val said quietly to Merle, "though I can't blame her."

Merle heaved a sigh and turned his head so he could eyeball Val. "Actually, by sending both of us with you for at least a small part of your journey, she's saying that she has great faith in you."

Val felt much better about this. "How will she know what we're doing?"

"Well, we're still within her circle of power—it extends in a radius of a hundred miles of her home—so she will know what we're doing when she chooses to look through my eyes or Missy's. That's all you need to know for now."

Val pulled the planchette out from under his shirt. It rose of its own accord and pointed ahead. At Missy.

"Is Missy our target?" he asked without thinking.

"I retract my earlier compliment," Merle said, derision clear. "Missy is leading us towards your first mission. The planchette is pointing towards the place where we're next needed. That the two align seems remarkably obvious. To *me*, at least."

Missy flicked her tail in what Val felt was a dismissive way. Meaning she'd heard all of this and felt he was as stupid as Merle did.

He patted Morty's neck. "Thanks for not telling me I'm a fool."

Morty whinnied in a way that sounded like the horse was laughing. But Val felt the horse was laughing with, not at, him, and so felt a little better.

Missy wasn't moving quickly because she was picking out a path that kept them reasonably dry. Sure, she could leap where Morty chose to walk, but at the highest the water was only up to the horse's forelocks. The swamp was still eerie, but Val decided to see it as a place of mystery versus horror. It took effort, but he managed it.

He didn't allow his vigilance to waver, though he did pull the planchette out of his shirt every so often to ensure it still rose and pointed in the direction Missy was heading.

After an hour or so the planchette tugged a bit against his neck. Soon enough they reached what could almost be called dry land, just as the sun began to rise. And in the first rays of the sun's light Val saw another thing he wouldn't have expected in about a thousand years.

* * *

There was a herd of animals, doing nothing much other than grazing on what looked like swamp muck. But they weren't animals as he'd ever seen before.

They looked something like buffalo, but not quite—they were a bit smaller, and the horns on their heads curled inwards so much that the points were in the center of a horn circle. They seemed docile, like slightly odd cattle, with a mane that looked more like Morty's than what Val would have said an ox or cow would have.

Missy came to a stop and sat down behind some large trees that hid them while still giving them a view of this weird herd. He reined Morty in behind her. "What are these?" he whispered to Merle, as Missy, satisfied that the others had stopped, leaped up into the tree nearest to Val's head.

Merle heaved another long-suffering sigh—Val had a suspicion he was going to hear that sigh a lot. "I suppose you can't be expected to know. They're bonnacons, related to European bison. And they're considered myths, since other than the ones you see here, they're extinct."

"What are European bison relations doing in the middle of the Louisiana swamplands?"

"Surviving." Merle fluffed his feathers and stopped speaking.

One of the bonnacons looked around, saw something that caused it to make a sound like a sick cow, then it turned its behind towards whatever it had seen, and Val heard what sounded like the bonnacon releasing gas.

He couldn't be sure, but it seemed like Merle had taken a deep breath and was holding it. Morty did the same. He looked up—Missy was crouched down on the large branch, front paws over her nose. And in about a second, Val found out why.

"What…" he gasped, "what is…that *smell?*"

"The bonnacon's protection," Merle said, wing over his beak. "Their gas can take your feathers off if you're too close. We're lucky it was aimed away from us *and* that the rest of the herd didn't panic."

Val managed not to gag, mostly because he didn't want Merle to see him do it. What he wanted to say—but didn't want to risk opening his mouth to do so—was that they needed to figure out where they were really supposed to be, because protecting a herd of stink monsters just didn't seem like what he'd signed up for.

Then again, he had to remind himself that "monsters" was indeed something he'd been recruited to handle. And that meant that maybe Missy, the planchette, and therefore Tanté Madia, wanted them here for a reason.

As soon as this thought occurred, he spotted something.

A man around Pa's age was moving towards the bonnacon herd in what seemed to be a stealthy manner. This man wasn't in uniform and he was almost as mucked up as Val, meaning he'd been in and out of the swamps. He was also wearing a kerchief over his lower face. Val didn't know if that indicated the man was a criminal or just smart enough to have some protection against bonnacon flatulence.

This man might be coming to herd the herd—a joke he'd laugh about later if he got to have a later—or might be up to no good. He felt the planchette stop tugging. Now was clearly the time for action. What action wasn't clear, of course, and neither Merle nor Missy were offering any suggestions, but he figured doing something was probably better than doing nothing. So he slowly slid his rifle out of the case.

He'd hoped that looking through the sight would give him a glimmer of an actual plan, but all this allowed was for him to verify that the man had a pistol on his hip, a rifle over his back, and what looked like a long length of rope slung over his shoulder.

Pa had taught him a few things, and how to spot a cattle rustler was one of them. This man looked like a rustler, and he was planning to rustle a herd of nearly extinct animals. But did that mean he shot the man or just shot above the herd to panic them?

Morty snorted—impatiently, if Val was any judge—and walked out from behind the tree. Then he whinnied, meaning that everyone's attention was now turned towards them. Miraculously, the bonnacons didn't panic, they just stood there, staring at him, Morty, and Merle. Missy, as far as he knew, was still in the tree.

The man aimed his gun—at Val. "You just put that rifle down and git on your way, boy. This ain't none of your concern." Val still had the rifle up and aimed, and he was looking at the man through the sight. He saw the man's eyes narrow. "You here to steal their horns out from under me? I'm Landry Montagu and this is my territory, ain't it? So you just move along."

"If it's your territory," Val asked, "why are you sneaking around?"

Montagu seemed to notice Merle for the first time. "Why you trotting around with a cockerel for a familiar? I'm the magic man in these parts, not you, boy."

A few things were vying for Val's attention. The first was that Montagu seemed to know that Merle was a familiar, meaning that him saying he was a magic man was probably truth.

The second was that the bonnacon herd was currently quiet and most of their rears were faced towards Montagu.

And third, he knew that this man would shoot Morty first, because Montagu had his pistol in his hand and that meant he couldn't be as accurate over the distance as Val, so he'd have to aim for the bigger target.

All of a sudden his vision changed and—just as he'd seen Merle look very different when he'd first laid eyes on him—Montagu changed. He looked dangerous in a different way than he had before, and he had a sickly greenish-brown glow around him.

Val had two choices, and he chose the one that, hopefully, wouldn't make him a murderer.

He fired over the bonnacons' heads.

* * *

Results were immediate. The bonnacons, to a one, screamed—which sounded like the cross between a wail and a warble combined with a moo—and to a one they released gas. Directly at Montagu.

Some of the bonnacons released the gas at each other, of course, but their gas didn't seem to affect the others in the herd. The same could not be said of Montagu.

He screamed and Val watched in horror as the gas hit him. His clothes burned off first, then his skin, then the rest of him. In short order there was nothing left but a skeleton in some charred boots.

The herd had mostly remained in place, but some had run off. They were swiftly herded back by Missy. Once the herd was back together and the smoldering pile of what was left of the rustler had died down, she padded over and took a look. Then she came back to the rest of them.

Val was frozen from the shock of what had happened. "What did I do?" he whispered as the jaguar reached them.

"You protected your familiar from an evil magic-user threatening him," Missy replied calmly. "And you protected the helpless from one who would have destroyed them for nothing."

"Bonnacon horn is reputed to be the supreme aphrodisiac," Merle added. "It's not, but fools will believe anything they're told, especially if that means they can harm something rare and helpless while getting it."

"They're not helpless!" Val realized he had shouted and forced himself to calm down—the bonnacons were watching them, and he didn't want to risk frightening any of them and having them fart in his direction. "They killed him. And I made them do it."

"You did what was necessary," Missy replied. "You didn't know that the bonnacons' release would kill him. You planned to stink him away. A good plan. It just worked better than you imagined it would."

"But now I'm a murderer."

"You were in the War," Merle said. "You killed people far more innocent than this man ever was. Get over it. You'll have to do it again, guaranteed."

Val knew Merle was right—Tanté Madia had said the same, essentially.

Something Missy had said finally registered. "You said I was protecting my familiar, but Merle belongs to Tanté Madia."

Morty whinnied, and now Val was sure the horse was laughing at him.

Missy gave a growl that also sounded like she was laughing. "Merle is not your familiar, Val, he is your guide through the new world you find yourself in. Morty, on the other paw..."

He patted the horse's neck. "You're my familiar? I can do magic because of you?"

"In a way," Merle corrected, as Morty did the horse head-bob that made it look like he was saying yes. "You'll channel magic through him. As you did when you saw the dead man there for what he was—evil. You'll both get better at it as time goes on."

"I saw you for what you really are when I first laid eyes on you," Val countered. "But I only see you the way I think you want to be seen now."

Merle fluffed his wings. "Yes, you can see the truth. I am more powerful than you, so for now you can only see me as I wish it to be."

"That will change in time," Missy added.

"What do the bonnacons look like for those who can't see what's real?" Val asked.

"Skinny cows," Merle replied. "But Landry saw them for what they are— and you stopped him."

"Just in time," Missy said. "For your first mission you needed three familiars, to ensure no mistakes. As you travel on, you will not always have me, but you will always have Merle." She sounded very satisfied.

"And why is *that*?" Merle asked haughtily.

"Because," Missy said with a flick of her tail. "Tanté Madia likes me better and cannot do without me for long." And with that, she disappeared.

They stood there in silence, other than the soft lowing the bonnacon made. It was obvious Merle was stung by Missy's words by the way the bird huddled in on himself.

Val cleared his throat. "Merle, I bet it's a lot safer and easier for you to travel out of the circle of power than for a big cat like Missy. It's clear how much Tanté Madia cares about you. And...and I'm honored that you'll be my companion."

Merle took a deep breath and fluffed up his feathers. "I knew you were smarter than you looked."

Val took the planchette out from under his shirt. "Reckon this will lead us to a meal? I haven't eaten since before I knew there were monsters, familiars, and a Voodoo Queen."

The planchette lifted and pointed in the direction of Merle.

"Ah...even if the planchette tells me to, I'm not eating you, Merle."

Merle heaved that long-suffering sigh again. "And once again, I take it back. Morty arrived with full saddlebags, no doubt containing provisions. Magic isn't necessary when common sense and planning will do. Though I'm still waiting to see if you have any sense at all."

Val reached into a saddlebag and rummaged around until he discovered a supply of beef jerky. The planchette immediately stopped pointing at Merle—now it pointed to the right of the bonnacon herd. "My sense tells me that the planchette pointed to you for a reason, Merle. Probably because it knew you'd know that there was food nearby."

"Well, the planchette does work in its own mysterious ways," Merle muttered as he rearranged himself on the pommel.

Val took a bite of jerky, then clucked to Morty. "Let's get a move on, then. Per those mysterious ways, looks like there's more trouble ahead."

"And while we ride," Merle said, "I'll explain to you why you should never, ever consider eating a familiar. Especially me."

Special Delivery

Russell Hugh McConnell

Gord leans across Meryl's old desk, holding the three of clubs, and I notice with relief that I can't see his brain anymore. On the downside, now I can see most of his sinus cavity, and about half of his teeth. Uvula, but no tongue. It's pretty gross, but it's nowhere near as bad as when his brain was showing. That's what made Meryl throw up, and it must have been the last straw, because she finally made good on her perennial threat and quit on the spot. It's a lot quieter and more relaxed around here with her desk empty, but there's also a lot less work getting done.

Gord is fine, by the way. Three days ago, he carelessly ripped open an envelope and got a big puff of invisibility powder in the face. At first his whole head went invisible, which was a lot more attractive than the current situation. That was tough for Gord, though, because an invisible head means invisible retinas, which means that light passed straight through his photoreceptors and he couldn't see anything. (At least that's how he explained it. He's the nerd, not me.) Now the invisibility is wearing off gradually from back to front, so for a while only the back half of his head was visible, including the back half of his brain, pulsing away for the world to see. Hence Meryl throwing up and quitting, hence the empty desk.

On the plus side, for at least the next six months we can blame almost everything that goes wrong around here on Meryl leaving. It's just like three years ago, when Barry got sucked into the ninth-dimensional puzzle box, along with two of the big filing cabinets; for over a year after that, we had a perfect excuse for never having the right paperwork for anything. It was a bit of a raw deal for Barry, but Gord says that he's not actually dead, because time slows down infinitely when you enter the ninth dimension, so he's actually frozen forever in a single moment and has no idea what's happening. So I don't feel too bad for Barry. I mean he's basically immortal now.

This is the Dead Letter Office. All postal systems need one, and the Mystic Post is no exception. This is where all the undeliverable letters and packages go. Some are marked with addresses that don't exist. Others are marked illegibly. In some cases, the intended recipient is deceased, and there's no return address.

In the Mystic Post, mail can travel in a lot of different ways, through a lot of different times and places, even through different ontological states, and if it can't be delivered, then we get it. There are actually a lot of undeliverables, probably because there are so many different systems of distribution and transport. We use passenger pigeons, passenger owls, and passenger griffons. We use phantom trains, ghost trains, steam engines that operate only in the past, and, occasionally, regular old trains. The Bone-man rides his skeletal horse with his sack of clattering packages. The Poste with a Packet of Mad Letters is still in business. There are so many different systems, operating on different schedules—and on different metaphysical principles—that it's no wonder that the occasional item goes astray.

Some packages go missing, some arrive too late, still others are deemed not to exist, or never to have existed. Metaphysically admissible or not, they all end up here. Our job is to open them, remove anything of value, attempt to determine where the contents were supposed to go (a task with a success rate of substantially less than one percent), and file whatever we can't deal with. So mostly we file stuff. There's lots of forms to fill out, but since no one ever really looks at them, I have to admit we can get a little lax.

We're still reeling a bit from the excitement a week ago when we opened a package with a smeared address and recovered a disassembled Contingency Pump. Even the fully functional ones are supposed to be pretty dangerous, and this one looks wonky to me, not that I'm an expert. It certainly should never have been sent just wrapped up in brown packing-paper; these things normally require a triple-sealed, hermetically-warded, runed iron box. Those are expensive, sure, but there are rules about this stuff for a reason.

A Contingency Pump is an example of a heavily controlled item. Certain reality-breaking objects and substances get special treatment, at least in theory. But that's a lot of work, you know? The truth is that we haven't finished the paperwork on it yet, so it's still just sitting on my desk. At the moment we're taking a break to work on our sixteen-deck house of cards—hence Gord leaning across the table with his three of clubs, showing off his newly half-visible sinuses.

I decide to take a pause from looking at the insides of Gord's head and make a quick trip down the hall to the break room, with the consequence that I don't even see the big box when it arrives. I'm just standing in front of the open fridge, trying to decide whether or not to steal something out of Gord's lunch bag, when I hear him yell, "Woah, we've got a live one!"

I groan aloud. One of the worst things at the Dead Letter Office is a live delivery. They're even worse than the dead ones. Sometimes you can guess that's what you're going to get, because the package has a "Live Specimen" label, or because it's a pet crate, or has air holes, or something. But when wizards transport creatures, the biological requirements are all over the place. Some things don't breathe at all, or are frozen in magical stasis. Last year, we got an unlabeled package that turned out to contain a living human head which floated up to the rafters and screamed for three days straight before we could get a containment crew to come pick it up. You can tell how unimportant this office is: when we make an emergency call it takes three days before anything happens. God help us if we get anything *really* dangerous.

When I get back to the mailroom, I see that Gord hasn't even opened the package yet. But it's moving, thumping up and down on the concrete floor, while Gord does his best to read the label. "Might be an unclaimed familiar," he says, shaking his head regretfully. "It's sad, but it happens. Good thing it's your turn to open it."

I sigh. It *is* my turn, isn't it? Normally I would at least attempt to argue, but Gord is a better arguer than me at the best of times, and it's hard to come up with anything clever when I'm looking into his wet mucous membrane.

I can't remember all of the procedures for opening a live package, but I do my best. First, I lay a big plastic sheet on the floor—at least we still have lots of plastic sheets. We don't have any hazmat suits, because most of them were melted when Gord accidentally dropped that wand of fireballs and then stepped on it. We don't even have any disposable vinyl gloves, even though I ordered a new box weeks ago. The last time we did a live opening, Meryl wore the rubber kitchen gloves from the break room, and those ended up getting mostly dissolved by the sentient protoplasm that oozed out of an improperly sealed bio-cannister.

This box seems to be just reinforced cardboard, so I carefully use a box-cutter along the edges, jerking back nervously every time it moves. No, I'm not being wimpy. There could be literally *anything* in there.

I gingerly fold down one side of the box, reflecting that I'm really not paid enough for this, and then let out an involuntary gasp of cuteness-inspired shock as I reveal a brown furry creature, about the size of a large housecat, crouched on a soft mat. It is *incredibly* cute. Meryl would be sorry if she knew she had missed it. It looks kind of like a wombat, but with longer legs, two stubby little black horns, and extraordinary eyes—large, pupilless, and iridescent—like two opals. I have seen a few creatures over the years with no pupils in their eyes, and this usually lends them a frightening appearance: blank, without personality. But this is different. Somehow the creature manages to look friendly, even kindly. It doesn't even seem frightened by Gord's hideous appearance as he leans in to have a look, his red head-innards and exposed white teeth being the sort of thing that might cause nightmares in children. (And, let's face it, adults.)

Completely forgetting all the safety regulations, I look into the creature's warm opal eyes and say, "You had me worried there for a second, buddy. But you're no trouble at all, are you?" Then, impulsively, I reach out and scratch it under the chin. When my finger touches its fur there is a loud ZAP and a big purple spark, and I jerk my hand back with an involuntary cry of "Waaugh!"

Gord springs to his feet. "Dude, are you okay?"

"I, uh, yeah. I am, actually," I say, feeling a bit silly. "It didn't hurt."

"Murgle?" says the creature.

I lift the tag around his neck and read it aloud: "I am Secundus, the Zeittier. Please look after me!"

"Zeittier," says Gord thoughtfully. "That's probably in the bestiary." He turns and begins rummaging in his desk drawer.

"He's pretty cute," I say. "Maybe we can keep him around the office."

Gord gives a hollow laugh. "I don't even want to think about how much paperwork that would involve."

"Oh, come on," I say. "We could keep him off the books. Like when you decided to keep that cool-looking paperweight that turned out to be a miniature black hole encased in crystallized acroamite." As soon as I say it, I realize it's a bad example. Once we figured out what the cube really was, we knew it was way too dangerous to keep—but we also knew that it was too late to report it without getting in major trouble. We ended up dumping it in the puzzle box after Barry. The universe didn't implode, so I figure we got away with it.

I look at the opal-eyed creature and feel a deep connection to him. There's no way I'm giving him up if I can help it, even if this is just about the last place an orphaned familiar would ever be allowed. Nevertheless, I've probably got to do at least a bit of the usual paperwork, to appease Gord and to make sure that the file we submit at the end of this quarter is thick enough. So I head into the supply closet to get a TJ1023-9. But when I try to turn on the light, I can't reach the light switch, because there's a stack of boxes in the way. I turn to yell at Gord but I remember just in time that I'm the one who put them there. So I just prop the door open with my foot and grab the whole box of forms, setting it on the floor of the hallway and letting the closet door swing shut.

Even out in the brighter light I have to rummage for a minute before I find the TJ1023-9s, and then when I pull one out I get a paper cut across the pad of my right index finger. The most used part of the most used finger. Isn't that always how it goes?

Manfully resisting the urge to say "ow," and wondering if I can come up with a plausible way to blame Gord for this, I leave the box on the floor, take the TJ1023-9 in my uninjured left hand and head to the break room, where I put a bright green SpongeBob band-aid on my finger. Are these really the only ones we have? We must have recovered them from one of the dead packages.

As I walk back down the hall towards the mailroom, I hear Gord saying, "I don't know, he seems okay now." I enter and see him kneeling down by the box, concernedly examining the furry creature. Next to him, in a low crouch, gently petting the creature's soft fur, is me.

I blink, and stand there, staring. The guy is definitely me. He's even dressed the same, in an unlicensed Formula One fan t-shirt with a picture of Guenther Steiner swearing. I open and shut my mouth a few times, and then say "Whaa...?"

Gord glances in my direction and says, "He started shaking and puffing up, and then he shot purple sparks out of his eyes and horns. I was afraid he was choking or having a seizure or something, but..." He trails off and stares at me, then at the other me, and then back again at *me* me.

None of the three of us is the panicky type. No one screams or faints. I just stand there, as Gord and the other me rise slowly to their feet. We all stare dumbfoundedly at one another. Although anything is possible, I feel in my heart that I am not confronting a reflection, or an illusion, or a doppelganger. The other me standing here is *me*. Plus, he doesn't seem sickened or horrified by Gord's face, which proves that he, like me, has been looking at it for the last three days.

I look myself in the eye and the two of us say, "Okay," in perfect unison, then break off. Then, in unison, we both turn to Gord, and both discover simultaneously that he's no longer standing there.

"Gord?" I ask. I look over to see him sitting at his desk, flipping through a big green binder. At moments of intense concentration he usually has his tongue stuck out, but as his tongue is still invisible, I have to just assume. "What are you doing?" I ask crossly. "This is an emergency."

He looks up. "Dude," he says. "This is the bestiary." He picks up the heavy binder, which is thick with laminated pages. "I don't think it's a wild stab in the dark to say that we need to figure out what a Zeittier is. Immediately." After a minute of page-flipping, he holds it open to show us a picture. It's a crappy photocopy, but it clearly shows the same kind of creature as Secundus. "It turns out," says Gord, "this might be the most rare and coveted familiar of all time. The photo is from 1923, and it's the last recorded instance of there being one of these in circulation."

"Are they legal?" my double and I ask at the same time, and then we glare irritably at one another.

"Technically yes, practically no. The paperwork you would need to fill out to even be allowed to apply for a license to own one of these makes the Contingency Pump stuff look like a customer service survey."

"What do Zeittiers do?" I ask urgently.

"Dude, take it easy," says Gord. "I only just found the entry. Give me a minute." He glances uncertainly between the two versions of me.

"I'm the real one!" my double and I say in unison. We turn to look at each other, both horrified.

"Look, be reasonable," I say. "I was here first. You didn't show up until after I went to the break room."

"Murgle," says Secundus.

"Never mind who was first—" Gord begins, and the two of me jerk our heads in unison to glare at him. "Um," he says. "Okay, look, I'm just going to read this. Why don't the two of you look in the box and see if there's any identifying materials. You know, standard Live Delivery procedure, Step Three."

The other me and I approach the open cardboard box, eyeing one another cautiously. We both see the envelope at the same time, taped to the inside of the box, and we both go for it, but he gets there first, possibly because he isn't being slowed down by the debilitating effects of a paper cut. He reads the note aloud:

Here you go, Mordy! Just in time, I hope. It's going to take more than a death curse to stop you, buddy. We've got to keep this whole thing on the low-low, but you know what to do. Once you've Bonded with him, you'll be in the clear forever.

This seems important. A death curse is serious business—rare and highly illegal. But what does this Zeittier have to do with that? And who is Mordy? With so little to go on, there's really no way—

"I know who the package was for," says Gord.

"What? How?" I'm completely baffled.

"Oh for corn's sake, Phil, it was all over the news." Gord rummages in one of his many drawers and pulls out a copy of the *Thaumic Times* from last week. The headline reads: *Mordechai Findler Dies in Bizarre Tuna Fish Mishap*. I quickly skim down the page, my eyes wide. I hadn't noticed this at the time, or maybe I had forgotten, but yeah, I do know who Mordechai Findler is. Everybody does. Heir of the Findler estate, a proven descendant of Merlin and Vivien. Practically royalty, insofar as we have that kind of thing. And according to the article, he died in an accident so strange and unlikely that there was immediate suspicion of a death curse. No one could prove it, of course. Once a curse has activated and killed its victim, it vanishes without a trace. No fingerprint.

Death curses are rare, and there aren't a lot of guys around named Mordechai. Clearly, Secundus was supposed to be some kind of countermeasure against a death curse. We need to study up on Zeittiers!

Fortunately, there's some info in the bestiary binder—more than one page, actually, which is pretty unusual. The binder is really just for quick checks; the real bestiary is the 31-volume *Gwydion's Unabridged Compendium of Magical Beasts*, and we have a copy of that filed over in Stack 71B, Shelf L. It was recovered from a misdirected shipping crate full of books nearly fifteen years ago— before my time working here. Apparently sorting that out was Meryl's first big job.

But anyway, even in the dumbed-down, Dick-and-Jane version of the bestiary that we have here, there's six pages of explanation that seem hopelessly dense and technical to me. The sentences are really long, and they're full of words like "supervenience," "endurantism," and "Gestalt." I turn to look at the other me, who of course turns to look my way at exactly the same time, wearing an expression that I assume is identical to my own. His brows are furrowed and his mouth is turned down in a frown which, I am dismayed to observe, somewhat resembles a pout. Do I really pout? I immediately stop frowning, and so does the other me. I guess we just learned something about ourselves we didn't like. But can you really blame us for pulling faces? How could anyone understand this crap?

"Wow," says Gord, "that makes perfect sense."

"What?" my double and I say in unison. Then we add, "You *understood* that?" We glare at one another in annoyance, but we're both more annoyed with Gord, so we quickly decide to glare at him instead.

"Murgle," says Secundus, and rubs against my leg. Without even thinking, I pick him up and hug him.

"God," says Gord, and rolls his eyes (a pretty wild sight with half his face invisible). "A Zeittier is basically a reality Xerox machine. It's making copies of you." He points to a passage of gobbledygook. "Look, it says right here. When a Zeittier bonds with a human and becomes its familiar, it creates sort of a save file of you. And it keeps renewing that save file. So if something really terrible happens to you the Zeittier loads a backup. It's not quite illegal, but it's rigidly controlled, like the Contingency Pump. But…"

I finish the thought. "But if you're Mordechai Findler under a death curse, it's exactly the sort of familiar you would need. Even if it were a persistent curse that went off multiple times, the Zeittier could just keep reuploading the old save file of you. So this guy got special dispensation from the High Council to—"

Gord laughs. "Of course he didn't! If he got special dispensation, this would have arrived with a stack of paperwork the size of the *Codex of Celestial*

Certainties. Plus, it would have had a return address. No, this was an under-the-counter job."

Both of me gasp, and I notice that the other me looks a little silly with that wide-eyed, innocent look of shock. It's very annoying to realize that I must look exactly the same. We both turn to the Zeittier in my arms, who looks back and forth between us. "So Secundus is contraband," says the other me.

"I guess the curse got Mordechai before the familiar arrived," said Gord. "Or maybe the package would have got there in time, but the address was wrong. Anyway, it doesn't matter now." He looks down at my SpongeBob-wrapped finger. "He really shouldn't have created a new copy of you unless you were killed or mortally wounded."

"But he did it for a paper cut..." I say.

"Yeah, something's definitely wrong."

The chime sounds, indicating that another round of post has arrived. My double and I emit identical groans of annoyance. I mean, I usually groan when the chime sounds, because I'm lazy and I don't like working, but the groan is greatly intensified this time. We really don't have time to be processing mail while trying to deal with this situation.

"Look," says Gord, "let's face it: I'm the one who's actually going to figure this out. I'll head to Stack 71B and consult *Gwydion's*, plus maybe some other stuff. Give me a couple of hours. You and you start unloading the packages so we don't fall behind. The two of you working together should be about half as fast as you and me combined, and that will just have to do."

"Hey!" the two of me say in unison. But we don't try to argue. Gord has probably actually run the numbers on this.

Gord strides out of the room, shaking his head with an emotion I'm not sure how to label. Whatever. Let him get on with his nerd stuff. Secundus starts wriggling so I put him down on the floor. Then the two of me crouch down to look at the Zeittier who, now that I think of it, must be bonded to both of us. One familiar with two humans. This might actually never have happened before.

The Zeittier looks up at us and says "Murgle!" In unison, the two of us lean forward to pet him and knock our heads together like Larry and Curly.

"Ow!" we say in unison.

Immediately, the Zeittier starts quaking from side to side. Its fur puffs up hugely, making it look like twice its normal size, and its opal eyes crackle with purple sparks.

"Oh no," me and I say together, as the supply closet door opens behind us.

* * *

"I think he's looking stressed," says Phil 17, kneeling down by Secundus and scratching his chin. At least I think it's Phil 17. Like a lot of the Phils around here he seems to have lost his number. I guess that *is* the kind of thing

I would do. I'm only really making a special effort to keep my own number on because I'm number 1, which I think should give me some authority. Opinions vary on this point, however, which is why some of me are not following my instructions and processing packages, but are instead finding various other activities—activities that include removing and even falsifying their assigned numbers.

My concern with the numbers is, however, eclipsed by my concern for Secundus. I sit down next to the Phil who may-or-may-not be 17 and examine our furry friend. It's very hard to read subtle emotional states in another species, but he does give off an impression of tiredness and stress. All that puffing and sparking must take it out of you. We Phils keep telling one another to be careful, but every bumped head, stubbed toe, or other minor mishap kicks off another spasm from our Zeittier, which is always followed by another me emerging from the supply closet.

Secundus has nibbled a bit of the peanut butter sandwich that we put out, but he hasn't touched the apple. I have no idea what a Zeittier normally likes to eat, but it's not as if we have a lot of options, so we just gave it the contents of Gord's lunch bag. Possibly it doesn't really need to eat anything at all, given that this one has apparently been living in a box for weeks with no food or air.

I know how Secundus must be feeling; I'm kind of stressed myself. The mailroom is a cacophony of voices. I stand up on a chair, and out before me is spread a sea of Guenther Steiner t-shirts. One of the Phils starts shouting, "Look, I'm the real one! I'm the original, because I'm the one with a paper cut!" He holds up a bandaged finger. What a fraud! *I'm* the one with the paper cut!

Immediately, a dozen copies of me all grab pieces of paper and start swiping them across their fingers.

"No! Stop, you assholes!" I yell at myselves. Although I'm not sure how this is all going to work out, I feel it's extremely important that I retain my status as Phil 1.

"I have a paper cut too!" says one of them. "I must be the real one."

"No, *I* am!" shout half a dozen others in unison.

Secundus puffs and sparks furiously, and another seven Phils (without paper cuts) tumble out of the closet.

"You idiots don't even have band-aids on your fingers!" I roar at the self-mutilators. At that, at least two-dozen Phils immediately charge towards the break room, towards the cupboard with the band-aids. There definitely won't be enough to go around, and I hope a fight doesn't break out. If we all start punching each other, then there's going to be another thirty or forty Phils in a minute.

I step down from the chair, stumble as my foot catches on one of the legs, and fall over. "Ow," I say. I can neither see nor hear Secundus from here, but I know he must be puffing and sparking, because a moment later, as the crowd of mes passes by the supply closet door, it opens and another me comes out. Phil 97 at this point? I think?

"Gaah!" he says, when he sees the horde of metaphysically Xeroxed clones charging past. He jumps back and barely avoids getting trampled.

It's at this moment that Gord comes back in the room. For the first time in three days, I'm actually glad that I can't see the expression on his face. But if a nasal cavity can look shocked, this one does. Remarkably, his presence actually quiets the room down quite a bit. It's as if Dad just came home and caught us making a mess. Quite a lot of me look abruptly chastened. It's actually kind of pathetic, seeing so many of me evidently intimidated by a half-faced nerd like Gord. I try to play it more cool than the rest of me. But then I feel a sudden stomach-turning rush of anxiety. What if Gord doesn't recognize me? I mean obviously all the versions of me are me, but what if he can't recognize that I'm the *original* me? What if one of me deceives him, and usurps my rightful place as myself?

But before I can decide what to do, Gord strides over towards me and asks, "What the hell is going on here? I was only gone for two hours."

"You recognize me!" I blurt out, and spontaneously hug him. I've never felt so relieved to have Gord know who I am. Hugging him does bring his exposed nasal cavities within a few inches of my face, though, which makes me gag a little and withdraw. "Ahem," I say. "You know it's me, though. The *original* me." Maybe my mother was right after all. Maybe I *am* special. "How did you know?"

"You have the number 1 pinned to your shirt," says Gord flatly.

Oh, right. Maybe my mother was wrong. Good. Back to normal then.

"I'm sorry," I say, trying not to sound pathetic. "But I keep coming out of the closet. I mean…well, you know what I mean."

"Yeah, I know. And it's not supposed to work that way. When Secundus first recorded your ipseity, he locked onto the closet as point-zero on the haeccity grid, so that's where all the copies come from."

I decide not to ask Gord to explain what that means. I have a terrible feeling that he might tell me.

"Also," says Gord, "you can tell he's malfunctioning because he keeps generating uploads from the same original copy. Notice how none of the other versions of you have paper cuts? The poor thing is stuck in a groove."

"So what do we do?" I ask.

"Well first of all, we lose his paperwork. It should be easy. I mean the whole point of this office is that no one really knows what's here."

Despite everything that has happened, I am momentarily scandalized. I can't believe Gord of all people is saying this. "That's interfering with the mail!" I exclaim. "ThePostmagister says that every letter is a spark of life, and the deliberate sabotage of the mail is like a murder!"

"It's only interfering with dead mail," he says, reasonably. "Which has already been interred in the Dead Letter Office. It's not murder, it' s more like, uh…"

"Necrophilia?" pipes up Phil 44, brightly.

Gord sighs. "Anyway, it's either that or we have to explain to the Postmagister at the end of the month why there's about a billion yous walking around. Every little paper cut, hangnail, stubbed toe…"

"Hey, my toe is still sore," says one of the crowd of Phils. "It's not nothing, you know."

"I'm worried about Secundus," I say. "He seems stressed out."

"Well of course he is!" says Gord. "He's just duplicated you about a hundred times. You're running the poor thing ragged. And it's not just that. He's bonded with you—or at least partially bonded to you. That means he's *your* familiar now, kind of. But he's also a partial familiar to a hundred different version of you at the same time. The bond is stretched across all of you."

"How do you know we're only partially bonded?" I ask. "And why did he bond with me at all? Why not you? Is it because I touched him?"

"Partly," says Gord.

"Do you mean that's partly why he bonded to me, or do you mean that's partly why he's partially bonded?"

"Shut up," says Gord, and holds up the thick book that he came in carrying. "This is Volume 31 of *Gwydion's*. Look: Familiar Bonding Procedure for Zeittiers. It says here that you have to place both hands on his head and say his name, clearly and correctly. If you don't do that, the bonding won't work properly."

"Hmm," I say. "I touched him with one hand, under his chin…" I struggle to remember exactly how the first interaction went.

"We know from his label that his name is Secundus," Gord says. "And when you touched him you said, *You had me worried there for a second.*"

Arg. That's it. I touched him with one hand and not two, and I said "second" instead of "Secundus." That's why the bond was imperfect. That's why poor Secundus is malfunctioning— uploading copies of me even when the previous version is still alive and well. And that's why he's somehow only making new versions of me in the supply closet. "Okay," I say, "so what if I bond with him properly now?"

"Honestly, I'm not sure what that would do," says Gord. "At the moment he's imperfectly bonded with all of you at once. Unsurprisingly, there doesn't seem to be anything in the Bestiary about what happens if you bond with a familiar when there's more than one of you. Apparently, this kind of thing hasn't happened before."

"Great. I'm an amazing precedent." I sigh.

"No doubt someone could write a fascinating research paper about you, but that won't happen unless they find out. And we've got to make sure no one does, or we're in very big trouble," says Gord. He sees me opening my mouth and says, "No, it won't matter if we explain that it's not our fault. Something this bad has to be *someone's* fault, and we're the chumps at Ground Zero. Step One for us now is that you have absolutely nothing further to do with that Zeittier. Don't look at me like that; I know he's cute, but you have to leave him alone. Step Two for us is that we have to erase this problem. Luckily, there's one thing that just might fix it."

I'm about to ask what, but when he looks to the side I follow his gaze and see that he's looking at the undocumented Contingency Pump that's sitting on my desk.

"Oh God, we're going to use *that?*" I say. "Isn't that some kind of time machine? So the plan is to erase about a hundred versions of me from existence?"

Gord rolls his eyes again—and once again it's a nightmarish sight. "God, you are such an idiot. I thought you had a BA in Magic Resource Management. No. The Contingency Pump is not a time machine. It's more like a time siphon. Or, even better, a reality siphon. The Contingency Pump doesn't erase anything from existence. It siphons anomalous things—or people—off into their own separate realities. This universe goes on just the way it did before, and the other universes go on their merry way, and we don't get any metaphysical collisions."

I furrow my brow. "So...it sends an inconvenient bit of our reality off into a different universe?"

"No," sighs Gord, "it sends an inconvenient bit of our reality off into its *own* universe."

"But the other versions of me come from *our* universe," I say. "They don't have home universes of their own to go back to." I'm worried about how the other versions of me might react to what I'm saying, but at the moment they're too busy squabbling amongst themselves to pay much attention to us. I guess my habit of totally ignoring what Gord says most of the time is actually kind of advantageous here. All the same, the two of us sidle over to the corner of the room and lower our voices.

"They're not going back; they're going forward," says Gord. Seeing my face, he explains. "That's why this is such a heavily controlled item. It might be finding pre-existing alternate universes in which there is a missing you, who can just be slotted into a suitable role. Or it might actually be creating entirely new alternate universes every time you use it. A whole new universe coming into being, just to accommodate one odd bit of metaphysical flotsam that we're kicking out of ours. The ethical implications are staggering. But..." He looks around the room at all the Phils, and I know what he's thinking. Just at the moment, the staggering ethical implications of possibly creating a hundred new universes pales in comparison to the trouble we're going to get into if the Postmagister finds out about all this. Although I'm not sure how I feel about copies of me being called "metaphysical flotsam."

"Look," says Gord. "You and me using the Contingency Pump isn't time travel, but legally and administratively it might as well be. It's one of the big no-nos. But improperly activating a Zeittier is also one of the big no-nos. I figure using the Contingency Pump can't possibly get us into *more* trouble than we're already in. I mean they can't banish us to the Outer Darkness *twice*."

"Hey," says one of the other Phils who has been listening in. He's got an upside-down 9 stuck on his shirt. "I won't be banished anywhere. I didn't cause any of this; *you* did."

"You're me, you dickhead," I say. "We both did it. I both did it."

"Hey, hey, hey," pipes up another one of me. "I *all* did it. After all, I'm all in this together."

"There's no 'I' in team," says Phil 15 pointlessly.

"There's no 'I' in 'we' or in 'me,'" said another one, who is slightly limping and who therefore might possibly be Phil 31.

"There's a 'me' in 'time'!" says another.

"And in 'metaphysics,'" says yet another.

"Look, let's just do this while everyone's in a good mood," says Gord. "If this crowd gets ugly, you're going to end up killing yourself. If you see what I mean."

The Contingency Pump, to my surprise, is a fundamentally simple device to operate. I was expecting quite a bit of assembly, but all you have to do is snap the bits together. It looks kind of like a cluster of copper pipes, only slightly more complicated than what you would find under a bathroom sink, with a round green gemstone at the center. One quick glance at the manual satisfies me that Gord is the only one who ought to read it.

By the time we get this all set up, there are definitely over a hundred Phils. We're milling around the mailroom, walking up and down the halls, lounging in the break room, and wandering the storage shelves. This place is huge, but it has a limit, and I'm worried Secundus might have a limit, too. While Gord is reading the Contingency Pump manual, I ignore his earlier instruction and sit with my part-familiar under Meryl's desk, cuddling him on my lap—although I have to quickly put him down on the floor for his periodic puffing and sparking routine. I don't leave him until Gord calls me for the big moment, and only at this point do I feel what might be called a surge of existential dread. "Gord, are you *sure* we're not killing any of me here? I couldn't live with myself if I killed myself." I look around at all the other Phils. "I mean if I wasn't so lazy and distractable, then some of me might be trying to stop us right now."

Gord sighs. "Dude," he says, "look on the bright side. This probably won't work anyway." And he touches his finger to the green gem at the center of the Contingency Pump.

The effect isn't actually all that amazing. It is plenty flashy though— basically like a bunch of multicolored spotlights rapidly turning on and off. I blink like crazy. All I can hear are a series of soft pops and crackles, which I imagine must be what it sounds like when one of me leaves my wrong universe and goes into my right one. His right one, that is. The one in which he's the real me and I'd be the wrong me.

After about a minute the popping and crackling stops, but it feels like ages before I can see anything other than floating blobs of color. Eventually things clear up enough that I can scan around the room and feel at least 90% confident that I'm the only me here. The only other human being around is Gord, and he's doing the same blinking performance that I'm doing. I wonder if he wishes his photoreceptors could go invisible again for a minute. It's a while before we stop blinking and can actually search properly. We check the break room. The storage closet. Every single row of the storage stacks. Not a me in sight.

Gord and I reconvene in the mailroom, and for a moment I feel a sudden irrational urge to apologize for stealing his lunch. But that would be stupid. I have the perfect alibi. I can say that a different me stole it, and I can't be held responsible. Why confess? It's better to let sleeping sandwiches lie.

"I think we got away with it," says Gord. He takes three deep, slow breaths and says, "I need to throw up now." He heads for the men's room.

And then, from under my desk, I hear a faint "Murgle?"

Ah yes. There's just one thing left to take care of— before Gord gets back and tells me I'm not allowed.

I kneel and hold out my hands. Secundus shuffles forward and rubs his face into them, making a noise that seems poised somewhere between a murgle and a purr. "Secundus," I say simply, making sure both of my hands are touching him. He squeals with joy and emits a veritable explosion of purple sparks that burst all over both of us and scatter across the concrete floor.

After a moment, Gord comes running. "Phil!" he shouts. "What happened?"

"We're bonded!" I say happily, scooping up Secundus and hugging him.

"Murgle!" says my Zeittier familiar, joyously.

"What?" says Gord. "That wasn't the plan."

"We didn't come up with a plan for this part," I say. "So the two of us improvised. Didn't we Secundus?" I tousle the top of his head. "It's a done deal now."

My Zeittier nuzzles my hand.

* * *

Sometimes I still feel as though I can hear the voices of my clones echoing around the Dead Letter Office, even though they've been gone for three weeks now. Actually, even that statement might not be quite right, because from what Gord says, I'm pretty sure they technically never existed. I mean they *used* to exist, but now they no longer have ever existed. I think. I get the grammar of it mixed up, and Gord says he's sick of trying to explain it to me. Anyway, it still kind of feels like the other versions of me might be around here somewhere. I really hope we didn't miss any.

Gord's face is fully visible again. Meryl still hasn't been replaced. More importantly, the Postmagister hasn't shown up to have us fired, arrested, shot, immolated, and then cast into the Outer Darkness. So it looks as though we've got away with everything.

The job's still kind of a drag, but it's a lot better with Secundus around. When he's not sleeping under my desk, he follows me around, or rides on my shoulder. He makes me feel safe. After all, he's got a Xerox copy of me ready to go at a moment's notice—one that he's saving for a real emergency, not just for when I stub my toe. So I'm not as bothered as I used to be about the shortage of hazmat suits and rubber gloves.

Gord says I'm opening all the dangerous-looking packages from now on, though.

Time and the Bell

Kari Sperring

The bell hung at the end of the causeway, where the low bump of land swelled up from the marsh. Water spread out on all sides, muddy and speckled with clumps of rushes, with sedge and hair grass, betony and iris and water fern. Here and there, bumps of stone broke through, moss-garbed and water-smoothed. Willow and birch swayed with transient wind, dropping leaves that lured fish to the surface to mouth at them. The trees, or their ancestors, provided the wood that built the causeway and palisades: long poles sunk into the mud, row upon row upon row. The same wood made the planking on which men walked to reach the center of the shrine; bound together by rope of twisted bast and wooden pegs. And within the palisades, the round houses—mud and rush and reed mingled to form thick walls, roofed over with reed bundles, doors guarded by woven hurdles; circles within circles of defenses and dwellings and, at the heart of all, the shrine where the bones of the ancestors lay, and the gods rested, watching over the bounty of the marsh and the descendants who drew sustenance from it.

The bell watched over it all, hanging on its stout rope at the center of the gateway into the inner shrine. Its low sweet voice told the comings and goings of the blue-faced priests who served the spirits, recalled the tales that bound the people, marked dawn and dusk, sun-height and moon-passage. It held them all under its care, from the smallest of the barefoot children to the most senior of the elders and the first ancestor. It was the voice of the people and the voice of the marsh, god and memory and protector. It had always hung there, long and long, years reaching back beyond the lifetimes of the oldest inhabitants, older than the rushes and the willows and the dry graying skulls that topped the palisades, than the cracked bones that hung from the staves to give sound to the wind. It was the bell, and for all the settlement knew, it had always been right there.

The bell itself knew better. It was, after all, Eldest. It had been forged to last, long before the causeways and palisades. The first ancestor had carried it here, wrapped in deerskin and bound to her breast like a child. She was the first to find the islet amidst the mud, the first to settle there, the first to raise a primitive palisade. But not the first to serve the bell, though the blood of its maker flowed through her veins and, indeed, had smeared its surface anew over the course of her journey east and north. Perhaps she knew this. Perhaps she did not. Such things didn't matter to the bell. It had been shaped and tuned to serve the folk and be served by them, generation upon generation, as its maker ordained.

A bell does not ask to be made, does not crave purpose nor seek change. It simply *is*. Intent, for this bell, had begun with the hands that made it. Lean brown hands dug copper and tin from the earth, shedding blood to do so, mingling with the metals. The same hands crushed the ores and dug the firepit for the charcoal; set the fire and worked the leathern bellows. Those hands—calloused and scarred—shaped the mold and poured the metal, admixed with a little more blood. They freed the cooled shape from its earthen cocoon, polished and tooled and refined it until it rang sweet and true, infused with the charms that the maker sang while working, binding the bell to the bloodline and the bloodline to the bell. Perhaps it was the first bell the crafter had made, perhaps the last. The bell neither knew nor cared. All that mattered was the bond, blood and bell and people. In those early days, it had no sense of place. That came later, with the flight north and east, the renewed blood seeping through the deerskin, the prayers of the first ancestor for security and home. It grew, it encrusted, through the long years in which the bell hung in the gateway, watching over the islet, the people, the marsh, season upon season; each birth, each death binding the bell closer to the people and the people to the bell.

A bell does not breathe, yet it has a voice. A bell does not live, yet it endures through time. A bell does not think or feel, not as humans or spirits do. It is made of the substance of the earth and the labor of the living. And earth… earth has its own kind of remembering.

This matters. It mattered then. It will matter again. Thus, then, like the bell, it will find a form of remembrance.

* * *

That was the winter the iron men came, skimming fang-faced and bloody-handed over the frozen marsh on bone-bladed feet. A bad winter, that one, already, even before this. A bitter winter, braided with gnawing cold and harsh rains, so that fires smoked and guttered and gave but scanty heat. Already, several of the people had joined the ancestors, carried hence by coughing sickness. The blue-faced priests drank down bitter herbs, sought answers from fish bones, and found none. The elders muttered and spat and fretted. The marsh gave little sustenance this season, sullen with ice. The bell tolled the deaths and voiced the winds, and waited. A bell, after all, does not control the weather nor can it heal. It endures and watches and warns.

That last morning dawned misty; the marsh hid itself under a gray veil, turning trees and rushes to shadows. At this season, the sun is mean with its light: dawn made a sickly ochre line to the east. On its wooden arch, the bell stirred, moved by the light salt breeze that came with the mist. Soft, its voice, that morning, while the iron men sped onwards, over the ice. Along the causeway, the skulls muttered among themselves. Inside the roundhouses, the people stirred, breath white in the air, shivering on their rush pallets and seeking the return of sleep. The bell stirred again, voice a little louder, and the blue-faced priests turned in their huts but did not wake. Perhaps the ancestors were displeased, by some deed performed or left undone. Perhaps the ancestors of the iron men were stronger, had already sought them out in ghostly battle. The bell did not know. It was not, after all, made to know such things, any things outside the bloodline and the marsh. It was not concerned with anything else. It sounded a third time, louder now, as the iron men broke through the outmost palisade, waking the people to fire and pain and fear. The bell cried out, now, in its loudest tones, as iron sliced through tender flesh and shattered bone, torches laid flame to thatch, set to leap from roof to roof, and the people screamed and ran and died, blood spilling onto the frozen soil. Fire lit up the skulls from within, before they toppled into the marsh as the staves fell. The blue-faced priests rushed hither and yon, chanting their spells and wielding their axes, fighting and dying with the people they ruled. The iron men made no distinctions, save only to pull aside the younger women as part of their spoils. They sought only precious metals and weapons and food. Their blades bit through living bodies and lifeless wood, until at last the great arch fell, and the bell tumbled, rolling to lie in the mingled blood and soil, silent now in the face of slaughter.

It lay next to the body of the youngest of the blue-faced priests, her blood washing over the metal, familiar, still warm at first, flavored in fear and distress and need. The bell might have lain there forever, to be swallowed over time by the marsh. But torchlight struck patterns from the bronze, and one of the iron men leaned down and scooped the bell up to join his other gains.

And that was the start of the second journey for the bell, tied by a thong to the belt of a warrior, rattling and jangling as the iron men skated back across the marsh to their encampment on the high ground to the south. The bell bounced and thumped, painting a bruise on the hip of its captor. He did not belong; his blood did not belong, and the bell cared nothing for him and his pains. The new land was the same: unfamiliar, unbound, outside the duty spelled into the bell. Perhaps it was this change that soured the bell's voice. Perhaps it had been damaged by the fall to the ground. Perhaps it was the bitterness of loss. The settlement was gone, the bloodline scattered and spilled, and the bell…the bell spoke in darker tones, now, low and unpleasant, hanging from the rafters in the smoke of the iron men's fire. And more seasons came and went, and more years, and the iron men too began to die, as the army men spread into their lands from the south, and the ship men from the east, and the herders and the farmers and the chanting followers of the new god, in their long robes. The bell passed from hand to hand, people to people, hung in this place and that, sometimes treasured, sometimes ignored, turning green and dull with time. A bell does not grieve, and yet…its cracked voice called out for the bloodline, thin and lost and alone.

No-one, it seemed, ever thought to cast it into a fire pit, to render it once more molten, to be shaped anew. Perhaps the maker had laid some charm within it, perhaps it was a quality of the blood, protecting it from change. Perhaps it was no more than chance. Seasons became years became centuries, counted now in the fashion of the brown-robed priests of the new god. War came, and settlements burned. Storms came, and settlements flooded or vanished under sand and mud, until one day the bell too sank into the soil. Not marshland, this. Not the homeland. But a place of rolling chalk and growing grass, which slowly swallowed what remained of older homesteads. Earth calls to earth and the bell was born of earth. Perhaps, there under the turf, it reached out, seeking the lost familiar taste of the fen, the mulch of sedge and reed, the thin distant flavor of the bloodline. It had a duty, after all. It had a purpose it must serve.

A bell can measure time, at least as the brown-robed priests would have it. A bell can count time and yet know nothing of its passage. A bell, as we know, endures, like the land and the blood, thin now and mingled with many other strands, other peoples. Did they know, these fragments of the blood, where they came from? Did some faint memory of the causeway and the palisade and the bell run through their marrow? The bell could not know. Bones mingled with the bronze in that long burial: old stone bones, of forgotten sea-creatures, newer bones of birds and rodents, sheep and goats and cattle and humankind. None belonged to the bloodline, and yet perhaps these, too, told their stories, there in the cool earth. Perhaps the bell heard and absorbed, drew into itself traces of these peoples. A bell, after all, is likewise made from earth, which changes and grows, shrinks and warps, with the passage of water and wind, pressure and heat, decay and time. Wind and water carry messages, sometimes, and there in its chalky grave, the bell heard once again the echoes of the marshland to the north, as men built dikes and dug ditches, made sluices and used strange panting engines to drain away the water. They uncovered old histories, these busy new men, dredging up belt buckles and collapsed bronze vessels, bent nails and leather shoes, cattle horns and bone combs and loom weights. And, every once in a while, the cramped remains of one of the ancient people, peat-stained and cured by time, calling in faint whispers to the bell, in need of protection and always out of reach. The new men kept the greenish metals, the carved bone, treasures of the marsh, but the bodies they shuddered from, muttering prayers and blessings in their own tongue. Some, they burned; others they reburied, at crossroads alongside the corpses of felons and the unbaptised. A bell cannot weep, but there in its chalky tomb, the loss registered. And more years came and went, and more men came and went with new ideas and interests.

A ploughboy raised the bell, ploughshare catching on something in the soil. He dug down with his two calloused tanned hands, expecting to find a lump of stone. Warm, those hands, though the blood that coursed through them bore no trace of the bloodline. He tugged the bell free from its chalky cocoon and took it home as an object of interest for his mother to clean. It was dull, its patterns hidden under the coating of earth, mouth clogged and silent. The woman cleaned the worst of it away, muttering to herself that her son had brought home such an uncanny, ugly thing. In the morning, once he was away to his toil, she wrapped it in her apron and took it to the village priest, to rid her house of ill-luck. But this was a different age: she still clung to superstition, but the priest—who wore black clothes and called himself a minister—considered himself a rational, scientific man, an antiquary and a scholar. He gave the woman sixpence for her trouble and sent her away. Then he placed the bell on his great oaken desk to study and describe.

He sent an account of it, complete with measurements and sketches, to a colleague at the Royal Society. Letters were exchanged, visits made, papers published in learned journals, and the bell was wrapped again in cloth and placed in a sturdy box, to be transported south to the great new museum of antiquities. *Bronze Age Ritual Bell,* read the hand-printed label now attached to it. *Discovered at R_____ East Downs. Gift of the Reverend Wm N_____.* The bell stood now on green woollen cloth, in a case of polished wood and glass, and people came to peer at it and argue as to its function. Not that the bell cared, of course. None of those who came belonged to the bloodline. They were not the people. They were no part of its duty and its purpose. The suggestions, the hypotheses, were no more than a thin reflection of the truth, not that the bell could have told them that. The blue-faced priests had offered more than ritual, with their chants and trances and sacrifices. They defined the people. They defined the land. And the bell marked their duties, speaking the bond of man and blood and land. The bell guarded, once. And now…now it held memory, held within its mouth the last word they might speak, long and long after the fire and the slaughter and the burning of the settlement.

Coincidences are more common than you may think. And then, not so many things survive millennia. Humankind likes to categorize and compare, collect and analyze and speculate and show off their conclusions. New engines drained more land, made more discoveries. Men invented new professions and new means to examine what they found. Here, an ancient midden told the tale of meals gone by. There, pieces of ancient wood described a structure, a home, a defensive enclosure. They found the settlement in the marsh, with its broken causeways and palisades. And, at the foot of the islet, a body, leathery and contorted, with traces of pigment yet clinging to its skin.

Blue, that pigment, once upon a time, harvested with a bronze knife, ground by work-worn old hands, applied with careful fingers to brow and cheekbones and chin. "Sacrificial victim," the curator printed on the label, referring to the dry gash across the throat. "Possibly killed to appease the gods."

The bell knew better. Even here, in this place of glass and speculation, the bell knew its own. Here at last, after so many moons and seasons and years, so many changes of people and place and intent; here the bell was reunited with the bloodline, with a blue-faced priest. Which one, exactly, did not matter, only that they were of the blood, the substance, of the bell. All that was wanting was the land, and yet that too had seeped its way into the preserved bone and muscle and skin of the priest, dyed peat-dark by the marsh. Familiar, known, bound.

Under the glass, under its patina of age, the bell stirred. Softly, slowly, it began to speak, too low at first to be discerned by any living thing. Memory slithered through the bronze, shivered its way into the glass and the wood. Wood had burned, reduced to charcoal to melt the ores for the bell. From wood the sound passed, into the stone body of the building, louder now, setting fear among the pigeons that roosted on its lintels and ledges and roof. Out through the packed sour earth of the great settlement that circled the building went the bell's voice, seeking water, rush and read, birch and willow, sedge and betony and soft fertile mud. Here and there, under the sleeping sky, humans stirred in their beds, some deep knowledge twined through their ancestry responding to that song. They dreamed then of waters, seeping and oozing upwards, slipping around foundations and under roads, finding tunnels and fissures through which to travel, mingling with the earth and dust. Through the roots of ancient trees, the song travelled, into the shallower roots of grasses, awakening memory of the islet, the causeways, the palisades. Dark staves, hard now as iron, broke through the topsoil, split roads and pathways, broke dikes and banks. Ancient earthworks trembled, ghosts under the skin of the land. One by one, streams and rivers rose, spilling outside their banks, each echoing the song of the bell, land becoming water, water returning to marsh.

Beside the bell, the blue-faced priest, last of the people, stirred, uncoiling cramped limbs, and opened water-washed eyes.

And the bell...the bell rang its people home.

Shine and Beam, Burn and Bleed

Alicia Cay

I am a woman on fire. A matchstick girl with a blaze of red hair, angry pink circles beneath the abundance of freckles on my cheeks, and a temper like a solar flare that saw me kicked out of every foster home—except the last one. That one I ran from in the dead of night, my torn nightgown the only thing I took with me.

I worked the sky-docks for a few years before Bosun, my first captain, called in a favor and got me a job on an off-planet merchant ship. Haven't been back to Earth since. I planned to go back one day, settle down in a proper home. That won't happen now.

I'm sitting in the brig, saber-light tethers slicing into my wrists, waiting to be transported in the morning. They want me to feel bad for what I've done, but I don't. I don't feel bad at all.

* * *

I elbowed my way through the other crew gathered in the ship's receiving bay, trying to get to the open cargo doors to catch a glimpse. We'd docked early this morning to take on a routine delegation headed to Lilium for the Primary, and rumor had it we'd also be taking on a special delivery. No one knew what.

I pushed past a tall sailor with uncombed greasy brown hair, wearing a gray rigging maintenance jumper.

"Hey, no cramming," he yelled. "What's the matter with you?"

I'd been asking myself that question for years, along with a slew of social workers. I still didn't have an answer. But I grew up fighting for every step forward I'd taken, and I'd be damned before I let some rig-boy who thinks he's better than a lowly deckhand disrespect me.

I turned, Bosun's voice in my head pleading with me not to, and smashed my fist into Greasy's pimple-covered face. My knuckles cracked across his cheekbone, splitting the skin. The crew surged in tight around us, their excited and panicked voices echoing in the double-story, alloy-lined bay.

Blood oozed from Greasy's cheek. He thumbed his nose, then swung an arm at my head. His reach was long, but he was slow. I ducked, came up, and plowed a right hook up and into the side of his chest. The crack of rib reverberated up my arm. Greasy doubled over.

Bosun's voice dulled, drowned out by the indignation flooding through my veins. I pulled back to deliver the blow that would drop this fool-idiot where he stood.

A wall of flesh and feathers moved in front of me—the master-at-arms. Dryornis pressed her armored body against mine, shoving me back. She slammed a knee into my solar plexus and I crumpled to the deck.

I glared up at her, struggling to pull in air through my gritted teeth.

Our master-at-arms was an Avem with golden eyes and the hooked, razor beak of a predator species. She collected weapons from every corner of the Six Galaxies and separated herself from her own species by wearing human armor, which required cutting back her remiges, those long flight feathers that lined her hands and legs; a brutal process that only made her meaner.

If I was fire, Dryornis was glacier ice.

"Next time, I'll drag your ass to the brig," Dryornis said. She spit a wad of undigested carrion onto the deck next to me.

I stayed down until she'd turned and stalked off, crew in blue-and-gray jumpsuits parting before her like weeping lovegrass.

Greasy's buddies picked him up, mumbling about getting him to medical bay and how insane folk were these days.

No one helped me up.

I sat there a moment longer, aching and pissed off, then wiped the remains of dead mouse off my arm and got to my feet.

The crowd let me through and I made my way to the open cargo hatch. I sucked in the fresh, cool air, trying to calm the adrenaline shakes racking my body.

Bosun's voice came again, *Long, slow breaths, Ryh.* The same words he'd offered each time I came back bruised from some bar fight I'd picked the night before. *One day you'll go too far and really hurt someone.*

But I couldn't always help it. I'd taken my share of hits growing up the way I did, and sometimes I needed to hit back.

Voices called from the deck below.

Several longshoremen were leading a pair of graceful creatures toward our ship. They resembled seahorses, with long vertical bodies and a single curled leg that ended in an odd-toed hoof. Their heads were small, snouts shaped like peonies on short stems, and they hovered above the ground using long waving fins, like banana leaves fluttering in a breeze that wasn't there.

My hands unclenched. They were the most beautiful things I'd ever seen.

These were animals so rare even our captain, a dog-chewed veteran of space hauling, came down from the bridge to see them.

"Where they headed, Cap'?" Flemming asked.

"Lilium, with the rest of the cargo." The captain shifted his tricorn cap back, the faintest smirk curling the corner of a lip. "A gift for the Primary's daughter."

Flemming, in proper second mate fashion, said not a word, but his eyebrows shot up and bounced off his hairline.

The Primary's daughter, Dianthus, was about my age and as wickedly spoiled as they came. Her tantrums were legendary, and her reputation for wanting, then discarding, all the pretty things she spied was known throughout the Six.

I sighed. What must that feel like? To have everything your heart desires and want none of it?

When the longshoremen had packed the animals into their transport orbs and loaded them onto the holding platforms in our ship, the captain and Flemming turned to leave.

I'd lived with a pet once, a Canis named Dax, in one of the homes. He'd licked our sticky faces, eaten the broccoli snuck to him beneath the dinner table, and curled against our tummies to sleep at night. Dax was patience and kindness in a world where such things seldom survived. He was probably the first living thing I'd ever loved.

I could tell by the way these creatures shifted in their transport orbs, letting out tiny whickers, that they were anxious to be let out. Something raw inside of me suddenly felt exposed to the air. It stung.

I pushed through the gawking crew until I was behind the captain. "Sir?" I flexed my fingers. The knuckles on my right hand were sore and swelling. "Could I take watch over them?"

The captain's gaze landed on me like a buzzard on roadkill, then he cocked a crooked eyebrow at Flemming.

The tiny turquoise fins behind Flemming's ears waved to and fro. "Ryhlee Arua, Deckhand," he said to the captain. "Been with us for—" He flicked on his Lectro-board and scanned my left eye. "—three rotations. Nothing of note in her file, sir."

Thank the Divine I'd asked before Dryornis' report hit the boards.

The captain didn't bother to look at me again. He shot a glance at Flemming and then left.

Being dismissed by the captain like that made my cheeks hot and I had to press my fingertips tight along the seams of my pants to keep them from curling into fists.

Flemming swiped his muck-rag at the yellow and pink tipped gills on the back of his neck and swiveled an eye at my fingers. "Not going to have any trouble with you, am I, Ryh?"

He knew my history. Three years ago, after a few crates of Malört had gone missing from a clipper ship docked next to us, Bosun thought it'd do me good to get off Earth for a while. He'd called in a favor with his old friend Flemming and got me assigned here on *The Scelus*.

"No, sir," I said, and meant it.

"They'll be moved up there." Flemming indicated a storage stall in the corner of the second deck.

"What do they eat?" I asked.

He shrugged. "The scientists from the refuge place sent over some data on them. I'll forward it to your board."

I vaulted up the stairs. The flush beneath my freckles this time was all excitement.

* * *

I opened the scientists' care notes on my Lectro-board. The animals were called Celestroequus. They formed intense bonds with their nest mates, and this pair was one of only a handful known to exist in all of Galaxy Four. They were being studied at a celestial animal refuge on Equus when Dianthus had found out about them and demanded a pair for her stables.

The first few days neither of the Celestroequus would eat, so I hand-fed them stalks of the fragrant grasses supplied for their feed. When they drank, they'd fill their water bladders, small pouches of loose skin under their trunk rings, and then staunchly refuse any offers of water for the next week.

I added my observations to the scientists' notes, per their request, including my discovery of their fondness for sugar cubes, which I began sneaking to them from my daily ration.

The female I called Shine 'cause she was bright yellow, like sunshine in summer, except the ends of her leaf-fins which faded into emerald-green. Her mate I called Beam 'cause he shone blue as a moonbeam on a snowy night.

Their bodies were covered in the softest hair, like velvet and cream. Sometimes when I got close, brushing them or rubbing down their curled legs when they got restless, they'd start to sort of glow, the way the light does when it dances off the ice crystals around the winter planets. They way they lit up made me feel close to them, like they were letting me in on a secret that only we shared.

We were five weeks in. I'd just finished laying fresh straw for Shine and Beam when I got an alert on my board. I headed to my bunk and found a private message from Bosun waiting for me on the comm-link.

His face, haggard and gray, appeared on the screen. I sucked a breath in between my teeth. When had he gotten so thin?

He lay in bed, bouts of coughing breaking his words into jagged shards. "Ryhlee…daughter I never had…*cough*…*breathe*…*cough*…stay out of trouble."

It didn't fully hit me what was happening until a woman stepped into view, dressed in hospital scrubs.

"Ms. Arua," she said. "If you're able to catch a shuttle back to Earth, he'd like to see you." The video skipped, a line of static distorting the nurse's face. "To say goodbye." She raised a hand toward the screen and the video blinked off.

I stared at my reflection in the darkness of that blank screen. I frowned at the clusters of freckles crowded on my nose and cheeks, at my bright red hair—the cause of so much teasing growing up—and at the feelings twisting in my belly that made my brown eyes damp. I bit my lower lip. I wanted to hit something.

I stood. I ran. Straight to the cargo bay and into the farthest corner of Shine and Beam's stall. I dropped onto the straw and pulled my legs to my chest, eyes shut tight against the things threatening to explode out of me. *Long breaths, Ryh. Slow breaths.* Bosun couldn't be dying.

My old captain was probably the only one who'd ever thought I was worth worrying about. After I ran away at fifteen, I ended up on the sky-docks begging for pocket change. He found me and put me to work—honest, hard work, not the kind expected of desperate women—and taught me everything he knew about sky-boats and off-planet rigs.

I *had* planned to return to Earth one day, make a home of my own, spend time with Bosun in his retirement, fishing in that dirty puddle he called a pond in his backyard. I could beg my way onto a shuttle by tomorrow latest to get back to him in time to…say goodbye.

But, going to Bosun would mean leaving the Celestroequus. I chewed at the corner of my mouth. I owed him so much. Who would I have if he left me?

Shine leaned over and nuzzled me, her long pink tongue tickling the back of my neck. It was time for their dinner. I uncurled and got up, heart heavy, cheeks hot.

Beam watched me, wariness in his bright blue eyes. I patted his neck to reassure him. Something about the softness of his fur, or the way his ears relaxed at my touch, and suddenly my face was buried in the velvet nap of his neck.

The hairs on my arms stood on end as a warm waterfall sensation tingled along my skin and across my scalp. I pulled back.

Beam was glowing. Not in the moonbeam way I'd seen before, but full on, like a star from the Eighteenth Dimension, blinding and brilliant. Shine lit up, too, blazing like hand-spun gold. She stretched her snout forward and nuzzled my pocket, searching for my stash of sugar cubes. A small current of electricity, like static buildup, zapped through me. "Ouch!" I yelped.

Beam nudged my arm. Either concerned I'd been hurt, or it was feeding time. A bubble of laughter forced its way from me involuntarily and my anger ebbed, leaving behind a feeling of belonging. They'd lit up for me, let me into their little circle. The three of us, far from our own homes, had come together out here.

I rubbed their foreheads, their favorite scratchy spot, until their eyelids drooped.

After work I strolled along the rear observation deck, watching starlight flicker past the ship's moonraker sails. Nothing in the care notes mentioned these animals could produce an energy field or…whatever that had been. Proof of how little we knew about them.

I wondered what would happen when the time came to turn Shine and Beam over to their new caretakers. I considered sending a message ahead to Primary's people, asking to join their staff—it wouldn't really be lying to say I was the only Celestroequus expert this side of the Luminous Rivers—but that would mean working for that spoiled brat, Dianthus. A sigh broke across my lips. How was it girls like her got to own such fantastic creatures, and girls like me spent their lives mucking up after them?

* * *

My head would have slammed into the top bunk when the ship's engine alarms went off had I not spent the last eight years sleeping in confined spaces.

I stepped into my shoes at a run and made for the cargo bay.

Chaos reigned in the bottom deck. The chief engineer shouted commands over the alarm to shut down the engines and lock all ventilation. Crew ran to their stations. I dashed upstairs.

Shine and Beam had pressed themselves into the corner of their stall, their long necks intertwined. When Beam saw me, a flicker of sapphire light shivered across his blue fur. Shine let out a whicker.

"Hey, you two. It's alright." I stroked their heads.

Shine's tongue flicked across my palm, searching for a treat. "Always the opportunist." I grinned and scratched behind her ears.

After they'd settled, I went down to investigate.

Worry warbled in my guts. The captain was down from the bridge, huddled in a meeting with Flemming, the first mate, and the chief engineer.

As I moved around them, the captain shouted, "We're dead, blasted dead! No one has ever made it out of a doldrum storm before—ever!"

My breath whistled on its way out as my throat seized. He wasn't wrong. Doldrum storms were things of myth. An old sailor I'd worked with on Earth once told a group of us how they'd come by their name.

Thousands of years before us, folk sailed on expansive bodies of water in ships made of wood. I'd thought he was pulling our legs, but later Bosun confirmed both water and wood. In the middle of these oceans, ill-fortuned sailors sometimes found themselves in spots of sea called the doldrums. All wind vanished, their sails hung slack, and the water around the boat was smooth as ice in every direction. Sometimes these doldrums lasted for days, or weeks, or didn't end at all, and the crew murdered each other out of sheer madness.

Then, the salty sailor leaned in and said, "Only one ship I ever heard tell of made it out of them doldrums." His breath smelled like death and peanuts. "Was sailing to the new world an' had horses with 'em, they did. Hooked 'em all in lines an' dropped 'em in the water like oars."

I circled the officers a solid minute before getting up the nerve to speak. "Um, sir?"

Flemming glanced at me. "We're in the middle of something, Ryh. Get to your station. Wait for orders."

"But...I have an idea. To get us out of the storm."

They stopped speaking. The first mate grunted for me to continue.

The doldrums in space aren't a windless place, but a kind of dark-matter fungus that gets ahold of ships and eats them away from the inside. They think. No one knows for sure. So, the first thing we're taught is to shut down the ship to keep from sucking in...whatever that stuff is. But, if we had an outside source of power that didn't *need* to be ventilated, maybe...

"The Celestroequus. They give off an energy field or an electrical charge or something. Maybe we could attach them or their orbs directly to the stern propellers, move them that way?"

The chief engineer squinted.

"It wouldn't be a lot of power," I said. "Not much more than an outboard motor, but if we got a drift going—"

"Could that work?" Flemming interrupted, looking at the chief engineer.

He lifted a shoulder. "No idea, but it's worth trying."

"Do it," the captain said. "I don't care how, get it done."

Flemming and the first mate called in more crew and together we came up with a plan.

* * *

The deckhands gathered in the cargo bay. We loaded Shine and Beam into their transport orbs, then used the hover crane to move them through the bottom hatchway and attach them beneath the ship using magnetic holds.

Shine and Beam shifted nervously, but Shine's small whinnies of worry were the only sound they made.

"Ready, Ryh?" Flemming asked.

I nodded.

"Let's hope this works," he said. "Ericka! Get over here and help Ryh get suited up."

Half an hour later, I was dangling at the end of a tether beneath the stern of the ship, between Shine and Beam in their orbs, the expanse of pitch-black space pushing in on us.

"Alright guys. Time to shine." I rubbed a heavy-gloved hand along the plex material of their encasements. I talked to them, made soothing sounds. Nothing happened.

Flemming's worried face popped onto my vis-comm. "Ryh, what's going on?"

"Nothing yet, sir." My voice warbled. "Getting them warmed up is all." The comm clicked off.

Shit. I'd always been touching them when they lit up. They hadn't been locked in their orbs. *Shit, shit!* No way could I go back inside and tell them I'd forgotten to mention a major detail. I really was good for nothing more than mopping decks and shoveling shit. I wanted to scream and break my knuckles on something.

Bosun's voice came. *Slow breaths, Ryhlee. Getting fired up won't solve your problems.*

Heat crept up my neck onto my cheeks. How could Bosun be dying? How could I be dangling beneath a ship stranded in a blasted doldrum storm? Was this really the way I was going to die? My throat tightened. Even if all this did work, and we made it to Lilium, then what? I was going to lose Shine and Beam and...tears crept into my eyes.

Blue light spread over Beam's body, soft and slow, like a sunrise over Arpina's crescent mountains. I gasped. Things I wanted to express jammed in my throat. The tears grew heavy and slipped from my eyes. Shine lit up. Her golden glow exploded as though we'd caught a miniature sun beneath the ship. I laughed as I cried, choking on the emotion rising to my surface.

Shine and Beam were responding to me. They could feel me even without touch. My heart swelled. They were ablaze now, and the plex-material of their orbs conducted their energy exactly as the chief engineer had hoped. It flowed through the magnetic holds wired directly into the rear shafts and, slowly, the ship's propellers began to turn.

Flemming shouted through the comm. "Something's happening! Keep it going, Ryh. We need more."

"Aye-aye." I locked my vis-screen. They didn't need to see my face for this.

I took a deep breath—*they need more*—and closed my eyes.

I thought of the woman who threw me away when I was five, abandoning me for addiction. I thought of Bosun, who'd been like a father, and even when he was angry with me, he was always kind. He was as good as folk come, and the Six would be poorer for his departure. I thought of the rotating homes, uncaring faces, the slaps and fights that made up my life—and Shine and Beam burned like creatures on fire.

Our ship moved on, out of the doldrums.

* * *

"All clear!" Flemming shouted in my helmet. The crew were cheering in the background. "Bringing you back in, Ryh."

My cheeks were soaked, and snot ran from my nose. "Good boy, Beam." I sniffled. "Sweet girl, Shine."

They pulled me in, and before I could get my helmet off, the crew surrounded me, applauding.

The captain stepped through the crowd. "Back to your stations, everyone. We need to get a move on, make up for lost time. Primary's waiting." He looked me straight in the eye. "Good job, then, deckhand."

My cheeks burned a shade of crimson to match my hair. The captain had congratulated me. Right there, in front of the entire crew.

As they returned to their stations, I began to work the crane out to retrieve Shine and Beam.

Suddenly, the ship lurched violently to port. A damage-indicator alarm wailed. Yellow lights flashed. The hatchway began to close with the Celestroequus still outside.

"No!" I hit the switch, trying to make it stop.

Something slammed into our hull. I was flung off my feet and slid a quarter of a meter on my ass. Another alarm went off, a different pitch, and the two wailed like sirens on a city street. The flashing lights turned red.

Flemming was yelling, his hands pressed to his ears trying to listen to his headset.

I grabbed him. "The doors are closing! We've got to get Shine and Beam!"

He shook his head, tried to push me off. My jaw clenched. I dug my nails into his scale-covered arm.

"Dammit, Ryhlee." He pulled his headset off. "We've hit a draconid cluster. The shields aren't back up and we're taking real damage."

The captain rushed in. Spittle flew from his mouth as he shouted. "Those meteors are going to tear a hole in our asses if we don't get these engines going, now! Flemming, turn the blasted alarms off. Robertson, get up to the bridge—go!" He hurried to the aft controls.

I ran over to him. "Captain, I need your override for the doors. To get the Celestroequus back inside."

He shook his head. "Not now, deckhand. We're getting killed."

"But, sir!"

He stopped me in my tracks with a look so scathing I might have been something stuck to the bottom of his shoe. "I make the decisions on this ship, and right now it's the lives of everyone on board, or those two animals." He hollered over his shoulder to Flemming. "Those orbs'll throw the ship's balance off. Cut them loose!"

My breath snagged on my ribs like torn paper on a dead tree limb. His words clanged around inside my skull like the clapper in a bell. *Cut. Them. Loose.*

He went back to the controls, barking commands without another glance at me, more concerned with murdering Shine and Beam than with a lowly deckhand.

A gnarled growl leapt from my throat. I angled my body and slammed into the captain with my shoulder, hitting him like a dred-tank. He landed hard on his back half a meter from where I'd felled him.

"Give me the codes!" I demanded.

Outrage lined the deep creases of his face. He'd been an *old* captain longer than I'd been alive. "No," he said.

The smell of melting wires filled my sinuses. The alarms faded into a background buzz of static. I grabbed one of the rig-boy's grizzly bars and raised it over my head. There would be no more straightened fingers or deep breaths to keep my temper in check. I was a woman on fire. The captain had tossed Shine and Beam aside, just like the world had done to me.

"Ryhlee!" Flemming yelled, his voice amplified by the echo in the ship's hold. "Ryhlee Arua, stop!"

I didn't bring the bar down, but I didn't move away from the captain either. He lay beneath me and, to his credit, managed to look more pissed off than afraid, even with his hands covering his face.

"I know about Bosun," Flemming said.

Bosun? The name penetrated the layer of lava roiling inside my skull.

"Put it down, Ryh." Flemming walked into my line of sight. "Is this what he wanted for you?"

That wasn't fair. To bring my only friend into this.

My eyelids fluttered. If I did this, I would be put to death. Decompressed. My lungs ruptured. No more breaths.

Long, slow breaths, Ryh.

I'd never set foot on Earth again. No Bosun, no good-byes, nothing.

"Give me the toolbar, Ryhlee," Flemming said.

I glanced around. The crew were watching us, silent and still, like frozen marionettes in some vintage Punch and Judy scene.

I'd been so ready to discard all these lives the way I had been discarded. Not the captain, though. He'd made the hard decision—sacrifice Shine and Beam in order to try and save all of us.

Long, slow breaths, Ryh.

The long breath I inhaled rattled in my tightened chest like metal wheels clacking across rusted tracks. How had I gotten here?

I exhaled, wheezy and unsteady. My hands dropped, still clutching the grizzly bar. The captain scurried out from beneath me, sliding backward until he hit the bulkhead.

Flemming grabbed the toolbar from my hands, then reached for my shoulder. I pulled away from him and approached the captain, offering an outstretched hand. He took it cautiously, letting me help him to his feet.

My words caught on the sharp barbs of emotion stuck in my throat. "I'm sorry," I said, wrenching them out in a hoarse whisper. "You made the right decision."

The captain trapped my gaze with his and squeezed my hand ever-so-slightly before the coarse glare of leadership returned to his eyes. "I'll deal with you later, sailor." Then he was moving, running, shouting. "Move, you rantallions! We aren't in the clear yet. Flemming, turn that dracking alarm off!"

Embarrassment held me in place for a few moments until a small static charge slid down my arms, the way it had when I'd sought shelter in the Celestroequus' stall, heart aching with the news about Bosun. The same way it ached now.

I shoved past Flemming, bolted up the stairs to the aft windows, and pressed my face to the quartz-glass, searching through the starlight for any sign of them.

There in the distance, a glint of light. I could just make them out—Shine and Beam ablaze in their orbs. I could feel the static electricity of their touch on my skin fading as I stood there, frozen, unable to do anything but watch them fall further away, growing smaller and smaller—our circle being torn apart.

Meteors flew past, some made contact and rocked the ship as we picked up speed. My hands curled into fists on the window. Despair clawed at my insides. "Good boy," I whispered. "Sweet girl."

There was a flash of light, as pale and bright as a moonbeam, way off in the darkness. Beam. He was trying to get to me—following the cry of my broken heart.

The passing stars blurred in my vision, but I couldn't cry. I'd spent all my tears to save this ship, and now there were none left for Shine and Beam.

They were gone.

I was fighting to stay upright when a heavy hand landed on my shoulder. Severed feather quills dug into my flesh.

* * *

So, here I sit, saber-light tethers slicing into my wrists, waiting to be transported in the morning. Tomorrow they're shipping me back to Earth on the next Wellerman supply shuttle, where I'll be put on trial for mutiny.

Dryornis' smug voice still sticks in the crevices of my mind. *Told you I'd throw your ass in the brig, didn't I?*

Screaming white walls reflect the bright overhead light, searing my eyes. The tiny cell reeks of piss and bleach.

Flemming steps through the glare and appears at the square-hatched bars. He heaves a sigh in my direction. "I asked if I was going to have trouble with you over these animals."

I open my mouth to respond. The barely-there-smirk on his face stops me. His ear-fins flip up and down in a chuckle. He's making a joke. I try to smile, but it won't take. I'm not used to having friends.

"I reached out to Bosun," he says.

I wrap my hands around the black bars.

Flemming places a webbed hand on mine.

"He's proud of you, Ryhlee, and he understands why you won't make it back to see him."

I half-snort. "Where else have I got to go?"

Flemming looks down the hall with his swiveling eyes. "I called in a favor. The Wellerman pilot coming for you in the morning, well…she might not actually work for the supply company."

I suck a sharp breath through my teeth.

"She'll help you find what you're looking for."

"What is it I'm looking for?"

Flemming passes a folded piece of yellowed paper between the bars. I slip it into my pocket. He turns to leave, then stops. "I saw you with those animals, Ryhlee. Seems our old friend was right about you after all." Flemming smiles. Then he's gone.

I sit on the bed-shelf and unfold the paper. Two sugar cubes fall into my lap. I gasp. Written on the paper in webbed-fingered handwriting are coordinates; the location where they'd cut Shine and Beam loose!

I can't pull the rank air into my lungs fast enough. My breathing grows ragged. Black spots appear in my vision.

Long, slow breaths, Ryh.

I watered the Celestroequus two days ago, which means I have roughly five days to locate them. That's *if* their transport orbs haven't been damaged by any of the meteors, and *if* the air exchangers haven't clogged.

On Earth, I'd planned to request a last visit with Bosun, have a proper goodbye and thank him for believing in me. That won't happen now.

Long, slow breaths, Ryh.

I can live with that. I made him proud and that's the best thanks I've got to give.

My hands tremble. My mind spins.

The coordinates weren't the entire answer, but they gave me a starting point. I *would* find them.

The embers of a smile begin to glow on my lips. I'm sure it's an unsightly thing, being so uncertain, but it continues to grow, lighting up my face like the dawn of a new day. I am a woman on fire.

Unfamiliar Magic

Jim C. Hines

Veka had spent her whole life trying to learn magic.

Most recently, she'd attended a school called Os-Webra. Her first term had gone well. She'd even learned a few spells. And then...well, those schools might *say* they welcomed students of all races and cultures, but if you made one mistake—if you ate one kid's pet owl—suddenly it was all, "The school board feels goblins are a disruptive influence" and "Too many parents have threatened to pull their children from the school."

They kicked her out, but not before stealing any memories of magic she'd learned. She'd been expelled and ex-spelled.

Veka didn't need their stupid school with their stupid rules about who you couldn't eat. She'd found someone better, an elf mage called Ember, who'd looked past the blue skin and the fangs jutting from her lower jaw to see her potential.

Ember wasn't a withered old teacher who hid behind his desk smoking his pipe and grooming his beard. He was a wizard of the fifth circle. Veka wasn't sure what that meant, but it sounded impressive. She was more impressed by the way he used his power to punish his enemies, and by his drive to become the very best wizard throughout the land.

And he'd chosen to share his knowledge with Veka. For that gift, she'd do anything he asked. Even climbing a stupid pine tree.

"Don't start the spell until you reach the top."

Ember's words cut through her thoughts, carried by the polished pebble that hung on a cord around her neck. He'd given her the little marble of green quartz when he took her as an apprentice. Not only did the necklace mark her as Ember's student, it created a mental bond between them. *"I know, Master."*

Their meeting had been destiny. Ember had attended Os-Webra too. He'd dropped out years before Veka was born. Rather, he'd been hounded out by jealous students and uncaring teachers. The final blow had come when a group of students stole and killed his dog. Which was apparently a big deal among elves and humans and other "civilized" people.

After hearing about the dog, Veka had carefully avoided mentioning the owl incident.

She pushed her snarled black hair out of her eyes and kept climbing. Pine trees meant pine needles and pine sap. Scratched and sticky, she pulled herself higher, until the tree began to wobble from her not-insubstantial weight.

She clung to the swaying spire with one hand and wiped her face with her sleeve. *"I'm here."*

"Good. Give me your eyes."

The first time he'd said that, Veka had nearly soiled herself. She knew there was always a price for magic, but she liked her eyes and very much wanted to keep them. She'd offered to fetch someone else's eyes for him instead. Maybe some nice green ones. Elves liked green, didn't they?

Ember had stared at her like she'd pulled a swamp mole from her nose.

Veka gripped the tree with both hands as Ember borrowed her sight to study their surroundings. Her eyes shifted to and fro, no longer under her control. A short distance to the south, the wagon that served as their traveling home waited in the shade of a giant oak.

Ember turned her head to study the woods to the east. A stream flowed through a cluster of birch trees. Her eyes began to burn—Ember sometimes forgot to blink. She—or rather he—had split his attention between the treetops swaying in the wind and a group of birds circling in the distance.

Finally, Ember freed her. Her vision blurred and doubled. She hugged the tree until the worst had passed. Her body always felt wrong for hours after Ember released her, like her muscles didn't fit her bones anymore.

"It's time to work the spell," he said. *"Just as we practiced. The wind will carry its effects to our prey."*

Veka forgot about the pain in her eyes, the pinecones tangled in her hair, the sap on her clothes, the needles and branches that jabbed her exposed skin. *This* was why she'd left her home. It was what she'd dreamed about for as long as she could remember.

Magic was the ability to change the world. It was power and freedom and respect and security…*if* you had the strength of will to control it and knew the gestures and words to unlock it. Any day now, according to Ember, Veka would be strong enough to cast spells again.

But despite all her practice, she wasn't there yet.

"Clear your thoughts of distraction. Feed the flames of your will."

Veka closed her eyes and imagined a fire burning in her stomach. The flame was sickly green like the muck lamps back home.

"Begin the gestures."

She raised a clenched fist, turned it from vertical to horizontal, and extended four fingers. Spreading fingers and thumb, she traced three circles through the air, each larger than the one before.

"Now the words."

Veka recited the elvish words she'd practiced every night for the past five days. Nothing happened until Ember took control. His mind guided her gestures, and his thoughts spoke the words from Veka's mouth, casting the spell known as *Martin's Malodorous Miasma*.

Veka's stomach rumbled and cramped like she'd eaten a carrion beetle without making sure it was dead first. Every spell had an effect on the caster, and while Ember might be guiding the spell, the magic was flowing through her mind and body.

She ignored the discomfort, concentrating on the green fire of her will and channeling that power into the cloud of yellow smoke spreading from her hand.

The spell book she'd studied had described the effect as "a stench like two-week-old death." Veka would have said a month. But maybe that was a mistranslation. All Ember's books were in elvish and, even with their bond, it was hard for her to translate the spells into goblin.

"More," said Ember.

Veka kept the spell going even as her hand cramped and her stomach felt like it was boiling in its own juices. A cloud of foul smoke surrounded her, blotting out the sunlight. Her legs shook. Spots crawled across her vision.

Finally, the green fire of her will fizzled and sparked out. Her body sagged. She could *taste* the stink of the spell, but she'd lived through worse back at the goblin lair.

"Can I come down?" she asked.

"Not yet. The spell will attract our prey, but it's more likely to approach if it sees a body."

A raspy shriek made her jump. She wrapped both arms around the tree to keep from falling. Through the smoke, she saw the shape of a large bird circling closer and closer.

"It sees you now," said Ember. *"Climb down, quickly."*

Veka tried. Like so many things in her life, it didn't go as she'd hoped. Her legs gave out, and she dropped through the branches with a yelp. The impacts got harder as she went from the thin upper branches to the thicker, clublike ones near the bottom. She struck the ground hard enough to make her vision flash. Twigs and pine needles showered her as she fought to force air into her flattened lungs.

Near the treetop, talons like black sickles sliced the branches. White and black wings beat the air. The bird was almost as tall as Veka herself. The thick black beak was bigger than a dagger. The bird attacked the tree again and again, searching for its meal.

Ember stepped over Veka. He was a slender fellow, even for an elf. A foot taller than Veka, he probably weighed fifty pounds less. He wore a wine-red robe over black silk clothes. His thinning blond hair was pulled into a thin braid. His shoulders were tight, like he was constantly bracing against an attack.

In one hand, he held a polished stone a little smaller than Veka's fist. Half was glassy black. The other half was gray crystal, like rainclouds.

Ember threw the stone.

It struck the center of the bird's speckled breast and clung like it was coated in glue. White light crackled over the feathers. The bird tried to take off, but the light acted as a magical net, binding it tighter and tighter. It fell from the tree with a squawk.

The light contracted, pulling the bird *into* the stone just before it hit the ground.

"The carrion crow." Ember's voice was thinner and higher-pitched when he spoke out loud. He picked up the stone. "Intelligent creatures with a keen sense of smell. They're lazy beasts—scavengers—but when they can't find a nice corpse, they'll mimic other birds' songs. They lure smaller birds in close, and then…"

He used his free hand like a beak, gobbling up an imaginary feathery snack.

Veka sat up and brushed debris from her shirt. "What next, Master?"

He pushed back his cloak and touched the stone to a polished metal plate on his belt. The gray crystal half of the stone was now a dull green. It clicked into place and clung there, held by magic Veka hadn't yet learned. He carried eight such stones now, each one containing a different creature. He called them his Belt Beasts.

"Next, we challenge a master bard, an egotistical dwarf who twists the hearts and minds of those around him." He started toward their horse and wagon. "It's half a day's journey to the port town of Olvine, and then we'll make the world safe from his magic and his cruelty."

* * *

Veka sat in the wagon, squeezed between boxes and barrels and tied-up bundles. A dusty tarp hid everything—including Veka—from view. She'd propped up one edge of the tarp to get a little light and fresh air, though the fresh air smelled more and more fishy the closer they got to Olvine.

She'd never imagined she could have so much in common with an elf. Ember's story could have been a goblin's. He'd been looked down upon, bullied and mocked, chased away by those with more power…but unlike most goblins, he'd fought back. He'd spent years mastering the magic he needed—or inventing it, as he'd done with his enchanted stones. Now he was proving himself to the world.

Veka shared the same dream. One day she would return to the goblin lair, and everyone who'd laughed would see how wrong they'd been. Especially after she turned them into cave frogs.

She was jolted from that daydream when the wagon lurched from muddy ruts onto paving stones. They must be getting close.

She sighed and went back to the scroll she'd been studying. Ember's handwriting was cramped and messy, full of unnecessary loops and swirls. His spelling wasn't great, either.

Veka checked her notebook, where she'd written how to pronounce the different words and what they meant. It wasn't enough to make the sounds; she had to understand their meaning.

The sounds of the town grew louder. Shouts and conversations jumbled together. She heard raucous laughter and townsfolk offering everything from fresh fish to laundry services.

The wagon stopped. Veka squeezed out from under the tarp and blinked against the evening sunlight. They stood outside a seedy one-story building. The sign, its paint faded and chipped, showed what looked like a cross-eyed catfish.

"The Bottom Feeder Tavern." Ember strode toward the door. "How fitting."

Inside, every table was full, and more people stood along the walls. Nobody noticed an elf and a goblin coming in off from the street. Their attention was captivated by the four dwarves on the stage.

One beat a sideways drum almost as tall as she was. The second used tiny hammers to assail a heavy, iron-framed harp. The third played a thick, metal flute, while the fourth stood with hands on his hips, singing.

Veka had met dwarves before, but never one with a voice so pure and smooth. He sang in the human language, a song about frozen rivers shattering the ice, about spring sunlight hammering the glaciers, and something about splitting a mountainside with your skull. Veka thought that must be a metaphor for strength or persistence, but you never knew with dwarves.

She tapped her foot to the drumbeat. Her head bobbed with the swells and ebbs of the flute. And that voice…it cocooned her in silk and lifted her away. The dwarf's song was impossible, stretching on and on, never breaking for a breath.

"Cheap bardic tricks." Ember's words in her head made her jump. *"Don't let yourself be drawn into his spell."*

The elf stood with his thumbs jammed in his ears. Veka grabbed her own ears and pulled them flat, dulling the sounds.

"How does bardic magic work?" Veka asked, fascinated. *"Are the lyrics the same as the words of a spell? Does he have to do gestures, too? Can you still do bard magic if your voice sounds like a bear throwing up its dinner?"*

"Hush," snapped Ember.

The song came to an end. Deafening applause filled the tavern. People stomped and banged their dishes and whistled. Coins clattered onto the stage, mostly silver, but Veka spotted some gold as well. With one performance, the band had earned enough money to last for weeks…thanks to the bard's enchantment, no doubt.

"Thank you, Olvine!" yelled the dwarf. "I'm Duke Hellhound, and we are the Gelatinous Spheres! We'll be at the Distended Donkey tomorrow night. The show starts at sixth bell. Tell your friends!"

"Duke Hellhound?" Ember called out. His voice sounded thinner and weaker than usual after the dwarf's music. It was like drinking the smoothest honey tea and then downing a chaser of dirty dishwater. "Is that what you're calling yourself these days, Herbert Shale?"

The dwarf climbed down from the stage, leaving his band to gather their coins. He plowed through the crowd toward Ember and Veka. He wore stylized armor of black leather, covered in polished silver studs and spikes. "Ember Silvermoon! I'd recognize that nasal whine anywhere. Look at you, dressed up like a real wizard."

"I'll show you what a real wizard can do."

Duke sighed and brushed his fingers through his beard. "I heard you've been causing trouble. How about I buy you a drink? Then you and your… friend…can be on your way."

"And let you go back to using your limited magic to charm coins from drunks?"

"Limited magic, is it?" Duke chuckled, but it was a hard, flinty laugh. "Ever the talker, you were. But you never had the magical strength to light your own farts. We both know you don't have the balls to start trouble. Especially here, surrounded by my adoring fans."

"You still think you're better than me?" asked Ember.

"I still think the sun rises in the east, too."

"Be ready, goblin."

Veka concentrated on the spell she'd been studying. She flattened her ears to try to shut out any distractions.

"All these years and you're still preying on the weak," said Ember. "Well, I'm not weak anymore."

"Now."

Veka barely had time to focus her will before Ember took charge of her hands and mouth. Together, they cast *Terrence's Terrific Soporific.*

Exhaustion wracked her body, backlash from the spell. She sagged against the wall. But the magic worked. One by one, the crowd dropped off to sleep, until only Ember, Duke, and Veka were left standing. Or slumping, in Veka's case. So much for the dwarf's "adoring fans."

"Not bad," said Duke. "Easy enough to deflect if you've been trained. And it helps that they were all drunk and half unconscious already. It's a shame you've got so little power of your own. All these years, and you're still stealing from others, the same as always."

Veka frowned. Ember hadn't been stealing from her. He just needed his wits to face Duke Hellhound. He couldn't afford the sleepiness that came with casting that spell.

"*You* stole *my* dog!" snapped Ember. "You dragged him into the desert to die. I challenge you, Herbert Shale, bardic wizard of the fourth circle."

"You talk too much. It's one of the reasons nobody could stand you. And we *freed* that poor beast. Aye, we should have kept a better watch on the dog, but how were we to know the daft animal would run straight into a sandsnake pit?"

Ember pushed back his cloak, revealing the stones on his belt. He pulled two free. "Today, I avenge poor Birchbark."

"Ridiculous name for a dog," muttered Duke. Then, before Veka or Ember could act, he began to sing.

The words were in a language Veka didn't know, but the music hit her like a kick from a horse. A really big horse. Duke's power bounced her against the wall. She collapsed to the floor as the tavern spun around her.

Ember staggered a step, then smiled. Raising the stone in his right hand, he sang Duke's song right back, perfectly mimicking every note.

Duke was blasted to the floor by the power of his own song.

"The power of the carrion crow," said Ember. "All of my Belt Beasts' gifts are mine to command. Impressive, no? I can also do this."

He threw the other stone at Duke's feet. White light flashed; when it faded, an orange lizard three feet long stood before the dwarf.

"Jungle gecko." Ember pointed at Duke. The lizard charged. Duke tried to roll out of the way, but the lizard's tongue snapped out, long and thin. The tip slapped Duke's exposed wrist.

Veka and Ember had trapped this creature a month ago, a quest that involved hiking through hot swamps and enduring far too many bug bites. The lizard's sticky tongue could capture insects and small rodents, and its spit was toxic enough to paralyze a child.

"Bastard." The word came out slurred. Duke's face looked stiff, like hardening clay. He tried to sing, but the tune was distorted.

"Witness my victory, Herbert Shale," said Ember. "Witness my defeat of a fourth circle wizard."

Veka could never remember exactly how the circle system worked. Were bigger numbers better, or were the smaller numbers the most powerful magic users? All she knew was that beating a ranked wizard gave Ember the right to claim the same rank for himself.

"Herbert Shale," said Ember. "The pride of Os-Webra. If only our teachers could see you now."

"Os-Webra was a school for *real* wizards," mumbled Duke. "Ye didn't deserve to be there."

"You're right. I deserved better." Ember clutched the carrion crow's stone close and sniffed the air. "I recognize that smell. You're still lugging around that old lungtoad?"

"Your gripe's with me," Duke said weakly. "Leave poor Wartbottom out of it."

"Like you left Birchbark?" Ember returned the carrion crow's stone to his belt and removed a different stone. This one was empty; the crystal half was still a cloudy gray. "At least Wartbottom will be safe."

Ember climbed up onto the stage and picked up a wide, shallow bowl from behind the drum. Inside the bowl was a yellow and brown toad the size of Veka's head. "Lungtoads like Wartbottom breathe through their skin. And they can hold their breath for half an hour. 'Duke Hellhound' used his familiar's power to sing without stopping to breathe."

He touched the stone to Wartbottom. Crackling white light enveloped the toad, and it disappeared.

Ember placed the stone with the trapped toad on his belt, then picked up the one he'd thrown at Duke Hellhound. He pointed it at the jungle gecko and spoke the elvish word for *return*. The lizard vanished into its stone. "Come, goblin. With that disgusting toad, we have everything we need. Our next foe is a wizard of the first circle. Once I've beaten her, I'll be known far and wide as a true master."

Oh, right. The *lower*-numbered circles were more powerful. It didn't make sense that less was better, but a lot of things about civilized people were backward.

With that finally cleared up, Veka swiped a bowl of pretzels from the closest table and followed Ember out of the tavern.

* * *

They made camp a mile outside of Olvine. Veka slept curled beneath the wagon, an old blanket pulled around her body. It wasn't comfortable, but the wagon protected her from the rain, and it was better than fighting for space back at the goblin lair.

She was dreaming about the elusive *Great Ball of Fire* spell when something struck her ear and startled her awake.

She groaned and rolled onto her side.

A stone hit her chin. She cursed and sat up, banging her head against the underside of the wagon.

"Keep it down, goblin."

"Sorry, Master." Veka tensed. The words hadn't come from Ember, who was resting comfortably in the wagon, but from the bushes on the far side of their camp. She fumbled for her weapon, an old dagger with a rope-wrapped handle.

"Easy, lass." Duke Hellhound crawled from the bushes. "I'm not here to fight."

"You're here to steal your familiar back." Ember really needed to start killing his foes. Or at least cutting off their feet so they couldn't chase him as easily. Veka touched her necklace. She could wake the elf with a single thought, and this time he'd do more than tongue-stun the dwarf.

"I wish I were," said Duke. "But I know better than to kick a dragon in the snout, no matter how much he might deserve it. I'll let someone else put old Ember the Member in his place. No, I'm here for you."

"If you hurt me, Ember will—"

"I'm here to help you, you daft goblin."

Veka crawled out from under the wagon, keeping her knife pointed at Duke. His hands were empty, but that meant nothing to a magic user.

"That's better," he said. "Let me take a look at that necklace."

"Touch it and I'll kill you."

Duke raised his hands. "I don't blame you for being afraid. I messed up with Birchbark all those years ago, and that was unforgivable. I can't change the past, but I promise I'll take more care this time. We'll steer clear of any sandsnakes."

Sandsnakes? What was he babbling about?

"If you stay, he'll squeeze you like a giant blueberry until there's nothing left. Same as he did to the rest of his familiars."

"Familiar?" Fury simmered Veka's blood as she realized what he thought. "I'm his apprentice!"

"But you're a—" Duke looked her over. "I saw how he used you, back at the Bottom Feeder."

"We worked together. To beat you." Forget waking Ember. She'd stab this arrogant dwarf herself.

Duke folded his arms. "All right, *apprentice*. Show me what he's taught you. Hit me with a spell."

Veka hesitated. "I can't. Not without Ember's help. I'm not strong enough yet. He says the more we use my power to cast spells, the stronger my will becomes. Like exercising a muscle."

"Oh, lass. You've more strength than you know. That's why he chose you." He pointed to Veka's necklace. "Do you know what that trinket is?"

"It's a bond between master and apprentice."

"Birchbark's collar had a pebble exactly like it. They're called bondage beads. That's why you can't remove it."

"You're wrong! I can't take it off because the contract between master and apprentice is unbreakable." She grimaced. "Bondage beads?"

"Unfortunate name, I know. No self-respecting wizard uses the silly things. They're for novices who can't work a binding spell. It chains the familiar who wears it to a master. Ember needs them because he has the magical power of a moldy potato."

"You're lying." Veka felt like a statue frozen in place. Every time Duke spoke, he chipped away at her anger and her certainty. "Ember invented the magical stones he uses to capture his Belt Beasts."

"Belt Beasts. It's a worse name than Birchbark." Duke shook his head. "He's clever enough to have designed those stones of his. But I wager he hired a real mage to do the spellwork. Just like he paid people to do his homework back at Os-Webra. Tell me this: have you *ever* seen him cast a spell by himself?"

"I…" Veka's knife wavered. "I haven't, no. Only through me."

"Using *your* strength of will, and letting *you* bear the brunt of the spell's kickback."

Or using her as bait to attract the carrion crow. The thought widened the cracks of her doubt.

Humiliation and shame burned her ears. If this dwarf was right, it meant Veka was just another animal, no better than the Belt Beasts she'd helped catch. Just a goblin who'd been stupid enough to believe Ember's lies, stupid enough to believe he'd seen something worthy in her.

She wanted to argue, to stab Duke's stupid words back into his stupid mouth. Instead, she slumped to the ground and asked, "Why would you help me?"

"I'd like to say it's because I'm a purehearted fellow, and you deserve better. And I suppose you do, true enough. Even goblins have songs, and that makes 'em worth saving. But truth be told, the pointy-eared bastard stole my familiar, and I wanted to pay him back in kind."

Veka sniffed. Any goblin would understand that motivation. "He deserves worse."

"Aye, but neither of us are a match for him and those stones. You're better off getting far away from him and starting over."

Veka yanked her ears until her eyes watered. How many times had she started over in her quest to learn magic? How many times had she failed? She was too tired to do it all again. She didn't have the strength for another defeat.

"Goblin?" Ember's voice, bleary and half-asleep, crept into her thoughts.

Veka jumped. "He's waking up."

"He probably senses your distress. Hurry and let me get that thing off you."

"There's no time. Go."

Duke hesitated. "What do you mean to do?"

Veka clenched her knife. "I'm going to stab him in the face."

* * *

Ember climbed out of the wagon and used one of his belt stones to light the darkness. Veka recognized the blue light from the fairy jellyfish they'd captured three weeks ago. The jellyfish *she'd* captured. She'd been the one who got jellyfish stings all over her arms so he could collect another stupid Belt Beast.

"What's this commotion, goblin?"

At least the light made it easier to see her target. Veka gripped her knife, snarled, and charged.

Ember blinked, looking both weary and annoyed. *"Stop."*

Her muscles locked. She tumbled forward, and her face smacked the dirt. So much for the face-stabbing.

Ember plucked the knife from her hand and tucked it away in his robe. *"What's gotten into you?"*

"I'm not your familiar," she mumbled through clenched teeth.

"Ah. I wondered how long it would take you to figure that out." He crouched in front of her, just out of reach. *"I'm afraid that's exactly what you are. You willingly accepted the collar, after all."*

"You said it was an apprentice's necklace."

He ignored her words. *"The bondage bead came with a free summoning. I was skeptical when you responded. I thought the summoning was defective and almost sent you away. But you've been more useful than the snakes and toads and rats I used in the past."*

"You *summoned* me?" She'd been searching for a wizard to learn from. She'd found him, not the other way around.

Hadn't she?

"You can't remove the collar, and as long as you wear it, you can't harm or disobey me. Try to accept the situation with dignity."

Dignity? It was like he'd never met a goblin before. "Set me free, or I'll bite off your—"

"I paid a great deal for that bead, and I intend to get my money's worth. You're going to help me finish my quest."

"Your *quest?*" Veka laughed. "You'll never be a first circle wizard, Ember. You're a fraud and a cheat. You need a goblin's help to cast even the simplest spell."

Ember took an empty stone from his belt. "I'm a genius. I may be the smartest wizard that ever was. And I'm tired of your disrespect."

"Wait!" Veka tried to scramble away as she realized what he was about to do, but her body wouldn't obey. The last thing she felt was the pain of the stone striking her stomach, and then the world vanished in a web of white lightning.

* * *

Veka didn't know how long she was trapped in the stone. From time to time, Ember would use her strength and willpower to work magic. Whenever he did, she felt faint. *Thin*, like lizard blood soup diluted to little more than water. But most of the time, there was just...nothing.

Her imprisonment was worse than torture. It was *boring*. Stuck in the dark with nothing but her thoughts and her memories and her failures.

Failures like her inability to do magic on her own. She'd been able to cast spells at Os-Webra, hadn't she? If she'd done it once, why was it so hard to do it again?

Gestures, words, and will. She'd practiced the movements until her hands and fingers cramped. She'd repeated the stupid elf words until her tongue was numb. Her will was strong enough for Ember to use. She was doing everything right, so why did it never work?

Seconds passed, or maybe years, before she heard Ember's voice again.

"We approach the home of Ellnior, elvish wizard of the first circle and former headmaster of Os-Webra. After today, no one will question my power."

Veka doubted that very much, but she kept the thought to herself.

Weakness rippled through her as Ember tapped into her power. *"Goblin, recite* Delilah's Discount Disappearance.*"*

"Elf, go suck a cactus." But she couldn't fight his command. The words of the spell flowed through her thoughts like spoiled meat through a goblin.

Delilah's Discount Disappearance wasn't even a real invisibility spell. It just planted suggestions in the mind of anyone who looked your way. Suggestions like, "That's not an enemy spy sneaking around behind your lines; it's just a rabbit" or "That isn't a thief scaling the tower wall; it's just a rabbit that jumped *really* high."

Delilah had obviously had a thing about rabbits.

What kind of name was Delilah, anyway? It wasn't an elf name. But the spell, like all magic, was in that overly melodic, tongue-knotting elvish.

She concentrated on Ember's thoughts. She picked up eagerness... excitement...fear. She couldn't tap into his senses the way he could borrow hers, but their connection remained, and it was easier to focus here, with no distractions.

She caught the impression of a hunched elf woman in a hastily-tied robe: Ellnior. The disappearance spell must have worked well enough for Ember to reach his target.

Ellnior gestured and snapped something in elvish. A cloud of noxious gas roiled forth.

Ember touched the stone with the lungtoad on his belt, borrowing its power. Had he guessed she might use this spell? Veka grudgingly gave him credit for planning ahead and making sure he wouldn't have to breathe.

Now it was Ember's turn. He grabbed more of his stones, directing his Belt Beasts' power at Ellnior. With so many beasts, it took all his concentration to juggle their different abilities.

Wouldn't it be a shame if something were to break that concentration? Veka focused on their bond and began to sing.

"Not all who are lost end up eaten
By dragons who lurk in the dark.
Not all goblin fighters are beaten
By heroes out making their mark.

"But if you're a pointy-eared goblin,
You're born with most terrible luck.
You dream of the battles you might win
When the truth is you're thoroughly——"

"Silence," snapped Ember. Veka could tell the song had distracted him. He'd dropped one of the stones, and he couldn't remember if the one in his left hand was the musclepede or the long-haired staticat.

Veka laughed to herself. Like any other familiar, she had to obey her master, but Ember hadn't specifically ordered her to stop singing. Only to be silent. What was more silent than a goblin trapped in a rock? Her song was nothing but thought, after all. She switched to a pirate ditty she'd learned as a child.

"There once was a gob with a pirate crew.
The name o' that gob was Brock the Blue.
But his crew didn't do what a crew should do.
So Brock cracked his whip. 'It's the lash for you!'

"Crack, crack for the chef Larink,
Burned the rat-tail stew and made a mighty stink.

"Crack, crack for one-fanged Jek,
Had too much to drink and threw up on the deck.

"Crack, crack for first mate Glot.
Thought the captain's hat was a chamber pot.

"Crack, Crack for—"

Colors and sounds and sensations crashed over her. White light flickered and flashed. She breathed in cool, putrid air.

Ember had called her from the stone—directly into the middle of his magical battle with Ellnior.

Goblin instincts took over. Veka squawked, dropped flat, and covered her head. To her left, an ice gator breathed frost at the old elf woman in her tweed cloak. The carrion crow was beating its wings about Ellnior's head.

"Goblin, bite her!"

Typical. All her knowledge and skills, and the only thing Ember saw was a big-fanged goblin. Veka got to her feet, compelled to attack.

Ellnior barely glanced at her. She pointed two fingers and rattled off something elvish.

Veka's legs gave out.

"Useless," snarled Ember, then ducked as Ellnior sent a streak of green fire at his face. From the scorch marks on his cloak, Ellnior had scored several hits already.

Veka glanced around. The rooftop was circular, twenty feet wide, with a low stone wall around the edge. Beyond, she saw nothing but cloudy sky. They must be atop a tower.

Ember tapped Veka's will to cast *Darnak's Distracting Detritus*. Dust and dirt swirled around Ellnior.

The spell's backlash left Veka coughing and cotton-mouthed, with a gritty feeling in her throat. But her thoughts were on the spell. *Darnak* was a dwarf name. What self-respecting dwarf would create a spell in elvish?

The answer hit her like a rock. None would. Which meant these spells didn't have to be in elvish to work. They only had to be in elvish to work *for Ember*. That was the language he'd grown up with. That was the language he thought in. And that was why the magic never worked for her.

She rolled away from the fighting. Her hands still worked, and her will was strong. She had Ember to thank for that—he'd been working her for months, exercising her willpower. She stoked her will, fueling it with all her anger and humiliation. She traced the gestures. Finally, she spoke the words of *Delilah's Discount Disappearance*—not in the beautiful tongue of the elves, but in the harsh, angry, gravel-grinding syllables of the goblin language.

Ember whirled. *"What have you done?"*

"Magic." Veka spat the word. He'd known why she couldn't do magic by herself. He must have. He'd just assumed she'd never figure it out on her own.

Veka looked down at herself and laughed at the sight of her furry legs and paws. She'd cast her illusion over them all, everyone except for Ember. Where his Belt Beasts had battled Ellnior a moment before, now there were nothing but rabbits. Rabbits bouncing at each other, breathing frost and shooting sparks and tossing flames. Rabbits flying about overhead.

Ember glared at the rabbits, probably trying to guess which one was his enemy. Before he could act, one of the rabbits wiggled its nose and shot a bolt of green fire that struck Ember's chest.

He stumbled backward, tripped over the low wall, and fell.

That same rabbit spoke a quick spell, and the illusion vanished. Ellnior strode to the wall and looked down.

"Is he dead?" asked Veka.

"Hardly." Ellnior studied Veka for a moment, then waved a hand. The spell paralyzing Veka's legs ended.

Veka joined her and peered over the edge. "Oh."

Ember lay groaning in the grass fifteen feet below. What Veka had taken to be a great tower was in fact a rather modest stone house, surrounded by a well-tended garden and a small orchard.

Ember looked to have twisted his ankle but was otherwise very much alive. His face turned red with fury when he spotted Veka. *"You!"*

She was still bound to him. He could order her to attack Ellnior again, or to jump headfirst off the roof, or to eat her own hands. She looked for a weapon, anything she might use to stop him. Her gaze fell on one of Ember's magical stones lying near her. She snatched it up and returned to the edge.

Ember laughed. *"You don't know the secrets of my stones. You can't possibly hope to use the complex magics I devised to—"*

The stone struck the center of Ember's forehead. There was no magical light, no enchanted entrapment…but it was still a stone, and Veka had a good throwing arm. Ember blinked once and lost consciousness.

Veka looked for more stones.

"I wouldn't have expected spellwork from one of your kind." Ellnior studied her closely. "You have potential."

"I know." Veka's heart beat like a rabbit's. Would Ellnior attack her next? Veka didn't know how to deflect magical fire.

Behind them, Ember's Belt Beasts puttered about the roof, confused and aimless. The carrion crow chased the staticat, who hissed and sent sparks flying at the crow's beak.

"I used to run a magical school," said Ellnior. "I retired ten years ago, but I still have connections on the board. If you'd like, I could try to find a place for you at Os——"

"No thank you," Veka said quickly. She'd rather face magic fire than go back there again. She lifted the pebble on her necklace. "But maybe you could do something about this?"

Ellnior touched a burning finger to the cord. It sizzled and separated. Veka pulled the necklace off and threw it as far as she could. Only after it disappeared into the field did she think she should have thrown it at Ember's face instead.

"What will you do now, goblin?"

"My name is Veka. I'll keep studying magic. It's all I've ever wanted. And look for ways to get back the memories they took from me at—at school." She hesitated. "Could you——?"

"I'm sorry, but memories pulled from the mind are like smoke, and dissipate quickly."

Disappointment twisted her stomach, but she pushed it aside. She was free, and she'd beaten Ember. That was worth something.

"What of these creatures?" asked Ellnior.

Veka picked up another stone. What was the command Ember had used? "Return," she said in goblin.

The carrion crow squawked and vanished.

"I'll take them back where they belong." Starting with Wartbottom the lungtoad. Veka grinned, thinking about what Ember would say when he woke up to find his precious Belt Beasts gone.

"You don't want to keep their power?" asked Ellnior.

"I want my own magic." She searched through the different stones until she found the one that felt...*familiar*. Like a lingering scent of goblin. That had to be the one Ember had used on her. She tucked it into her pocket. She didn't know if Ember could call her back into the stone, but she wasn't going to risk it.

"Visit me from time to time, Veka. I could help you with your studies." She raised her hands before Veka could protest. "Not as a familiar, or even an apprentice. Consider me an occasional advisor for your...independent study."

"Maybe," Veka said warily.

"What about him?" Ellnior pointed down at Ember.

Veka's thoughts were like debris clogging a drain. There were so many possibilities that none could make it through. She could stab him or hit him with more rocks or trap him in one of his own stones or drag him back to the goblin lair for barbeque night. But one idea squeezed past the rest.

She imagined all of Ember's books and notes and gadgets tucked away in the wagon, waiting for her. "I'm going to become the wizard he never could."

"I thought you'd want revenge."

"One day I'll be famous, and Ember will hear stories about me," Veka continued. "He'll know even a goblin is more powerful than him. And he'll cry like an infant who just lost his baby fangs."

"I see." Ellnior chuckled. "Good luck, Veka."

"I don't need luck." Veka stepped away to start collecting the rest of the Belt Beasts. "I can do magic."

Familiarity

Sharon Lee & Steve Miller

At least it was Friday, Trixie thought. It was important to acknowledge the good things that happened, and not dwell on the negative. She'd learned that from her grandma, and if she'd managed to miss it there, the books repeated it over and over.

So—Friday was a good thing. And, because it was Friday, she wouldn't have to see Beth McCaffrey and her new eagle familiar for two whole days—another good thing. Not quite enough to balance out the…disappointing things, like there being no mail at the box for her, despite her grandmother's warning that she'd sent something special from the Flow Country in Scotland for her favorite granddaughter's birthday. Admittedly, Trixie's birthday was three months past. She still kept hoping for the arrival of that present, but, really, after three months, the edge had kind of worn off.

What had made her sad was that there hadn't been any crows to commune with—not even Mr. Frodo and Samwise, who so often greeted her at the trade-tree inside the crow-field she'd built. Worse, there hadn't been any trades on the table. There hadn't been any trades for nearly a week. Trixie hoped nothing bad had happened. More likely, it was probably too noisy, even for crows, she thought, trying to be practical and not sour. She refreshed the seed and the cat food, chanting while she did, to renew her intentions and desires.

Then, she went into the house, and instead of a hello got a distracted look from her mother. "Oh, Trix—good. Go out to the garage and get me a package of chops, a package of burger, and some buns, will you? Thanks!"

At least, Trixie thought darkly, she'd said *thanks*.

She pulled the packages out, juggling them as she pushed the freezer door shut with her hip, and—

"Hey!"

The skinny calico cat stood tall on two white back feet, beige front paws against the freezer door. Trixie frowned at her—no, at *him*! she thought; a male calico.

There'd been a time, not too long ago, when Trixie had wanted a cat, like Grandma's Flann, who was her companion and her guide. That was before she'd gotten side-tracked into crows, and before—

"Can you talk?" she asked softly.

The cat brought his front feet down to the garage floor and looked up at her, silently.

Of *course* he couldn't talk, Trixie thought. Why should he talk to *her*, the only person in the whole house with an aptitude—a strong aptitude, Grandma said!—for majick?

Trixie took a deep breath and reminded herself that it was Friday, and that the world was better served by positive thoughts and actions.

"So, you're a stray," Trixie said, trying not to sound like she was judging his lifestyle choice. "This isn't a good time. Really. We're kind of full up. Maybe you should go somewhere else."

Juggling the food, she opened the side garage door with one awkward hand and stepped aside so the cat could go out. It walked to the threshold and looked up at her. She brought her foot gently up under the lean stomach, meaning to urge him on his way, but he simply stepped aside, still looking at her.

The stuff in her arms was starting to remind her that it was frozen and she wasn't. She stepped out, the cat ducking between her feet, as the door closed behind them. Fine. At least the cat wasn't trapped in the garage, that was positive.

The kitchen had gotten crowded in the time it took her to get the stuff out of the freezer. Mom was still at the counter, chopping. Her brother was fiddling with the remote for the big wall-screen, and her sister was standing in the middle of everything, staring at the images.

Nobody looked around to say hi. After all, Trixie thought, it wasn't like she was as important as *the news*.

She dumped her burdens on the counter, opened the fridge, and noisily shoved them onto a mostly empty shelf.

Turning, she nearly fell over the calico cat and let out an exasperated sigh.

"A cat followed me into the kitchen!" she said loudly.

Mom looked round from her chopping.

"I see," she said calmly. "Is it your cat?"

Of course Mom didn't yell at her for bringing a stray in. Yelling hadn't worked with the ponies or the snake, or the other "bog strays."

"It followed me in, didn't it?" Trixie said.

"Observably," Mom said, "but *is it yours?* Has it spoken to you?"

Well, Mom *would* ask that. Grandma had raised her, after all, even though Mom was about as science-y as you could get.

Trixie looked down at the cat. The cat, sitting neatly next to the fridge, fluffy tail wrapped prettily around his toes, looked up at Trixie.

"Well—no," Trixie said. "Not in so many words. Not in *any* words, actually. So, how would I tell?"

"Does it *feel like* a sign or a portent?"

That was another question her grandmother would ask, and suddenly Trixie didn't *care* that it was Friday.

"*I* don't know!" she said, flinging her hands up in frustration. "Seems to me we're surrounded by signs and portents. All of you with your new familiars, can't you tell me if a cat following me into the house is a portent?"

Trixie glared around the room.

Her mother looked thoughtful; her brother, still staring at the screen, shrugged; but her older and *looooong* suffering bigger sister, Amery, rolled her eyes, the parrot on her shoulder muttering, "Cats are more often flea-bitten than they are portents! And they're always mangy!"

The parrot, Bucko, was a mean summabitch—that was what Trixie's dad said, with a touch of pride, perhaps. Easy for *him* Trixie thought, with his twin mini-ponies tied up outside the back door.

Mom—Dr. Loralee Lincoln Robertson, the artist and science historian to the academic world; Loralee to friends; and Lee to husband Jason—reached up to pull a mixing bowl down from the cabinet.

"Bucko, be kind, please," she said over her shoulder. "You're not helping."

Trixie, not one of Bucko's fans, turned her glare on him. "That's right, be *helpful!*" she said. "And he doesn't have mange! He's skinny, but there isn't anything wrong with him."

Trixie looked at the cat again. The cat squinted its eyes at her.

"He doesn't have a collar," she said weakly.

"Mangy anyhow, I bet, or fleas!" the parrot squawked.

"Shh…Bucko!" Am scolded.

"Not my rules, not my rules, not my rules," Bucko said, and turned ostentatiously around on Am's shoulder. "Pirates were my family! We don't do helpful!"

"That cat looks familiar," Am said, stepping closer. She caught Trixie's gaze and rolled her eyes at her use of *familiar.* "It looks like one we saw at the end of last winter, hanging around the bird feeder when the Schmealys moved away."

"No," Trixie said, "that one was orange, and her tail wasn't fluffy."

"We at least know what to feed a cat," Mom said, "and you've been getting the high-grade stuff for your crows." She turned and directed a frown at her youngest daughter. "I thought you *wanted* a cat, before all this started."

Well, no, Trixie thought; she hadn't wanted *a cat*. She'd *wanted* a familiar. Everybody knew that familiars came when they were needed. Except now—

Behind them, Dando—short for Daniel Donald Oliver—fiddled with the remote, bringing the volume on the big screen up as the map at *Newsquirt's* "Your Daily Oddity" showed where the complaints about a talking animal infestation were coming from. Dando was wearing a windbreaker, and mom was ignoring that—the rules had gotten stretched pretty thin, ever since the local "infestation" had begun.

"Looks like there are thirteen anomalous sites around the world, Biff," the reporter on the spot was saying, "with one right here near the confluence of Three Rivers! Now back to you!"

"I love how nobody wants to talk about what set this off," Am said.

"Well, the Smithsonian says ancient shamans—"

"What's the Smithsonian know?" Am demanded heatedly. "Wasn't it one of their expeditions that started this? Talk about bad technique—"

"A lot people think it was the Russians messing around in Siberia, trying to weaponize a sinkhole…"

"That's just a rumor, Dando," said Jason, sometimes known as Dad, as he entered the kitchen, followed by a three-foot tall pony, hooves making light clipping noises on the poured custom floor.

"My people," said the pony, "are not taking sides until we find out if we're all going to evaporate like the Burmese goats did in Washington State. Fifteen days and poof—gone like never been, not even a bone!"

"Has Dando been leaving talk radio on for you at night?" Jason asked, throwing a sharp glance at his son, who ignored it by staying focused on the screen.

Bowl in hand, Mom turned around.

"Didn't we ask you to guard the driveway?" Mom asked, apparently talking to the pony, but sparing an exasperated look at her husband, who was fondling the silky mane. "I'd prefer not to have company right now."

"You let the cat in." The pony shook his head, striking Jason's knee with an audible *clunk*. "Jason didn't even see it. Cats are sneaky."

Jason took a step forward, looking down. Trixie saw the exact moment he did see the cat, even before he lifted his eyes to the ceiling.

"Always room for one more," he muttered.

"So, Trix, what *should* the cat do?" Am said. "Ask for a safe place to live, like Finzie?"

Finzie roused himself, poking his head out from Dando's windbreaker.

"*I* asked politely. I hung on the trellis over the front door until Dando came home and made sure he was the right one. *Bucko* snooped and listened to you for days before he flew to the window and said he was here for Amery. I saw it happen; I was here first!"

Finzie's tongue flickered as he leaned down across Dando's waist.

"Hey, you! Fur spot!" he called. "Who are you? Speak, whisker beast!"

The cat looked over his shoulder, saw the big blacksnake—and yawned before settling closer to the floor, stretching one paw out to touch Trixie's shoe.

"I am fixing this family's dinner," Mom said, loud enough to be heard over the news report about the bogs in Nova Scotia. "Can I get some room? And maybe some help?"

In the quiet that followed this, she smiled at Trixie. "Thanks for bringing those packages, Trix."

Trixie ducked her head.

"I am looking for a volunteer to make garlic bread," Mom said.

"Just let me put Rouncy outside," said Jason, moving toward the door.

"Ugh," Bucko said. "Garlic makes my eyes water."

"Not your meal," Mom said. "Am, I need room to work, so move Bucko now. I've got renders coming in, and I need to send them to the big CNC printer at the tech center, so, Dando, I need that remote. You can take vulpine rumors elsewhere."

Dando put the remote on the kitchen table.

"Don't you think the news is important? Somebody must know the truth, and as soon as we know it, we can—!"

"Be even more confused than we are now," said Jason, returning from exiling the pony. "Give your mother room for the sauce!"

Dando took a deep breath, but before he could say anything, Finzie chuckled lightly and said, "You wanted to check out that new Steam game."

"Yeah," Dando said, "I did." He left the kitchen.

"The bread needs to be sliced, Jason," Mom said.

"On it," he answered, grabbing a cutting board and heading for the work center.

"But," Trixie said, "why is it happening? The whole world is infested, and—"

"Well, no," Dad said quietly, "the *whole world* is *not* infested. In fact, there isn't much evidence for an *infestation*. Just because some people you know personally are talking about this as an *infestation* doesn't mean the whole world is experiencing one. That's a bias in observation—you should look it up to see which one, right?"

Trixie rolled her eyes, knowing that this would be a question at breakfast tomorrow.

"There are charts online," Dad continued, as he used the knife against the Italian loaf. "Orbital images—the boggy gasses that are being released are thick enough to show up on camera. We happen to be directly in the path of those clouds, thanks to the jet stream. But only a small portion of the world is experiencing the effects."

Trixie, relaxing somewhat from her frustration, made a foosh noise, waving an imaginary jet stream overhead.

"Have you practiced your guitar today, Trix?" Mom asked in that tone of voice that suggested the best answer was—

"No, ma'am."

"Then maybe you ought to do that. Take your friend with you."

* * *

Trixie kicked off her shoes and got the guitar into her lap. The cat stretched out across the discarded New Balance runners. She glanced at him when she hit a sour note in her practice, half-expecting a sarcastic comment, but he only stared at her. Experimentally, she hit another wrong note and he flicked an ear before he rolled half onto his back and started cleaning his belly.

When her official practice was done, Trixie donned finger picks to try to emulate Jorma Kaukonen doing his "Water Song." She still had a lot to learn there; her thumb pick was still not quite in the right spot. She adjusted it and tried again, and one more time, before her concentration broke and she looked up.

In her attention to the music, she'd missed the cat moving to the hollow of centered pillows on her bed, where he was now carefully cleaning the pink toe pads of his front foot.

Trixie shook her head. "If you want to sleep on my pillows, you could at least come across with your name. My grandmother says that indifference is a given with cats, but if you want to be treated right you can tell me your favorite foods. Grandma's always saying that Flann—"

The cat yawned, widely.

"Don't be that way! It's not flan like the food, but with two ns, OK? Like Flann O'Brien! Anyway, Grandma's Flann talks to her when no one's around. He's—I guess we'll have to call him a *traditional* familiar—" She waved her hand, meaning to include the recent additions to her family, and all the others who had suddenly just appeared. "These new guys, they'll talk to *any*body."

She leaned forward and met the cat's green gaze.

"We're all alone," she murmured.

The cat surveyed the room regally, gaze alighting on a pair of plush cats and a Father Christmas that hadn't been put away in three years.

"They don't count. I might talk to them, but I know they won't answer me, OK? If you're going to stay, I'm going to have to call you something, so it'll be easier on us all if you just tell me your name."

The cat rose and leapt to the end of the bed, clearly judging the jump from there to her lap. Trixie unslung the guitar just in time.

Her lap was full of calico; she got a head butt to her belly, then one higher, and the cat curled against her where the guitar's waist and lower bout had been, a good, secure, balancing act.

If Trixie had heard a purr before, now her strokes brought a rumble that shook her in her seat, while she used her finger picks to good effect.

The cat scrunched around in her lap, and now there was a belly in view. Did she dare?

She thought for a moment of her Grandmother's example—she'd shown Trixie not to rapidly dig in to a cat belly, but to let her hand rest before starting, slow.

The cat blinked smiley eyes at her.

She *did* dare then, and the cat stretched even longer, starting a low rumbling purr. Trixie playfully finger-picked the intro to a ghostly "Embryonic Journey" on that belly to find both sound and vibration much increased...

"I'm going to call you Jorma until you tell me otherwise," Trixie said.

The cat turned over and stood on her lap, extending his head to bump her firmly on the chin.

"So, Jorma's fine with you?"

Came another bump as Trixie finished the intro to the song on the side of the cat's neck and forehead. Without fanfare the cat—Jorma!—jumped down and curled against her feet, looking smug. Trixie sighed. Maybe it wouldn't be so bad, to just...have a cat.

"Well, I guess that's settled." She glanced at the clock. "Still a couple minutes 'til dinner. I can finish reading that chapter—" She made a long arm, managed to grab the book off her desk without disturbing the cat, and flipped it open.

It was a book on the properties of stones, a particular interest of hers. It didn't agree with the book she'd been working with when she set up the crow-field, and she'd been disagreeing with it because of her own fondness for garnets and peridot, both of which this author deprecated. Not only that, she'd made a pentagram in the crow-field using a peridot and garnet pendulum to help set boundaries, and she knew—from experience!—that wasn't something jade could *ever* match. Jade was far too brittle for—

"The dinner bell is ringing, ladies and gentleman!" Dad called up the stairs, and Trixie put her book down.

* * *

Despite house rules to the contrary, Dando sat at the table with his phone at his right hand and an app open to a news feed. He adjusted the butter dish out of his way as Am asked, "Any more on the invasion story?" while leaning in to look.

He shook his head. "They're calling it a migration now, not an invasion—that's what the ranger they were interviewing called it. 'Infestation' is a big buzzword on a couple channels. There's a lot of pets—talking pets, that would be—and they're migrating to, well…here! We're in one of the thirteen whatever they are—loci or foci or centers—they think they've identified."

Mom looked hard at the pony trying to hide behind Jason's chair.

"You! No familiars at dinner. You'll be left out until after we eat, and this time guard the door like I asked. We don't need anyone else coming in unless they've got hands and permission."

"What about the cat?"

Mom put a hand to her forehead.

"The cat's a nameless visitor, OK? Probably not guard material."

"The dog doesn't guard! As big a brute as he is…"

"My Puppy is a Bernese Mountain Dog, and the wikis all say that is a very intelligent *and helpful* breed. Also, he says he's watching for someone already. Maybe he'll help you if you give him a little direction. *We* have to eat—Jason?"

Trixie felt a bit guilty about the no familiars rule, because Jorma *did* have a name. On the other hand, he was obviously *not* a familiar, so—

Dad nodded and moved toward the door. "C'mon Rouncy, we'll get you posted. I promise you three will have the heater tonight, if the temperature gets below sixty!"

Rouncy moved from behind the chair, following Dad, still muttering.

Trixie looked at the table and saw it still wanted place settings. She moved to take care of that, Jorma half a step ahead, elegantly not being quite in the way or quite out of the way, either.

Mom glanced at Dando's windbreaker.

"Please hang Finzie in your room, Dando. No familiars at dinner tonight."

Dando suffered his way out of the kitchen and was back a moment later in his Monaco Grand Prix t-shirt. Clearly Finzie had been hung on the coat rack by the door and not upstairs in Dando's room, but Mom let it pass.

Jason returned from outside, shaking his head.

"Lee, have you checked in recently—like in the last five minutes?"

"No. I told them I needed a couple hours for dinner and family."

"There's three SUVs and a cop car up the road, at the corner toward the outlet, and what looks like a couple of animal control vans. I *told you* a cul de sac could be blocked. They've left about a half lane clear. Right now, they're talking to Mrs. Finifter, who wants to go down to her driveway."

"Right." Mom opened the oven, pulling out two steamy trays. "Mrs. Finifter will keep them busy while we eat."

"C'mon kids. Lasagna. White dish is meat, clear dish is mushroom. Self-serve. Garlic bread in the toaster oven."

Trixie was still on her feet, so she got ahead of Dando, which was a good thing, since he seemed to expand according to available pasta. Jason was right behind her, cutting a slice from each tray for himself, and the same for another plate which he brought to the table for Lee, who was patting her pockets.

"There. Eat up, but everyone quiet! "

"Easy for you to say," Dando muttered, earning him dark looks from both parents as Mom's cell appeared in her hand—which *never* happened at dinner.

She tapped, frowned, frowned again, tapped *hard*—and grimaced. Then she leaned in Jason's direction, lips pursed, and brows drawn...

"Purdy's put my in-office back-office render on secure link only. Doesn't want anyone not already involved to even see it!"

Jason rolled his eyes.

"Still clueless after all these years? They ask us to do a job and then think they're going to interfere when we get to the end? They're about fifteen minutes behind your machine here, aren't they? We can see it in a minute and twenty seconds in your office or here on the big screen."

Lee looked around the table.

"I'm hungry, but I need to see this. You can take your meals into the family room, or you can sit here and pretend you're not looking at the screen."

Jason looked hard at Dando.

"If you stay, eighteen or not, you have to agree to be deputized to the Bureau of Hermetic Affairs. You can't talk about this with anyone outside this family or the Bureau. You, too, Amery. Trixie, you already know better than to deal your Grandma's business in public."

Trixie stared—this was *Grandma's* business now? But, yeah, she didn't tell anybody all of Grandma's business. Not even Mom and Dad.

"I thought you worked for the Department of State!" Dando said, clearly surprised.

"I do, and the Bureau's my job at the Department. Just like your mom's a Neo Godard Professor who happens to be doing grant work for the Bureau."

Mom laughed her low accepting-the-inevitable laugh like she was playing Scrabble or Boggle against an impossible board.

"There are more secrets you can't share, right?" offered Mom, 'There are secrets in all families' is what Farquhar said..."

"Hey!" Am argued, "that was Jane Austen!"

"Nope, said Mom, "Austen always was a copycat! That was George Farquhar, many years before Austen was born. Pretty popular in his day, too. Anyhow, family secrets, right, everyone? That means you, too, cat!"

She glanced up at the big screen, still empty, and shook her head.

"I have a feeling," she murmured, and looked at Trixie.

"If your Grandmother calls you, answer it. Be careful what you say." She said to the room at large, "No one picks up a call from anyone else, no one takes an email, no one sends anything to anyone about this. Ever. Turn off your phones, kids, and dig in!"

* * *

Trying not to look up at the screen was like trying not to think about ping pong balls after someone says, "Whatever you do, don't think about ping pong balls!" At least eating at the same time as they looked made it easier to act like they weren't.

In fact, everyone was studying the rendering of the three...devices... shown on the screen, in 3D, with a projection from each one demonstrating what they might be used for. The images rotated around one axis and then another. Showing detail all the way around. The first and simplest looked to be a representation of an...

"Astrolabe," Dando said. "Maybe one of the stripped down ones they used on ships in the middle ages."

"Good observation," Jason said, "I took the pictures that's based on when your mother and I traveled to the History of Science Museum at Oxford for our honeymoon...world's biggest collection of astrolabes and orreries, and—" He cut himself off with a laugh. "Like I haven't told this story before." He dove into the vegetarian side of his plate.

"Then that middle jobbie *is* the Antikythera device, almost entirely reconstructed," suggested Am. "I recognize the dial from my archeology classes after they tried a computer reconstruction that was incomplete. Looks like they found the other forty pieces or so for the full rebuild. I think I see the moon settings, the Mars setting, the ... anyway, I don't understand what the link to that other thing is. Wasn't the original a standalone?"

Mom shook her head.

"Incomplete *means* incomplete. The researchers knew that what they had was only the astronomical side of the calculators—the basic moon calculations, exact to the hour if not the minute, the yearly cycles, the thirteen year cycles, the nineteen year cycles, the two hundred thirty-three year cycles—those have been known since Babylonian times. What they didn't have was the astrological side."

Trixie gasped. "Astrological? You mean like horoscopes? Fortune telling and majick?"

"Yes, exactly. I know your grandmother lent you some books, and has talked to you about...majick. She talked to me, too, when I was your age, but it didn't resonate with me like it seems to do for you."

Mom took a bite of garlic bread. "Your Dad and I were attracted to the science side. I wanted something I could study in school, but I never forgot that modern science all started off as the study of alchemy and magic, with majick on the fringes. The Babylonians, Greeks, Mayans, Hebrews; the Kabllah, Cahokia, the Druids, the Nagual...the entire worldwide pre-Christian net of magic used calculators and math—until they stopped, within a century or two of each other, when the European invasions disrupted history across the world."

"This is going to be your next book, isn't it?" Dando said, and raised his hands in front of him, like that would protect him from Mom's stare. "The drawing looks really cool, Mom; not nearly as gaumy as that thing in the basement!"

"Dando, have some respect," Dad said. "And don't admit you've been peeking, that's bad form!"

Mom waved her hand. "Yes, the prototype is in the basement. The final device will be much smaller—handheld."

It was at this point that the cat leapt into Trixie's lap, surprising a squeak and a scolded, "Jorma! You never even asked!"

"Jorma, is it?" Mom said. "As rude as Flann, too, I see."

The cat ignored this, stropping the top of his head on Trixie's chin before turning to study the screen.

Jason's phone rang; he stabbed it into silence without looking. Mom's phone rang and she did the same.

Trixie's phone, deep in her front pocket, began to play out the broom's line from the "Sorcerer's Apprentice".

"Yes, I *did* have a feeling," Mom said, calmly, and folded her hands on the table.

Trixie tried to get her phone out of her pocket without dislodging Jorma, the broom's dance getting more energetic.

Dando shook his head. "At least it isn't 'Witchy Woman'!"

"Dando," Jason said quietly, and Dando suddenly found his lasagna very interesting.

"Hello, Grandma," Trixie said, the phone finally at her ear.

"Listen to me, Trixie. There's a mysterious force acting against our work here in Scotland. You need to know that someone near where you live is affecting the bond we share with our familiars. That's what all the nonsense in the news is—"

"It's happening to us!" Trixie interrupted. "Dando's got a snake, and Am's got a parrot, and Jason has—"

"Stop" Grandma said. "Let me think."

The sigh that eventually came out of the phone was long and complicated.

"This is probably an accident, because I doubt your mother would do it on purpose. She's been after the secret flows of power since before she was your age. She thinks that *seeing* where the magic is will lead to the ability to manipulate it. Only, that's not how magic works. Knowing the phases of the moon doesn't give you power over the moon. Insight, yes; power no—Selene's going to do what Selene's going to do.

"Part of this mess is my fault. She talked to me about building a machine that would let her extrapolate the underlying flows and power—and harvest them, too!—by attaching it to the Antikythera device...and I stupidly told her it wouldn't work. Let that be a lesson to you, Trix; never tell a woman of our family that something they believe in won't work. Ask her if her machine can see the power that's been stored in the bogs."

"Bogs," Trixie said, looking at Mom. "Power flows? Can your machine—"

"Ask your mother if she's used her device, tried to predict the flows."

Trixie repeated the question. Jason shook his head.

"The device we built doesn't *do* anything."

Mom put her hand on his arm. "Speaker?"

Trixie hit the button—and Jason repeated himself.

"You can't say that it doesn't *do* anything," Grandma said. "Is it measuring? Is it watching? Do you get directional information? Do you see patterns?"

"Of course we see patterns," Mom said, "but seeing the timing of power flows isn't exact with the prototype. We've got hints of under-patterns that we'll be able to measure, eventually, but—"

"Is it portable? Your device?"

"It's heavy," Jason said. "Lee needs my help to move it. This is all kinds of cobbled together, and the connections to the other device are pretty flimsy. But the theory, the theory looks good. There's a resistance we haven't figured out, but—"

"I think I understand," Grandma said. "Trixie?"

"Grandma?"

"What have you been doing, Trix? Spells? Wards? Devices or equipment?"

"Not equipment, just a couple of pendulums—garnet and peridot. I used them to measure where to put the pentagram in the crow-field."

Mom and Jason both looked at her.

"In the crow-field," Grandma said. "How big is that, honey? And why a pentagram?"

Trixie gathered her thoughts, aware of Jorma curled, purring, into her lap.

"I trade with the crows, and I was trying to help us talk to each other. I thought maybe one of them would be my familiar, but we get a whole flock sometimes, mostly Sammy and Mr. Frodo's kids, and all they want to do is eat and trade shiny things. Anyway, the pentagram's centered on the oak stump we use as a trade table."

"Ah," said Grandma gently. "The trade table is the center, and it's an oak stump. Good choice, oak. How big is the pentagram?"

Trixie laughed.

"About the size of a softball infield."

"Oh, dear." That was Mom.

"When did you do this working?" Grandma asked.

"On my birthday. It was a perfect daytime full moon, sitting as high as you can ever see it here. I used a compatibility spell—more a chant, really. I closed the pentagram at noon, and used quartz scrying balls and mirrors instead of candles. That afternoon was the first time the crows brought me shiny things—a bright new penny, a nail, and a silver earring. "

"Which book did you get the chant from, Trix?" Grandma asked, and Trixie told her, even the edition number, pointing out that she'd had to ad lib parts of it, because you almost always do if you're doing day magic, and—

"And you plumb-lined the power center using peridot and garnet—with peridot your birth stone, on your birthday," Grandma finished.

Trixie nodded, then realized they weren't on video, and said, "Yes."

Jason started to say something about the size of the pentagram, and Mom tried to talk over him about day magic being a different kettle of fish than she was used to thinking about, until Grandma said, sharply, "Quiet!" and everybody stopped talking, though Trixie could still feel Jorma purring against her stomach.

"Root, mean, square," Grandma said then, and it sounded like a chant. "Centered in rooted oak at a fullest moon, with speech intended. Are you reinforcing your spell, Trix?"

"Yes, ma'am, every time I put out new food."

"Of course you are. Loralee?"

"Mother?"

"When did you start working with your device?"

Mom kind of huffed a laugh.

"I've been *working on it* for years. I finished building the prototype and did a first calibration on Trixie's birthday. Jason helped me power the thing with button batteries so it could precisely match up with the button-powered Antikythera copy I'd been working on. Today I'm rendering the cleaned-up design."

"Did you account for observer effect?"

"The observer sees what they expect!" Dando broke in.

Grandma sighed. "Not *that* one, grandson."

"Wait," Amery said. "You mean that by measuring something, you affect it. Waves and particles, right? The more delicate the thing you're observing is, the more *precise*, the more likely it is that you'll affect its function, just by watching it."

"Yes. Louis de Broglie might not have put it that way, but that's what he had to put up when he was figuring things out."

Grandma sighed.

"My work-group's been exploring Flow Country bog magic for years. It's delicate, precise work with pattern and flow. What we do has worldwide effect, so we work very slowly, and very carefully, to try to keep change manageable."

She laughed suddenly.

"What a bunch of old women we are! In one day, Trixie creates a ginormous daylight pentagram aimed at making—or letting—potential guides talk to her, and renews her spell every day. At the same time, Loralee's trying to measure the minutest of barely recognized magical energies, using a half-built, untested device."

She laughed again.

"I think what we have here," she said, "is a failure to communicate. Trixie's working over her head with strong intent, Loralee's working with an imperfect instrument, Jason's using silver—watch batteries right?—to power magic interactions, and all kinds of significant timing bound up with oak and creatures who tend to familiarize themselves with magic seekers on occasion. I figure Trixie's pentagram and spells have contaminated your prototype by now, Loralee."

Trixie muttered, "Over my head?" while Jason said, "I didn't *think* about the silver!" and Mom said, "Well, it seemed like a good idea to test it!"

"If you'll take my advice, this is what I think you should do now," Grandma said.

"Jason—take the batteries out. Loralee—disconnect the devices…and maybe move them seven feet apart. Make sure they don't line up with Trixie's crow-field or pentagram. Trixie—stop renewing the chants. Don't try to undo them, just don't add any more. If you've got chants wrapped around your pendulums, separate them. I'd start right now, if I were you."

"But," said Jason, "will we lose our familiars?"

"Yes? Or maybe no, if you want them, and they want you—that's the ancient contract. Does it hold in these circumstances? Interesting question. I'll do some research and call you back."

A plaintive meow came over the phone and Grandma sighed.

"Flann's on me about dinner. I better go. I'll check in tomorrow, children. Goddess bless."

Everybody got up for seconds. Then Jason asked Trixie why she hadn't mentioned what she was doing, while Am pointed out that the whole house was affected, and maybe Lee should have *explained* what she was doing, and Jason should have known better, and really, if they were all too busy to check in on what they did daily with the rest of the family…

Eventually dinner was done. Mom and Jason went downstairs; Trixie and Jorma went out to the crow-field.

* * *

Jorma jumped up on to the bed when they got back to Trixie's room and settled himself, sphinx-like among the blankets. She sat next to him and scritched his ears. He leaned into her fingers and began to purr.

"So," Trixie said lazily, "what've you go to say for yourself, Jorma?"

The cat rose and arched his back into her hand.

"Hello, Trixie," he said in a pleasant baritone. "I'd like to stay with you."

More Than Life

Shanna Germain

I thought, when my end came, I would meet it fiercely, sword and shield. Not that I've wielded a sword or shield ever in my life, but I believe it's terribly human to think of our future selves, even our future dying selves, as something better than we have ever been or ever will be.

So no sword now, as the end comes. No shield.

Magic is more my forte anyway.

But I am tired and this bed next to the fire is cozy and the magic words for asking, once my bread and butter, seem less and less important. I don't believe in an afterlife, per se. The kind of magic I do, the life and death of it, doesn't leave much room for that. I do believe in rest, though. In bodies and bones. In becoming the moss and loam and little black beetles. I am ready to be a green inchworm across the back of a leaf, the crimson mushroom pushing through the loam, that bit of snow that falls upon someone's tongue.

I am so ready.

Except.

Except there is one thing I must accomplish before I go. It is proving to be the hardest thing. And so, every spring, my mahogany bird and I walk into the woods, where I creak my knees down into the snow to dig up the earliest of hemlock, carrot-feathered and newly green. Every spring, I pass my magic into the hemlock and ask it to do what it was never made to do: to bring life instead of death. And then I eat it down. Everything that kills also saves, if you know how to ask it properly.

"Celese?" As if summoned by my thinking of her, Vervain wings herself from the corner of the room and settles upon my quilted knee, beady black eyes paying the utmost attention, as if my every expression is a shiny object, ready for careful inspection and collection. "The day grows. We should go."

I do not want to get up and go into the woods. What I want is for her to go away. My bones ache. My one eye has gone wobbly in the socket, my sight a blurry dream of sharpness. There is something new happening in my back, not the forever-one in my spine, but deeper inside me. A dull pressure that sometimes makes me dream of the old giants with their feet on my bones. There have been a hundred thousand mornings just like this one, and if Vervain has her way, there will be a hundred thousand mornings more.

It is not Vervain's fault that she wishes me to live. She was created for the sole purpose of being my protector, my guardian, my lifeline. My father crafted her before I was born, spending months carving her carefully from mahogany, telling her stories of who I was to be, nestling the black bird into the curve of my mother's stomach to hear my heartbeat. Vervain would come to mimic it over time, a natural stethoscope, always letting my parents know the state of their unborn child.

The first time Vervain saved my life, I was only months along, a wiggling bump in my mother's belly. My heartrate dropped to almost nothing and Vervain, still wordless then, mimicked the slowing lub-dub. And my mother, a magic-user as I am, as all my maternal ancestors have been, sent my father to the woods. Then she asked the hemlock to save me and she ate it down.

It was the first time I tasted asked hemlock, passed down through my mother's blood and body into my own.

* * *

The first time I tried to fool Vervain, I was stupid about it. But the scent of near-spring coming through the windows made my mind tremble with the years past, the people past, the over-and-over of this so-long life. I didn't know if I could bear to rise again, to light the fire, to stir the breakfast, to wash my single plate and set it aside to dry. There was life in me, yes, but it was not alive. A husked seed, a rotten egg, a berry too long forgotten in the back of the cupboard.

But there, as ever, was Vervain, and so we set forth to the woods and collected the spring hemlock, as we always did, enough for a year's worth of my life.

When we got home, I laid out a huge buffet of coins and jewels and buttons and beads, a thousand things I'd collected through the years. She is not a raven, but my father imbued her with the tendencies of one—long memory, loyal to a fault, a love of all things that sparkle in the light.

"Why?" Vervain asked. She trusted me fully then, thought she'd done something wonderful or perhaps it was a celebration she'd forgotten about.

I did that sometimes, made up a reason to throw ourselves a party, to drink elderberry tea out of the gold-rimmed glasses that Vervain loved. Although there was only one left now, and much of the gold was long-gone.

"Because I love you more than life itself," I said. It was true, but I didn't know the whole of it then. Still, something in my body knew, for my eyes welled with tears. I pressed my fingers to the pin-prickle at the bridge of my nose, holding them back.

"Thank you," she said, and her simple trust and joy almost stopped me. I wish it had.

Instead, I left her to her trinkets and this time, I did not ask the hemlock to heal me as I swallowed it down.

Vervain, ever vigilant to me in the way my father had made her, soon found me behind the bed, stuffing my mouth full of feathered strands, a furtive mouse hoarding her own death.

She dropped the jeweled button from her bill, only fluttering her feathers once as it smashed to the floor, and then she reached in and pulled the plant from my mouth, my throat, my blood and bones. An invasive reverse-feeding, the magic of her most powerful in these moments of saving.

"Why?" she asked after, and this time there was no hope for celebration, no hint of joy in the question.

I blame my beak-ravaged mouth, my hemlock-ravaged throat, for not being able to answer, but the truth was I didn't know. I could have said I was tired. But I suspect Vervain would have heard *tired of her* and I could not bear that.

"I am made to protect you," she said when I did not answer her.

That was four springs ago. She has rarely let me out of her sight since.

* * *

I have always known Vervain would outlast me. She is, after all, not an actual living raven, but a construct of one, a being built of love and hope and magic. She will go on forever. She will never be moss or beetles or snow.

Which is, of course, the problem. It's not enough that she is trying so desperately to keep me alive. It's not enough for me to stay. I must find her someone else to love and protect, someone young enough to give her purpose for a long time.

If I had ever had a child, that would be the easy choice. Or even siblings with nieces. But I am an only child, and I never craved being a mother. There has only ever been the two of us.

From her perch on my knee, Vervain ruffles her feathers open and digs her beak into the in-between spaces.

"Shall we read?" I ask. It's a stalling tactic, and she knows it. But she loves stories of far-away places and creatures she has never seen, loves to hear me do the voices. It is how we spend our nights now, although I don't reveal to her that I can barely see the words anymore, that I know them only because I have memorized them over the tellings.

"No," she says, unmoved by my offer. If there is one thing we share, the two of us, it is a stubbornness to our purpose. I wonder if my father knew this when he made her, or if we have become each other across the years. Or if it matters at all. But this is where my mind goes these days, musings toward those who are long dead, who left me and this bird as their accidental too-long legacy.

"Shall we roast nuts before we go?" I brush the soft curve of her head to show her I am teasing, so that she doesn't get her feathers in a ruffle. She dips her beak into the curve of my palm, opens and closes it in the gentlest of kisses. "I'd be up already if you weren't sitting on me, bird."

"Celese," she says, and it's not quite a reprimand, but she flutters away to alight on the back of a chair.

I push back the quilt and ask my body and my brain to do the things they do not wish to do, and find there is no magic there. Just will and determination and those, too, run empty. No amount of asking magic will fill those and I do not know what happens when they are gone.

* * *

The second time Vervain saved my life I was a teenager, stupid and wild. Trying to find my body's edges in the danger and the dark. I met an older boy who scared me, as much wolf as man, and still I believed my power exceeded his. I let my hands linger and tease, my voice a promise I did not yet know I could not fulfill. We went into the darkness, him behind me, and I thought, again, that I was the one in charge.

Vervain was less watchful then. Perhaps she had thought her duties would wane as I grew into an adult. Or perhaps I had not yet given her reason to stay close. She let me go down the path into the shadows, and it wasn't until I screamed that she came, a flurry of feathers and talons, a caw of beak that echoed my own bone break.

She blamed herself, though I told her again and again that it was not her fault. It was mine. Although I know now that was not true either—it was his fault, in the end. His fault and the fault of his fathers, who did not teach him better.

Vervain stayed beside me as I healed and I promised her I would never go anywhere without her again.

* * *

It takes me ages to get ready. Vervain is nervous that we will miss the day, that dark will be upon us and I will use it as an excuse not to go. She attempts to hide her impatience by flitting from bed to windowsill to the edge of her nest in tiny bursts of wings and energy.

Outside, the drifts are deeper than I realized, but already beginning to melt, the tops crusted with frozen water. And still, snow drifts down around us like sifted sugar. Time has compressed, a spine sinking beneath its years, and I suddenly can't remember the last time I walked this path toward the woods. Surely it wasn't last year at this time? Surely not that long?

In the forest, I touch the trees I recognize, say hello. Step around the small hole of the rabbit den, those long tracks in the white. Vervain, to hide her nerves, I suspect, pecks at a branch of snow-bent rosehips, crimson drops in the process of forever falling.

There is so much magic here for the asking, and once I would have been overjoyed by the possibilities. I might have asked the snow to open itself before me, asked the rabbit to be unafraid so that I might check on her winter babies, asked the rosehips to lift themselves toward the sun for another year. Instead, I am this tiny crocus, head crushed by snow and an accidental footstep, dreaming of returning to the soil.

"Nearly there!" Vervain calls as she rises up, does a circle in the sky, returns to me.

"Nearly there," I repeat in a huff of breath that does not feel at all warm leaving my mouth.

* * *

The second time I tried to die, I tried to talk to Vervain. Explain. Persuade. Convince. Beg. Plead. Coerce.

"Please," I said. "I am ready to go."

"No," she said, again and again, pecking at the word like it was a seed she wished to break forever. "I am made to protect you."

It didn't take long to realize the futility of my words, to understand that I was attempting to unwind the very essence of her. An impossible task, even for an asking witch like me.

That year, we barely made it to the woods before dark, and she watched me every moment, her eyes dark with something that I could not begin to guess at.

* * *

The hemlock is scarce this spring, only a few handfuls. It's not nearly enough and for a long moment, I am filled with relief, like the drowsy well-being after a long nap full of good dreams. Perhaps this year...

Then Vervain says, "Here," and digs with her tiny raven feet and there's another young growth beneath the snow.

I do not let my disappointment show on my face. I pile the hemlock all together and wrap the stems like a bouquet, my gloved hands too numb not to crush the fronds. This fresh, the hemlock would kill me whether I asked it to or not. It needs time to settle into itself, to become open to other possibilities of what it could be.

The snow has stopped and for a moment there is stillness in the forest, a hush of things turning in their sleep. I break off a dead branch from a nearby tree and its crack is a thunder through the quiet. Vervain cocks her head at me. "My knee," I say.

We begin to retrace our steps, Vervain perched upon my shoulder, her weight a counterbalance and a comfort. My stick slips off balance, and I right myself, but not before I've blown up a puff of snow.

"Oh," Vervain says. She takes off in a batter of wings and swoops low over my head, landing to the side of the trail in the freshly shifted snow, shaking her tail feathers the way she does when she is most pleased. "Look."

I do. In the dim light, my failing eyes first register what she's found as a snake of gold slithering into the snow. And then I realize it's a length of jewelry.

Vervain uses her beak and lifts it from the snow with the kind of reverence she reserves for the best of things—fresh corn from the field, a book being read to her by firelight, me.

It's a necklace. Expensive and still shined gold despite the weather. It's broken, links separated by force, but it still bears its single charm: the head of a wolf wrought in gold with a single ruby eye.

Magicked to protect its wearer, but the ruby eye has cracked. It's done its duty well, but could only do it once. I could ask it to become whole again, but I suspect I should not. There is a story here, in its brokenness, and it would not do to end it without hearing it first.

* * *

The third time I tried to die, I made a plan in secret. Only in my head because otherwise Vervain would know, and even then I thought she might sense it. Those long winter months before the first thaw I stoked the fire and roasted corn upon the flames and read Vervain's favorite stories to her over and over in the flickering light.

Meanwhile in my head, I planned.

Because everything that saves also kills, if you know how to ask it properly. Even birds crafted with love and care.

The last night of winter, I could smell the thaw coming. When Vervain came to me and rested upon my lap, spreading her wings to ask for gentle stroking in the softest place along her back, I knew it was time.

* * *

Vervain flies and flies, tighter and tighter circles, the necklace winking off what little light still remains, until she finds what she is seeking. Then she comes back and alights up on my shoulder. She allows me to hold the necklace so she can speak—it is searing cold from the snow and the sky, but I can feel the magic it had once, biting into my skin.

"We can go?" Her beak already pointing the direction we must travel, through the highest of drifts. My knees sigh at the prospect, my barely-there toes wiggle in protest.

"Of course," I say. She asks for so few things. For shinies and stories and for me to stay alive and now for this.

The trees become their shadow selves as we go. I do not say darkness is about to fall. I do not say it has surely been years since I last felt my toes or fingers. I do not say what I truly hope, that we will walk so long we will walk straight into my resting place, finally, a hollow in the snow where I may sink.

Instead, we go until we find what Vervain seeks: the charm's former owner.

* * *

In the end, I couldn't ask a dark bird of life to bring about my death. Of course I couldn't and I felt foolish and stupid for even thinking that I might be able to. But we all hold these ideas of ourselves, don't we? These beautiful, dark promises of who we might become.

Instead, I sent word to everyone I knew, which wasn't as many people as before. So many had already gone to moss, or moved away, or lost touch. I thought I might find Vervain someone new to watch over. I asked them all, "Do you know of a child with magic? A niece, perhaps? A friend's baby? Even someone older, maybe?"

No one did. Children born with magic have grown rarer and rarer, as if even they are running as fast as they can toward extinction.

That night, I read Vervain her favorite story in the dying light with my dying eyes and I crawled into bed and I ached in all the places that one can. And the next morning, we rose once again and went into the snow and the woods.

* * *

It's a girl, barely a teen, curled into the hollow of an ancient tree as much as she will fit, which is mostly. It is a big tree and she is a small girl. Her whole being shivers, a constant low movement that shakes the topmost layer of snow from the crimson cloak she has wrapped herself in. Her dark curls drag wetly down her face and there is blood, too. Her nose, her face.

She does not look up when we approach, but shrinks instinctively back, farther into the open trunk. That she is alive at all surprises me, but it also makes sense. Surely Vervain knows she is putting me in danger coming here. She would not come for anything less than life.

But there is death here, too. Nearby, the body of a man rests still and silent upon the crust of snow. There is no mark on him, save a few long scratches upon one cheek. You could be convinced they are from briers as long as you didn't look to see the blood beneath the girl's nails. He looks almost peaceful, as if he has put himself down there for a long winter's nap.

When the girl turns her face up, her eyes are so pale blue they echo the shadows of the ice. It is clear what has happened—the broken necklace, the dark marks at her throat, the way she starts like a trapped kit at every sound—and so I do not ask.

"I am Celese," I say. "This is Vervain. We wish you no harm."

Vervain pulls the necklace from the shirt pocket where I tucked it. She lands next to the girl with a shiver of tail feathers and holds the necklace out, an offering of great import. For Vervain to give up a shiny thing willingly means something, and I find myself struck by it. Struck and thinking of what it might come to mean.

The girl reaches for it, but her shivers wrack her and she cannot take hold of it. Vervain hops forward and lays it gently into her open hand, then cants her head, those black eyes looking and looking.

"I killed him," the girl says, and I do not think she knows what she is saying, and I'm glad it is us who found her in this state of telling all. Who knows what might cross the minds of others, others who have not been in the dark woods with dark men. Although I do not know what to do with her now that we have found her. Night comes and home is farther away every moment.

"Where is your home?" I ask. "Your family?"

The shake of her head is nearly imperceptible. She closes her fist tight around the necklace, so tight I'm sure the edges of it are breaking the layers of her skin. "I asked him to want to die," she says, so low her voice nearly bleeds into the fall of snow. "And then he did."

"Why?" Vervain asks.

"Because I wanted to live," the girl says simply.

I bury the body of the man. It takes me ages, as everything does these days. But the frozen ground does what I ask it to do and it does what it wants to do, which is swallow things whole and keep them hidden. When it is done, there is nothing left but a wolf's ghosted shape upon the crust of snow.

I return to find Vervain telling the girl a story, one of her favorites that she has heard me tell a thousand times. She doesn't have all of the words, but she has the essence and she has the voices, and in truth, it doesn't matter, because we can both see the girl is dying.

We can both see that I am, too.

My black bird and the pale girl stare at each other a long time, and I stare at the two of them.

A plan is beginning. No, a plan has already hatched, grown feathers, and begun to fly.

* * *

The last time Vervain saves my life is in the dark of the night, at the frozen thaw of spring, in the deep wilds of the woods.

The girl's shivering has turned into something else, a bone-shattering shake that cascades the snow from the trees. A cough deep in her chest barks like a wild dog caught on a leash. Her fist around the necklace blooms bright red.

One of her eyes has grown misty, already dreaming of becoming soil and seed, loam and earth.

I let myself down into the snow next to the two of them with as much grace as I can muster, which is very little, and am grateful for the softness that catches me halfway down.

"Vervain," I say.

It's time. No sword. No shield. Just magic and truth. I pull the bouquet of hemlock from my pocket. It will be enough, just barely, for one of us. "You must choose."

"No," she says. Then, "Why?"

"You know why."

"She wants to live." She hops onto my shoulder with a flutter of wings and settles where she can crane her head around and look at me. "But I am made to protect you."

I lift my stiff and frozen hand to stroke her small, black head as best I can. "I think…maybe you are made to protect that which needs protection."

Even through the cold, I can feel the softness of her beak resting against my neck. "You don't, anymore?"

"I don't anymore," I say. And there is so much else I would say now, about a life well lived with someone who loves you so deeply and guards you so carefully, but that ache is my own and I know I must give her the space to choose.

Vervain hops down, paces between us on the snow, feathers ruffling as she considers. My face is numb with cold and my hands shake holding the hemlock bouquet, but I do not hurry her.

She casts her black eyes on me, and this time I can read everything in her gaze: love, loss, purpose, a decision.

"Okay, Celese," she says, bobbing her head again and again. "Yes."

Vervain watches close as I feed the asked hemlock to the girl. It might be too early—the hemlock is freshly picked and still holding tight to its original purpose—but she will surely die without it.

Together, we watch as her face grows still, as the cough in her chest becomes quiet through the lack of breath. Vervain presses her head to the girl's chest and mimics her heartbeat. It is too fast and too slow and then, finally, it is just right.

The girl coughs once into her hand and what comes out is not bright red but yellow green, the remnants of the hemlock doing its work. She breathes in and out a long time, as if breathing is all her body can handle, and then finally, she lifts her head. She is still bruised and battered, and her eyes are shot with blood, but when she sees Vervain, she smiles, and in that smile is her sword and the shield, her magic and her might. "Thank you," she says.

"Come," Vervain says to the girl. "We should go."

Which is when I realize that I am already going, already gone. I am leaving behind body and bone, becoming this earth and loam, this leaf, this crocus, this tiny beetle.

I am the hemlock. I am the berries. I am the snow, falling upon the head of a small black bird and the girl she protects.

The Wager

Jacey Bedford

The red squirrel felt a little smug. It had worked. She watched the new-made witch squint into the cracked sliver of mirror-glass, feel at her ears, twitch her nose, and brush the side of her mouth with a knuckle.

Sitting on the kitchen table, the squirrel wobbled and dropped to all fours, finding her tail automatically sticking out to balance her furry body. She marvelled that her spell had crammed a whole human being into this small, furry, and decidedly strange-feeling body. She ran her tongue around her mouth, suppressing the urge to gnaw on the edge of the scrubbed pine table with her long, sharp teeth. That would never do. She was a civilized squirrel, or would be when she got used to her new shape.

I wish we didn't need the money, she thought. *This is not my brightest moment.*

She inched forwards and sniffed at the witch. Whoa, her nose was much more sensitive than usual. The witch appeared perfect in all respects, even down to the musty scent of old clothes, but the change must be disorienting for her, too. How would she be feeling?

The witch was still staring into the mirror as if she could hardly believe it. She cleared her throat and touched her hat.

"P-p-pointy h-hat."

The squirrel tried to form the word, yes, but she didn't have the mouth shape for human speech any more. She nodded instead.

The witch let her gnarly fingers slide down her face. "R-r-wrinkles."

The squirrel made a wild and slightly uncoordinated leap to the witch's arm and ran up it to crouch on her shoulder. She stared at the witch in the mirror's rippled image. It had all worked exactly as planned. That surprised her. It was one of the spells she'd inherited from her late father, one he'd never used to her knowledge, at least, not in his later years when his spellcasting skills had diminished considerably, probably due to his over-fondness of hard liquor.

The squirrel continued to assess the witch.

Straggly gray hair, check.

Wart on the side of her nose, check.

Missing front tooth, check.

Sharp chin, check.

Sparse whiskers sprouting from a brown mole, check.

The squirrel looked down. Raggedy black from neck to ankles, check.

Diamond encrusted shoes peeping out from under dusty skirts.

Oops.

"Yes?" the witch asked hopefully.

Ah, if only those diamonds were real, that would solve all their financial problems. The squirrel shook her head, chittered angrily and stared at the shoes.

"Worth a try." The witch's speech was noticeably stronger, now, and the initial stammer had gone.

The witch screwed up her eyes in concentration. Her sparkly shoes turned to worn work boots with creased toes and mismatched laces. "Better? Yes?"

The squirrel settled back and gave a tiny kuk-kuk which sounded like a small dog yapping very far away.

The witch sighed. "I liked the s-sparkly. Can I—"

The squirrel bared needle-sharp teeth, which cut off that question before it was fully formed.

"Name. Need new name," the witch said. "Witchy name." She touched her right hand to her cheek and tapped her lips with her pinky finger. "Seraphina?"

The squirrel didn't respond.

"Katerina?" She shook her head. "Too like the old queen. How 'bout Jemima?"

The squirrel managed to convey a shrug, even though it was more like a head-bob.

"Jemima it is, then." The witch straightened her hat. "Now you? Need your name."

The squirrel gave her a hard stare. It had better be a good name, or else.

Jemima tried to laugh. It came out more like a squeak. She clapped her hand across her mouth, eyes wide.

It was an awful sound to sensitive ears. The squirrel raised her paws to her tufted ears, but discovered she couldn't block out the sound. She should have decided on names before relinquishing her human form, then she wouldn't be subject to Jemima's sense of humor. It was easy to have a sense of humor when you were so much bigger. Never mind. She would endure it for a day. A wager was a wager, and they needed to win if they were to pay off her father's debt. He'd owed Lady Ellandine's land agent fifty crowns for unpaid rent when he'd dropped down dead, suddenly and unexpectedly, with half a bottle of the finest rhenish un-drunk. How inconvenient of the old sot. She sighed, as much as a squirrel can sigh, which sounded more like a huffed-out breath. If she was honest she didn't miss her father. He'd been away from the beginning of spring to the end of autumn each year, doing what he called his wizarding circuit. Which meant he was drinking with old friends and performing the occasional easy spell to earn little more than his keep. When he'd come home for winter, he'd spent his days snoring in the chair, and his nights at whichever tavern would still give him credit. A very small part of her mourned the man he might have been if Mama had lived, but *what-if* didn't pay the rent.

"Nutkin?" Jemima said. She was speaking much more easily now, as if getting used to the way her mouth and throat worked.

The squirrel yanked her thoughts back to the present and showed her teeth.

"Miss Bushy-Tail?"

The squirrel managed an angry kuk-kuk-kuk.

"Peanut?"

This time the squirrel simply stared, unblinking.

"Red?"

That would do. The squirrel nodded once, ran down the witch's body and bounded purposefully towards the open door, tail out, with the twitching tip plainly saying, "Follow me." Jemima gathered up a large leather satchel, slung it over her shoulder, and followed into the early morning light.

The squirrel, Red, didn't look back.

A flea-bitten gray pony waited patiently by the cottage door, saddlebags bulging. He dropped his head to examine the squirrel, who bumped nose to nose, gave a kind of chirruping squeak, then leaped clean over the pony's long face to land between his ears. The pony threw up his head in surprise, but Red clung tenaciously. Turning once, she settled in the scrubby mane with her tail hanging down for balance, back legs draped to either side of the pony's neck and front paws hooked around the headband of the bridle.

With less elegance than the squirrel, Jemima scrambled into the saddle like a novice, felt for the stirrups, and gathered her reins. The squirrel made a squeak and the pony set off at a steady walk, out of the cottage's open gate and onto the rutted track towards town, a league hence.

The track nestled deep between hedgerows, then climbed a gentle rise into the sunshine. In the rolling fields on either side, bearded barley waved in the breeze. As they crested the last hill, the low morning sun bounced off the turrets of Lady Ellandine's castle, its pearl and pink towers rising to meet a pale blue sky streaked with cirrus clouds. It looked magical in the morning light.

The town, however, was just a town: gray-brown stone and half-timbered buildings, cobbled streets with open drains down the center flowing with water diverted from the river, taking away the detritus of a couple of thousand people living in close proximity to each other. The houses leaned across the street, jettied floors reaching out towards each other. Jemima nudged the pony to the side of the street so as to avoid the potential deluge from chamber pots being emptied, illegally, from upper windows directly into the drain. The cry of "Ware below!" rarely gave enough time to duck beneath the overhang.

Ruswarp Armitage's apothecary's shop stood on the corner of Marygate and the market square, where traders were already setting up their stalls for the day. A narrow snickleway down the side of the shop led to a walled back yard. The pony knew his way to the apothecary's stable and Jemima dismounted with a grunt and rubbed her arse with one hand.

"Good morning, mistress." A boy of about fourteen came out into the yard and took the pony's rein. "I know these here..." He patted the pony's nose and then ran a careful finger down the squirrel's head between her tufted ears, but looked slightly askance at Jemima. "But do I know 'ee?" He jumped when Red leaped from the pony's poll to the boy's shoulder and then ran down his arm and dropped to the hard-packed dirt of the yard.

"Your father will," Jemima said. "I know the way, boy."

Red ran ahead, as before, bobbing through the gap in the back door. By the time Jemima negotiated the tiny kitchen and the corridor to the shop at the front of the building, Red was already sitting on the apothecary's counter, tail bushed out.

The apothecary, Ruswarp Armitage, a heavyset man in his fifties with thinning hair and a close-cropped grizzled beard, stared at the squirrel, then looked up when Jemima entered and dumped her bags on the counter. At first his face showed puzzlement, then he nodded and began to laugh.

"Oh, you've done it. Clever."

The squirrel stared pointedly at Jemima and waved a paw impatiently.

Jemima reached into her satchel to hand Ruswarp a folded paper.

He took it, perched a pair of metal-rimmed spectacles on the end of his nose and read out loud:

To Mr. Ruswarp Armitage, Apothecary.

This is to state my acceptance of the terms of our wager.

The sum wagered: Five crowns.

The wager: That my squirrel, Climbs Like the Wind, and I will exchange places and remain in our changed forms for one full trading day, during which we will attend the Wednesday Market and carry out business as usual. The wager to be complete on returning to your premises after the market's closing bell.

My signature is my word

Susan, Witch of White Cottage

"Well, Miss Susan, this note'll do nicely," Ruswarp said, addressing the squirrel directly.

"If anyone asks, her name is Red, and mine is Jemima," the witch said.

Red nodded to emphasise the new names.

"Red and Jemima," Ruswarp said. "Until after the market closes, at least."

"That was the wager." Jamima set the satchel down on the counter. "Will I pass?"

"Oh, aye, indeed. You look like a perfect witch. But if she looks like you..." He beetled his brows, "Why don't you look like her?"

"An experiment. You yourself said she'd sell more potions if she looked like people expected a witch to look, and the change was not so difficult once the main transformation had been achieved."

"I did say that, aye." Ruswarp took off his spectacles and folded them carefully into a small leather case. "I'll get our Tommy and Nate to bring your usual trestle and set it up. I expect you to sell out of potions and lotions. Speaking of which, you've brought my order?"

"Oh yes, now, which bag is it in?"

Red tapped one of the saddle bags with a delicate front paw.

"Ah, right, so it is. Thank you, Red," Jemima said with exaggerated politeness.

Squeak.

Jemima handed the small package over. Ruswarp took it without checking the contents and popped it under the counter before emerging into the body of the shop. He unlocked the front door, ready for the day's customers, and held it open for the witch and her familiar.

"Good luck to you...both," he called after them as Jemima headed across to the market square, with the squirrel sitting on her shoulder.

Tommy, the boy who'd taken their pony into the apothecary's stable, and Nate, a skinny little thing maybe a year shy of eleven, trotted past with a wooden board and the trestle legs to support it balanced on a hand-cart. By the time Jemima arrived, they'd erected the table and positioned it about six feet from the nearest neighbor, a dumpy woman selling brown-glazed terracotta dishes and beakers. Jemima nodded a thanks to the boys and took a small bundle of green silk from her satchel. She tossed it on to the table. Released from captivity, it blossomed to cover the whole table.

Red leaped up on to the table and, as Jemima unpacked bottles, vials, and packets of dried herbs and powders from the bags, she patted items into place with deft paws. The stall was set up in time for the market bell to ring to open the day's trading.

All good, so far, Red thought. If their luck held, they'd have good takings today and an extra five crowns from Ruswarp to add to their savings. If the land agent would let them pay in instalments, they could stave off eviction from the cottage for a little longer and clear the rent arrears in a few months.

Soon the crowds began to gather. Some people arrived early, hunting for the best bargains, others headed for a particular stall, bought what they'd come for, and marched off. The really annoying ones ambled around, picking goods up, putting them down again without the slightest intention of buying.

The potter, a middle-aged woman who looked as though she was made out of cushions beneath her loose-fitting dress, watched one of the amblers put a pot down in the wrong place, and pointedly rearranged it. She folded her arms, sidled up to Jemima, and said in a tone that was meant to carry to another idler, "It's a three-pee day today, love: pick up, put down, and piss off. That's all they're doing. I haven't seen you before, have I?"

"No, I usually send my assistant."

"Pretty little girl with fair curls?"

"Susan, yes."

Jemima edged away. Red approved. Jemina didn't have a lot of practice at talking to people.

The potter wasn't put off by Jemima's reluctance to chat. She nodded to the empty space on the far side of Jemima's stall. "He's late."

"Who?" Jemima asked.

"New fellow. The market-master said old Billow had given up his pitch to a new man. Calls himself The Great Adeeno, but between you and me his real name is Cuthbert Sidebottom. I stand Sawby Market on a Friday and his auntie has a butcher's stall. Best fat-back bacon this side of the moor, and she knows a lot about everything."

"You mean she's a gossip?"

"The best. She told me he'd negotiated for Billow's pitch."

"What does this Great Adeeno sell?"

"Magic spells and potions. It's all rubbish if you ask me. His auntie says he doesn't have a magic bone in his body, but he talks a good talk."

Red hoped he wasn't a true magician, or he might see through her and Jemima swapping forms. The potter hadn't noticed anything strange about them, but an experienced magic-user might.

A customer hovered by the potter's basket of seconds, taking her attention.

"You hear that, Red?" Jemima muttered. "Sounds like we have competition."

Red chittered very softly, took up position on the back corner of the table and sat, tail fluffed out, watching passers-by intently. When one picked up an item, put it down, picked up another, and another, the squirrel would suffer the timewaster for only so long before standing and barking kuk-kuk-kuk in her throat, intent clear. But when someone asked timidly if there was a potion to cure insomnia and bring kindly dreams, Red stepped carefully over the assembled goods and patted a potion with one paw, then retreated to the corner again. Jemima smiled her best gap-toothed smile and took the money, muttering kindly words as she pressed the bottle into the customer's hands with a heartfelt blessing.

The Abbey church bell rang Terce some time after trading had begun. There was a commotion on the edge of the market place, and a striking figure pushed his way through the crowd. He wore a surcoat of midnight blue velvet and a matching soft hat with gold braid around the rim. Beneath the surcoat he wore a bulky doublet that might have been made for a man two sizes larger, and close-fitting hose which might have better fitted a man two sizes smaller. Red chittered loudly as he took up position in the empty space next door.

A skinny boy of nine or ten arrived, panting, with a rolled rug, and spread it on the cobbles with a flourish. An older man hefted a wooden chair with polished arms, obviously meant to resemble a throne. A third man set up an easel with a painted board covered in astrological symbols, and a fourth brought a polished mahogany box with a brass clasp and set it on a folding frame at table height. The Great Adeeno, for it could be no one else, nodded his approval and waved the servants away, all but the boy who'd brought the carpet, who stood like a little statue behind Adeeno's chair.

"I don't know that one." The potter sidled up to Jemima again and nodded at the boy. "But the other three are just muscle for hire, employed by the hour or, in Adeeno's case, probably the half-hour. He's not rich enough to employ four servants, it's all show. He's all codpiece and no braies."

Red made a noise that was half yowl and half growl. The best she could do for a chuckle

Within the hour Jemima had sold half a dozen remedies to five women of varying ages, and to one old man. She had accrued the princely sum of four shillings and nine copper pennies. Her customers gave the Great Adeeno a sideways glance and avoided looking him in the eye. They stood at Jemima's stall with their backs half-turned towards the newcomer. Only one of them, the oldest of the women, said, "He looks as though he'll be a bit expensive and, well, you know, probably not sympathetic to women's troubles."

Red patted a small pot of cream. Jemima handed it over and took the proffered pennies.

A runner for the roast pig stand came around all the stalls before the noon bell, taking orders for nuncheon. Jemima paid up for hot roast pig on a trencher, and the boy promised to return before the hour was out. The Great Adeeno didn't order and sent the boy away with a harsh word.

"No need for that," the potter said quietly. "The lad's only doing his job. It wouldn't surprise me if the fellow didn't have a penny to his name."

Red squeaked.

"You know what I'm saying little squirrel, don't you?"

The squirrel nodded.

Before the roast pig boy returned, the crowds in the market parted to let though a bustling, well-dressed man, short in stature and pigeon-chested, attended by a single herald and four palace guards in deep burgundy livery, armed with swords and carrying pikes.

"Make way for the Lord Chamberlain," the herald cried, and everyone did. The Lord Chamberlain paused in front of Jemima's table, glanced at the packets, bottles, and phials. He looked up and studied Jemima with the air of a man who had just had a servant scrape something smelly off his shoe. Then his eyes slid to the Great Adeeno. He pursed his lips and looked from Jemima to Adeeno and back again.

He stood in the no-man's-land between the two stalls and said to the air, "Something for ladies' troubles?"

Red was reaching a paw to pat the willow-bark powder when Adeeno stepped forward, took the Lord Chamberlain by the sleeve, and led him onto the carpet, to the mahogany box. "Sir, I have just the thing, but the remedy is not cheap, infused as it is with my own special magical talent." He lowered his voice for privacy, to the point Red couldn't hear him.

Talent, indeed, Red had detected not a whisker of magic in the man, yet the Chamberlain had immediately been drawn to all his show. How like a man to turn to another man for women's troubles. Red was annoyed by fancy doctors putting on airs and graces and attending women in childbirth when they hardly dare touch a woman's nethers. And yet the wealthy looked down on common midwives who had years of experience and didn't mind getting their hands bloody when the need arose.

She ran down the table leg and crept around the side of Adeeno's stall in time to see him take a bottle of something dark from his mahogany box and press it into the Lord Chamberlain's hand. "Fifteen crowns for this, good sir, and cheap at twice the price. It will give the Lady's daughter some relief. Trust me on this." Then with a flourish he drew out a second, smaller bottle. "And this, good sir, is just the very thing for a young lady's monthly cramps. It's rare, though, so thirty crowns. But if that's too much—" He began to put the bottle back into the box.

"No. No. Not at all." The Lord Chamberlain put out his hand. Adeeno duly delivered the bottle.

The Lord Chamberlain took the stopper from the first bottle and sniffed. Red's sensitive nose caught a whiff reminiscent of sweet coffee. She yowled. That was exactly the thing to exacerbate menstrual cramps.

Then the Lord Chamberlain took the stopper from the smaller bottle. Another sniff revealed a minty overtone. Red stiffened. That aroma was oil of pennyroyal. Just a small teaspoon of the stuff was very dangerous, deadly even. Pennyroyal tea in small quantities was fine, but not the oil. Never the oil.

Squeak! Squeak!

Red scampered back to Jemima, leaped up onto the table, and chittered for attention as the Lord Chamberlain and his entourage marched away.

"Is your squirrel all right?" the potter asked.

Red chittered, louder this time and more insistent.

"I don't know," Jemima said. Then she looked directly at Red and, eyebrows raised, said again, "I don't know."

Red looked to Adeeno's stall, where he was pocketing the crowns. Forty-five crowns! In one transaction he'd done better than she'd ever done in a whole day's trading. But it was wrong, and there was no way to tell Jemima or anyone. Damn this wager.

Adeeno smirked at Jemima and patted down his fine robe before closing the lid on his box of potions. "It's all about image, old crone," he said, and with that he snapped his fingers at his boy-servant who promptly rolled up the carpet. They left the chair where it was and went.

The potter sniffed. "Chair must have been rented," she said. "Wonder why he's gone so early?"

Gone before they discover he's a fraud. Red paced up and down the length of the table, tail quivering, then sat and chittered at Jemima.

A customer arrived at this inopportune moment, and then another, taking Jemima's attention.

Red continued to pace and chitter.

"I don't know what you're trying to tell me," Jemima said. "We should have figured this speech thing out ahead of time."

Squeak!

"Do you always talk to your squirrel?" The potter asked, offering Jemima half a slab of raisin-heavy journeycake.

Jemima nibbled at the journeycake with her front teeth, taking her time with each crumb.

Red ran up and down the table agitatedly. That potion could kill the Lady's daughter. Dammit, they'd only needed willow bark and a warm wheat-bag. It didn't take magic to ease women's pains, just a bit of common sense. Red jumped up on Jemima's shoulder and then on to the top of her head, perching upright to see if she could see the departing Lord Chamberlain, but he was long gone. What could she do?

She ran down the table leg, then back and forth several times. Eventually she ran up Jemima's body and chittered directly into her ear. Dropping to the table she looked pointedly towards the latrines. There was nothing for it, they would have to swap back into their own bodies. Wager be damned. There was a life on the line.

"Oh, I get it," Jemima said. She turned to the potter. "Will you keep an eye on my things? Call of nature."

"Surely," the potter said.

Red set off, and Jemima turned to follow, when there was a commotion at the castle end of the marketplace. Eight soldiers, marching in smart formation, headed for Jemima's stall.

"You there, halt!" the guard captain said to the potter. "Are you the potion seller?"

The potter shook her head and pointed at Jemima, mouthing, "Sorry."

"Arrest the witch," the captain said.

Jemima stood, frozen to the spot.

"What's she supposed to have done?" the potter asked.

"Tried to murder Lady Ellandine's daughter."

The soldier moved quickly, but so did Red. The squirrel leaped on to Jemima's shoulder, chittering and kuk-kukking at the guard captain. He was having none of it. He swiped a mailed fist with such force that Red flew through the air and landed on the cobbles twelve feet away.

She could hear Jemima sobbing as they dragged her away, her sobs sounding more like kuk-kuk-kuks than actual human sobs.

Blast-it. In her panic she was reverting to squirrel in her head.

* * *

Red's ribs hurt. She tried to wriggle but the potter had her firmly wrapped in a shawl and was holding her tight as if she'd never let go.

"Poor little thing. Hold still. You might have hurt something inside."

Never mind that. The castle guards had Jemima. Poor innocent Jemima who didn't know what had happened, and who wouldn't be able to defend herself against any accusations.

Red needed to follow. And quickly.

She relaxed in the potter's arms and curled up, pretending to sleep.

"There's a good squirrel," the potter said, and settled Red down in one of the baskets she'd brought her pots to market in. A potential customer started to pick up a couple of stoneware beakers and compare one to the other.

Red heard the woman ask, "Will these hold hot tea?" and the potter started to explain that they'd been fired in a kiln, so hot tea was no problem. Red wriggled and shuffled until the shawl worked loose and then, as the woman was handing a sixpence over to the potter, she slipped from the basket and set off for the castle gate at a bounding run. Where would they have taken Jemima?

Squirrels were popular pets amongst court ladies, but farmers regarded wild ones as vermin. It wasn't like she was a cat. Cats could go anywhere. It was worth a try, though. *Just walk in past the guards as if you own the place,* Red told herself.

She kept to the shadow of the wall and approached the gatehouse's drum towers. The portcullis was raised and there was a guardsman on either side of the opening. The entrance was through a barbican, forty feet of killing ground with holes in the roof, through which boiling oil or hot sand could be poured on to hapless invaders, or arrows could be loosed, or even newfangled muskets fired if the shooter wanted to risk getting his hand blown off by the unreliable mechanism. Red had once had to amputate a soldier's hand for that very reason. She wasn't a squirrel, then, of course.

Swapping places with her familiar in order to win a five-crown wager had seemed like a simple thing. She could still direct everything, or so she'd thought.

Dammit, this had been a stupid idea. It had all been going so well until Adeeno showed up. Oil of pennyroyal! Had he prescribed it because he knew no better, or had he been up to deadly mischief? Was he an idiot con-man, or an assassin?

No one could have known the Chamberlain would arrive with such a request, so con-man with no scruples and even less knowledge was probably the answer. Hopefully someone had noticed the pennyroyal before the poor child swallowed it. The guard did say *tried to murder*, not *murdered*.

Red managed to walk, stop-start, behind the nearest guard and into the cool depths of the barbican. The far end of the stone-walled tunnel was protected by another portcullis, also raised, and another pair of guards. One of them was more alert than the guards at the front of the gatehouse had been.

"Get out of it." He stamped his big boot in front of Red's face. She turned and fled before she got a kick in her poor bruised ribs.

She ran between the outer guards and retreated towards the market once more, heart thumping. She tucked herself into a pile of rubbish and watched the comings and goings. The guards challenged everyone, asking their business, or saluting if it was someone of higher rank. She missed an opportunity when a cart full of logs passed through, but then was glad she had when the guards pulled off the tarred canvas and poked amongst the logs with the tips of their swords.

Several more people entered the castle, and some came out again. Red saw no opportunity to slip by the guards. Maybe they were extra alert because they thought someone else might try to murder Lady Ellandine's daughter.

A surge of brown caught her attention, cruising through the market crowd like a ship in full sail.

Friars! Four of them in plain brown habits walked two by two. They halted at the outer gate, but the guard greeted the older of the two leading monks by name. Brother Anselm muttered a short blessing and all four moved on, in step. Red made a dash and tucked herself between the swirling hems of the two hindmost, keeping close as they walked beneath the murder holes and under the second portcullis.

The castle's outer ward was thronged with people, most of them looking as though they had jobs to do, but a few standing around gossiping. Red hesitated, dropped back, and the friars walked on, oblivious. She bounded out from under a set of hooves as big as soup plates and dodged around a pair of booted feet.

Red could see very little from down here. The world was all slick cobbles, heavy boots, women's skirts, cartwheels, iron-shod hooves, slopping buckets, wisps of straw, a barefoot boy with a broom. She vowed never to grumble about being barely five feet tall again.

"Squirl." A small child reached for her, but was pulled along by a woman, mother or nursemaid. Red began to have a lot more respect for squirrels in general. How on earth did they manage to survive? Everything seemed designed to inflict injury. Oh, for a nice serene tree. Dammit she was even thinking like a squirrel, now.

She desperately hoped she wouldn't encounter a dog. She edged past the gossiping women and would have carried on, but caught the words, "A witch tried to murder Lady Ellandine's daughter. They've got her o'course. Finest guards this side o' York."

Red scurried around behind the hem of one of the women. It was gray and none too clean, but with luck the women wouldn't notice her.

"My Robert's wife's brother's son is in the palace guard. I had it direct from him to his pa, his pa to his sister, and from her mouth to my ear. First to know, I am."

"Is there going to be a trial?" the owner of the dusty brown hem asked.

"Foregone conclusion, I reckon," the woman with the dark green hem said. "Hang her for sure. Apparently, she's not said one word. Just makes little barking noises. Mad, I expect. Magic makes you mad, I heard."

Got the witch. Hang her. That didn't sound good. Surely there'd be a trial? Red's little heart raced in her chest. Did Lady Ellandine's castle have a dungeon? Where would it be?

Red circled around the outer ward. Against the inside of the stout wall were stables, a blacksmith's workshop, and assorted buildings that might have been single-roomed houses or longer barracks. The smell of cooking came from one. By the door, a mangy dog chewed at what might have been a kitchen scrap. Dog! Red's first instinct was to turn and run, but the dog only snarled, not willing to leave its prize to chase her.

She came to an entrance to the inner ward, this one up a dozen steps worn by the passing of many feet. There was nothing out here; she was going to have to risk going in there. The steps led to an arch with grooves either side for another portcullis. Two guards were on duty. Where were friars when you needed them?

A loud bark startled her. A broad-chested dog with serious square jowls hurtled in her direction. She didn't even think about it, just let instinct take over. She leaped for the gateway and ran straight up the nearest guard, the dog's jaws snapping at her tail. The guard jumped in surprise and tried to brush her off, but the dog was on him. Shouts, barks, growls. More shouts and a yelp as the guard's boot hit the dog's chest. Red leaped for the cobbles, streaked under the archway, and across the shady inner courtyard dominated by a tall yew tree, glad there were no magical wards in place. She leaped for the trunk and climbed nimbly up to the lowest branch, flattening herself to make a small target. She wasn't sure what had happened to the dog, but she couldn't see it, and the guards didn't seem bothered about a stray squirrel.

She wasn't sure how long she stayed there while her pounding heart steadied. This inner courtyard, completely enclosed by stone buildings on all four sides, was less busy than the outer one. No horses for starters, and no dogs that she could see. There was an external stone stair leading up to the great hall on the upper floor of the range to the left of the gate-arch. A door beneath likely led to storerooms. Opposite the gate-arch there were domestic apartments. A neatly-dressed lady with a small child sat on a wooden bench beside an open door. The lady stitched at a piece of linen while the child danced two tiny wooden dolls across the flagstones.

By the smell and the activity, the building across from the great hall was a kitchen. And the range of buildings on the fourth side, through which the entrance archway cleaved, looked to be guard rooms. Red could hear voices, but not make out speech.

Perhaps Jemima was in there.

Red stayed as still as she could and watched as people came and went. She began to make out patterns of movement, but there was still no clue as to where Jemima might be. The castle seemed to have swallowed her up completely. Maybe she wasn't even in the inner court.

Then, at last, a clue. The Lord Chamberlain, he who had paid so many crowns for a potion that could have killed Lady Ellandine's daughter, emerged from the domestic apartments and hailed a guard captain who attended him with some deference and, after a short conversation, called over a bullish-looking soldier and sent him through a narrow door in the corner, by the archway entrance. The door began to swing shut behind him. Red took her chance. She ran out along the yew branch, dropped to the top of the great hall stair, ran down, and squeaked through the closing door, almost losing a few tail hairs.

She was in a storeroom, with crates and barrels pushed up against the walls. The bullish man took up a position by an arch that led to steps descending into darkness. A lantern on the wall above and behind him cast a weak light across the floor. Red settled down in the shadow between two barrels and studied the guard. He looked tough in leather body-armor, a pudding basin helmet, and stout woollen trousers. He was armed with a short sword and had an all-purpose knife tucked into his belt. A pike rested against the wall, within easy reach.

He didn't look like anyone who would stand for any nonsense.

She waited and watched. After an hour, or maybe more, he began to fidget, shifting from one foot to the other and glancing towards the door as if waiting for someone to arrive. Ah, Red interpreted the movements, maybe he was regretting that last cup of small beer at noon-tide. The man needed the jakes.

Another ten minutes passed, and still no one came to relieve him. Red reckoned relieve might be the important word. Another ten minutes and the guard stepped across the storeroom to a narrow door in what was likely the outer wall of the castle. Behind the door was a garderobe. The man fumbled with the laces on his trousers, presented himself to the hole in the wooden seat and sighed as piss flowed like a small waterfall. Apart from one brief glance to orient himself over the hole, he kept looking over his shoulder, ever vigilant. Damn.

With a sigh, he finished what he was doing, and just for a few seconds looked down to tie his laces. Red took the opportunity and bounded across the middle of the floor and through the archway. The stairs were narrow. It was immediately obvious that there was no other guard down there. It was simply a hole with a small area at the bottom of the steps and an iron-barred door enclosing a cell that was barely six feet by four. Red blinked. There was only a faint glow from the lantern upstairs, but she could just make out Jemima sitting slumped on a pile of straw on the floor making kuk-kuk noises in the back of her throat.

She sat by the bars and gave the smallest chitter. Jemima twisted to her knees instantly, pushing against the bars and reaching through to touch Red with a little gasp and a muffled cry.

Red tried the bars for size. She could squeeze through them. Through and back again.

"Change back?" Jemima whispered.

"Kuk-kuk."

Jemima reached through the bars. Red touched her hand with an outstretched paw, then leaned over and bit into Jemima's soft palm with her sharp front teeth. Jemima winced, but didn't cry out. The guard was too close and would be able to hear the slightest sound echoing around the stone walls.

Red tasted blood. Jemima squeezed her paw hard, too hard. Then, where paw met hand, the change began. Red's tiny squirrel hand extended and Jemima's hand shrank to a paw. Sharp squirrel teeth bit into Red's now human hand and blood flowed. Magic swirled around their joined flesh and fur. The change happened instantly, bones and flesh compressing for one and expanding for the other until a small red squirrel sat inside the prison cell and a young, blonde girl lay on the narrow strip of floor between the bars and the bottom step. The squirrel, formerly Jemima the witch, slipped out from between the bars and the young witch, formerly the squirrel, sat up carefully and rubbed her bleeding hand.

Susan. She was Susan, not Red. She felt so big and clumsy.

She put a finger to her lips and pointed up the steps. The squirrel, Climbs-Like-The-Wind, sat on the bottom step and began to smooth her whiskers.

How were they going to get past the guard and out of the castle?

They needed to either get rid of the guard or render him insensible. It was too much to hope that he would make another trip to the jakes. Besides, the jakes was their way out, or at least it was the squirrel's. They couldn't both get out that way.

Susan took a deep breath and pulled together the shreds of her regained identity. She tugged at a blonde ringlet. "I guess we've lost the wager," she whispered, "but better to get out of here in one piece."

Climbs-Like chirped quietly.

"Top of the steps and to your left there's the jakes. Door was ajar when last I saw. You'll have to climb down the channel in the outer wall. It won't be pleasant. Wait for me at Ruswarp's shop."

The squirrel didn't like that idea.

"I know, I know, but someone has to sort out this mess, otherwise Lady Ellandine's guard will be at our door. We can't just disappear. The market-master knows where we live. We're in danger of losing the cottage as it is. Let's not make it any worse."

Climbs-Like chittered.

"Yes, I know. How the Lord Chamberlain can let his guards arrest a woman when clearly he dealt with a man is a mystery to me, too. It's obviously mistaken identity."

Climbs-Like's chittering calmed down.

"I'll cause a fuss. When the guard comes down, you make a run for it. Now, go!"

Susan began to scream, and the squirrel made a dash for the steps as the guard clomped down.

"What? Who? Where's the crone?" The guard held the lantern above his head.

"She's gone. I'm her assistant, here to explain. Please take me to Lady Ellandine."

It didn't take long before Susan was brought before not only Lady Ellandine, but her Chamberlain as well, together with the bullish soldier and the guard captain. The bullish soldier gripped her elbow tightly to the point of pain and shoved her forward to stand before the Lady.

"What have you to say, child?" Lady Ellandine, every inch the ruler of this province in deep blue velvet, sounded stern.

Susan tried not to let her voice shake. "It wasn't my mistress, Lady. Your Chamberlain bought the potions from a man. Can he not tell the difference between a man and a woman?"

Lady Ellandine swivelled around to the Chamberlain, who looked to the guard captain. "I said to arrest the man who sold me the potions."

The guard captain looked to the Lady, obviously not willing to take the blame. "He told me to arrest the potion seller. He didn't say whether it was a man or a woman."

"The man you want calls himself The Great Adeeno," Susan said. "His real name is Cuthbert Sidebottom. His auntie has a butcher's stall on Sawby Market."

Lady Ellandine looked to the captain. "Go! And don't come back without him."

The captain bowed, spun on his heel, and marched out, taking the bullish soldier.

"You may leave." Lady Ellandine said to Susan.

Susan rubbed her elbow where the soldier's grip had likely left a bruise.

"Well, what are you waiting for?"

"I don't believe there was any malice behind the potions Adeeno sold, my lady. He was a fraudster who knew no better. He had just enough knowledge to be dangerous. He might deserve some time behind bars, but not a short swing on the end of a rope."

"I will decide that."

Susan nodded. "Your daughter's troubles can be easily eased. Let me send something to soothe her bellyache."

"How do I know I can trust you?"

"You know where we live, my lady, or at least your land agent does."

"And how much will you charge for your magic?" the Lord Chamberlain asked.

"Not magic, my lord. It doesn't take magic to make willow bark tea. Your own kitchen staff could brew it, but..." She swallowed hard. "For the inconvenience of locking up my mistress and her losing a day's trading, not to mention me telling you how to find the real miscreant..."

"Yes?"

Susan turned to Lady Ellandine. "Fifty-five crowns, my lady, though only five in coin. The rest to cancel my late father's debt for the rent arrears on our cottage."

* * *

"So, the Chamberlain was very embarrassed. He and the guard captain blamed each other." Susan put her nearly empty wine cup down on Ruswarp's kitchen table.

Climbs-Like chittered.

"Yes, dear friend, I know you tried to tell them, but you were reverting to squirrel in your head, and Lady Ellandine's guard didn't understand kuk-kuk-kuk."

"So, you sorted it out." Ruswarp topped up her wine cup.

Ruswarp's boys entered the kitchen, pushing and shoving each other to be the first with the news.

"Did you deliver Miss Susan's package?" Ruswarp asked.

"Aye, Dada," Tommy, the fourteen-year-old said. But before he could take a breath to say more, little Nate piped up, "And they gave us a purse to give to you, Miss Susan."

"A purse," Tommy said, "that clinks like gold crowns."

"We didn't look, of course," Nate said, eyes not meeting hers, suggesting that he might have taken the tiniest peek.

Susan laughed and held out her hand for the purse. Yes, definitely gold. She opened it up. Ten crowns rather than five, and a note to say her rent arrears had been cancelled.

"That's a lot for willowbark tea," Ruswarp said.

"And for the inconvenience of my mistress, the crone, being arrested by accident," Susan said. "I'm glad they didn't want to interview her in person."

Climbs-Like kuk-kuk-kukked. It could have been a laugh, or it could have been relief.

"At least I have enough to cover my lost wager," Susan said, handing over five crowns to Ruswarp.

He scooped them up. "You might have done it if it hadn't been for that charlatan."

"Maybe. Who knows? But I think I've learned my lesson, unless..." She looked at the squirrel and back at Ruswarp, then weighed the remaining five crowns in her hand. "Unless you'd like to double your bet..."

Girl, Bot, and the 200th Goat

A. Katherine Black

This is the story of Girl and her metaly-bendy friend Bot. Girl was born on Station Grimm-7 and raised in the shadows on level Zee-Zed. She was fed out of trash bins and bathed in the wastewater, until one day her parent was taken, and then Girl was alone. Until she was not. But this story is not about where Girl came from, because Girl's circumstances had been, until very recently, far from unique. This is not a story about where they came *from*, but about where Girl and her friend Bot were going. It begins with an oddity strange enough to draw Girl out from hiding. And why would Girl take such a risk? Why would she jump from the rafters above Zee-Zed's main crossing bay, during high transit time, no less? Why drop right smack in the middle of a thick mid-day crowd of passersthru, risking a twisted ankle or, worse, a run-in with an enforcer? There were many reasons. More reasons than Girl had fingers and toes. Maybe more than Bot had metaly-bendy legs. (Girl counted twenty-six legs the first time they met.) More than all the sweetpops in all the marketstands on Grimm-7. (Girl'd often speculated about how many pops there might be, but the answer could never be known without exploring far beyond level Zee-Zed.)

A big reason Girl decided to take such a risk was the goats (soft, strange, and curiously half-clothed, Girl counted exactly one hundred and ninety-nine) who gathered and milled right under Girl's rafter perch and looked up, all of them, *right at her*, before they began to file away.

Mostly, though, Girl jumped down because Bot told her not to.

To be clear, Girl loved Bot. Loved it as much as she loved sweetpops, as much as she loved numbers. As much as she loved watching the holomaps in Zee-Zed's crossing bay and calculating endless ship routes from anywhere to everywhere.

Ever since Bot had been told by its owner to get lost, ever since it heard Girl's tapping patterns whisper across the pipes and tracked down the source of the satisfying sounds, it had been Girl's entire family. It could play number games better than anyone else, and it had all sorts of dataknow tucked into its rectangular body. It even knew what goats were, and it told her so when they appeared on level Zee-Zed. Still, Bot didn't know everything. Neither did Girl, of course.

Which was precisely why she needed a closer look.

So, immediately after Bot said, with its best stern-person voice, that it was not safe, that she should not, by any means, *under any circumstances*, approach those one hundred and ninety-nine goats, Girl slipped from her favorite rafter beam. She shimmied down one pipe, then another, and dropped two full Girl-lengths down into the middle of the busy bustle of people and goats.

As it turned out, Bot was right. And then, he was not.

Bot had been purchased, like manufactured ones usually are, to serve as teacher on a transport ship. This meant it was expected to keep children quiet while adults did various Important Things. Bot performed its job quite well, and for quite some time, until an innocent but excited child broke its holo-projector. As a result, Bot was instructed to get itself "good and lost" at the next port, so the owners could file a claim with insurance. Bot did as it was told.

But as things had been done for many a generation, just in case Bot was a rare one who eventually realized it had a choice, it was programmed to freeze all motor functions if discovered by station authorities. To freeze all motor functions, forever. This would prove Bot to be the defective bot its owners claimed it to be, and no one, not the authorities, not the owners, not the insurance company, would be put out if Bot were discovered. No one would be put out except Bot itself, of course.

Bot's motor functions were still working when the goats arrived.

It had been a typical day, at first. Girl and Bot held their normal perch, small human body and rectangular alloy shell straddling a pair of wide beams that crossed above the heads of so many passersthru. Ships docked at Zee-Zed's cheap slots. People disembarked to gather supplies or "do business" (which meant next to nothing to Girl and Bot), before climbing back through their hatches and scooting off to some other station, in some other system.

Every day since Bot had found Girl, it stretched along the rafters beside her, using many of its twenty-six legs for bracing, and craning a few free toe-cameras this way and that. It monitored the activity below, looking out for anything Girl might find interesting, and of course looking out for enforcers (with their shoulder sashes and angry postures) so it could warn Girl as needed.

Girl's spot provided an excellent view of Zee-Zed's central holo nav. Passersthru gathered at the console below, tapped in coordinates, and a star map would burst to life. Stars and planets, asteroid belts and molecular clouds filled the space, nearly to the rafters. Huge and colorful, spinning and zooming in and out, Girl found every single display beautiful. And so her days were spent, soaking in maps and imagining routes.

Bot had never met a child so attentive. Feet curled around the rim of her metal rafter beam, she watched the holo, one hand holding a few of Bot's legs, the other tapping away on the beam.

Like all the unnamed, the uncounted homeless inhabiting the rafters and subfloors of Station Grimm-7 and hundreds of other stations strung along this swath of people-infested systems, Girl communicated through tapping. Huddled in small groups, the unnamed sent each other warnings through the station by way of quiet rap-a-tap-taps, an attempt to evade the many enforcers eager to deliver them to a slow death on worklevel. The unnamed were all eventually caught; excepting the fortunate few who were not.

Like all unnamed communications, Girl's taps were quiet enough to hide within the noise and chatter below. Quiet enough to avoid an enforcer's notice. Of course, Girl's taps went way beyond the simple codes used by the rest of the hidden masses on Zee-Zed. She'd long ago taken those codes and expanded them, stretched them, overlapped them until they became something new. Balanced and beautiful, these wonderfully complex communications were entirely unique to Girl.

Bot had stopped worrying long ago about Girl attracting attention with her intricate and ever-shifting tappings. But then, one day, someone noticed after all. Not only did they notice, but they tapped right back, much to Bot's surprise. And much to Girl's surprise.

There they were, Girl and Bot, inhabiting a normal day of watching and tapping, when a mass of goats suddenly began swarming the bay.

Now Girl and Bot had definitely seen a thing-or-two over their many rafter-dwelling days, and Bot had seen even more things-or-twos when teaching on that transport ship. They'd seen people with extra limbs and people missing noses, people with mechanical parts and people sharing parts, but neither had ever seen anything quite like a goat.

The goats poured across the bay, streaming alongside some people and in-between other people, filling the gaps between clumps of passersthru, who yelped and excused themselves and tried their best not to stare, as if a great collection of hairy creatures with four legs, zero arms, stretched-out faces, and an odd smattering of miscellaneous clothing visited Grimm-7 on a regular basis.

A tapped message came just then, whispering across the pipes, warning of an enforcer raid in the subfloors clear on the other end of Zee-Zed. At that moment, somewhere down one of the long station corridors, floorboards were being ripped off and unnamed were being carted away while passersthru ignored the obvious scene better than they ignored the swirl of goats just below.

As always, Girl wondered if she knew anyone being taken at that moment, never to be seen again. She was tired of hiding. She was tired of running away. She watched the goats below and felt a wish burst within her belly like a newborn star, a wish to run *toward*. And just as this wish grew behind her wide eyes, the goats, all one hundred and ninety-nine of them, turned their faces up to the rafters and began to stomp.

Seven-hundred and ninety-six hard feet (give or take, because some people had fewer feet than others, and with goats Girl assumed it was the same) pounded at the station floorboards in what first seemed a meaningless mess, until, curiously, wonderfully, the goats' stomps began to take form. The clops of hundreds of feet gathered and swirled, layered and spaced, until they were amazingly similar to Girl's very own taps.

These goats were saying hello.

Bot's functions spun into high alert as it watched its only friend drop to the floor and walk with outstretched hands among the goats. Girl assumed all the enforcers would be busy with the raid, that she'd be okay, but Bot wasn't the type to assume. Girl's giggles danced among the regular noise of the bay, wafting up to meet Bot's microphones, as the goats gently jostled her to and fro, as her fingertips drifted across the tippy ends of their short hair. It was when the goats began to file away, toward the far end of Zee-Zed, that Bot first spotted an enforcer closing in.

The one-hundred-ninety-ninth goat finally gone, Girl seemed to shake herself awake, eyes scanning as she made her way to the closest climbing point. But it was no use. The enforcer was closing in, tracking his prize through the crowd.

Bot tapped the pipes as hard as it could, but Girl, passing through the noise of the bay's bustle, didn't seem to notice. It gave up tapping and called out in its best-disguised person voice. "Girl!" But it had to be careful. Words like "watch out" or "run" or "enforcer" were much too risky, so Bot repeated, helplessly, "Girl!" Until the enforcer was only a few steps from its best and only friend.

Girl finally noticed the reaction of passersthru, how they averted their eyes and scooted away, but it was too late. The enforcer was only a few strides away.

Girl was about to be taken away. Away from Zee-Zed and away from Bot, to be slaved to death on worklevel.

If only Bot could help. If *only*.

That was it. Bot was going to jump, right then. It *would* jump. Bouncing on all its legs, it calculated the trajectory to land squarely on the enforcer's head. *It. Would. Jump.*

But nothing happened. It couldn't. Thanks to the final order from its owner, Bot couldn't move.

Girl was brave, mouth shut and eyes narrowed, as the enforcer snatched her by the arm. She didn't look up, even a smidge, when he dragged her away, determined not to betray her best friend, her only friend, Bot.

* * *

A miniscule blip in the known universe, Grimm7 twirls in ragged disrepair above a bland planet. For those inhabiting the collection of ramshackle bubbles dubbed The Grimm, though, it was all of the universe they ever expected to see. Workers doomsmiled at passersthru popping in and out of shops and offices. Enforcers winked friendly-like at passersthru before snatching unnamed and hauling them to worklevel. The unnamed, the uncounted, watched from the shadows, meeting hushlike behind giant machines that kept the whole place stuffed with acrid, metallic smelling air. Such was the monotony of Grimm-7.

But then there were those rare times when something new arrived. When something strange and unknown docked at The Grimm to spark a curious twinkle inside its otherwise dull, gray walls. For Girl, this shiny unknown appeared that very day in the form of an odd stream of creatures. Girl and Bot watched from the rafters as the furry, many-legged spectacle poured forth, and Girl's soft voice curled around the metal beams like a dream. "Mysterythis."

Bot explained that these creatures were goats and then apologized for knowing very little about them. It had been filled with only the knowledge its owners had decided it should have, and apparently goats weren't interesting enough. By then, Bot's words had begun shifting into a warning, just before Girl began to move.

And we know how that turned out.

Which left Bot doing something no one had ever programmed it to do. It ran. Across the rafters of level Zee-Zed, using all twenty-six of its standard, bendable legs, with a speed that would have made Girl whistle.

* * *

Now, we know Girl is a watcher, and we know she's a tapper. Most of all, though, Girl is a thinker. And every time she watched an enforcer drag someone away to worklevel, she took all that fear and all that sadness and reshaped it into a plan. Enforcers, all rough and meanlike with their scarves and their tasers, pulled people from under the floors and behind the walls, and Girl would watch until a plan sprung within her mind, unfolding like the slow-mo star explosions that played on the main bay holo when no one was using the navs. Girl would examine each new plan that appeared, would shift and stretch it, would tighten it until she liked its shape, and then she'd tuck it away in a side pocket of her mind, ready for access later.

Now, it appeared, her later had come.

She'd never communicated with her feet before, but as the enforcer dragged Girl down a long corridor, pulling her arm so high she was afraid it might pop off, she had no easy way to tap. Plus, it was dangerous, tapping so close to an enforcer. If the unnamed communication method was ever discovered, it might mean the end of all of them. There would be ears and sensors laid across every metal beam on every level of The Grimm, and maybe even on other stations, as well, and the quiet community of unnamed might be silenced forever.

But a little scuff of feet here and there? That would mean nothing to an enforcer. Or so Girl hoped.

If it weren't for all the danger, if it weren't for Girl being dragged past her favorite sweetpop shop for the very last time, destined for a slow death on worklevel, she would have delighted at this new toe tapping talk the goats had introduced. She would have wanted to see those wonderful goats again, to thank them for sharing their idea. But now was not the time for delight, there were no longer any goats in sight.

Girl had to concentrate.

She had to not just tap, but she had to listen. Listen for any clinks and clanks above that might be Bot. She'd never asked Bot how it came to Zee-Zed, but every unnamed knew the kinds of programming done to bots before they were abandoned.

Despite the certain danger ahead and all the swirling unknown of the looming worklevel, Girl opened the pockets of her mind and unleashed a constellation of wonderful ideas. They overflowed, spilling out through her scuffling, tapping toes. It was her tapping that first led Bot to Girl, when no one else had recognized her thoughts translated into vibration. And now she hoped Bot would notice this new, rough, scuffy tapping of her tattered rubber soles against the hard station floor.

Final programming or not, Girl had ideas of how Bot could help.

* * *

Bot moved quickly, hopping from beam to beam, stretching from this pipe to that, all the while pointing toe-cameras down at the passerthru crowd. The enforcer, with his blue and gold striped shoulder scarf, towed Girl with a grip that bent her arm wrong at the shoulder and must have hurt. They entered the corridor where Girl and Bot often scrounged for tasty leftover scraps. Bot was determined to keep up.

It hadn't pushed its legs to their limits or climbed much of anything before it was left on The Grimm, but here it had seen other bots use their legs in curious ways, like the shop bots stretching this way and that and crawling right up the front of impressively tall shelving. Back when Bot's holo-projector had broken beyond repair, it hadn't even imagined there might be another way to be useful.

Bot eventually learned that the purposeful losing of bots was quite commonplace. After all, children couldn't be expected to experience stories only in audio. Although Girl didn't mind.

Then again, life within the shadows of The Grimm was different than life on a transport coach offering "moderately decent" accommodations. And Girl was really quite different than the children Bot had met before. She didn't interrupt. She didn't climb all over Bot. And not even once, in all their time together, did she try to pry Bot's body apart.

When Bot first found Girl, captivated by her tapping patterns that echoed across Zee-Zed, Girl had appeared to be captivated right back. She tapped at Bot's legs lightly, counting them once and counting them again. She rarely made eye contact with its cameras, though, too busy scanning the area for enforcers and watching the stellar holo-displays. And her fingers never stopped moving. They drummed on any surface and every surface, sometimes even on Bot's smooth alloy back. And now an enforcer was dragging her away.

If Bot didn't do something, it might never hear her tapping again.

Bot knew exactly where they were headed. Straight for the nearest lift, to escape the gaze of passersthru and get Girl to worklevel, where she'd be slaved until she was entirely spent. She couldn't run for centuries on a single battery, not like Bot. Humans required upkeep: good sleep, nutrients, and a variety of stimulation, or else they flickered until they sparked out completely. Bot had seen this happen to many an unnamed, withering to a sad stillness within the shadows of Zee-Zed.

The enforcer's progress toward the lift was slow, as he politely dodged clumps of passersthru with a pause here, a side-step there, allowing Bot to skitter ahead of them across the rafters.

It arrived at the lift at a loss about what to do next. A thick metal barrier prevented entry into the shaft. But Bot couldn't just drop onto the floor and casually step in like a person would. Its motor functions would freeze if it was seen by an official. To prevent invalidation of its owner's insurance claim, Bot would be forced to play dead. Forever.

How to solve such a problem? Bot was not a problem solver. Its entire existence had been about storing and communicating dataknow for entertainment.

Of course, it *had* devised new ways to communicate with Girl, who preferred using taps instead of voice. Although this deviation was not a part of its original programming, it was easy to reason that it was necessary for Bot's audience to be entertained. And Girl's tapping language fit easily into Bot's existing linguistic framework. Syntax, semantics, and pragmatics were all there, conveyed through intensity and tone, through clumping of sounds and the spaces between.

Bot had been surprised to learn that the rest of the unnamed had no grasp of Girl's language. Maybe because Girl lived apart from other unnamed. Or maybe that was *why* she lived apart everyone else. Everyone except Bot.

It was then, as Bot perched on the edge of desperation, that it caught a hint of Girl's toe-tapping words. These were different than the higher-pitched clinks and the deeper metallic throngs. These toe-taps were dull, rough. But they were there, and once it knew what to scan for, all the swipes and skids of Girl's ratty scavenged shoes emerged from the babble of the passerthru crowd.

Bot zoomed its camera on Girl's partially visible feet as it parsed out her taps. They had the familiar cadence of alarm used by the unnamed, but Girl was saying more than just "stay away or die." She had suggestions. Instructions.

After a moment of listening intently, Bot began to move.

* * *

Girl balanced on tippy toes as best she could, as the enforcer jerked her arm higher, making it difficult to tap out instructions. It hurt like everything. Not just her arm, but knowing where she was headed, foreveraway from Zee-Zed, foreveraway from Bot. So many plans in her head, but what if nothing worked?

The enforcer dragged her to one side of the lift, allowing a group of passersthru the next ride. That was good. It gave Bot more time to prepare. *If* it had received her instructions. The enforcer's grip tightened. She wanted to kick, to twist and wriggle free, but this wasn't the time. Not yet.

Girl dared not look up toward the rafters, but as she listened for any sign of Bot above, she heard something curious. Not coming from above, but from down the corridor. Not the clinking of Bot's feet, but more of a hollow sound. A clopping. A long, hairy nose poked between groups of passersthru.

The goat shimmied past some passersthru, then clopped sideways until it was almost directly behind the enforcer. It wore a vest, like a person might wear. Girl wondered how it secured snaps with only those thick, hard feet. That's exactly when the goat's feet began to stomp. First one light clop, then another, and then several in succession, in a pattern. Just like they had before, this goat was talking to Girl.

"Mysterythis," Girl whispered.

The goat danced in response. *Mysterythis,* it said. A perfect translation.

Why more passersthru didn't turn at the curious clip-clop dance of this four-legged, no-armed goat was just another mystery that lit up Girl's mind. But then people were very good at ignoring things they couldn't explain, just as they were especially good at ignoring problems they didn't want to solve. This was why the unnamed are widely ignored, why the worklevels and enforcers are widely accepted.

But it wasn't just that the goat was talking with its strange, thick feet, *or* that passersthru were barely even reacting. It was what the goat was *saying* that most especially caught Girl's attention. She was indeed so distracted that she lost her tip-toe footing and slipped, annoying the enforcer. He pulled her up so hard that her shoulder popped. Sharp pain burst across her body, and Girl screamed.

* * *

Bot had almost worked its way through the crack in the sheeting that enclosed the lift (right in the back corner as Girl had directed) when a scream sounded from the corridor. Bot froze, but the bundle it carried kept moving on its own momentum, nearly falling from Bot's grip and onto the lift floor. Bot had never heard Girl's voice above a whisper, but it was sure that was her. And now the entire corridor was silent.

Bot imagined all the passerthru eyes turned on the enforcer, holding Girl in such a horrible manner.

The lift door opened below Bot. The enforcer's voice floated in as he reassured the crowd with clashing tones of joviality and authority, a crowd that could no longer pretend not to notice, not with a scream like that still ringing in their ears. And then the enforcer stepped into the lift, carrying Girl in both arms. Her face was slack, with a green tint, and one of her own arms swung disturbingly loose. If Bot had lungs it would have held its breath. Girl wouldn't survive long on worklevel now.

This changed everything. How could Bot stick to the plan? Girl might end up with still worse injuries, and even if Bot could carry her to safety, it was no sort of medic.

Tossing a few last words of reassurance to the crowd, the enforcer stepped to the panel and awkwardly shifted his hold on Girl in an attempt to free a hand for the keypad. She whimpered, staring at nothing as her arm swung in an unnaturally wide arc.

Having stopped to process the new information, Bot hadn't yet reached its position, and any second the enforcer would activate the lift. It had precious little time to cross above the lift and open the box labeled "maintenance." It moved as fast, as quiet, as it could, carefully balancing its burlap bundle that hissed as sand shifted inside.

Only seconds left.

Girl was now slung over the enforcer's shoulder. He reached for the lift controls just as Bot made it to the other side and pressed several legs at once on the bright red button. Then Bot froze, hoping with all its metal parts that some version of Girl's plan might still work.

The enforcer pressed the pad. Nothing happened. The lift stayed open.

He tried again, apologizing to passersthru standing on the other side of the door. Girl whimpered as the enforcer jostled her small body, pressing at the pad again and again, this way and that, with fingers this time and open palm that time, finally with a hard fist.

Nothing.

His laugh jittered as he held a finger to the passersthru looking on and turned, walking to the back corner of the lift, and clumsily tried to pull the com from the pocket that was right under Girl.

He was going to call for reinforcements.

Bot had to act. Had to throw the bundle on the enforcer's head, and knock him out. But what if he moved and the bundle hit Girl instead? If Bot did nothing, though, more enforcers would show up, and what hope was there, then?

There was only one thing to do, and Bot was going to do it.

It crossed the rafter until it stood directly above the enforcer and Girl.

Bot was *going* to do it. It dropped the sandbag to the floor. *Thunk.* The enforcer looked down, and that's when Bot jumped. It landed perfectly square on the back of the enforcer's head, quickly wrapped its arms around the enforcer's face, and held.

The enforcer dropped Girl with a thud that twisted Bot's insides. He reached for Bot's arms. But Bot was frozen. It had been discovered by an authority, after all, and its body responded exactly as programmed.

Bot's mind still churned, but its body would never move, never speak, again.

The enforcer mumbled under layers of legs, thrashing back and forth, while the crowd milled away, apparently deciding if they couldn't ignore the messy situation, it must be time to leave. Bot could see everything through its cameras, could hear Girl moaning from her crumpled spot on the floor, but it couldn't make itself call out to her. It couldn't tell her to get up and run.

Run!

The enforcer threw its head back against the lift wall, trying to knock Bot free, but Bot was going nowhere. The enforcer threw itself back again and again. Bot felt the human's head slam against the inside of its body with each impact, until the enforcer crumpled to the floor, probably knocked out.

And there lay the three of them. An unnamed girl, an abandoned bot discovered, and an unconscious enforcer, tangled on the floor of the open lift, deserted by passersthru.

Bot wondered how long it would take for someone to call for help. Passersthru had demonstrated a striking ability to ignore important things happening right in front of their faces, so it might be awhile. But would Girl get up and run before that call was made? It worried immensely about Girl, who shuddered with ragged, uneven breaths. No matter how much it tried, it couldn't move to help, couldn't even offer a reassuring word.

But then came an odd sound echoing down the corridor. A clopping. Faint at first, but suddenly there it was, right outside the lift. There *they* were, right outside the lift.

A torrent of hair and legs, of long snouts and odd bits of clothing, swarmed in, silent apart from their tapping feet. Tapping feet. Were they talking? It sounded like Girl's language, but not the dull, slippery way she'd produced it under the enforcer's drag. This stomping was sharp and uniform, neat and clear. And from the sound of it, the goats were stomping together, their many legs merging with wonderful coordination into one tapping voice, their words layering to spring forth all at once. *Hold still,* they said. *It will be okay.*

Girl whimpered as the goats nudged their long noses under her curled body and, after a few tries, they successfully scooped her up and onto one of their backs. She managed to grip the goat's hair with one hand as she lay limp against its neck, looking straight at Bot, eyes filled with tears. The goat carrying Girl trotted out of the lift, flanked by its companions.

Relief flooded every circuit within Bot. Wherever she was going, wherever the goats took her, it hoped Girl would be safe.

It sent adrift a silent farewell. Girl was a better friend than Bot could have ever imagined, and it would miss her for as long as its battery lasted. It would miss her until the enforcers carried it off and disassembled it for parts.

But then there was movement. Under Bot, under the body of the enforcer.

The goats' thick feet tapped reassurance, this time to Bot. *It will be okay,* they said.

And just like that, Bot and the enforcer were stretched across the backs of two goats and whisked through the market corridor, past clumps of passersthru who had resumed their well-practiced ignoring of the strangeness all around.

* * *

Bot had only been on one other ship before this, and it had never ever been on a ship's main bridge. The room was round and tall, and at that moment it was filled with a stellar map bigger than any holo-display Bot had ever seen. Girl stood in the center of the room, hands raised and moving fast, spinning the display, tilting it this way and zooming it that. Bot watched from its perfectly-sized rectangular stool, shaking a leg every few seconds, just because it could.

When the goats brought them on board, Girl, Bot, and the enforcer were taken to some sort of medical bay. Girl was placed on a bed and given a puff of relaxing gas. Bot watched with joy from the next bed as bendy arms dropped from the ceiling and gently but swiftly slipped her shoulder back into place.

Resolved as Bot was to live forever within its newly frozen shell, it observed with curiosity as one arm then turned in its direction and attached to Bot's side with a hiss. Bot's insides shifted as its programming morphed, as if such a task was really so easy. Seconds later, Bot fell wonderfully free from the enforcer, all its legs back under its own control.

More goats led Girl and Bot out of the medical bay and past room upon room upon room, each one with an open door. Past people, some of whom Bot recognized as unnamed from level Zee-Zed, sitting at tables and playing with toys, wearing clean clothes and relaxed expressions. They passed bots of all shapes, some dented and chipped, but all of them hovering and walking, all of them unfrozen. All of them free.

And then, as if they hadn't endured enough surprise, the goats led Girl and Bot to the main bridge, where they sat just now. And that's when Ship said hello.

It used Girl's own language, flooding the room with tones that were quick and precise, soft and refined. Ship had heard Girl's tapping after docking at The Grimm, and it knew right away she was meant to be crew. Now that Ship's belly was full of people no longer neglected, it was time to leave The Grimm.

A display of the stars burst to fill the room, and Ship invited Girl to pick their destination. There were many possibilities. Many nice spots to settle the unnamed and the discarded, before heading to another station and doing it all again.

Once Ship was underway, Bot and Girl relaxed into their seats to watch the distant stars go by. Bot rested a leg on Girl's arm, she leaned her head against its side, and their thoughts sifted through all that had happened, and through all the mysteries that remained.

The door opened, and in came a trample of goats. Two had trays strapped to their backs. One tray was piled with food so colorful as to rival any sweetpop back on level Zee-Zed. The other held a small cube that flashed and strobed like a tiny, endless rainbow. Girl squealed and reached for a tasty morsel, while Bot stretched legs to pick up the datacube. It hadn't seen one since it was last programmed by its former owner. What wonders of information Ship was offering Bot, it could barely begin to imagine.

Just before snapping the cube into its belly, Bot noticed something odd about the goat holding Girl's tray. Not odd as in unfamiliar, but odd as in *too* familiar. Strangely, impossibly familiar. The goat wore a scarf wrapped around one shoulder. A scarf striped with blue and gold, like an enforcer's. Like *the* enforcer who tried to drag Girl to worklevel back on Zee-Zed.

Bot looked to Girl, who also looked at the goat, eyes as wide as the large treat in her hand. It leaned forward to examine the goat's eyes, which looked distinctly human-like. The goat leaned in as well, tilted its nose down, and gave Bot a jovial bop with its forehead. And then the goat, its enforcer days clearly at an end, danced a clopping friendly *Good day!* before leaving with its new companions.

Clearly, there were many things Bot had yet to learn.

And so, there was nothing left to do but slip Ship's cube into its belly and sit back, as a universe of wonderful, fascinating tidbits burst across Bot's joyful mind. Girl giggled through her mouthful of sweets.

Soul Mate

Jason Palmatier

Trace opened his eyes to the familiar, cold, gray sky. Artillery boomed in the distance as it battered the line to his left in the closing light of dusk. Constance crouched low on his shoulder, small squirrel eyes tense as she listened to the clank and rustle of enemy troops in the trenches across no man's land, a mere five hundred yards over the top before them. Her bushy gray tail twitched as voices sounded, carrying on the brisk autumn air, past the mangled barbed wire hung with torn uniforms and over the waterlogged craters where rats scurried looking for flesh.

"Look lively! Get to it!" Sergeant O'Connell shouted, squelching through the thick mud and shoving kneeling soldiers to their feet. The one eye that wasn't covered with a blood-soaked bandage flicked to the squirrel on Trace's shoulder and he leaned in conspiratorially, head wound smelling of sulfur.

"You got the voodoo workin' tonight, lad?"

Trace turned his eyes on the Irishman, who didn't even blink under their thousand-yard gaze, and replied, "Yes."

O'Connell nodded, his chapped lips cracking as he pursed them and flicked his eye in the direction of the German lines.

"Alright, then. You get across there and take out their Minnies, just like the lieutenant said, and you fire that flare, but—" O'Connell leaned in even closer, the rot of his corned beef breath brushing Trace's ear "—before you come back, put an extra one in their shell stash, if your furry friend can find it, aye?"

Trace nodded, feeling Constance's tail twitch as she saw his thoughts of O'Connell's plan play out in his mind. She chirped three times in protest, eyes narrowed into a disapproving frown.

O'Connell patted Trace on the shoulder and continued limping down the trench, shouting "Look lively!" again as he disappeared around the next zig-zag.

Trace shifted the canteen at his waist and picked up his rifle, flicking mud off the wooden butt and checking that the breach was clear of debris. His shirt hung loosely on his arms, snagging the short cartridge just in front of the trigger, which he had stuffed with ten rounds, against regulations. He checked his bootlaces, tightening one and retying the mud-caked double knot before squaring up the final length of the puttees that wrapped around his leg from the ankle up to the knee.

Constance deftly hopped onto his back and back to his shoulder as he did all this.

Ready? He thought.

Constance chirped once.

Go.

Constance sprang from his shoulder onto the top of the trench, immediately flattening herself out as she scurried into no man's land.

Trace took a deep breath, fortifying himself, and turned to the men strung out along the trench beside him. He ran his gaze over their mud-caked and bloodied faces, taking in the haunted eyes next to the terrified ones, the slack jaws next to the grimly determined ones. He saw the uniforms patched and frayed and stained with gunpowder and blood and filth, whose sleeves ended in rifles clutched tightly to keep fingers from trembling. He let his eyes go vague and heard their screams in his mind, felt the concussion of the shells that blew them apart and knocked the air from his lungs, smelled the sickly-sweet scent of rotting bodies, burning flesh, and exploded gunpowder, tasted the tang of blood and the bitterness of bile at the back of his throat. He surrounded himself with these things, let them crush in on him, suffocating him, pulling him down into the darkness that grew within him every day.

Then he closed his eyes.

A cavern yawned around him, unseen, echoing faintly with drips of water. Trace felt outward into the blackness with his mind, seeking the presence that was always there, just beyond sight, yet near enough to drive its preternatural power deep into his heart. He shuddered, mind wanting to flee back to the purgatory of the trenches where it could crouch and whimper as the pounding of the artillery drew nearer and nearer. But he pushed on, into the nothingness that suddenly held a presence, a vague field of power and menace whose tendrils drifted out towards him, curious and hungry.

"Strength, fog, vision," Trace said, voice booming into the silence, only to die away as if never spoken.

The tendrils twisted around him with airy sounds like breath laboriously sucked through gas mask filters or the final exhalations of the dead. Slowly, the sounds resolved into words.

Offer?

"Six months. Fifty souls." Trace said, swallowing against the dread of extended servitude. But the German *Minenwerfer* mortars the Allies called "Minnies" had devastated their lines and would do so again if they were not destroyed. He, and the men in the trench with him, would be dead if they didn't take them out.

The tendrils converged around his face, inches from it, twisted ends burning his skin with their abyssal cold.

One innocent.

The faces of four men—some mere boys—flashed in his mind, all sharp, clear, as if still alive despite the final look of horror that overtook them as his benefactor extracted its eternal price.

"One innocent," Trace confirmed, swallowing hard.

The tendrils hovered, drinking in the fear he had clamped his jaw tight to control, waiting for the slim thread of sanity connecting him to the stinking mire of the trench to snap, stranding him in the dark for eternity.

Done.

The tendrils withdrew, the darkness faded.

Trace sagged forward, hand rising to catch himself against the wooden reinforcement on the side of the trench. He stood for a moment, braced against the fatigue of contact, hearing the voices of those around him with unnatural clarity.

"Is it done?"

"God help us."

"Look, a fog's rollin' in!"

Trace opened his eyes and shoved himself back from the wall. A chill slowly flowed outward from the darkness within him, rolling like gas vapors down into the trenches, invigorating his arms and legs with a false strength that would leave him helpless when it ran out. But nothing else would do. The bargain had been struck and the deal set in motion. If he did not complete it, he'd suffer the consequences.

Trace pulled the rifle from his shoulder and pulled himself over the top of the trench into no man's land.

"God speed, sir," someone whispered behind him.

Not even close, Trace thought grimly.

He crawled the first few feet, navigating around the offset barbed wire barricade with care before levering himself up into a crouch.

An eerie, reddish glow washed over his vision, bringing into stark relief everything that lay shrouded by the unnatural fog that billowed up from the forlorn craters as if pushed from Beyond.

Because it is.

Staying low, he jogged into the thick vapors, seeing through them with ease, though to an unaided eye they would have been impenetrable. Halfway across the torn expanse he slid down into a crater and called to his familiar.

Constance. Show me.

A vision of shattered timbers protruding from thick mud filled his mind, viewed from two inches above the ground. Trace squinted against the disorienting perspective, concentrating on the sound of voices and puffs of breath Constance could hear and see.

"Woher kommt dieser Nebel?" an unnerved voice asked in midlands German. *Where has this fog come from?*

"Ich weiß es nicht, aber es gefällt mir nicht. Es ist nicht natürlich," another voice answered. *I don't know, but I don't like it. It isn't natural.*

Trace shuddered, feeling the icy tentacles reaching for him, hearing the hiss of avarice through the mists around him. He concentrated on his link to Constance, on her warm reception and patient waiting.

Too many. Too alert. Find another spot.

A bob of the head and the view crept away from the trench, back into the mist. Then it began to bound through the veil of white, leaping through bloodied barbed wire and over half-buried helmets that materialized with startling clarity before flashing away. A fall into a crater initiated a sharp turn to the left and a final leap up to the lip. Then the slinking resumed, an inch from the ground, nose sniffing for the smell of guard dog or trench cat.

Nothing.

A cautious move forward led to sandbags piled around a cutout, the snub nose of a machine gun sticking out from it. A peek past the barrel revealed two soldiers sitting on old ammo bins with scrap wood on top for insulation, hands stuffed in pockets against the cold. One snored; the other's head drooped, jerked back up, then drooped again.

Good. I am coming.

Trace crept from the crater and jogged, bent over, towards the warm beacon that was Constance in his mind. She glowed brightly against both the darkness of the night and that which grew within him.

Shattered tree trunks, mere splintered logs rooted in the earth now, told him he was at the North Copse and he turned towards the German line knowing exactly where he would intersect it.

Constance had chosen well. The concentration of German machine gun pits had made the line here taboo for command and they had ceased to directly attack it. Consequently, the Germans who manned it had become complacent, slacking off in their watches.

Trace slowed his pace, crouching low, placing his feet carefully. As lazy as the enemy had become, no one on the front shook off an odd noise on a foggy night. A dozen yards from Constance's warmth he lowered himself to the ground and began a painstaking crawl around barbed wire and x-barriers until his face brushed Constance's fluffy tail. She twitched it and shifted slightly to one side.

One soldier still slept but his companion had just shaken his head and stood, slapping himself on the cheek and muttering as he shoved his hands under his armpits.

Trace slid his knife from its leather scabbard at his waist. He rolled over the edge of the trench, landed in a deep squat behind the standing soldier, and leapt up, hand sweeping around to clamp over the man's mouth.

"Mmmpphhhh!"

Trace's blade slid across the man's throat. He held him upright, struggling to keep his thrashings from making noise, but the German pounded the wooden walkway with his boot.

Trace flung the man aside and dove forward, stabbing his knife to the hilt in the throat of the sleeping soldier just as his eyes sprang open. The man toppled backwards, ammo crate seat clattering out onto the walkway.

"Was war das?" a voice called from the mist, further down the trench line. *What was that?*

Trace shoved the dying soldier's head back and yanked the round medallion out from under the soldier's coat by its tie while air bubbled around the knife in his neck.

"Wilhelm ist eingeschlafen und umgefallen! Ha, ha!" Trace yelled back, reading the soldier's name from his id tags. *Wilhelm fell asleep and fell over! Ha, ha!*

"Bah, Wilhelm. Er ist nutzlos," the voice called back. *Bah, Wilhelm. He is useless.*

Trace glimpsed the life fading from Wilhelm's eyes as he pulled his knife free, seeing dozens of other eyes doing the same in his mind from bodies torn apart by shrapnel, shot through with bullets, bloated with fluids from organs ruptured by shock waves. He turned, creeping past the first soldier's hand as it fell away from his gaping throat, pausing only briefly to listen for footsteps from either direction down the trench.

Constance. Find.

Trace concentrated on an image of a squat *Minenwerfer*, emphasizing its large round base, short barrel, small aiming wheels, and the massive shells it launched, which looked like gargantuan bullets.

Constant squeaked and bobbed her head, jumping down into the trench and scaling the opposite wall. She disappeared over the top, tail twitching.

Trace moved further down the line, listening intently. He wanted to sink into Constance's view, see the layout of the trenches from her vantage point, but the separation he would experience from his immediate surroundings made it too dangerous. He waited, squatted down, alternating between spinning and squeezing the handle of the knife in his hand until he began to shake from the nerves. A rustle from behind spooked him into an about-face that only revealed a rat fattened on battlefield spoils waddling up to lick the spilled blood.

A single squeak.

Trace backed up against the trench wall, heart pounding, Constance's voice in his head momentarily confusing him.

People? He finally managed to ask.

An angry chatter.

Trace's stomach turned, seeing images of soldiers' heads from a top-trench vantage point as Constance thought about her progress so far. A series of leaps and bounds dove deeper and deeper into the labyrinth until Constance stopped at a cluster of mortar positions well back from the front line.

There was no time to get there by stealth, not with the false strength burning through his veins, threatening to strand him in convalescence at any moment.

He glanced back at the uniforms on the two bodies behind him, seeing the dark, spreading stain of blood on them even from this distance. They would not do.

Amidst a mounting dread he closed his eyes and searched the darkness.

Illusion. Disguise.

A hiss, hungry for fresh blood, answered.

One month…

Trace swallowed against bile, a part of him dying inside as he responded.

Agreed.

A hiss of satisfaction.

Granted…

Trace opened his eyes and looked down at his uniform. Gray-green wool, held together by a close row of brass buttons, covered his torso. The baggy gray pants around his legs ended in wrappings over knee-high boots. He stood, checking that his gun had been transformed, too, then let it hang loosely in a carry position. He walked briskly, taking the first left that led deeper into the maze of trenches.

The repaired walkway behind the machine gun nests gave way to mud paths and shattered embankments as he worked his way up into the areas they had attempted to take in the last great push. The soldiers that sat huddled in alcoves around makeshift fires looked up at him with the same distant, shell-shocked eyes as his own mates and he experienced a strange vertigo, unable to tell in the gloom if the faces he saw were familiar or foreign. Only the greetings in short clipped German reminded him that he was in enemy lands.

An officer smoking a curled pipe and reading an outdated newspaper addressed him at a major intersection deep in the trenches: "Hallo, Soldat." *Hello, private.*

"Hallo, Hauptmann," Trace replied, saluting crisply. *Hello, Captain.*

The officer raised a questioning eyebrow and Trace patted the illusory side pocket of his coat while passing briskly, saying, "Versenden. Dringend." *Dispatch. Urgent.*

"Ahh," the officer replied, puffing further on his pipe and returning to his reading.

The warmth of Constance grew closer and he only had to backtrack once, muttering excuses to those he passed again to cover his error, before he felt her presence above him just out of sight over the edge of the trench.

On the walkway before him, the first of the mortar pits opened up, extra shells standing sentinel behind the platform on which the squat gun stood. The trench ran behind it, leading to the next emplacement, zig-zagging slightly so there was no line of fire down its entire length.

Good. He told Constance. *Find others.*

Trace imagined row upon row of shells, some stacked on each other, sitting under cover. Constance chittered softly, agitated, and Trace knew she felt the errand folly. They were too far behind enemy lines and should not head any farther back for the ammo dump. But Sergeant O'Connell wanted them gone; Trace did, too. It was something that might turn the tide of this never-ending battle.

Please.

Constance chirped a final short protest and hopped off towards the rear.

Trace turned his attention to the mortars before him, attempting to look at them casually as he took out a cigarette from his pack and lit it.

The crews rested about their guns, one or two awake in the darkness, the others sleeping as best they could on the cold ground or on makeshift cots. Trace began a purposeful walk down the line, noting the general position of each person and fixing it in his mind. A few glanced up at him, some nodding in greeting, which he returned, careful to not let their faces register and blank out his memory of those he had already passed. When he got to the end of the line of twelve guns he turned, closed his eyes, and dove fully into the darkness.

Souls. Take them.

The hissing in the dark turned to a warping screech as he remembered his walk and the artillerymen he had passed. Violent forces whipped past him, staggering him, and he discerned in the blackness around him thick tentacles, their twisted musculature stretching and popping as they extended from the Otherworld into his own.

He opened his eyes to the hell that was his own Earth and witnessed the carnage he had brought upon it.

Black tentacles from beyond erupted from the mud, splintering walkways and knocking aside shells as they lashed out to grab the stunned soldiers. Screams of mortal terror and gurgles of strangulation quickly gave way to shouts of alarm and gunshots and the sounding of whistles.

Trace stood for a moment, seeing the life crushed from men, their eyes bulging, their mouths gaping open for air, their arms thrashing against a foe that saw them as nothing more than fodder for its inhuman existence. He watched as they were dragged downward, disappearing into the mud as if they had never been, erased in the blink of an eye by an implacable foe who knew nothing of them and did not care to.

It looked like any other day in this war.

A squad of soldiers rushed past him, shouting, pulling their rifles from their shoulders before faltering at the sight of the unnatural horrors before them.

Trace swung the backpack on his back to one side, pulled the flare gun from inside, loaded it with a single shell from his right ammo pouch, and fired it into the air.

A soldier next to him ducked at the unfamiliar bang and swung his rifle around.

Trace looked at him, watched as the flare ignited overhead to illuminate his startled face, and thought, *Another soul.*

Sinewy black tentacles erupted from the ground, wrapping around the soldier's face, muffling his existential screams as they pulled him down, down, down into the shapeless Beyond.

Trace puffed on his cigarette, placed the flare gun in the backpack, and grabbed a stick grenade off the belt of a German sergeant who grimly fired rounds at the first batch of tentacles as they pulled the last artilleryman down through the earth.

"Was an Hölle!" the sergeant cursed as his bullets impacted to no effect. *What in Hell!*

Trace squeezed the ball from the bottom of the stick grenade, yanked the string attached to it down, and hurled the grenade into the toppled over shells of the nearest mortar pit. Then he ran.

Gray-green uniforms swept past him in the twinkling artificial light as he pounded on canted walkways and splashed through mud, shouting as he ran, "Die Briten sind hier, in den Schützengräben!" *The British are here, in the trenches!*

Confusion followed in his wake. Shots rang out, orders were shouted.

The flare's light died away.

The first boom of British artillery filled the blackness that followed.

Trace doubled his speed as German soldiers stopped what they were doing and threw themselves against the sides of the trench, clutching at their helmets with their heads held down. One peeked out at the sound of Trace's pounding feet and yelled, "Was machst du? Runter!" *What are you doing? Get down!*

The grenade exploded behind him, setting off one mortar shell, which begat detonations in the others. The blasts that followed threw Trace to the ground, showering him with dirt and timbers and the left arm of the sergeant, continuing on and on, the sound so loud, the concussions so relentless, that Trace's mind screamed on the edge of insanity, the grasping tentacles of the being that used him as a conduit reaching eagerly for him, until a simultaneous detonation of mortar shells blasted his mind to white static. The air was crushed from his lungs and his heart was shocked to stillness.

He lay, staring straight into the orange- and red-tinged sky as his limp body jerked and shuddered to forces that killed with pressure and fire, fragments and force, tearing the paltry flesh and bone of humanity apart with uninterested efficiency.

On and on the roaring went, stuttering out in fits and spurts that reminded Trace of the backfires of the lorry that had brought him and Constance to the front. She, wagging her tail, tongue hanging out, eager golden retriever eyes taking in the bustle of activity around her, the medical cross on the first aid kit strapped to her back bright red against muslin white. He had rubbed her head, apprehensive, but somewhat relieved that he was finally here and it didn't look that bad. His dark brown eyes had shown with a glimmer of hope.

Then the first shelling came, the first feel of the indescribable and unstoppable forces hurled at them for hours that spanned lifetimes, the first cries of the broken, mentally and physically, the first blood splattered, the first limb found, its owner lost, the first taste of carnage so great, suffering so severe, that it attracted the attention of Them.

Constance had looked up at him, her soft, dog eyes still full of innocence after months of blood and death. His fingers had scratched behind her muddy ears; his hand rubbed her head. He concentrated on those eyes, the last thing that felt familiar to the small part of Trace that was left from before, willing them to stay, to just stay.

But they closed anyway.

And when he pulled her torn body close to him and rocked back and forth as the earth erupted around him and men fell and the last hope in him died, he felt the tendrils touch him. They whispered into his roaring grief, into his shattered soul.

She can live.

He had screwed his eyes shut, wanting her back so badly that even the burning cold of the words that penetrated his mind did not dissuade him.

How?

Different...but familiar.

Anything. Anything to get her back, the last thing that was familiar from before. But...

What cost?

Servitude. Souls.

A man had fallen beside him, clutching at a throat that was no longer there, glassy eyes fading as he died for an imaginary line that divided something that belonged to no one. All in service to…what?

I will do anything.

A satisfied hiss.

Done.

Something blasted him into a pure whiteness that wrapped about him like a blanket, soothing and soft. Constance had stood afar in that dimensionless space, looking away, tongue hanging out. He spoke her name and she turned, eyes brightening, tail springing up and wagging. She began to run to him, but as she did something grabbed him, pulling him backwards, away from her, ripping him from the encompassing whiteness into a deep, silent darkness.

He had opened his eyes to a gray sky with a scraggly trench cat nestled against him. At first, he had grabbed it roughly, thinking it was a rat attempting to feast on him, but when he saw its eyes, he knew.

Constance…

A purring chirp.

He picked her up and stroked the matted fur on the back of her neck, the joy at having her back tempered by the change in her and the otherworldly darkness that lingered inside of him. He worried on that until the soldiers near him spoke, their voices sharp and clear in the twilight air. Bile rose as he looked down at his mud-spattered uniform and realized where he was and what must have transpired as part of the deal. He'd clutched Constance to him and screwed his eyes shut, praying for a forgiveness he knew he would not receive.

And so it had gone. Each time Constance came back she was smaller, different but familiar, and connected to him far more than before. But each time she came back, his fear of losing her grew.

And now she was sitting next to acres of shells as the first of the British artillery rounds fell among the German trenches.

Trace rolled to his side, dirt and splinters falling from him as he stood. His chest ached, bruised on the inside and out, a sharp stabbing pain indicating a broken rib. He staggered towards the warmth that sat alone and exposed deep behind the lines.

Flares lit the landscape with their hellish red light, shells exploded around him, men fell before him, whistles blew in the distance as his mates charged over the top and finally, finally, finally, he reached her. She jumped down from the top of the trench onto his shoulder and looked out at the neatly stacked pallets of mortar shells that spread out before them, ready to arc into the sky and deliver death as soon as replacement mortars were delivered.

He reached in his pack to rig their destruction, but the darkness surged in him.

One innocent!

He felt the menace in the words, remembered the deal, but saw no one around who could satisfy it.

Soon.

A screech, a hiss.

Now!

Trace staggered, clutching at his midsection as shards of ice pierced his insides.

There is no one!

The airy voice growled with avarice.

Her!

Trace fell to his knees clutching his head as the icy tentacles lashed it from within, questing to break out, to seize Constance and drag her back to its unholy domain. But it could not do so. Trace was its conduit, its portal to this world, and without him this arcane force—no matter how powerful, no matter how angry—could not access it. It must induce Trace to do its bidding.

Or so he thought.

He felt his finger twitch, unbidden. Before the alien horror of that movement could fully set in, his clenched fist suddenly burst open, reaching, fingers arched at obscene angles.

"Constance, run!" Trace yelled, shoving his hand to the ground and pinning it with his knee.

Constance chattered angrily, feeling the presence in Trace's head, trying to bark at it as she would have in her first form, to protect her pack mate, her human. But Trace's struggle against his own body finally spurred her on as she felt his fear of losing control and saw his final plan.

"Go!"

She leapt onto the top of the trench, running away from the fighting towards the tree line pocked with errant shell holes, toward a country not yet torn by war.

A screech of rage swayed Trace as he shouldered his backpack onto the ground and fumbled to pull the flare gun from it, feeling his false strength failing rapidly. The tang of metal and char of spent powder struck his tongue as he bit down on the fat barrel, yanking with his good hand to separate it from the handle. He tossed the old flare to the side and shoved a new one in while it dangled from his teeth. Then he clapped it shut and pulled back the hammer.

You will repay your debt!

The voice screeched in his head as he staggered forward and fell among the shells nearest him, rolling onto his errant arm to pin it beneath him. He placed the flare gun barrel against the side of the heavy mortar shell, knowing that the explosives packed behind the shell's thin wall were vulnerable to shocks. He paused, feeling to see if Constance had made it far enough to survive what was to come, but the fingers of the possessed hand snatched the sleeve of his shirt, attempting to yank it down and grab the gun.

Trace whispered a prayer for her, the one part of him still worth saving, and pulled the trigger.

* * *

Silence.

Beautiful and clean.

He turned in the blinding light toward Constance, who ran to him, fur flowing about her, tongue hanging out, joy in her deep brown eyes. She leapt for him and he spread his arms wide, her name echoing in that liminal space that held nothing but peace and hope.

Then the tentacles snatched her, yanking her away with a yelp that Trace matched with a forlorn cry, muffled by the thick sinew that slid across his mouth and wrapped around his chest. It yanked him backwards, out of the beautiful, clean light, into a world of darkness.

* * *

Trace opened his eyes to the familiar, cold, gray sky. Artillery boomed in the distance as it battered the line to his right in the closing light of dusk. Constance crouched low on his shoulder, small mouse eyes tense as she listened to the clank and rustle of enemy troops in the trenches across no man's land, a mere five hundred meters over the top before them. Her thin pink tail twitched as voices sounded, carrying on the brisk autumn air, past the mangled barbed wire hung with torn uniforms and over the water-logged craters where rats scurried looking for flesh.

"Sehen Sie lebendig aus! Mach es!" Sergeant Wolff shouted, squelching through the thick mud and shoving kneeling soldiers to their feet. *Look lively! Get to it!* The one eye that wasn't covered with a mud-caked bandage flicked to the mouse on Trace's shoulder and he leaned in conspiratorially, head wound smelling of iodine.

"Heute Abend hast du den Voodoo zum Laufen gebracht, Junge?" *You got the voodoo working tonight, lad?*

Trace turned his eyes on the Bavarian, who didn't even blink under their thousand-yard gaze, and replied, "Ja." *Yes.*

Wolff nodded, his chapped lips cracking as he pursed them and flicked his eye in the direction of the British lines.

"Alles klar dann..." *Alright, then...*

About the Authors

BEBE BAYLISS is a California-born Canadian author writing mystery & suspense, science fiction, fantasy, paranormal, weird west, and horror, with stories featured in anthologies from Zombies Need Brains, Flame Tree Publishing, Brigids Gate Press, and Air and Nothingness Press (as Sonya Carlin.) She and co-writer Gini Koch bonded over a shared love of snark and sci-fi conventions and they now write short stories, novellas, and novels together, including FALL'S GIRL, first in their Fall's Girl Mystery series from Ginger Blue Publishing. Bebe lives in British Columbia with a very tall husband and a very small dog. http://www.bebebayliss.com

JACEY BEDFORD is a British writer of science fiction and fantasy with novels (seven so far) published by DAW. Her short stories have appeared on both sides of the Atlantic. She lives a thousand feet up on the edge of the Yorkshire Pennines in an old stone house that takes the first hit when the wind howls off the moor. She has been a librarian and a folk singer. Her claim to fame is that she once sang live on BBC Radio 4 accompanied by the Doctor (Who?) playing spoons. Catch up with her at www.jaceybedford.co.uk and https://linktr.ee/jaceybedford_writer

A. KATHERINE BLACK lives in Northern Minnesota with her family, their cats, and her overworked coffee machines. She loves making snow angels and dreaming up stories about creatures with bunches of legs, tentacles, and wings. Find her at flywithpigs.com or on bluesky @akatherineblack.bsky.social.

JORDAN BRICCO lives in the Land of Enchantment with her family and dog in a house full of overflowing bookcases. She writes stories shaped by every book she's read and every day she's lived, hoping others will find a place for her tales on their bookcases. The majority of her writing time is spent on rewriting her novel yet again. Short stories are a newer passion, but are becoming a favorite. You can follow her writing journey on Instagram at @ authorjordanb

ALICIA CAY is a writer of speculative and mystery stories. Her short fiction has appeared in Galaxy's Edge magazine, and in several anthologies including Unmasked from WordFire Press and The Wild Hunt from Air and Nothingness Press. She suffers from wanderlust, collects quotes, and lives beneath the shadows of the Rocky Mountains. Find her at aliciacay.com

If **SHANNA GERMAIN** were a god, she'd be the Benevolent God of Rainbow Sprinkles. Sadly, she's only human. Her award-winning body of work encompasses stories, games, poems, and essays about lust, lies, and leviathans, and includes Predation, No Thank You, Evil!, Invisible Sun, *As Kinky as You Wanna Be*, The Old Gods of Appalachia Roleplaying Game, and *The Poison Eater*. She lives in a rainforest with a dog named &. Follow her down the rabbit hole at shannagermain.com and on all the socials as shannagermain.

ALEXANDER G.R. GIDEON's writing style can best be described by the phrase, "...and many people died." He's a multi-genre author of Historical Fantasy, Dark Fantasy, Sci-Fi, and Horror. As the world's only Pan Librarian Wizard, he's an expert on most things, from High Magick and spirit summoning, to eldritch texts, to making you look like the Kings, Queens, and various other Monarchs you know you are! You can find him across all social media as @PanLibrarianWizard.

LAWRENCE HARDING is a recovering medievalist from Cambridge, England. When not befriending pigeons, she enjoys weaving together fantasy, horror and gothic in her writing. She runs a small hand-illustrated fiction zine called Endless Otherwheres, and can be found on Twitter and Bluesky as @ lhardingwrites.

JIM C. HINES' first novel was *Goblin Quest*, the humorous tale of a nearsighted goblin and his fire-spider companion. Wil Wheaton described the book as "too f***ing cool for words." After finishing the goblin trilogy, Jim went on to write the Princess series of fairy tale retellings and the Magic ex Libris books, a modern-day fantasy series about a magic-wielding librarian. He's also the author of the Fable Legends tie-in *Blood of Heroes*, the Janitors of the Post-Apocalypse trilogy, and two middle grade books. His short fiction has appeared in more than 50 magazines and anthologies. Find him at www. jimchines.com.

BRIAN HUGENBRUCH is the author of more than forty speculative fiction stories and poems. His fiction has most recently appeared in the ZNB Presents Year 2 anthology, Cast of Wonders, and Analog. He lives in Upstate New York with his wife and their daughter. He enjoys fishing (but only in video games); Scotch (but only in real life); and he spends his days trying to explain quantum cryptography to other nerds. You can find him on Bluesky @ the-lettersea.com, on IG/Threads @the_lettersea, and on the web at https:// the-lettersea.com. No, he's not certain how to say his last name either.

GINI KOCH writes the fast, fresh, and funny Alien/Katherine "Kitty" Katt series for DAW Books, the Necropolis Enforcement Files, and the Martian Alliance Chronicles. As G.J. Koch she writes the Alexander Outland series and she's made the most of multiple personality disorder by writing novels, novellas, novelettes, and short stories in all the genres out there and under a variety of other pen names as well, including Anita Ensal, Jemma Chase, A.E. Stanton, and J.C. Koch. She now enjoys expanding the fun co-writing with Bebe Bayliss. Their first mystery novel, FALL'S GIRL, released from Ginger Blue Publishing in 2024. http://www.ginikoch.com

SHARON LEE and **STEVE MILLER** have been writing stories together since the 1980s, with over 100 works of fantastic fiction to their joint credit. Sharon is the only person to consecutively hold office as executive director, vice president, and president of the Science Fiction and Fantasy Writers of America. Steve was Founding Curator of Science Fiction at the University of Maryland's SF Research Collection. Their awards include the Skylark, the Prism, and the Hal Clement Award. Sharon and Steve's newest Liaden Universe®, and 30th joint, novel, Ribbon Dance, was published by Baen in June 2024. More at https://www.korval.com

RUSSELL HUGH McCONNELL was born in Toronto, Canada. Over the years, time and chance have taken him to prairies and mountains, to great metropolises, to swamps and beaches, and (most recently) to the magical land of east Texas. Throughout this time he has had several careers, or possibly one, or none. When he is not drinking and brawling, he teaches literature, philosophy, and writing to university students, and when he is not doing that he writes things.

JASON PALMATIER is a speculative fiction author and stay at home dad who has written for screenplay projects (the short film "Hunter"), independent comics (*Lords of the Cosmos*, Ugli Studios), graphic novels (*Plague*, Markosia Enterprises Ltd.), and short story anthologies (Zombies Need Brains, LLC.). His award-winning story "Under My Cypresses" placed second in the L. Ron Hubbard Writers of the Future Contest for the 4th quarter of the 2023 contest year, and appears in volume 39 of the anthology. See details of his various projects at http://www.jasonpalmatier.com.

KARI SPERRING is the author of two novels (*Living with* Ghosts [DAW 2009] and *The Grass King's* Concubine [DAW 2012], the novella collection, *The Book of Gaheris* se [NewCon Press 2023] and numerous short stories. As Kari Maund, she has written and published five books and many articles on Celtic and Viking history and co-authored a book on the history and real people behind her favourite novel, *The Three Musketeers* (with Phil Nanson). She's British and lives in Cambridge, England, with her partner Phil and three very determined cats, who guarantee that everything she writes will have been thoroughly sat upon.

JEAN MARIE WARD writes fiction, nonfiction, and everything in between. Her credits include a multi-award nominated novel, numerous short stories and two popular art books. The former editor of CrescentBlues.com, she is the author interviewer for BookBale.com and a frequent contributor to the online convention ConTinual. Find her at JeanMarieWard.com, BlueSky @ jeanmarieward.bsky.social, Facebook.com/JeanMarieWardWriter, Instagram @jean_marie_ward, and Twitter @Jean_Marie_Ward.

About the Editors

PATRICIA BRAY was there when Zombies Needs Brains was born, and has the t-shirt to prove it. The author of a dozen novels, her storytelling skills also come in handy in her day job as a business intelligence analyst. She lives in New Hampshire, where she balances her time at a keyboard with cycling, hiking and curling. Find her on the web at www.patriciabray.com.

****

JOSHUA PALMATIER is a fantasy author with a PhD in mathematics. He currently teaches at SUNY Oneonta in upstate New York while writing in his "spare" time, editing anthologies, and running the anthology-producing small press Zombies Need Brains LLC. His most recent fantasy series, releasing Spring/Summer 2024 is called the "Crystal Cities" and includes *Crystal Lattice*, *Crystal Rebel*, and *Crystal War*. You can also find his "Throne of Amenkor" series, the "Well of Sorrows" series, and the "Ley" series still on the shelves. He is currently hard at work writing his next fantasy and designing the Kickstarter for the next Zombies Need Brains anthology projects. You can find out more at www.joshuapalmatier.com or at the small press' site www.zombiesneedbrains.com. Or follow him on Blue Sky at joshuapalmatier.bsky.social or on X as @bentateauthor or @ZNBLLC. And check out the Zombies Need Brains Patreon at www.patreon.com/zombiesneedbrains.

Acknowledgments

This anthology would not have been possible without the tremendous support of those who pledged during the Kickstarter. Everyone who contributed not only helped create this anthology, they also helped support the small press Zombies Need Brains LLC, which I hope will be bringing SF&F themed anthologies to the reading public for years to come. I want to thank each and every one of them for helping to bring this small dream into reality. Thank you, my zombie horde.

The Zombie Horde: Cory Williams, Axisor and Firestar, Lisa Kruse, Chris Matosky, Ian Chung, Kathryn Smith, Karen M, Sheryl, John Markley, Jaq Greenspon, Raymond Lowell, Beth Coll, Jamieson Cobleigh, Sarah Cornell, Kerri Regan, Henry W. Schubert, Anne Burner, Kris W, Robyn DeRocchis, Richard O'Shea, Jeremy Audet, Rowan Stone, Andrew Hatchell, Nicholas Stephenson, Ian Harvey, Becky Boyer, Stephen Ballentine, Phillip Spencer, Cindy Cripps-Prawak, Andrija Popovic, Millie Calistri-Yeh, Eva Jayet Alaminos, LetoTheTooth, Miranda Floyd, Wulf Moon Enterprises, Michael Axe, Lindsay Knight, Claire Sims, Taia Hartman, Cathy Green, Wolf SilverOak, Beth LaClair, Duncan and Andrea Rittschof, Patricia Bray, Megan Beauchemin, Stephanie Lucas, Mark A Kiraly, Rich 'Razmus' Weissler, Michael Kohne, Beth Lobdell, David Rowe, David Lahner, Michael Hanscom, Edward Ellis, Mary Jo Rabe, J.R. Murdock, Arej N Howlett, David Hankins, R.J.H., Niall Gordon, Michael D'Auben, Jakub Narębski, Ezra Lee, Juanita J Nesbitt, Piet Wenings,

R. Hunter, Dina S Willner, Jenny Barber, Todd V. Ehrenfels, E.M. Middel, Sasha, Tania, L.C., Rory King, Joe Hauser, Dino Hicks, Charles E Norton, Stephannie Tallent, Mustela, Jennifer Berk, Michele Hall, Owen Blacker, Jeff Eppenbach, Kit Rodgers, Jason Swensen, Leah Webber, Random Yarning, Jörg Tremmel, Carol J. Guess, Kerry aka Trouble, Jen1701D, Shayne Easson, Hoose Family, Richard Leis, Jenn Whitworth, Jackie Coleman, Curtis Frye, Helen Ellison, Jacen Leonard, Angie Hogencamp, Joanne B Burrows, Jessica A. Enfante, Colette Reap, Maggie Laigaie, Vulpecula, Colleen Feeney, T Lynn P, Kat Feete, Vana Smith, Sandy Bryant, Ruth Ann Orlansky, Samantha Sendele, Craig "Stevo" Stephenson, Margaret Killeen, Ron Currens, Alicia henness, A. Kristina Casasent, Kelly Snyder, Jo Beere, Cherie Livingston, Chad Bowden, Keith E. Hartman, Kate Stuppy, A.H. Gillett, Brenda Rezk, Ryan C, Rebecca Buchanan, Darren Lipman, Lorri-Lynne Brown, Andy F, Margot Harris, Rebecca M, Lace, Christopher Wheeling, Susan Simko, Bonnie Warford, Heidi Lambert, Tina M Noe Good, S Horvat, Brynn, Sheryl R. Hayes, Robert B Tharp, Annette Agostini, Charlie Russel, MykeTea, Debbie Matsuura, Trisha J. Wooldridge, Anthony R. Cardno, Svend Andersen, John 'Doc' Strange, Howard J. Bampton, Robin Hill, John H. Bookwalter Jr., rissatoo, Ilene Tsuruoka, Tris Lawrence, Jim Gotaas, Cyn Armistead, Margaret Bumby, Keith West, Future Potentate of the Solar System, Sonya R.Lawson, Katy Manck - BooksYALove, Brita Hill, Elaine McMillan, Ane-Marte Mortensen, Chris McLaren, Crysella, Randall Brent Martin II, G. M. Persbacker, Simon Dick, Ashley Clouser Leonard, Sidney Whitaker, Elyse M Grasso, Senhina, Mary Alice Wuerz, Chantelle Wilson, Jerrie the filkferengi, Elektra Hammond, Patrick Osbaldeston, Lou/justloux2, Niall Spain, Mark Carter, Bess Turner, Stephanie Cranford, Ryan Hunter and Cameron Alexander, R.G. Roberts, Bona Books, Adam Goldstein, Jesse N. Klein, Scott Raun, Brad L. Kicklighter, Penny Ramirez, Lynn R, Joshua McGinnis, Ian F Bell, Craig Hackl, Konstanze Tants, Eric B, Michael Fedrowitz, Terry Williams, Eric, Brendan Lonehawk, Anonymous Reader, Ronald H. Miller, Steve Arensberg, Steve & Beckey Sanchez, Patrick Dugan, K. Hodghead, Caroline Westra, Chris Huning, Sharan Volin, Kari Blackmoore, Robert Claney, Jonathan Brown, Krystal Bohannan, Cliff Winnig, John Senn, Kat Haines, Jim Landis, Jamie M. Boyd, Nathan Turner, Helen Cameron, Jeanne Talbourdet, KennyBoy, Robert Bull, RJ Hopkinson, Heidegger Dart, JMC, Janet Piele, Sue Phillips, GMarkC, Vicki Greer, Leane Verhulst, Dana Carson, Chris Munroe, Jenni P., L.C. Parfomak, Kate Malloy, Tanya K., Joshua Hair, Brooks Moses, Melissa Tabon, Lisa Dees, Mark Newman, Nightwing Whitehead, Tommy Acuff, Pamela Lunsford, Richard Hailey, Steve Blount, Gail Z. Martin, Craig Maylor, Kenyon Wensing, BOBBY ZAMARRON, Brent J, Olivia Montoya, PunkARTchick "Ruthenia", Brian, Kay, and Joshua Williams, Misha Dainiak, Yankton Robins, Bethany Jezerey, Tina Connell, Patti Montgomery, Jennifer Flora Black, Deborah

Nossaman, Kevin, Yosen Lin, Dagmar Baumann, Clarissa C. S. Ryan, Jessica Meade, Robert K. Barbour, Abi Scott, Mallory A. Haws, The Other Yvonne, Paul & Laura Trinies, Tara Paine, J.L. Gerrard, Shirley, Amanda Saville, Aysha Rehm, Daniel Hopersberger, Alice "Huskyteer" Dryden, Katie Mergener, Mike Rimar, Ryan Power, Bobbi Boyd, Taylor Munsell, Jackie Duckworth, Tasha Turner, Susanne Schörner, Joseph Jerome Connell, Shay Dinur, Steven Halter, Alice Bentley, Elaine Tindill-Rohr, Jonathan Olsson, Elise Power, Julia Hart, Risa Scranton, David Myers, Michelle P., Regis M. Donovan, Robert D. Stewart, Herbert Eder, John T. Sapienza, Jr., Thomas Booker, Rolf Laun, Max Kaehn, Lorraine J. Anderson, Donna Royston, Mervi Hamalainen, FOS Grace, Andrea Tatjana, Kristin EvensonHirst, In memory of Tammy Greco, Rob In AU, CL McCollum, BT McMenomy, Hayden Trenholm, Francesco Tehrani, Katherine, Barb Moermond, Tibs, Ian, Brenda Carre, Venessa Giunta, Andrew Foxx, Miriah Hetherington, jjmcgaffey, Emy Peters, Jacob H Joseph, Holly Elliott, Keith A. Kline, Joachim Verhagen, Paul Alex Gray, Sandy Komoroff, Michael M. Jones, Gail Morse, Fantastic Books, Edward K. Beale, V Hartman DiSanto, Yosef Kuperman, Meyari McFarland, Gary Ehrlich, M Glasser, Stephen Buchanan, Deborah A. Flores, J Millwood, Alison Scott, Sarah T, Cyn Wise, Karen Dubois, Pat Knuth, Dale Cozort, Blade McMicking, D.I., Jennifer Crow, Brad Roberts, K.tee Magrowski, kayliealien, Tim Jordan, Julie Pitzel, Lee Dalzell, Bob D. M, Adam Nemo, Anne Walker, Sheila Huijbregts, Abra Staffin-Wiebe, Matthew Egerton, Merav Hoffman, Mervi Mustonen, Arin Komins, Louisa Swann, Sylvia Greenwich, J.P. Goodwin, Michael Abbott, A. L. Kaplan, Arinn Dembo, Julie Halperson, Kathy Brady, RickyD, Tracy Popey, Darrell Z. Grizzle, Wingnut, R Kirkpatrick, Agnes Kormendi, Ellery Rhodes, Robin Schwarz, Alan Smale, Fred and Mimi Bailey, Mary Ann Shuman, James Enge, Caryn Cameron, Sarah L., Karen Fonville, Gavran, Tal S, Cat Ellison, Amelia Smith, Coleman bland, Winter Hart, Jason Palmatier, Will Gunderson, Geoffrey Willmoth, Cynthia Porter, Stuart Hall (aka Celt), Alexander Gent, Jeff G, David Keener, VikingSnail, Carol Mammano, Linnéa G, Lavinia Ceccarelli, David Futterrer, Bob Thibodeau, Alphonzs, Katelyn Cserjes, Carver Rapp, Mandy Stein, Connor Bliss, John Jason Lau, Tania Clucas, Holly J, AM Scott, Author, Robby Thrasher, CGJulian, Tracy 'Rayhne' Fretwell, Leah Smith, Stephen Kotowych, Gary Phillips, Lotta Fjelkegård, Katrina Knight, Kat D'Andrea, Powell Zucks, Michèle Laframboise, James Olsen, Jon Nepsha, Nick Mandujano III, Chris Vincent, Mike Smith, Jakiette, Acer R., Zalyn Schwartz, Fren & Edna, R. McKean

www.ingramcontent.com/pod-product-compliance
Lightning Source LLC
Chambersburg PA
CBHW030825020726
47499CB00006B/2069